Praise for the #1 *New York Times* bestselling A Court of Thorns and Roses series

A COURT OF THORNS AND ROSES

A Buzzfeed Best Fantasy Book
A Bustle Best Young Adult Book
A Huffington Post Best Young Adult Book

★ "Simply dazzles. . . . The clamor for a sequel will be deafening." —*Booklist*, starred review

"A true page-turner. . . . Not to be missed!" —*USA Today*

"Suspense, romance, intrigue and action. This is not a book to be missed!" —The Huffington Post

A COURT OF MIST AND FURY

The Goodreads Choice Award Winner for Best Young Adult Fantasy and Science Fiction for 2016

"A thrilling game changer that's fiercely romantic, irresistibly sexy and hypnotically magical. A veritable feast for the senses, Maas ratchets up tensions of all kind. . . . A flawless sequel." —*USA Today*

"Hits the spot for fans of dark, lush, sexy fantasy." —*Kirkus Reviews*

"As darkly sexy and thrilling as you have hoped and expected from your queen of YA fantasy." —Bustle

A COURT OF WINGS AND RUIN

"Side characters' romantic storylines are interwoven with the strategizing and even the war, pairing the expanded world with extended action sequences and character revelations, and the conclusion's ramifications will be felt in the next installments." —*Kirkus Reviews*

Books by Sarah J. Maas

THE THRONE OF GLASS SERIES

The Assassin's Blade
Throne of Glass
Crown of Midnight
Heir of Fire
Queen of Shadows
Empire of Storms
Tower of Dawn

•

The Throne of Glass Coloring Book

A COURT OF THORNS AND ROSES SERIES

A Court of Thorns and Roses
A Court of Mist and Fury
A Court of Wings and Ruin

•

A Court of Thorns and Roses Coloring Book

A COURT OF THORNS AND ROSES

SARAH J. MAAS

BLOOMSBURY
NEW YORK LONDON OXFORD NEW DELHI SYDNEY

First published in the United States of America in May 2015
by Bloomsbury Children's Books
Paperback edition published in May 2016
www.bloomsbury.com

The Library of Congress has cataloged the hardcover edition as follows:
Maas, Sarah J.
A court of thorns and roses / by Sarah J. Maas.
pages cm
Summary: Dragged to a treacherous magical land she knows about only from stories, Feyre discovers that her captor is not an animal but Tamlin, a High Lord of the faeries. As her feelings toward him transform from hostility to a fiery passion, the threats against the faerie lands grow. Feyre must fight to break an ancient curse, or she will lose Tamlin forever.
ISBN 978-1-61963-444-2 (hardcover) • ISBN 978-1-61963-445-9 (e-book)
[1. Fantasy. 2. Fairies—Fiction. 3. Blessing and cursing—Fiction.] I. Title.
PZ7.M111575Co 2015 [Fic]—dc23 2014020071

ISBN 978-1-61963-518-0 (paperback)

Book design by Donna Mark
Typeset by Westchester Book Composition
Printed and bound in the U.S.A. by Berryville Graphics Inc., Berryville, Virginia
10 9

For Josh—

Because you would go Under the Mountain for me.

I love you.

Prythian
Night Court
Day Court
Dawn Court
Under the Mountain
Winter Court
Summer Court
Autumn Court
Spring Court
The Wall
Feyre's Village
Hybern
Mortal Lands

Faerie Realms

North to Faerie Realms
South to Mortal Lands
The Wall
Mortal Lands

A COURT OF THORNS AND ROSES

CHAPTER 1

The forest had become a labyrinth of snow and ice.

I'd been monitoring the parameters of the thicket for an hour, and my vantage point in the crook of a tree branch had turned useless. The gusting wind blew thick flurries to sweep away my tracks, but buried along with them any signs of potential quarry.

Hunger had brought me farther from home than I usually risked, but winter was the hard time. The animals had pulled in, going deeper into the woods than I could follow, leaving me to pick off stragglers one by one, praying they'd last until spring.

They hadn't.

I wiped my numb fingers over my eyes, brushing away the flakes clinging to my lashes. Here there were no telltale trees stripped of bark to mark the deer's passing—they hadn't yet moved on. They would remain until the bark ran out, then travel north past the wolves' territory and perhaps into the faerie lands of Prythian—where no mortals would dare go, not unless they had a death wish.

A shudder skittered down my spine at the thought, and I shoved it away, focusing on my surroundings, on the task ahead. That was all I could do, all I'd been able to do for years: focus on surviving the week, the day, the hour ahead. And now, with the snow, I'd be lucky to spot anything—especially from my position up in the tree, scarcely able to see fifteen feet ahead. Stifling a groan as my stiff limbs protested at the movement, I unstrung my bow before easing off the tree.

The icy snow crunched under my fraying boots, and I ground my teeth. Low visibility, unnecessary noise—I was well on my way to yet another fruitless hunt.

Only a few hours of daylight remained. If I didn't leave soon, I'd have to navigate my way home in the dark, and the warnings of the town hunters still rang fresh in my mind: giant wolves were on the prowl, and in numbers. Not to mention whispers of strange folk spotted in the area, tall and eerie and deadly.

Anything but faeries, the hunters had beseeched our long-forgotten gods—and I had secretly prayed alongside them. In the eight years we'd been living in our village, two days' journey from the immortal border of Prythian, we'd been spared an attack—though traveling peddlers sometimes brought stories of distant border towns left in splinters and bones and ashes. These accounts, once rare enough to be dismissed by the village elders as hearsay, had in recent months become commonplace whisperings on every market day.

I had risked much in coming so far into the forest, but we'd finished our last loaf of bread yesterday, and the remainder of our dried meat the day before. Still, I would have rather spent another night with a hungry belly than found myself satisfying the appetite of a wolf. Or a faerie.

Not that there was much of me to feast on. I'd turned gangly by this time of the year, and could count a good number of my ribs. Moving as nimbly and quietly as I could between the trees, I pushed a hand against my hollow and aching stomach. I knew the expression that would be on my two elder sisters' faces when I returned to our cottage empty-handed yet again.

After a few minutes of careful searching, I crouched in a cluster of snow-heavy brambles. Through the thorns, I had a half-decent view of a clearing and the small brook flowing through it. A few holes in the ice suggested it was still frequently used. Hopefully something would come by. Hopefully.

I sighed through my nose, digging the tip of my bow into the ground, and leaned my forehead against the crude curve of wood. We wouldn't last another week without food. And too many families had already started begging for me to hope for handouts from the wealthier townsfolk. I'd witnessed firsthand exactly how far their charity went.

I eased into a more comfortable position and calmed my breathing, straining to listen to the forest over the wind. The snow fell and fell, dancing and curling like sparkling spindrifts, the white fresh and clean against the brown and gray of the world. And despite myself, despite my numb limbs, I quieted that relentless, vicious part of my mind to take in the snow-veiled woods.

Once it had been second nature to savor the contrast of new grass against dark, tilled soil, or an amethyst brooch nestled in folds of emerald silk; once I'd dreamed and breathed and thought in color and light and shape. Sometimes I would even indulge in envisioning a day when my sisters were married and it was only me and Father, with enough food to go around, enough money to buy some paint, and enough time to put those colors and shapes down on paper or canvas or the cottage walls.

Not likely to happen anytime soon—perhaps ever. So I was left with moments like this, admiring the glint of pale winter light on snow. I couldn't remember the last time I'd done it—bothered to notice anything lovely or interesting.

Stolen hours in a decrepit barn with Isaac Hale didn't count; those times were hungry and empty and sometimes cruel, but never lovely.

The howling wind calmed into a soft sighing. The snow fell lazily now, in big, fat clumps that gathered along every nook and bump of the trees.

Mesmerizing—the lethal, gentle beauty of the snow. I'd soon have to return to the muddy, frozen roads of the village, to the cramped heat of our cottage. Some small, fragmented part of me recoiled at the thought.

Bushes rustled across the clearing.

Drawing my bow was a matter of instinct. I peered through the thorns, and my breath caught.

Less than thirty paces away stood a small doe, not yet too scrawny from winter, but desperate enough to wrench bark from a tree in the clearing.

A deer like that could feed my family for a week or more.

My mouth watered. Quiet as the wind hissing through dead leaves, I took aim.

She continued tearing off strips of bark, chewing slowly, utterly unaware that her death waited yards away.

I could dry half the meat, and we could immediately eat the rest—stews, pies . . . Her skin could be sold, or perhaps turned into clothing for one of us. I needed new boots, but Elain needed a new cloak, and Nesta was prone to crave anything someone else possessed.

My fingers trembled. So much food—such salvation. I took a steadying breath, double-checking my aim.

But there was a pair of golden eyes shining from the brush adjacent to mine.

The forest went silent. The wind died. Even the snow paused.

We mortals no longer kept gods to worship, but if I had known their lost names, I would have prayed to them. All of them. Concealed in the thicket, the wolf inched closer, its gaze set on the oblivious doe.

He was enormous—the size of a pony—and though I'd been warned about their presence, my mouth turned bone-dry.

But worse than his size was his unnatural stealth: even as he inched closer in the brush, he remained unheard, unspotted by the doe. No animal that massive could be so quiet. But if he was no ordinary animal, if he was of Prythian origin, if he was somehow a faerie, then being eaten was the least of my concerns.

If he was a faerie, I should already be running.

Yet maybe . . . maybe it would be a favor to the world, to my village, to myself, to kill him while I remained undetected. Putting an arrow through his eye would be no burden.

But despite his size, he *looked* like a wolf, moved like a wolf. *Animal*, I reassured myself. *Just an animal*. I didn't let myself consider the alternative—not when I needed my head clear, my breathing steady.

I had a hunting knife and three arrows. The first two were ordinary arrows—simple and efficient, and likely no more than bee stings to a wolf that size. But the third arrow, the longest and heaviest one, I'd bought from a traveling peddler during a summer when we'd had enough coppers for extra luxuries. An arrow carved from mountain ash, armed with an iron head.

From songs sung to us as lullabies over our cradles, we all knew from infancy that faeries hated iron. But it was the ash wood that made their immortal, healing magic falter long enough for a human to make a killing blow. Or so legend and rumor claimed. The only proof we had of the ash's effectiveness was its sheer rarity. I'd seen drawings of the trees, but never one with my own eyes—not after the High Fae had burned them all long ago. So few remained, most of them small and sickly and hidden by the nobility within high-walled groves. I'd spent weeks after my purchase debating whether that overpriced bit of wood had been a waste of money, or a fake, and for three years, the ash arrow had sat unused in my quiver.

Now I drew it, keeping my movements minimal, efficient—anything to avoid that monstrous wolf looking in my direction. The arrow was long and heavy enough to inflict damage—possibly kill him, if I aimed right.

My chest became so tight it ached. And in that moment, I realized my life boiled down to one question: Was the wolf alone?

I gripped my bow and drew the string farther back. I was a decent shot, but I'd never faced a wolf. I'd thought it made me lucky—even blessed. But now . . . I didn't know where to hit or how fast they moved. I couldn't afford to miss. Not when I had only one ash arrow.

And if it was indeed a faerie's heart pounding under that fur, then good riddance. Good riddance, after all their kind had done to us. I wouldn't risk this one later creeping into our village to slaughter and maim and torment. Let him die here and now. I'd be glad to end him.

The wolf crept closer, and a twig snapped beneath one of his paws—each bigger than my hand. The doe went rigid. She glanced to either side, ears straining toward the gray sky. With the wolf's downwind position, she couldn't see or smell him.

His head lowered, and his massive silver body—so perfectly blended into the snow and shadows—sank onto its haunches. The doe was still staring in the wrong direction.

I glanced from the doe to the wolf and back again. At least he was alone—at least I'd been spared that much. But if the wolf scared the doe off, I was left with nothing but a starving, oversize wolf—possibly a faerie—looking for the next-best meal. And if he killed her, destroying precious amounts of hide and fat . . .

If I judged wrongly, my life wasn't the only one that would be lost. But my life had been reduced to nothing but risks these past eight years that I'd been hunting in the woods, and I'd picked correctly most of the time. Most of the time.

The wolf shot from the brush in a flash of gray and white and black, his yellow fangs gleaming. He was even more gargantuan in the open, a marvel of muscle and speed and brute strength. The doe didn't stand a chance.

I fired the ash arrow before he destroyed much else of her.

The arrow found its mark in his side, and I could have sworn the ground itself shuddered. He barked in pain, releasing the doe's neck as his blood sprayed on the snow—so ruby bright.

He whirled toward me, those yellow eyes wide, hackles raised. His low growl reverberated in the empty pit of my stomach as I surged to my feet, snow churning around me, another arrow drawn.

But the wolf merely looked at me, his maw stained with blood, my ash arrow protruding so vulgarly from his side. The snow began falling again. He *looked*, and with a sort of awareness and surprise that made me fire the second arrow. Just in case—just in case that intelligence was of the immortal, wicked sort.

He didn't try to dodge the arrow as it went clean through his wide yellow eye.

He collapsed to the ground.

Color and darkness whirled, eddying in my vision, mixing with the snow.

His legs were twitching as a low whine sliced through the wind. Impossible—he should be dead, not dying. The arrow was through his eye almost to the goose fletching.

But wolf or faerie, it didn't matter. Not with that ash arrow buried in his side. He'd be dead soon enough. Still, my hands shook as I brushed off snow and edged closer, still keeping a good distance. Blood gushed from the wounds I'd given him, staining the snow crimson.

He pawed at the ground, his breathing already slowing. Was he in much pain, or was his whimper just his attempt to shove death away? I wasn't sure I wanted to know.

The snow swirled around us. I stared at him until that coat of charcoal and obsidian and ivory ceased rising and falling. Wolf—definitely just a wolf, despite his size.

The tightness in my chest eased, and I loosed a sigh, my breath clouding in front of me. At least the ash arrow had proved itself to be lethal, regardless of who or what it took down.

A rapid examination of the doe told me I could carry only one animal—and even that would be a struggle. But it was a shame to leave the wolf.

Though it wasted precious minutes—minutes during which any predator could smell the fresh blood—I skinned him and cleaned my arrows as best I could.

If anything, it warmed my hands. I wrapped the bloody side of his pelt around the doe's death-wound before I hoisted her across my shoulders. It was several miles back to our cottage, and I didn't need a trail of blood leading every animal with fangs and claws straight to me.

Grunting against the weight, I grasped the legs of the deer and spared a final glance at the steaming carcass of the wolf. His remaining golden eye now stared at the snow-heavy sky, and for a moment, I wished I had it in me to feel remorse for the dead thing.

But this was the forest, and it was winter.

CHAPTER 2

The sun had set by the time I exited the forest, my knees shaking. My hands, stiff from clenching the legs of the deer, had gone utterly numb miles ago. Not even the carcass could ward off the deepening chill.

The world was awash in hues of dark blue, interrupted only by shafts of buttery light escaping from the shuttered windows of our dilapidated cottage. It was like striding through a living painting—a fleeting moment of stillness, the blues swiftly shifting to solid darkness.

As I trudged up the path, each step fueled only by near-dizzying hunger, my sisters' voices fluttered out to meet me. I didn't need to discern their words to know they most likely were chattering about some young man or the ribbons they'd spotted in the village when they should have been chopping wood, but I smiled a bit nonetheless.

I kicked my boots against the stone door frame, knocking the snow from them. Bits of ice came free from the gray stones of the cottage, revealing the faded ward-markings etched around the threshold. My father had once convinced a passing charlatan to trade the engravings against faerie harm in exchange for one of his wood carvings. There was so little that my father was ever able to do for us that I hadn't possessed the heart to tell him the engravings were useless . . . and undoubtedly fake. Mortals didn't possess magic—didn't possess any of the superior strength and speed of the faeries or High Fae. The man, claiming some High Fae blood in his ancestry, had just carved the whorls and swirls and runes around the door and windows, muttered a few nonsense words, and ambled on his way.

I yanked open the wooden door, the frozen iron handle biting my skin like an asp. Heat and light blinded me as I slipped inside.

"Feyre!" Elain's soft gasp scraped past my ears, and I blinked back the brightness of the fire to find my second-eldest sister before me. Though she was bundled in a threadbare blanket, her gold-brown hair—the hair all three of us had—was coiled perfectly about her head. Eight years of poverty hadn't stripped from her the desire to look lovely. "Where did you get that?" The undercurrent of hunger honed her words into a sharpness that had become too common in recent weeks. No mention of the blood on me. I'd long since given up hope of them actually noticing whether I came back from the woods every evening. At least until they got hungry again. But then again, my mother hadn't made *them* swear anything when they stood beside her deathbed.

I took a calming breath as I slung the doe off my shoulders. She hit the wooden table with a thud, rattling a ceramic cup on its other end.

"Where do you think I got it?" My voice had turned hoarse, each word burning as it came out. My father and Nesta still silently warmed their hands by the hearth, my eldest sister ignoring him, as usual. I peeled the wolf pelt from the doe's body, and after removing my boots and setting them by the door, I turned to Elain.

Her brown eyes—my father's eyes—remained pinned on the doe. "Will it take you long to clean it?" Me. Not her, not the others. I'd never once seen their hands sticky with blood and fur. I'd only learned to prepare and harvest my kills thanks to the instruction of others.

Elain pushed her hand against her belly, probably as empty and aching as my own. It wasn't that Elain was cruel. She wasn't like Nesta, who had been born with a sneer on her face. Elain sometimes just . . . didn't grasp things. It wasn't meanness that kept her from offering to help; it simply never occurred to her that she might be capable of getting her hands dirty. I'd never been able to decide whether she actually didn't understand that we were truly poor or if she just refused to accept it. It still hadn't stopped me from buying her seeds for the flower garden she tended in the milder months, whenever I could afford it.

And it hadn't stopped her from buying me three small tins of paint—red, yellow, and blue—during that same summer I'd had enough to buy the ash arrow. It was the only gift she'd ever given me, and our house still bore the marks of it, even if the paint was now fading and chipped: little vines and flowers along the windows and thresholds and edges of things, tiny curls of flame on the stones bordering the hearth. Any spare minutes I'd had that bountiful summer I used to bedeck our house in color, sometimes hiding clever decorations inside drawers, behind the threadbare curtains, underneath the chairs and table.

We hadn't had a summer that easy since.

"Feyre." My father's deep rumble came from the fire. His dark beard was neatly trimmed, his face spotless—like my sisters'. "What luck you had today—in bringing us such a feast."

From beside my father, Nesta snorted. Not surprising. Any bit of praise for anyone—me, Elain, other villagers—usually resulted in her dismissal. And any word from our father usually resulted in her ridicule as well.

I straightened, almost too tired to stand, but braced a hand on the table beside the doe as I shot Nesta a glare. Of us, Nesta had taken the loss of our fortune the hardest. She had quietly resented my father from the moment we'd fled our manor, even after that awful day one of the creditors had come to show just how displeased he was at the loss of his investment.

But at least Nesta didn't fill our heads with useless talk of regaining our wealth, like my father. No, she just spent whatever money I didn't hide from her, and rarely bothered to acknowledge my father's limping presence at all. Some days, I couldn't tell which of us was the most wretched and bitter.

"We can eat half the meat this week," I said, shifting my gaze to the doe. The deer took up the entirety of the rickety table that served as our dining area, workspace, and kitchen. "We can dry the other half," I went on, knowing that no matter how nicely I phrased it, I'd still do the bulk of it. "And I'll go to the market tomorrow to see how much I can get for the hides," I finished, more to myself than to them. No one bothered to confirm they'd heard me, anyway.

My father's ruined leg was stretched out before him, as close to the fire's heat as it could get. The cold, or the rain, or a change in temperature always aggravated the vicious, twisted wounds around his knee. His simply carved cane was propped up against his chair—a cane he'd made for himself . . . and that Nesta was sometimes prone to leaving far out of his reach.

He could find work if he wasn't so ashamed, Nesta always said when I hissed about it. She hated him for the injury, too—for not fighting back when that creditor and his thugs had burst into the cottage and smashed his knee again and again. Nesta and Elain had fled into the bedroom, barricading the door. I had stayed, begging and weeping through every scream of my father, every crunch of bone. I'd soiled myself—and then vomited right on the stones before the hearth. Only then did the men leave. We never saw them again.

We'd used a massive chunk of our remaining money to pay for the healer. It had taken my father six months to even walk, a year before he could go a mile. The coppers he brought in when someone pitied him enough to buy his wood carvings weren't enough to keep us fed. Five years ago, when the money was well and truly gone, when my father still couldn't—wouldn't—move much about, he hadn't argued when I announced that I was going hunting.

He hadn't bothered to attempt to stand from his seat by the fire, hadn't bothered to look up from his wood carving. He just let me walk into those deadly, eerie woods that even the most seasoned hunters were wary of. He'd become a little more aware now—sometimes offered signs of gratitude, sometimes hobbled all the way into town to sell his carvings—but not much.

"I'd love a new cloak," Elain said at last with a sigh, at the same moment Nesta rose and declared: "I need a new pair of boots."

I kept quiet, knowing better than to get in the middle of one of their arguments, but I glanced at Nesta's still-shiny pair by the door. Beside hers, my too-small boots were falling apart at the seams, held together only by fraying laces.

"But I'm freezing with my raggedy old cloak," Elain pleaded. "I'll shiver to death." She fixed her wide eyes on me and said, "Please, Feyre." She drew out the two syllables of my name—*fay-ruh*—into the most hideous whine I'd ever endured, and Nesta loudly clicked her tongue before ordering her to shut up.

I drowned them out as they began quarreling over who would get the money the hide would fetch tomorrow and found my father now standing at the table, one hand braced against it to support his weight as he inspected the deer. His attention slid to the giant wolf pelt. His fingers, still smooth and gentlemanly, turned over the pelt and traced a line through the bloody underside. I tensed.

His dark eyes flicked to mine. "Feyre," he murmured, and his mouth became a tight line. "Where did you get this?"

"The same place I got the deer," I replied with equal quiet, my words cool and sharp.

His gaze traveled over the bow and quiver strapped to my back, the wooden-hilted hunting knife at my side. His eyes turned damp. "Feyre . . . the risk . . ."

I jerked my chin at the pelt, unable to keep the snap from my voice as I said, "I had no other choice."

What I really wanted to say was: *You don't even bother to attempt to leave the house most days. Were it not for me, we would starve. Were it not for me, we'd be dead.*

"Feyre," he repeated, and closed his eyes.

My sisters had gone quiet, and I looked up in time to see Nesta crinkle her nose with a sniff. She picked at my cloak. "You stink like a pig covered in its own filth. Can't you at least *try* to pretend that you're not an ignorant peasant?"

I didn't let the sting and ache show. I'd been too young to learn more than the basics of manners and reading and writing when our family had fallen into misfortune, and she'd never let me forget it.

She stepped back to run a finger over the braided coils of her gold-brown hair. "Take those disgusting clothes off."

I took my time, swallowing the words I wanted to bark back at her. Older than me by three years, she somehow looked younger than I did, her golden cheeks always flushed with a delicate, vibrant pink. "Can you make a pot of hot water and add wood to the fire?" But even as I asked, I noticed the woodpile. There were only five logs left. "I thought you were going to chop wood today."

Nesta picked at her long, neat nails. "I hate chopping wood. I always get splinters." She glanced up from beneath her dark lashes. Of all of us, Nesta looked the most like our mother—especially when she wanted something. "Besides, Feyre," she said with a pout, "you're so much better at it! It takes you half the time it takes me. Your hands are suited for it—they're already so rough."

My jaw clenched. "Please," I asked, calming my breathing, knowing an argument was the last thing I needed or wanted. "Please get up at dawn to chop that wood." I unbuttoned the top of my tunic. "Or we'll be eating a cold breakfast."

Her brows narrowed. "I will do no such thing!"

But I was already walking toward the small second room where my sisters and I slept. Elain murmured a soft plea to Nesta, which earned her a hiss in response. I glanced over my shoulder at my father and pointed to the deer. "Get the knives ready," I said, not bothering to sound pleasant. "I'll be out soon." Without waiting for an answer, I shut the door behind me.

The room was large enough for a rickety dresser and the enormous ironwood bed we slept in. The sole remnant of our former wealth, it had been ordered as a wedding gift from my father to my mother. It was the bed in which we'd been born, and the bed in which my mother died. In all the painting I'd done to our house these past few years, I'd never touched it.

I slung off my outer clothes onto the sagging dresser—frowning at the violets and roses I'd painted around the knobs of Elain's drawer, the crackling flames I'd painted around Nesta's, and the night sky—whorls of yellow stars standing in for white—around mine. I'd done it to brighten the otherwise dark room. They'd never commented on it. I don't know why I'd ever expected them to.

Groaning, it was all I could do to keep from collapsing onto the bed.

⸸

We dined on roasted venison that night. Though I knew it was foolish, I didn't object when each of us had a small second helping until I declared the meat off-limits. I'd spend tomorrow preparing the deer's remaining parts for consumption, then I'd allot a few hours to currying up both hides before taking them to the market. I knew a few vendors who might be interested in such a purchase—though neither was likely to give me the fee I deserved. But money was money, and I didn't have the time or the funds to travel to the nearest large town to find a better offer.

I sucked on the tines of my fork, savoring the remnants of fat coating the metal. My tongue slipped over the crooked prongs—the fork was part of a shabby set my father had salvaged from the servants' quarters while the creditors ransacked our manor home. None of our utensils matched, but it was better than using our fingers. My mother's dowry flatware had long since been sold.

My mother. Imperious and cold with her children, joyous and dazzling among the peerage who frequented our former estate, doting on my father—the one person whom she truly loved and respected. But she also had truly loved parties—so much so that she didn't have time to do anything with me at all save contemplate how my budding abilities to sketch and paint might secure me a future husband. Had she lived long enough to see our wealth crumble, she would have been shattered by it—more so than my father. Perhaps it was a merciful thing that she died.

If anything, it left more food for us.

There was nothing left of her in the cottage beyond the ironwood bed—and the vow I'd made.

Every time I looked toward a horizon or wondered if I should just walk and walk and never look back, I'd hear that promise I made eleven years ago as she wasted away on her deathbed. *Stay together, and look after them*. I'd agreed, too young to ask why she hadn't begged my elder sisters, or my father. But I'd sworn it to her, and then she'd died, and in our miserable human world—shielded only by the promise made by the High Fae five centuries ago—in our world where we'd forgotten the names of our gods, a promise was law; a promise was currency; a promise was your bond.

There were times when I hated her for asking that vow of me. Perhaps, delirious with fever, she hadn't even known what she was demanding. Or maybe impending death had given her some clarity about the true nature of her children, her husband.

I set down the fork and watched the flames of our meager fire dance along the remaining logs, stretching out my aching legs beneath the table.

I turned to my sisters. As usual, Nesta was complaining about the villagers—they had no manners, they had no social graces, they had no idea just how shoddy the fabric of their clothes was, even though they pretended that it was as fine as silk or chiffon. Since we had lost our fortune, their former friends dutifully ignored them, so my sisters paraded about as though the young peasants of the town made up a second-rate social circle.

I took a sip from my cup of hot water—we couldn't even afford tea these days—as Nesta continued her story to Elain.

"Well, I said to *him*, 'If you think you can just ask me so nonchalantly, sir, I'm going to decline!' And you know what Tomas said?" Arms braced on the table and eyes wide, Elain shook her head.

"Tomas Mandray?" I interrupted. "The woodcutter's second son?"

Nesta's blue-gray eyes narrowed. "Yes," she said, and shifted to address Elain again.

"What does he want?" I glanced at my father. No reaction—no hint of alarm or sign that he was even listening. Lost to whatever fog of memory had crept over him, he was smiling mildly at his beloved Elain, the only one of us who bothered to really speak to him at all.

"He wants to marry her," Elain said dreamily. I blinked.

Nesta cocked her head. I'd seen predators use that movement before. I sometimes wondered if her unrelenting steel would have helped us better survive—thrive, even—if she hadn't been so preoccupied with our lost status. "Is there a problem, *Feyre*?" She flung my name like an insult, and my jaw ached from clenching it so hard.

My father shifted in his seat, blinking, and though I knew it was foolish to react to her taunts, I said, "You can't chop wood for us, but you want to marry a *woodcutter's* son?"

Nesta squared her shoulders. "I thought all you wanted was for us to get out of the house—to marry off me and Elain so you can have enough time to paint your glorious masterpieces." She sneered at the pillar of foxglove I'd painted along the edge of the table—the colors too dark and too blue, with none of the white freckling inside the trumpets, but I'd made do, even if it had killed me not to have white paint, to make something so flawed and lasting.

I drowned the urge to cover up the painting with my hand. Maybe tomorrow I'd just scrape it off the table altogether. "Believe me," I said to her, "the day you want to marry someone worthy, I'll march up to his house and hand you over. But you're not going to marry Tomas."

Nesta's nostrils delicately flared. "There's nothing you can do. Clare Beddor told me this afternoon that Tomas *is* going to propose to me any day now. And then I'll never have to eat these scraps again." She added with a small smile, "At least I don't have to resort to rutting in the hay with Isaac Hale like an animal."

My father let out an embarrassed cough, looking to his cot by the fire. He'd never said a word against Nesta, from either fear or guilt, and apparently he wasn't going to start now, even if this was the first he was hearing of Isaac.

I laid my palms flat on the table as I stared her down. Elain removed her hand from where it lay nearby, as if the dirt and blood beneath my fingernails would somehow jump onto her porcelain skin. "Tomas's family is barely better off than ours," I said, trying to keep from growling. "You'd be just another mouth to feed. If he doesn't know this, then his parents must."

But Tomas knew—we'd run into each other in the forest before. I'd seen the gleam of desperate hunger in his eyes when he spotted me sporting a brace of rabbits. I'd never killed another human, but that day, my hunting knife had felt like a weight at my side. I'd kept out of his way ever since.

"We can't afford a dowry," I continued, and though my tone was firm, my voice quieted. "For either of you." If Nesta wanted to leave, then fine. Good. I'd be one step closer to attaining that glorious, peaceful future, to attaining a quiet house and enough food and time to paint. But we had nothing—absolutely nothing—to entice any suitor to take my sisters off my hands.

"We're in love," Nesta declared, and Elain nodded her agreement. I almost laughed—when had they gone from mooning over aristos to making doe-eyes at peasants?

"Love won't feed a hungry belly," I countered, keeping my gaze as sturdy as possible.

As if I'd struck her, Nesta leaped from her seat on the bench. "You're just jealous. I heard them saying how Isaac is going to marry some Greenfield village girl for a handsome dowry."

So had I; Isaac had ranted about it the last time we'd met. "Jealous?" I said slowly, digging down deep to bury my fury. "We have nothing to offer them—no dowry; no livestock, even. While Tomas might want to marry you . . . you're a burden."

"What do you know?" Nesta breathed. "You're just a half-wild beast with the nerve to bark orders at all hours of the day and night. Keep it up, and someday—someday, Feyre, you'll have no one left to remember you, or to care that you ever existed." She stormed off, Elain darting after her, cooing her sympathy. They slammed the door to the bedroom hard enough to rattle the dishes.

I'd heard the words before—and knew she only repeated them because I'd flinched that first time she spat them. They still burned anyway.

I took a long sip from the chipped mug. The wooden bench beneath my father groaned as he shifted. I took another swallow and said, "You should talk some sense into her."

He examined a burn mark on the table. "What can I say? If it's love—"

"It *can't* be love, not on his part. Not with his wretched family. I've seen the way he acts around the village—there's one thing he wants from her, and it's *not* her hand in—"

"We need hope as much as we need bread and meat," he interrupted, his eyes clear for a rare moment. "We need hope, or else we cannot endure.

So let her keep this hope, Feyre. Let her imagine a better life. A better world."

I stood from the table, fingers curling into fists, but there was nowhere to run in our two-room cottage. I looked at the discolored foxglove painting at the edge of the table. The outer trumpets were already chipped and faded, the lower bit of the stem rubbed off entirely. Within a few years, it would be gone—leaving no mark that it had ever been there. That I'd ever been there.

When I looked at my father, my gaze was hard. "There is no such thing."

CHAPTER 3

The trampled snow coating the road into our village was speckled with brown and black from passing carts and horses. Elain and Nesta clicked their tongues and grimaced as we made our way along it, dodging the particularly disgusting parts. I knew why they'd come—they'd taken one look at the hides I'd folded into my satchel and grabbed their cloaks.

I didn't bother talking to them, as they hadn't deigned to speak to me after last night, though Nesta had awoken at dawn to chop wood. Probably because she knew I'd be selling the hides at the market today and would go home with money in my pocket. They trailed me down the lone road wending through the snow-covered fields, all the way into our ramshackle village.

The stone houses of the village were ordinary and dull, made grimmer by the bleakness of winter. But it was market day, which meant the tiny square in the center of town would be full of whatever vendors had braved the brisk morning.

From a block away, the scent of hot food wafted by—spices that tugged on the edge of my memory, beckoning. Elain let out a low moan behind me. Spices, salt, sugar—rare commodities for most of our village, impossible for us to afford.

If I did well at the market, perhaps I'd have enough to buy us something delicious. I opened my mouth to suggest it, but we turned the corner and nearly stumbled into one another as we all halted.

"May the Immortal Light shine upon thee, sisters," said the pale-robed young woman directly in our path.

Nesta and Elain clicked their tongues; I stifled a groan. Perfect. Exactly what I needed, to have the Children of the Blessed in town on market day, distracting and riling everyone. The village elders usually allowed them to stay for only a few hours, but the sheer presence of the fanatic fools who still worshipped the High Fae made people edgy. Made *me* edgy. Long ago, the High Fae had been our overlords—not gods. And they certainly hadn't been kind.

The young woman extended her moon-white hands in a gesture of greeting, a bracelet of silver bells—*real* silver—tinkling at her wrist. "Have you a moment to spare so that you might hear the Word of the Blessed?"

"No," Nesta sneered, ignoring the girl's hands and nudging Elain into a walk. "We don't."

The young woman's unbound dark hair gleamed in the morning light, and her clean, fresh face glowed as she smiled prettily. There were five other acolytes behind her, young men and women both, their hair long, uncut—all scanning the market beyond for young folk to pester. "It would take but a minute," the woman said, stepping into Nesta's path.

It was impressive—truly impressive—to see Nesta go ramrod straight, to square her shoulders and look down her nose at the young acolyte, a queen without a throne. "Go spew your fanatic nonsense to some ninny. You'll find no converts here."

The girl shrank back, a shadow flickering in her brown eyes. I reined in my wince. Perhaps not the best way to deal with them, since they could become a true nuisance if agitated—

Nesta lifted a hand, pushing down the sleeve of her coat to show the iron bracelet there. The same one Elain wore; they'd bought matching adornments years ago. The acolyte gasped, eyes wide. "You see this?" Nesta hissed, taking a step forward. The acolyte retreated a step. "This is what you *should* be wearing. Not some silver bells to attract those faerie monsters."

"How *dare* you wear that vile affront to our immortal friends—"

"Go preach in another town," Nesta spat.

Two plump and pretty farmers' wives strolled past on their way to the market, arm in arm. As they neared the acolytes, their faces twisted with identical expressions of disgust. "*Faerie-loving whore*," one of them hurled at the young woman. I couldn't disagree.

The acolytes kept silent. The other villager—wealthy enough to have a full necklace of braided iron around her throat—narrowed her eyes, her upper lip curling back from her teeth. "Don't you idiots understand what those monsters did to us for all those centuries? What they still do for sport, when they can get away with it? You deserve the end you'll meet at faerie hands. Fools and whores, all of you."

Nesta nodded her agreement to the women as they continued on their way. We turned back to the young woman still lingering before us, and even Elain frowned in distaste.

But the young woman took a breath, her face again becoming serene, and said, "I lived in such ignorance, too, until I heard the Word of the Blessed. I grew up in a village so similar to this—so bleak and grim. But not one month ago, a friend of my cousin went to the border as our offering to Prythian—and she has not been sent back. Now she dwells in riches and comfort as a High Fae's bride, and so might you, if you were to take a moment to—"

"She was likely eaten," Nesta said. "That's why she hasn't returned."

Or worse, I thought, if a High Fae truly was involved in spiriting a human into Prythian. I'd never encountered the cruel, human-looking High Fae who ruled Prythian itself, or the faeries who occupied their lands, with their scales and wings and long, spindly arms that could drag you deep, deep beneath the surface of a forgotten pond. I didn't know which would be worse to face.

The acolyte's face tightened. "Our benevolent masters would never harm us. Prythian is a land of peace and plenty. Should they bless you with their attention, you would be glad to live amongst them."

Nesta rolled her eyes. Elain was shooting glances between us and the market ahead—to the villagers now watching, too. Time to go.

Nesta opened her mouth again, but I stepped between them and ran an eye along the girl's pale blue robes, the silver jewelry on her, the utter cleanness of her skin. Not a mark or smudge to be found. "You're fighting an uphill battle," I said to her.

"A worthy cause." The girl beamed beatifically.

I gave Nesta a gentle push to get her walking and said to the acolyte, "No, it's not."

I could feel the acolytes' attention still fixed on us as we strode into the busy market square, but I didn't look back. They'd be gone soon enough, off to preach in another town. We'd have to take the long way out of the village to avoid them. When we were far enough away, I glanced over a shoulder at my sisters. Elain's face remained set in a wince, but Nesta's eyes were stormy, her lips thin. I wondered if she'd stomp back to the girl and pick a fight.

Not my problem—not right now. "I'll meet you here in an hour," I said, and didn't give them time to cling to me before slipping into the crowded square.

It took me ten minutes to contemplate my three options. There were my usual buyers: the weathered cobbler and the sharp-eyed clothier who came to our market from a nearby town. And then the unknown: a mountain of a woman sitting on the lip of our broken square fountain, without any cart or stall, but looking like she was holding court nonetheless. The scars and weapons on her marked her easily enough. A mercenary.

I could feel the eyes of the cobbler and clothier on me, sense their feigned disinterest as they took in the satchel I bore. Fine—it would be that sort of day, then.

I approached the mercenary, whose thick, dark hair was shorn to her chin. Her tan face seemed hewn of granite, and her black eyes narrowed slightly at the sight of me. Such interesting eyes—not just one shade of black, but . . . many, with hints of brown that glimmered amongst the shadows. I pushed against that useless part of my mind, the instincts that had me thinking about color and light and shape, and kept my shoulders back as she assessed me as a potential threat or employer. The weapons on her—gleaming and wicked—were enough to make me swallow. And stop a good two feet away.

"I don't barter goods for my services," she said, her voice clipped with an accent I'd never heard before. "I only accept coin."

A few passing villagers tried their best not to look too interested in our conversation, especially as I said, "Then you'll be out of luck in this sort of place."

She was massive even sitting down. "What is your business with me, girl?"

She could have been aged anywhere from twenty-five to thirty, but I supposed I looked like a girl to her in my layers, gangly from hunger. "I have a wolf pelt and a doe hide for sale. I thought you might be interested in purchasing them."

"You steal them?"

"No." I held her stare. "I hunted them myself. I swear it."

She ran those dark eyes down me again. "How." Not a question—a command. Perhaps someone who had encountered others who did not see vows as sacred, words as bonds. And had punished them accordingly.

So I told her how I'd brought them down, and when I finished, she flicked a hand toward my satchel. "Let me see." I pulled out both carefully folded hides. "You weren't lying about the wolf's size," she murmured. "Doesn't seem like a faerie, though." She examined them with an expert eye, running her hands over and under. She named her price.

I blinked—but stifled the urge to blink a second time. She was overpaying—by a lot.

She looked beyond me—past me. "I'm assuming those two girls watching from across the square are your sisters. You all have that brassy hair—and that hungry look about you." Indeed, they were still trying their best to eavesdrop without being spotted.

"I don't need your pity."

"No, but you need my money, and the other traders have been cheap all morning. Everyone's too distracted by those calf-eyed zealots bleating across the square." She jerked her chin toward the Children of the Blessed, still ringing their silver bells and jumping into the path of anyone who tried to walk by.

The mercenary was smiling faintly when I turned back to her. "Up to you, girl."

"Why?"

She shrugged. "Someone once did the same for me and mine, at a time when we needed it most. Figure it's time to repay what's due."

I watched her again, weighing. "My father has some wood carvings that I could give you as well—to make it more fair."

"I travel light and have no need for them. These, however"—she patted the pelts in her hands—"save me the trouble of killing them myself."

I nodded, my cheeks heating as she reached for the coin purse inside her heavy coat. It was full—and weighed down with at least silver, possibly gold, if the clinking was any indication. Mercenaries tended to be well paid in our territory.

Our territory was too small and poor to maintain a standing army to monitor the wall with Prythian, and we villagers could rely only on the strength of the Treaty forged five hundred years ago. But the upper class could afford hired swords, like this woman, to guard their lands bordering the immortal realm. It was an illusion of comfort, just as the markings on our threshold were. We all knew, deep down, that there was nothing to be done against the faeries. We'd all been told it, regardless of class or rank, from the moment we were born, the warnings sung to us while we rocked in cradles, the rhymes chanted in schoolyards. One of the High Fae could turn your bones to dust from a hundred yards away. Not that my sisters or I had ever seen it.

But we still tried to believe that something—anything—might work against them, if we ever were to encounter them. There were two stalls in the market catering to those fears, offering up charms and baubles and incantations and bits of iron. I couldn't afford them—and if they did indeed work, they would buy us only a few minutes to prepare ourselves. Running was futile; so was fighting. But Nesta and Elain still wore their iron bracelets whenever they left the cottage. Even Isaac had an iron cuff around one wrist, always tucked under his sleeve. He'd once offered to buy me one, but I'd refused. It had felt too personal, too much like payment, too . . . permanent a reminder of whatever we were and weren't to each other.

The mercenary transferred the coins to my waiting palm, and I tucked them into my pocket, their weight as heavy as a millstone. There was no possible chance that my sisters hadn't spotted the money—no chance they weren't already wondering how they might persuade me to give them some.

"Thank you," I said to the mercenary, trying and failing to keep the bite from my voice as I felt my sisters sweep closer, like vultures circling a carcass.

The mercenary stroked the wolf pelt. "A word of advice, from one hunter to another."

I lifted my brows.

"Don't go far into the woods. I wouldn't even get close to where you were yesterday. A wolf this size would be the least of your problems. More and more, I've been hearing stories about those *things* slipping through the wall."

A chill spider-walked down my spine. "Are they—are they going to attack?" If it were true, I'd find a way to get my family off our miserable, damp territory and head south—head far from the invisible wall that bisected our world before they could cross it.

Once—long ago and for millennia before that—we had been slaves to High Fae overlords. Once, we had built them glorious, sprawling civilizations from our blood and sweat, built them temples to their feral gods. Once, we had rebelled, across every land and territory. The War had been so bloody, so destructive, that it took six mortal queens crafting the Treaty for the slaughter to cease on both sides and for the wall to be constructed: the North of our world conceded to the High Fae and faeries, who took their magic with them; the South to we cowering mortals, forever forced to scratch out a living from the earth.

"No one knows what the Fae are planning," the mercenary said, her face like stone. "We don't know if the High Lords' leash on their beasts is slipping, or if these are targeted attacks. I guarded for an old nobleman who claimed it had been getting worse these past fifty years. He got on a boat south two weeks ago and told me I should leave if I was smart. Before he sailed off, he admitted that he'd had word from one of his friends that in the dead of night, a pack of martax crossed the wall and tore half his village apart."

"Martax?" I breathed. I knew there were different types of faeries, that they varied as much as any other species of animal, but I knew only a few by name.

The mercenary's night-dark eyes flickered. "Body big as a bear's, head something like a lion's—and three rows of teeth sharper than a shark's. And mean—meaner than all three put together. They left the villagers in literal ribbons, the nobleman said."

My stomach turned. Behind us, my sisters seemed so fragile—their pale skin so infinitely delicate and shredable. Against something like the martax, we'd never stand a chance. Those Children of the Blessed were fools—fanatic fools.

"So we don't know what all these attacks mean," the mercenary went on, "other than more hires for me, and you keeping well away from the wall. Especially if the High Fae start turning up—or worse, one of the High Lords. They would make the martax seem like dogs."

I studied her scarred hands, chapped from the cold. "Have you ever faced another type of faerie?"

Her eyes shuttered. "You don't want to know, girl—not unless you want to be hurling up your breakfast."

I was indeed feeling ill—ill and jumpy. "Was it deadlier than the martax?" I dared ask.

The woman pulled back the sleeve of her heavy jacket, revealing a tanned, muscled forearm flecked with gruesome, twisted scars. The arc of them so similar to—"Didn't have the brute force or size of a martax," she said, "but its bite was full of poison. Two months—that's how long I was down; four months until I had the strength to walk again." She pulled up the leg of her trousers. Beautiful, I thought, even as the horror of it writhed in my gut. Against her tanned skin, the veins were black—solid black, spiderwebbed, and creeping like frost. "Healer said there was nothing to be done for it—that I'm lucky to be walking with the poison still in my legs. Maybe it'll kill me one day, maybe it'll cripple me. But at least I'll go knowing I killed it first."

The blood in my own veins seemed to chill as she lowered the cuff of her pants. If anyone in the square had seen, no one dared speak about it—or to come closer. And I'd had enough for one day. So I took a step back, steadying myself against what she'd told me and shown me. "Thanks for the warnings," I said.

Her attention flicked behind me, and she gave a faintly amused smile. "Good luck."

Then a slender hand clamped onto my forearm, dragging me away. I knew it was Nesta before I even looked at her.

"They're dangerous," Nesta hissed, her fingers digging into my arm as she continued to pull me from the mercenary. "Don't go near them again."

I stared at her for a moment, then at Elain, whose face had gone pale and tight. "Is there something I need to know?" I asked quietly. I couldn't remember the last time Nesta had tried to warn me about anything; Elain was the only one she bothered to really look after.

"They're brutes, and will take any copper they can get, even if it's by force."

I glanced at the mercenary, who was still examining her new pelts. "She robbed you?"

"Not her," Elain murmured. "Some other one who passed through. We had only a few coins, and he got mad, but—"

"Why didn't you report him—or tell me?"

"What could you have done?" Nesta sneered. "Challenged him to a fight with your bow and arrows? And who in this sewer of a town would even care if we reported anything?"

"What about your Tomas Mandray?" I said coolly.

Nesta's eyes flashed, but a movement behind me caught her eye, and she gave me what I supposed was her attempt at a sweet smile—probably as she remembered the money I now carried. "Your friend is waiting for you."

I turned. Indeed, Isaac was watching from across the square, arms crossed as he leaned against a building. Though the eldest son of the only well-off farmer in our village, he was still lean from the winter, and his brown hair had turned shaggy. Relatively handsome, soft-spoken, and reserved, but with a sort of darkness running beneath it all that had drawn us to each other, that shared understanding of how wretched our lives were and would always be.

We'd vaguely known each other for years—since my family had moved to the village—but I had never thought much about him until we'd wound up walking down the main road together one afternoon. We'd only talked about the eggs he was bringing to market—and I'd admired the variation in colors within the basket he bore—browns and tans and the palest blues and greens. Simple, easy, perhaps a bit awkward, but he'd left me at my cottage feeling not quite so . . . alone. A week later, I pulled him into that decrepit barn.

He'd been my first and only lover in the two years since. Sometimes we'd meet every night for a week, others we'd go a month without setting eyes on each other. But every time was the same: a rush of shedding clothes and shared breaths and tongues and teeth. Occasionally we'd talk—or, rather, *he*'d talk about the pressures and burdens his father placed on him. Often, we wouldn't say a word the entire time. I couldn't say our lovemaking was particularly skilled, but it was still a release, a reprieve, a bit of selfishness.

There was no love between us, and never had been—at least what I assumed people meant when they talked about love—yet part of me had sunk when he'd said he would soon be married. I wasn't yet desperate enough to ask him to see me after he was wed.

Isaac inclined his head in a familiar gesture and then ambled off down the street—out of town and to the ancient barn, where he would be waiting. We were never inconspicuous about our dealings with each other, but we did take measures to keep it from being too obvious.

Nesta clicked her tongue, crossing her arms. "I do hope you two are taking precautions."

"It's a bit late to pretend to care," I said. But we were careful. Since I couldn't afford it, Isaac himself took the contraceptive brew. He knew I wouldn't have touched him otherwise. I reached into my pocket, drawing out a twenty-mark copper. Elain sucked in a breath, and I didn't bother to look at either of my sisters as I pushed it into her palm and said, "I'll see you at home."

⁜

Later, after another dinner of venison, when we were all gathered around the fire for the quiet hour before bed, I watched my sisters whispering and laughing together. They'd spent every copper I'd given them—on what, I didn't know, though Elain had brought back a new chisel for our father's wood carving. The cloak and boots they'd whined about the night before had been too expensive. But I hadn't scolded them for it, not when Nesta went out a second time to chop more wood without my asking. Mercifully, they'd avoided another confrontation with the Children of the Blessed.

My father was dozing in his chair, his cane laid across his gnarled knee. As good a time as any to broach the subject of Tomas Mandray with Nesta. I turned to her, opening my mouth.

But there was a roar that half deafened me, and my sisters screamed as snow burst into the room and an enormous, growling shape appeared in the doorway.

CHAPTER 4

I didn't know how the wooden hilt of my hunting knife had gotten into my hand. The first few moments were a blur of the snarling of a gigantic beast with golden fur, the shrieking of my sisters, the blistering cold cascading into the room, and my father's terror-stricken face.

Not a martax, I realized—though the relief was short-lived. The beast had to be as large as a horse, and while his body was somewhat feline, his head was distinctly wolfish. I didn't know what to make of the curled, elk-like horns that protruded from his head. But lion or hound or elk, there was no doubting the damage his black, daggerlike claws and yellow fangs could inflict.

Had I been alone in the woods, I might have let myself be swallowed by fear, might have fallen to my knees and wept for a clean, quick death. But I didn't have room for terror, wouldn't give it an inch of space, despite my heart's wild pounding in my ears. Somehow, I wound up in front of my sisters, even as the creature reared onto its hind legs and bellowed through a maw full of fangs: "*MURDERERS!*"

But it was another word that echoed through me:

Faerie.

Those ridiculous wards on our threshold were as good as cobwebs against him. I should have asked the mercenary how she'd killed that faerie. But the beast's thick neck—that looked like a good home for my knife.

I dared a glance over my shoulder. My sisters screamed, kneeling against the wall of the hearth, my father crouched in front of them. Another body for me to defend. Stupidly, I took another step toward the faerie, keeping the table between us, fighting the shaking in my hand. My bow and quiver were across the room—past the beast. I'd have to get around him to reach the ash arrow. And buy myself enough time to fire it.

"*MURDERERS!*" the beast roared again, hackles raised.

"P-please," my father babbled from behind me, failing to find it in himself to come to my side. "Whatever we have done, we did so unknowingly, and—"

"W-w-we didn't kill anyone," Nesta added, choking on her sobs, arm lifted over her head, as if that tiny iron bracelet would do anything against the creature.

I snatched another dinner knife off the table, the best I could do unless I found a way to get to the quiver. "Get out," I snapped at the creature, brandishing the knives before me. No iron in sight that I could use as a weapon—unless I chucked my sisters' bracelets at him. "Get out, and begone." With my trembling hands, I could barely keep my grip on the hilts. A nail—I'd take a damned iron nail, if it were available.

He bellowed at me in response, and the entire cottage shook, the plates and cups rattling against one another. But it left his massive neck exposed. I hurled my hunting knife.

Fast—so fast I could barely see it—he slashed out with a paw, sending it skittering away as he snapped for my face with his teeth.

I leaped back, almost stumbling over my cowering father. The faerie could have killed me—could have, yet the lunge had been a warning.

Nesta and Elain, weeping, prayed to whatever long-forgotten gods might still be skulking about.

"WHO KILLED HIM?" The creature stalked toward us. He set a paw on the table, and it groaned beneath him. His claws thudded as they embedded in the wood, one by one.

I dared another step forward as the beast stretched his snout over the table to sniff at us. His eyes were green and flecked with amber. Not animal eyes, not with their shape and coloring. My voice was surprisingly even as I challenged: "Killed who?"

He growled, low and vicious. "The wolf," he said, and my heart stumbled a beat. The roar was gone, but the wrath lingered—perhaps even traced with sorrow.

Elain's wail reached a high-pitched shriek. I kept my chin up. "A wolf?"

"A large wolf with a gray coat," he snarled in response. Would he know if I lied? Faeries couldn't lie—all mortals knew that—but could they smell the lies on human tongues? We had no chance of escaping this through fighting, but there might be other ways.

"If it was *mistakenly* killed," I said to the beast as calmly as I could, "what payment could we offer in exchange?" This was all a nightmare, and I'd awaken in a moment beside the fire, exhausted from my day at the market and my afternoon with Isaac.

The beast let out a bark that could have been a bitter laugh. He pushed off the table to pace in a small circle before the shattered door. The cold was so intense that I shivered. "The payment you must offer is the one demanded by the Treaty between our realms."

"For a wolf?" I retorted, and my father murmured my name in warning. I had vague memories of being read the Treaty during my childhood lessons, but could recall nothing about wolves.

The beast whirled on me. "Who killed the wolf?"

I stared into those jade eyes. "I did."

He blinked and glanced at my sisters, then back at me, at my thinness—no doubt seeing only frailness instead. "Surely you lie to save them."

"We didn't kill anything!" Elain wept. "Please . . . *please*, spare us!" Nesta hushed her sharply through her own sobbing, but pushed Elain farther behind her. My chest caved in at the sight of it.

My father climbed to his feet, grunting at the pain in his leg as he bobbled, but before he could limp toward me, I repeated: "I killed it." The beast, who had been sniffing at my sisters, studied me. I squared my shoulders. "I sold its hide at the market today. If I had known it was a faerie, I wouldn't have touched it."

"Liar," he snarled. "You knew. You would have been more tempted to slaughter it had you known it was one of my kind."

True, true, true. "Can you blame me?"

"Did it attack you? Were you provoked?"

I opened my mouth to say yes, but—"No," I said, letting out a snarl of my own. "But considering all that your kind has done to us, considering what your kind still likes to *do* to us, even if I *had* known beyond a doubt, it was deserved." Better to die with my chin held high than groveling like a cowering worm.

Even if his answering growl was the definition of wrath and rage.

The firelight shone upon his exposed fangs, and I wondered how they'd feel on my throat, and how loudly my sisters would scream before they, too, died. But I knew—with a sudden, uncoiling clarity—that Nesta would buy Elain time to run. Not my father, whom she resented with her entire steely heart. Not me, because Nesta had always known and hated that she and I were two sides of the same coin, and that I could fight my own battles. But Elain, the flower-grower, the gentle heart . . . Nesta would go down swinging for her.

It was that flash of understanding that had me angling my remaining knife at the beast. "What is the payment the Treaty requires?"

His eyes didn't leave my face as he said, "A life for a life. Any unprovoked attacks on faerie-kind by humans are to be paid only by a human life in exchange."

My sisters quieted their weeping. The mercenary in town had killed a faerie—but had attacked her first. "I didn't know," I said. "Didn't know about that part of the Treaty."

Faeries couldn't lie—and he spoke plainly enough, no word-twisting.

"Most of you mortals have chosen to forget that part of the Treaty," he said, "which makes punishing you far more enjoyable."

My knees quaked. I couldn't escape this, couldn't outrun this. Couldn't even try to run, since he blocked the way to the door. "Do it outside," I whispered, my voice trembling. "Not . . . here." Not where my family would have to wash away my blood and gore. If he even let them live.

The faerie huffed a vicious laugh. "Willing to accept your fate so easily?" When I just stared at him, he said, "For having the nerve to request *where* I slaughter you, I'll let you in on a secret, human: Prythian must claim your life in some way, for the life you took from it. So as a representative of the immortal realm, I can either gut you like swine, or . . . you can cross the wall and live out the remainder of your days in Prythian."

I blinked. "What?"

He said slowly, as if I were indeed as stupid as a swine, "You can either die tonight or offer your life to Prythian by living in it forever, forsaking the human realm."

"Do it, Feyre," my father whispered from behind me. "Go."

I didn't look at him as I said, "Live *where*? Every inch of Prythian is lethal to us." I'd be better off dying tonight than living in pure terror across the wall until I met my end in doubtlessly an even more awful way.

"I have lands," the faerie said quietly—almost reluctantly. "I will grant you permission to live there."

"Why bother?" Perhaps a fool's question, but—

"You murdered my friend," the beast snarled. "Murdered him, skinned his corpse, sold it at the market, and then said he *deserved* it, and yet you have the nerve to question my generosity?" *How typically human*, he seemed to silently add.

"You didn't need to mention the loophole." I stepped so close the faerie's breath heated my face. Faeries couldn't lie, but they could omit information.

The beast snarled again. "Foolish of me to forget that humans have such low opinions of us. Do you humans no longer understand mercy?" he said, his fangs inches from my throat. "Let me make this clear for you, girl: you can either come live at my home in Prythian—offer your life for the wolf's in that way—or you can walk outside right now and be shredded to ribbons. Your choice."

My father's hobbling steps sounded before he gripped my shoulder. "Please, good sir—Feyre is my youngest. I beseech you to spare her. She is all . . . she is all . . ." But whatever he meant to say died in his throat as the beast roared again. But hearing those few words he'd managed to get out, the effort he'd made . . . it was like a blade to my belly. My father cringed as he said, "Please—"

"*Silence*," the creature snapped, and rage boiled up in me so blistering it was an effort to keep from lunging to stab my dagger in his eye. But by the time I had so much as raised my arm, I knew he would have his maw around my neck.

"I can get gold—" my father said, and my rage guttered. The only way he would get money was by begging. Even then, he'd be lucky to get a few coppers. I'd seen how pitiless the well-off were in our village. The monsters in our mortal realm were just as bad as those across the wall.

The beast sneered. "How much is your daughter's life worth to you? Do you think it equates to a sum?"

Nesta still had Elain held behind her, Elain's face so pale it matched the snow drifting in from the open door. But Nesta monitored every move the beast made, her brows lowered. She didn't bother to look at my father—as if she knew his answer already.

When my father didn't reply, I dared another step toward the beast, drawing his attention to me. I had to get him out—get him away from my family. From the way he'd brushed away my knife, any hope of escaping lay in somehow sneaking up on him. With his hearing, I doubted I'd get a chance anytime soon, at least until he believed I was docile. If I tried to attack him or fled before then, he would destroy my family for the sheer enjoyment of it. Then he would find me again. I had no choice but to go. And then, later, I might find an opportunity to slit the beast's throat. Or at least disable him long enough to flee.

As long as the faeries couldn't find me again, they couldn't hold me to the Treaty. Even if it made me a cursed oath-breaker. But in going with him, I would be breaking the most important promise I'd ever made. Surely it trumped an ancient treaty that I hadn't even signed.

I loosened my grip on the hilt of my remaining dagger and stared into those green eyes for a long, silent while before I said, "When do we go?"

Those lupine features remained fierce—vicious. Any lingering hope I had of fighting died as he moved to the door—no, to the quiver I'd left behind it. He pulled out the ash arrow, sniffed, and snarled at it. With two movements, he snapped it in half and chucked it into the fire behind my sisters before turning back to me. I could smell my doom on his breath as he said, "Now."

Now.

Even Elain lifted her head to gape at me in mute horror. But I couldn't look at her, couldn't look at Nesta—not when they were still crouched there, still silent. I turned to my father. His eyes glistened, so I glanced to the few cabinets we had, faded too-yellow daffodils curving over the handles. *Now.*

The beast paced in the doorway. I didn't want to contemplate where

I was going or what he would do with me. Running would be foolish until it was the right time.

"The venison should hold you for two weeks," I said to my father as I gathered my clothes to bulk up against the cold. "Start on the fresh meat, then work your way through to the jerky—you know how to make it."

"Feyre—" my father breathed, but I continued as I fastened my cloak.

"I left the money from the pelts on the dresser," I said. "It will last you for a time, if you're careful." I finally looked at my father again and allowed myself to memorize the lines of his face. My eyes stung, but I blinked the moisture away as I stuffed my hands into my worn gloves. "When spring comes, hunt in the grove just south of the big bend in Silverspring Creek—the rabbits make their warrens there. Ask . . . ask Isaac Hale to show you how to make snares. I taught him last year."

My father nodded, covering his mouth with a hand. The beast growled his warning and prowled out into the night. I made to follow him but paused to look at my sisters, still crouched by the fire, as if they wouldn't dare to move until I was gone.

Elain mouthed my name but kept cowering, kept her head down. So I turned to Nesta, whose face was so similar to my mother's, so cold and unrelenting.

"Whatever you do," I said quietly, "don't marry Tomas Mandray. His father beats his wife, and none of his sons do anything to stop it." Nesta's eyes widened, but I added, "Bruises are harder to conceal than poverty."

Nesta stiffened but said nothing—both of my sisters said absolutely nothing—as I turned toward the open door. But a hand wrapped around my arm, tugging me into a stop.

Turning me around to face him, my father opened and closed his mouth. Outside, the beast, sensing I'd been detained, sent a snarl rumbling into the cottage.

"Feyre," my father said. His fingers trembled as he grasped my gloved hands, but his eyes became clearer and bolder than I'd seen them in years. "You were always too good for here, Feyre. Too good for us, too good for everyone." He squeezed my hands. "If you ever escape, ever convince them that you've paid the debt, don't return."

I hadn't expected a heart-wrenching good-bye, but I hadn't imagined *this*, either.

"Don't *ever* come back," my father said, releasing my hands to shake me by the shoulders. "Feyre." He stumbled over my name, his throat bobbing. "You go somewhere new—and you make a name for yourself."

Beyond, the beast was just a shadow. A life for a life—but what if the life offered as payment also meant losing three others? The thought alone was enough to steel me, anchor me.

I'd never told my father of the promise I'd made my mother, and there was no use explaining it now. So I shrugged off his grip and left.

I let the sounds of the snow crunching underfoot drive out my father's words as I followed the beast to the night-shrouded woods.

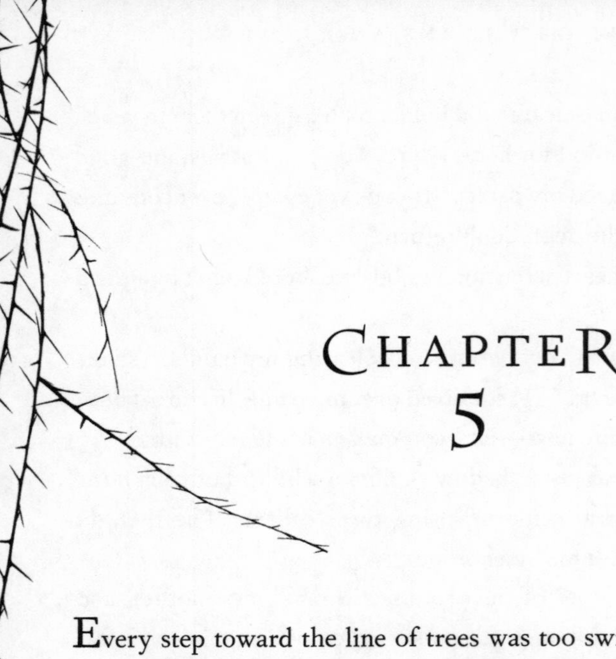

Chapter 5

Every step toward the line of trees was too swift, too light, too soon carrying me to whatever torment and misery awaited. I didn't dare look back at the cottage.

We entered the line of trees. Darkness beckoned beyond.

But a white mare was patiently waiting—unbound—beside a tree, her coat like fresh snow in the moonlight. She only lowered her head—as if in *respect*, of all things—as the beast lumbered up to her.

He motioned with a giant paw for me to mount. Still the horse remained calm, even as he passed close enough to gut her in one swipe. It had been years since I'd ridden, and I'd only ridden a pony at that, but I savored the warmth of the horse against my half-frozen body as I climbed into the saddle and she set into a walk. Without light to guide me, I let her trail the beast. They were nearly the same size. I wasn't surprised when we headed northward—toward faerie territory—though my stomach clenched so tightly it ached.

Live with him. I could live out the rest of my mortal life on his lands. Perhaps this was merciful—but then, he hadn't specified in what manner, exactly, I would live. The Treaty forbade faeries from taking us as slaves, but—perhaps that excluded humans who'd murdered faeries.

We'd likely go to whatever rift in the wall he'd used to get here, to steal me. And once we went through the invisible wall, once we were in Prythian, there was no way for my family to ever find me. I'd be little more than a lamb in a kingdom of wolves. Wolves—wolf.

Murdered a faerie. That was what I'd done.

My throat went dry. I'd killed a faerie. I couldn't bring myself to feel badly about it. Not with my family left behind me to surely starve; not when it meant one less wicked, awful creature in the world. The beast had burned my ash arrow—so I'd have to rely on luck to get even a splinter of the wood again, if I was to stand a chance of killing him. Or slowing him down.

Knowledge of that weakness, of their susceptibility to ash, was the only reason we'd ever survived against the High Fae during the ancient uprising, a secret betrayed by one of their own.

My blood chilled further as I uselessly scanned for any signs of the narrow trunk and explosion of branches that I'd learned marked ash trees. I'd never seen the forest so still. Whatever was out there had to be tame compared to the beast beside me, despite the horse's ease around him. Hopefully he would keep other faeries away after we entered his realm.

Prythian. The word was a death knell that echoed through me again and again.

Lands—he'd said he had lands, but what kind of dwelling? My horse was beautiful and its saddle was crafted of rich leather, which meant he had some sort of contact with civilized life. I'd never heard the specifics of what the lives of faeries or High Fae were like—never heard much about anything other than their deadly abilities and appetites. I clenched the reins to keep my hands from shaking.

There were few firsthand accounts of Prythian itself. The mortals who went over the wall—either willingly as tributes from the Children of the

Blessed or stolen—never came back. I'd learned most of the legends from villagers, though my father had occasionally offered up a milder tale or two on the nights he made an attempt to remember we existed.

As far as we knew, the High Fae still governed the northern parts of our world—from our enormous island over the narrow sea separating us from the massive continent, across depthless fjords and frozen wastelands and sandblasted deserts, all the way to the great ocean on the other side. Some faerie territories were empires; some were overseen by kings and queens. Then there were places like Prythian, divided and ruled by seven High Lords—beings of such unyielding power that legend claimed they could level buildings, break apart armies, and butcher you before you could blink. I didn't doubt it.

No one had ever told me why humans chose to linger in our territory, when so little space had been granted to us and we remained in such close proximity to Prythian. Fools—whatever humans had stayed here after the War must have been suicidal fools to live so close. Even with the centuries-old Treaty between the mortal and faerie realms, there were rifts in the warded wall separating our lands, holes big enough for those lethal creatures to slip into our territory to amuse themselves with tormenting us.

That was the side of Prythian that the Children of the Blessed never deigned to acknowledge—perhaps a side of Prythian I'd soon witness. My stomach turned. *Live with him*, I reminded myself, again and again and again. *Live*, not die.

Though I supposed I could also *live* in a dungeon. He would likely lock me up and forget that I was there, forget that humans needed things like food and water and warmth.

Prowling ahead of me, the beast's horns spiraled toward the night sky, and tendrils of hot breath curled from his snout. We had to make camp at some point; the border of Prythian was days away. Once we stopped, I would keep awake for the entirety of the night and never let him out of my sight. Even though he'd burned my ash arrow, I'd smuggled my remaining knife in my cloak. Maybe tonight would grant me an opportunity to use it.

But it was not my own doom I contemplated as I let myself tumble into dread and rage and despair. As we rode on—the only sounds snow crunching beneath paws and hooves—I alternated between a wretched smugness at the thought of my family starving and thus realizing how important I was, and a blinding agony at the thought of my father begging in the streets, his ruined leg giving out on him as he stumbled from person to person. Every time I looked at the beast, I could see my father limping through town, pleading for coppers to keep my sisters alive. Worse—what Nesta might resort to in order to keep Elain alive. She wouldn't mind my father's death. But she would lie and steal and sell anything for Elain's sake—and her own as well.

I took in the way the beast moved, trying to find any—*any*—weakness. I could detect none. "What manner of faerie are you?" I asked, the words nearly swallowed up by the snow and trees and star-heavy sky.

He didn't bother to turn around. He didn't bother to say anything at all. Fair enough. I'd killed his friend, after all.

I tried again. "Do you have a name?" Or anything to curse him by.

A huff of air that could have been a bitter laugh. "Does it even matter to you, human?"

I didn't answer. He might very well change his mind about sparing me.

But perhaps I would escape before he decided to gut me. I would grab my family and we'd stow away on a ship and sail far, far away. Perhaps I would try to kill him, regardless of the futility, regardless of whether it constituted another unprovoked attack, just for being the one who came to claim my life—my *life*, when these faeries valued ours so little. The mercenary had survived; maybe I could, too. Maybe.

I opened my mouth to again ask him for his name, but a growl of annoyance rippled out of him. I didn't have a chance to struggle, to fight back, when a charged, metallic tang stung my nose. Exhaustion slammed down upon me and blackness swallowed me whole.

✢

I awoke with a jolt atop the horse, secured by invisible bonds. The sun was already high.

Magic—that's what the tang had been, what was keeping my limbs tucked in tight, preventing me from going for my knife. I recognized the power deep in my bones, from some collective mortal memory and terror. How long had it kept me unconscious? How long had *he* kept me unconscious, rather than have to speak to me?

Gritting my teeth, I might have demanded answers from him—might have shouted to where he still lumbered ahead, heedless of me. But then chirping birds flitted past me, and a mild breeze kissed my face. I spied a hedge-bordered metal gate ahead.

My prison or my salvation—I couldn't decide which.

Two days—it took two days from my cottage to reach the wall and enter the southernmost border of Prythian. Had I been held in an enchanted sleep for that long? Bastard.

The gate swung open without porter or sentry, and the beast continued through. Whether I wanted to or not, my horse followed after him.

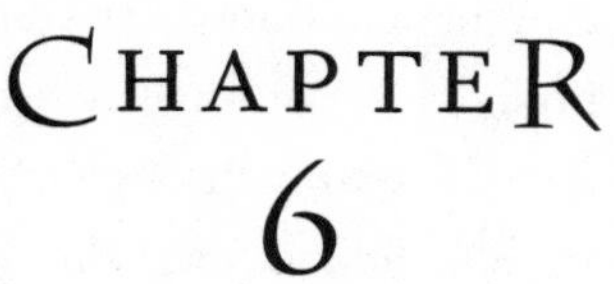

CHAPTER 6

The estate sprawled across a rolling green land. I'd never seen anything like it; even our former manor couldn't compare. It was veiled in roses and ivy, with patios and balconies and staircases sprouting from its alabaster sides. The grounds were encased by woods, but stretched so far that I could barely see the distant line of the forest. So much color, so much sunlight and movement and texture . . . I could hardly drink it in fast enough. To paint it would be useless, would never do it justice.

My awe might have subdued my fear had the place not been so wholly empty and silent. Even the garden through which we walked, following a gravel path to the main doors of the house, seemed hushed and sleeping. Above the array of amethyst irises and pale snowdrops and butter-yellow daffodils swaying in the balmy breeze, the faint stench of metal ticked my nostrils.

Of course it would be magic, because it was spring here. What wretched power did they possess to make their lands so different from ours, to control the seasons and weather as if they owned them? Sweat trickled down my spine as my layers of clothes turned suffocating. I rotated my wrists and shifted in the saddle. Whatever bonds had held me were gone.

The faerie meandered on ahead, leaping nimbly up the grand marble staircase that led to the giant oak doors in one mighty, fluid movement. The doors swung open for him on silent hinges, and he prowled inside. He'd planned this entire arrival, no doubt—keeping me unconscious so I didn't know where I was, didn't know the way home or what other deadly faerie territories might be lurking between me and the wall. I felt for my knife, but found only layers of frayed clothes.

The thought of those claws pawing through my cloak to find my knife made my mouth go dry. I shoved away the fury and terror and disgust as my horse came to a stop of her own accord at the foot of the stairs. The message was clear enough. The towering estate house seemed to be watching, waiting.

I glanced over my shoulder toward the still-open gates. If I were to bolt, it would have to be now.

South—all I had to do was go south, and I would eventually make it to the wall. If I didn't encounter anything before then. I tugged on the reins, but the mare remained stationary—even as I dug my heels into her sides. I let out a low, sharp hiss. Fine. On foot.

My knees buckled as I hit the ground, bits of light flashing in my vision. I grasped the saddle and winced as soreness and hunger racked my senses. Now—I had to go *now*. I made to move, but the world was still spinning and flashing.

Only a fool would run with no food, no strength.

I wouldn't get half a mile like this. I wouldn't get half a mile before he caught me and tore me to ribbons, as he'd promised.

I took a long, shuddering breath. Food—getting food, *then* running at the next opportune moment. It sounded like a solid plan.

When I was steady enough to walk, I left the horse at the bottom of the stairs, taking the steps one at a time. My breath tight in my chest, I passed through the open doors and into the shadows of the house.

Inside, it was even more opulent. Black-and-white checkered marble shone at my feet, flowing to countless doors and a sweeping staircase. A long hall stretched ahead to the giant glass doors at the other end of the house, and through them I glimpsed a second garden, grander than the one out front. No sign of a dungeon—no shouts or pleas rising up from hidden chambers below. No, just the low growl from a nearby room, so deep that it rattled the vases overflowing with fat clusters of hydrangea atop the scattered hall tables. As if in response, an open set of polished wooden doors swung wider to my left. A command to follow.

My fingers shook as I rubbed my eyes. I'd known the High Fae had once built themselves palaces and temples around the world—buildings that my mortal ancestors had destroyed after the War out of spite—but I'd never considered how they might live today, the elegance and wealth they might possess. Never contemplated that the faeries, these feral monsters, might own estates grander than any mortal dwelling.

I tensed as I entered the room.

A long table—longer than any we'd ever possessed at our manor—filled most of the space. It was laden with food and wine—so much food, some of it wafting tendrils of steam, that my mouth watered. At least it was familiar, and not some strange faerie delicacy: chicken, bread, peas, fish, asparagus, lamb . . . it could have been a feast at any mortal manor. Another surprise. The beast padded to the oversized chair at the head of the table.

I lingered by the threshold, gazing at the food—all that hot, glorious food—that I couldn't eat. That was the first rule we were taught as children, usually in songs or chants: If misfortune forced you to keep company with a faerie, you never drank their wine, never ate their food. Ever. Unless you wanted to wind up enslaved to them in mind and soul—unless you wanted to wind up dragged back to Prythian. Well, the second part had already happened, but I might stand a chance at avoiding the first.

The beast plopped into the chair, the wood groaning, and, in a flash of white light, turned into a golden-haired man.

I stifled a cry and pushed myself against the paneled wall beside the door, feeling for the molding of the threshold, trying to gauge the distance between me and escape. This beast was not a man, not a lesser faerie. He was one of the High Fae, one of their ruling nobility: beautiful, lethal, and merciless.

He was young—or at least what I could see of his face seemed young. His nose, cheeks, and brows were covered by an exquisite golden mask embedded with emeralds shaped like whorls of leaves. Some absurd High Fae fashion, no doubt. It left only his eyes—looking the same as they had in his beast form, strong jaw, and mouth for me to see, and the latter tightened into a thin line.

"You should eat something," he said. Unlike the elegance of his mask, the dark green tunic he wore was rather plain, accented only with a leather baldric across his broad chest. It was more for fighting than style, even though he bore no weapons I could detect. Not just one of the High Fae, but . . . a warrior, too.

I didn't want to consider what might require him to wear a warrior's attire and tried not to look too hard at the leather of the baldric gleaming in the sunlight streaming in through the bank of windows behind him. I hadn't seen a cloudless sky like that in months. He filled a glass of wine from an exquisitely cut crystal decanter and drank deeply. As if he needed it.

I inched toward the door, my heart beating so fast I thought I'd vomit. The cool metal of the door's hinges bit into my fingers. If I moved fast, I could be out of the house and sprinting for the gate within seconds. He was undoubtedly faster—but chucking some of those pretty pieces of hallway furniture in his path might slow him down. Though his Fae ears—with their delicate, pointed arches—would pick up any whisper of movement from me.

"Who are you?" I managed to say. His light golden hair was so similar to the color of his beast form's pelt. Those giant claws undoubtedly still lurked just below the surface of his skin.

"Sit," he said gruffly, waving a broad hand to encompass the table. "Eat."

I ran through the chants in my head, again and again. Not worth it—easing my ravenous hunger was definitely not worth the risk of being enslaved to him in mind and soul.

He let out a low growl. "Unless you'd rather faint?"

"It's not safe for humans," I managed to say, offense be damned.

He huffed a laugh—more feral than anything. "The food is fine for you to eat, human." Those strange green eyes pinned me to the spot, as if he could detect every muscle in my body that was priming to bolt. "Leave, if you want," he added with a flash of teeth. "I'm not your jailer. The gates are open—you can live anywhere in Prythian."

And no doubt be eaten or tormented by a wretched faerie. But while every inch of this place was civilized and clean and beautiful, I had to get out, had to get back. That promise to my mother, cold and vain as she was, was all I had. I made no move toward the food.

"Fine," he said, the word laced with a growl, and began serving himself.

I didn't have to face the consequences of refusing him another time, as someone strode past me, heading right for the head of the table.

"Well?" the stranger said—another High Fae: red-haired and finely dressed in a tunic of muted silver. He, too, wore a mask. He sketched a bow to the seated male and then crossed his arms. Somehow, he hadn't spotted me where I was still pressed against the wall.

"Well, *what?*" My captor cocked his head, the movement more animal than human.

"Is Andras dead, then?"

A nod from my captor—savior, whatever he was. "I'm sorry," he said quietly.

"How?" the stranger demanded, his knuckles white as he gripped his muscled arms.

"An ash arrow," said the other. His red-haired companion hissed. "The Treaty's summons led me to the mortal. I gave her safe haven."

"A girl—a mortal girl actually killed Andras." Not a question so much as a venom-coated string of words. He glanced at the end of the table, where my empty chair stood. "And the summons found the girl responsible."

The golden-masked one gave a low, bitter laugh and pointed at me. "The Treaty's magic brought me right to her doorstep."

The stranger whirled with fluid grace. His mask was bronze and fashioned after a fox's features, concealing all but the lower half of his face—along with most of what looked like a wicked, slashing scar from his brow down to his jaw. It didn't hide the eye that was missing—or the carved golden orb that had replaced it and *moved* as though he could use it. It fixed on me.

Even from across the room, I could see his remaining russet eye widen. He sniffed once, his lips curling a bit to reveal straight white teeth, and then he turned to the other faerie. "You're joking," he said quietly. "That scrawny thing brought down *Andras* with a single ash arrow?"

Bastard—an absolute bastard. A pity I didn't have the arrow now—so I could shoot him instead.

"She admitted to it," the golden-haired one said tightly, tracing the rim of his goblet with a finger. A long, lethal claw slid out, scraping against the metal. I fought to keep my breathing steady. Especially as he added, "She didn't try to deny it."

The fox-masked faerie sank onto the edge of the table, the light catching in his long fire-red hair. I could understand his mask, with that brutal scar and missing eye, but the other High Fae seemed fine. Perhaps he wore it out of solidarity. Maybe that explained the absurd fashion. "Well," the red-haired one seethed, "now we're stuck with *that*, thanks to your useless mercy, and you've ruined—"

I stepped forward—only a step. I wasn't sure what I was going to say, but being spoken about that way . . . I kept my mouth shut, but it was enough.

"Did you enjoy killing my friend, human?" the red-haired one said. "Did you hesitate, or was the hatred in your heart riding you too hard to consider sparing him? It must have been so satisfying for a small mortal thing like you to take him down."

The golden-haired one said nothing, but his jaw tightened. As they studied me, I reached for a knife that wasn't there.

"Anyway," the fox-masked one continued, facing his companion again with a sneer. He would likely laugh if I ever drew a weapon on him. "Perhaps there's a way to—"

"Lucien," my captor said quietly, the name echoing with a hint of a snarl. "Behave."

Lucien went rigid, but he hopped off the edge of the table and bowed deeply to me. "My apologies, lady." Another joke at my expense. "I'm Lucien. Courtier and emissary." He gestured to me with a flourish. "Your eyes are like stars, and your hair like burnished gold."

He cocked his head—waiting for me to give him my name. But telling him anything about me, about my family and where I came from—

"Her name is Feyre," said the one in charge—the beast. He must have learned my name at my cottage. Those striking green eyes met mine again and then flicked to the door. "Alis will take you to your room. You could use a bath and fresh clothes."

I couldn't decide whether it was an insult or not. There was a firm hand at my elbow, and I flinched. A rotund brown-haired woman in a simple brass bird mask tugged on my arm and inclined her head toward the open door behind us. Her white apron was crisp above her homespun brown dress—a servant. The masks had to be some sort of trend, then.

If they cared so much about their clothes, about what even their servants wore, maybe they were shallow and vain enough for me to deceive, despite their master's warrior clothes. Still, they were High Fae. I would have to be clever and quiet and bide my time until I could escape. So I let Alis lead me away. *Room*—not *cell*. A small relief, then.

I'd barely made it a few steps before Lucien growled, "That's the hand the Cauldron thought to deal us? *She* brought Andras down? We never should have sent him out there—none of them should have been out there. It was a fool's mission." His growl was more bitter than threatening. Could he shape-shift as well? "Maybe we should just take a stand—maybe it's time to say *enough*. Dump the girl somewhere, kill her, I don't care—she's nothing but a burden here. She'd sooner put a knife in your back than talk to you—or any of us." I kept my breathing calm, my spine locking, and—

"No," the other bit out. "Not until we know for certain that there is no other way will we make a move. And as for the girl, she stays. Unharmed. End of discussion. Her life in that hovel was Hell enough." My cheeks heated, even while I loosed a tight breath, and I avoided looking at Alis as I felt her eyes slide to me. A hovel—I suppose that's what our cottage was when compared to this place.

"Then you've got your work cut out for you, old son," Lucien said. "I'm sure her life will be a fine replacement for Andras's—maybe she can even train with the others on the border."

A snarl of irritation resonated through the air.

The shining, spotless halls swallowed me up before I could hear more.

✠

Alis led me through halls of gold and silver until we came to a lavish bedroom on the second level. I'll admit I didn't fight that hard when Alis and two other servants—also masked—bathed me, cut my hair, and then plucked me until I felt like a chicken being prepared for dinner. For all I knew, I might very well be their next meal.

It was only the High Fae's promise—to live out my days in Prythian instead of dying—that kept me from being sick at the thought. While these faeries also looked human, save for their ears, I'd never learned what the High Fae called their servants. But I didn't dare to ask, or to speak to them at all, not when just having their hands on me, having them so *close* was enough to make me focus solely on not trembling.

Still, I took one look at the velvet turquoise dress Alis had placed on the bed and wrapped my white dressing gown tightly around me, sinking into a chair and pleading for my old clothes to be returned. Alis refused, and when I begged again, trying my best to sound pathetic and sad and pitiful, she stormed out. I hadn't worn a dress in years. I wasn't about to start, not when escape was my main priority. I wouldn't be able to move freely in a gown.

Bundled in my robe, I sat for minute after minute, the chattering of small birds in the garden beyond the windows the only sounds. No screaming, no clashing weapons, no hint of any slaughter or torture.

The bedroom was larger than our entire cottage. Its walls were pale green, delicately sketched with patterns of gold, and the moldings were golden as well. I might have thought it tacky had the ivory furniture and rugs not complemented it so well. The gigantic bed was of a similar color scheme, and the curtains that hung from the towering headboard drifted in the faint breeze from the open windows. My dressing gown was of the finest silk, edged with lace—simple and exquisite enough that I ran a finger along the lapels.

The few stories I'd heard had been wrong—or five hundred years of separation had muddled them. Yes, I was still prey, still born weak and useless compared to them, but this place was . . . peaceful. Calm. Unless that was an illusion, too, and the loophole in the Treaty was a lie—a trick to set me at ease before they destroyed me. The High Fae liked to play with their food.

The door creaked, and Alis returned—a bundle of clothing in her hands. She lifted a sodden grayish shirt. "You want to wear this?" I gaped at the holes in the sides and sleeves. "It fell apart the moment the laundresses put it in water." She held up a few scraps of brown. "Here's what's left of your pants."

I clamped down on the curse building in my chest. She might be a servant, but she could easily kill me, too.

"Will you wear the dress now?" she demanded. I knew I should get up, should agree, but I slumped farther into my seat. Alis stared me down for a moment before leaving again.

She returned with trousers and a tunic that fit me well, both of them rich with color. A bit fancy, but I didn't complain when I donned the white shirt, nor when I buttoned the dark blue tunic and ran my hands over the scratchy, golden thread embroidered on the lapels. It had to cost a fortune in itself—and it tugged at that useless part of my mind that admired lovely and strange and colorful things.

I was too young to remember much before my father's downfall. He'd tolerated me enough to allow me to loiter about his offices, and sometimes even explained various goods and their worth, the details of which I'd long since forgotten. My time in his offices—full of the scents of exotic spices and the music of foreign tongues—made up the majority of my few happy memories. I didn't need to know the worth of everything in this room to understand that the emerald curtains alone—silk, with gold velvet—could have fed us for a lifetime.

A chill scuttled down my spine. It had been days since I'd left. The venison would be running low already.

Alis herded me into a low-backed chair before the darkened fireplace, and I didn't fight back as she ran a comb through my hair and began braiding it.

"You're hardly more than skin and bones," she said, her fingers luxurious against my scalp.

"Winter does that to poor mortals," I said, fighting to keep the sharpness from my tone.

She huffed a laugh. "If you're wise, you'll keep your mouth shut and your ears open. It'll do you more good here than a loose tongue. And keep your wits about you—even your senses will try to betray you here."

I tried not to cringe at the warning. Alis went on. "Some folk are bound to be upset about Andras. Yet if you ask me, Andras was a good sentinel, but he knew what he would face when he crossed the wall—knew he'd likely find trouble. And the others understand the terms of the Treaty, too—even if they might resent your presence here, thanks to the mercy of our master. So keep your head down, and none of them will bother you. Though Lucien—he could do with someone snapping at him, if you've the courage for it."

I didn't, and when I went to ask more about whom I should try to avoid, she had already finished with my hair and opened the door to the hall.

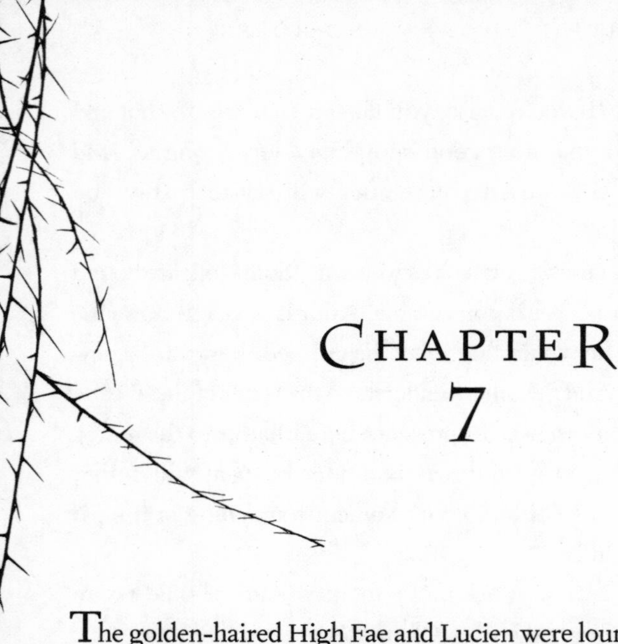

CHAPTER 7

The golden-haired High Fae and Lucien were lounging at the table when Alis returned me to the dining room. They no longer had plates before them, but still sipped from golden goblets. Real gold—not paint or foil. Our mismatched cutlery flashed through my mind as I paused in the middle of the room. Such wealth—such staggering wealth, when we had nothing.

A half-wild beast, Nesta had called me. But compared to him, compared to this place, compared to the elegant, easy way they held their goblets, the way the golden-haired one had called me *human* . . . we were all half-wild beasts to the High Fae. Even if they were the ones who could don fur and claws.

Food still remained on the table, the array of spices lingering in the air, beckoning. I was starving, my head unnervingly light.

The golden-haired High Fae's mask gleamed with the last rays of the afternoon sunshine. "Before you ask again: the food is safe for you to eat." He pointed to the chair at the other end of the table. No sign of his claws. When I didn't move, he sighed sharply. "What do you want, then?"

I said nothing. *To eat, flee, save my family* . . .

Lucien drawled from his seat along the length of the table, "I told you so, Tamlin." He flicked a glance toward his friend. "Your skills with females have definitely become rusty in recent decades."

Tamlin. He glowered at Lucien, shifting in his seat. I tried not to stiffen at the other bit of information Lucien had given away. *Decades*.

Tamlin didn't look much older than me, but his kind was immortal. He could be hundreds of years old. Thousands. My mouth dried up as I carefully studied their strange, masked faces—unearthly, primal, and imperious. Like immovable gods or feral courtiers.

"Well," Lucien said, his remaining russet eye fixed on me, "you don't look half as bad now. A relief, I suppose, since you're to live with us. Though the tunic isn't as pretty as a dress."

Wolves ready to pounce—that's what they were, just like their friend. I was all too aware of my diction, of the very breath I took as I said, "I'd prefer not to wear that dress."

"And why not?" Lucien crooned.

It was Tamlin who answered for me. "Because killing us is easier in pants."

I kept my face blank, willed my heart to calm as I said, "Now that I'm here, what . . . what do you plan to do with me?"

Lucien snorted, but Tamlin said with a snarl of annoyance, "Just sit down."

An empty seat had been pulled out at the end of the table. So many foods, piping hot and wafting those enticing spices. The servants had probably brought out new food while I'd washed. So much wasted. I clenched my hands into fists.

"We're not going to bite." Lucien's white teeth gleamed in a way that suggested otherwise. I avoided his gaze, avoided that strange, animated metal eye that focused on me as I inched to my seat and sat down.

Tamlin rose, stalking around the table—closer and closer, each movement smooth and lethal, a predator blooded with power. It was an effort to keep still—especially as he picked up a dish, brought it over to me, and piled some meat and sauce on my plate.

I said quietly, "I can serve myself." Anything, *anything* to keep him well away from me.

Tamlin paused, so close that one swipe of those claws lurking under his skin could rip my throat out. That was why the leather baldric bore no weapons: why use them when you were a weapon yourself? "It's an honor for a human to be served by a High Fae," he said roughly.

I swallowed hard. He continued piling various foods on my plate, stopping only when it was heaping with meat and sauce and bread, and then filled my glass with pale sparkling wine. I loosed a breath as he prowled back to his seat, though he could probably hear it.

I wanted nothing more than to bury my face in the plate and then eat my way down the table, but I pinned my hands beneath my thighs and stared at the two faeries.

They watched me, too closely to be casual. Tamlin straightened a bit and said, "You look . . . better than before."

Was that a compliment? I could have sworn Lucien gave Tamlin an encouraging nod.

"And your hair is . . . clean."

Perhaps it was my raging hunger making me hallucinate the piss-poor attempt at flattery. Still, I leaned back and kept my words calm and quiet, the way I might speak to any other predator. "You're High Fae—faerie nobility?"

Lucien coughed and looked to Tamlin. "You can take that question."

"Yes," Tamlin said, frowning—as if searching for anything to say to me. He settled on merely: "We are."

Fine. A man—faerie—of few words. I had killed his friend, was an unwanted guest. I wouldn't want to talk to me, either.

"What do you plan to do with me now that I'm here?"

Tamlin's eyes didn't leave my face. "Nothing. Do whatever you want."

"So I'm not to be your slave?" I dared ask.

Lucien choked on his wine. But Tamlin didn't smile. "I don't keep slaves."

I ignored the release of tightness in my chest at that. "But what am I to do with my *life* here?" I pressed. "Do you—do you wish me to earn my keep? To work?" A stupid question, if he hadn't considered it, but . . . but I had to know.

Tamlin stiffened. "What you do with your life isn't my problem."

Lucien pointedly cleared his throat, and Tamlin flashed him a glare. After an exchanged look I couldn't read, Tamlin sighed and said, "Don't you have any . . . interests?"

"No." Not entirely true, but I wasn't about to explain the painting to him. Not when he was apparently having a great deal of trouble just talking to me civilly.

Lucien muttered, "So typically human."

Tamlin's mouth quirked to the side. "Do whatever you want with your time. Just stay out of trouble."

"So you truly mean for me to stay here forever." What I meant was: *So I'm to stay in this luxury while my family starves to death?*

"I didn't make the rules," Tamlin said tersely.

"My family is *starving*," I said. I didn't mind begging—not for this. I'd given my word, and held to that word for so long that I was nothing and no one without it. "Please let me go. There must be—must be some other loophole out of the Treaty's rules—some other way to atone."

"Atone?" Lucien said. "Have you even apologized yet?"

Apparently, all attempts to flatter me were dead and gone. So I looked Lucien right in his remaining russet eye and said, "I'm sorry."

Lucien leaned back in his chair. "How did you kill him? Was it a bloody fight, or just cold-blooded murder?"

My spine stiffened. "I shot him with an ash arrow. And then an ordinary arrow through the eye. He didn't put up a fight. After the first shot, he just stared at me."

"Yet you killed him anyway—though he made no move to attack you. And then you *skinned* him," Lucien hissed.

"*Enough*, Lucien," Tamlin said to his courtier with a snarl. "I don't want to hear details." He turned to me, ancient and brutal and unyielding.

I spoke before he could say anything. "My family won't last a month without me." Lucien chuckled, and I gritted my teeth. "Do you know what it's like to be hungry?" I demanded, anger rising to devour any common sense. "Do you know what it's like to not know when your next meal will be?"

Tamlin's jaw tightened. "Your family is alive and well-cared for. You think so low of faeries that you believe I'd take their only source of income and nourishment and not replace it?"

I straightened. "You swear it?" Even if faeries couldn't lie, I had to hear it.

A low, incredulous laugh. "On everything that I am and possess."

"Why not tell me that when we left the cottage?"

"Would you have believed me? Do you even believe me now?" Tamlin's claws embedded in the arms of his chair.

"Why should I trust a word you say? You're all masters of spinning your truths to your own advantage."

"Some would say it's unwise to insult a Fae in his home," Tamlin ground out. "Some would say you should be grateful for me finding you before another one of my kind came to claim the debt, for sparing your life and then offering you the chance to live in comfort."

I shot to my feet, wisdom be damned, and was about to kick back my chair when invisible hands clapped on my arms and shoved me back into the seat.

"Do *not* do whatever it was you were contemplating," Tamlin said.

I went still as the tang of magic seared my nose. I tried to twist in the chair, testing the invisible bonds. But my arms were secured, and my back was pressed into the wood so hard that it ached. I glanced at the knife beside my plate. I should have gone for it first—futile effort or no.

"I'm going to warn you once," Tamlin said too softly. "Only once, and then it's on you, human. I don't care if you go live somewhere else in Prythian. But if you cross the wall, if you flee, your family will no longer be cared for."

His words were like a stone to the head. If I escaped, if I even *tried* to run, I might very well doom my family. And even if I dared risk it . . . even if I succeeded in reaching them, where would I take them? I couldn't stow my sisters away on a ship—and once we arrived somewhere else, somewhere safe, we'd have nowhere to live. But for him to hold my family's well-being against me, to throw away their survival if I stepped out of line . . .

I opened my mouth, but his snarl rattled the glasses. "Is that not a fair bargain? And if you flee, then you might not be so lucky with whoever comes to retrieve you next." His claws slipped back under his knuckles. "The food is not enchanted, or drugged, and it will be your own damn fault if you faint. So you're going to sit at this table and *eat*, Feyre. And *Lucien* will do his best to be polite." He threw a pointed look in his direction. Lucien shrugged.

The invisible bonds loosened, and I winced as I whacked my hands on the underside of the table. The bonds on my legs and middle remained intact. One glance at Tamlin's smoldering green eyes told me what I wanted to know: his guest or not, I wasn't going to get up from this table until I'd eaten something. I'd think about the sudden change in my plans to escape later. Now . . . for now I eyed the silver fork and carefully picked it up.

They still watched me—watched my every move, the flare of my nostrils as I sniffed the food on my plate. No metallic stench of magic.

And faeries couldn't lie. So he had to be right about the food, then. Stabbing a piece of chicken, I took a bite.

It was an effort to keep from grunting. I hadn't had food this good in years. Even the meals we'd had before our downfall were little more than ashes compared to this. I ate my entire plate in silence, too aware of the High Fae observing every bite, but as I reached for a second helping of chocolate torte, the food vanished. Just—vanished, as if it had never existed, not a crumb left behind.

Swallowing hard, I set my fork down so they wouldn't see my hand start to shake.

"One more bite and you'll hurl your guts up," Tamlin said, drinking deeply from his goblet.

The bonds holding me loosened. Silent permission to leave.

"Thank you for the meal," I said. It was all I could think of.

"Won't you stay for wine?" Lucien said with sweet venom from where he lounged in his seat.

I braced my hands on my chair to rise. "I'm tired. I'd like to sleep."

"It's been a few decades since I last saw one of you," Lucien drawled, "but you humans never change, so I don't think I'm wrong in asking *why* you find our company to be so unpleasant, when surely the men back home aren't much to look at."

At the other end of the table, Tamlin gave his emissary a long, warning look. Lucien ignored it.

"You're High Fae," I said tightly. "I'd ask why you'd even bother inviting me here at all—or dining with me." Fool—I really should have been killed ten times over already.

Lucien said, "True. But indulge me: you're a human woman, and yet you'd rather eat hot coals than sit here longer than necessary. Ignoring this"—he waved a hand at the metal eye and brutal scar on his face—"surely we're not so miserable to look at." Typical faerie vanity and arrogance. That, at least, the legends had been right about. I tucked the knowledge away. "Unless you have someone back home. Unless there's a line of suitors out the door of your hovel that makes us seem like worms in comparison."

There was enough dismissal there that I took a little bit of satisfaction in saying, "I was close with a man back in my village." *Before that Treaty ripped me away—before it became clear that* you *are allowed to do as you please to us, but we can hardly strike back against you.*

Tamlin and Lucien exchanged glances, but it was Tamlin who said, "Are you in love with this man?"

"No," I said as casually as I could. It wasn't a lie—but even if I'd felt anything like that for Isaac, my answer would have been the same. It was bad enough that High Fae now knew my family existed. I didn't need to add Isaac to that list.

Again, that shared look between the two males. "And do you . . . love anyone else?" Tamlin said through clenched teeth.

A laugh burst out of me, tinged with hysteria. "No." I looked between them. Nonsense. These lethal, immortal beings really had nothing better to do than this? "Is this really what you care to know about me? If I find you more handsome than human men, and if I have a man back home? Why bother to ask at all, when I'll be stuck here for the rest of my life?" A hot line of anger sliced through my senses.

"We wanted to learn more about you, since you'll be here for a good while," Tamlin said, his lips a thin line. "But Lucien's pride tends to get in the way of his manners." He sighed, as if ready to be done with me, and said, "Go rest. We're both busy most days, so if you need anything, ask the staff. They'll help you."

"Why?" I asked. "Why be so generous?" Lucien gave me a look that suggested he had no idea, either, given that I'd murdered their companion, but Tamlin stared at me for a long moment.

"I kill too often as it is," Tamlin said finally, shrugging his broad shoulders. "And you're insignificant enough to not ruffle this estate. Unless you decide to start killing us."

A faint warmth bloomed in my cheeks, my neck. Insignificant—yes, I was insignificant to their lives, their power. As insignificant as the fading, chipped designs I'd painted around the cottage. "Well . . . ," I said, not quite feeling grateful at all, "thank you."

He gave a distant nod and motioned for me to leave. Dismissed. Like the lowly human I was. Lucien propped his chin on a fist and gave me a lazy half smile.

Enough. I got to my feet and backed toward the door. Putting my back to them would have been like walking away from a wolf, sparing my life or no. They said nothing when I slipped out the door.

A moment later, Lucien's barking laugh echoed into the halls, followed by a sharp, vicious growl that shut him up.

I slept fitfully that night, and the lock on my bedroom door felt more like a joke than anything.

⸸

I was wide awake before dawn, but I remained staring at the filigreed ceiling, watching the growing light creep between the drapes, savoring the softness of the down mattress. I was usually out of the cottage by first light—though my sisters hissed at me every morning for waking them so early. If I were home, I'd already be entering the woods, not wasting a moment of precious sunlight, listening to the drowsy chatter of the few winter birds. Instead, this bedroom and the house beyond were silent, the enormous bed foreign and empty. A small part of me missed the warmth of my sisters' bodies overlapping with mine.

Nesta must be stretching her legs and smiling at the extra room. She was probably content imagining me in the belly of a faerie—probably using the news as a chance to be fussed over by the villagers. Maybe my fate would prompt them to give my family some handouts. Or maybe Tamlin had given them enough money—or food, or whatever he thought "taking care" of them consisted of—to last through the winter. Or maybe the villagers would turn on my family, not wanting to be associated with people tied with Prythian, and run them out of town.

I buried my face in the pillow, pulling the blankets higher. If Tamlin had indeed provided for them, if those benefits would cease the moment I crossed the wall, then they'd likely resent my return more than celebrate it.

Your hair is . . . clean.

A pathetic compliment. I supposed that if he'd invited me to live here, to spare my life, he couldn't be completely . . . wicked. Perhaps he'd just been trying to smooth over our very, very rough beginning. Maybe there would be some way to persuade him to find some loophole, to get whatever magic that bound the Treaty to spare me. And if not some way, then some*one* . . .

I was drifting from one thought to another, trying to sort through the jumble, when the lock on the door clicked, and—

There was a screech and a thud, and I bolted upright to find Alis in a heap on the floor. The length of rope I'd made from the curtain trimmings now hung loosely from where I'd rigged it to snap into anyone's face. It had been the best I could do with what I had.

"I'm sorry, I'm sorry," I blurted, leaping from the bed, but Alis was already up, hissing at me as she brushed off her apron. She frowned at the rope dangling from the light fixture.

"What in the bottomless depths of the Cauldron is—"

"I didn't think anyone would be in here so early, and I meant to take it down, and—"

Alis looked me over from head to toe. "You think a bit of rope snapping in my face will keep me from breaking your bones?" My blood went cold. "You think that will do anything against one of us?"

I might have kept apologizing were it not for the sneer she gave me. I crossed my arms. "It was a warning bell to give me time to run. Not a trap."

She seemed poised to spit on me, but then her sharp brown eyes narrowed. "You can't outrun us, either, girl."

"I know," I said, my heart calming at last. "But at least I wouldn't face my death unaware."

Alis barked out a laugh. "My master gave his word that you could live here—*live*, not die. We will obey." She studied the hanging bit of rope. "But did you have to wreck those lovely curtains?"

I didn't want to—tried not to, but a hint of a smile tugged on my lips. Alis strode over to the remnants of the curtains and threw them open, revealing a sky that was still a deep periwinkle, splashed with hues of pumpkin and magenta from the rising dawn. "I am sorry," I said again.

Alis clicked her tongue. "At least you're willing to put up a fight, girl. I'll give you that."

I opened my mouth to speak, but another female servant with a bird mask entered, a breakfast tray in hand. She bid me a curt good morning, set the tray on a small table by the window, and disappeared into the attached bathing chamber. The sound of running water filled the room.

I sat at the table and studied the porridge and eggs and bacon—*bacon*. Again, such similar food to what we ate across the wall. I don't know why I'd expected otherwise. Alis poured me a cup of what looked and smelled like tea: full-bodied, aromatic tea, no doubt imported at great expense. Prythian and my adjoining homeland weren't exactly easy to reach. "What is this place?" I asked her quietly. "*Where* is this place?"

"It's safe, and that's all you need to know," Alis said, setting down the teapot. "At least the house is. If you go poking about the grounds, keep your wits about you."

Fine—if she wouldn't answer *that* . . . I tried again. "What sort of—faeries should I look out for?"

"All of them," Alis said. "My master's protection only goes so far. They'll want to hunt and kill you just for being a human—regardless of what you did to Andras."

Another useless answer. I dug into my breakfast, savoring each rich sip of tea, and she slipped into the bathing chamber. When I was done eating and bathing, I refused Alis's offer and dressed myself in another exquisite tunic—this one of purple so deep it could have been black. I wished I knew the name for the color, but cataloged it anyway. I pulled on the brown boots I'd worn the night before, and as I sat before a marble vanity letting Alis braid my wet hair, I cringed at my reflection.

It wasn't pleasing—though not for its actual appearance. While my nose was relatively straight, it was the other feature I'd inherited from my mother. I could still remember how her nose would crinkle with feigned amusement when one of her fabulously wealthy friends made some unfunny joke.

At least I had my father's soft mouth, though it made a mockery of my too-sharp cheekbones and hollow cheeks. I couldn't bring myself to look at my slightly uptilted eyes. I knew I'd see Nesta or my mother looking back at me. I'd sometimes wondered if that was why my sister had insulted me about my looks. I was a far cry from ugly, but . . . I bore too much of the people we'd hated and loved for Nesta to stand it. For me to stand it, too.

Though I supposed that for Tamlin—for High Fae used to ethereal, flawless beauty—it *had* been a struggle to find a compliment. Faerie bastard.

Alis finished my plait, and I jumped from the bench before she could weave in little flowers from the basket she'd brought. I would have lived up to my namesake were it not for the effects of poverty, but I'd never particularly cared. Beauty didn't mean anything in the forest.

When I asked Alis what I was to do now—*what I was to do with the entirety of my mortal life*—she shrugged and suggested a walk in the gardens. I almost laughed, but I kept my tongue still. I'd be foolish to push aside potential allies. I doubted she had Tamlin's ear, and I couldn't press her about it yet, but . . . At least a walk provided a chance to glean some sense of my surroundings—and whether there was anyone else who might plead my case to Tamlin.

The halls were silent and empty—strange for such a large estate. They'd mentioned others the night before, but I saw and heard no sign of them. A balmy breeze scented with . . . hyacinth, I realized—if only from Elain's small garden—floated down the halls, carrying with it the pleasant chirping of a bunting, a bird I wouldn't hear back home for months—if I ever heard them at all.

I was almost to the grand staircase when I noticed the paintings.

I hadn't let myself really *look* yesterday, but now, in the empty hall with no one to see me . . . a flash of color amid a shadowy, gloomy background made me stop, a riot of color and texture that compelled me to face the gilded frame.

I'd never—never—seen anything like it.

It's just a still life, a part of me said. And it was: a green glass vase with an assortment of flowers drooping over its narrow top, blossoms and leaves of every shape and size and color—roses, tulips, morning glory, goldenrod, maiden's lace, peonies . . .

The skill it must have taken to make them look so lifelike, to make them *more* than lifelike . . . Just a vase of flowers against a dark background—but more than that; the flowers seemed to be vibrant with their own light, as if in defiance of the shadows gathered around them. The mastery needed to make the glass vase hold that light, to bend the light with the water within, as if the vase did indeed have weight to it atop its stone pedestal . . . Remarkable.

I could have stared at it for hours—and the countless paintings along this hall alone could have occupied my entire day—but . . . garden. Plans.

Still, as I moved on, I couldn't deny that this place was far more . . . civilized than I'd thought. Peaceful, even, if I was willing to admit it.

And if the High Fae were indeed gentler than human legend and rumor had led me to believe, then maybe convincing Alis of my misery might not be too hard. If I could win over Alis, convince her that the Treaty had been wrong to demand such payment from me, she might indeed see if there was anything to get me out of this debt and—

"You," someone said, and I jumped back a step. In the light of the open glass doors to the garden, a towering male figure stood silhouetted before me.

Tamlin. He wore those warrior's clothes, cut close to show off his toned body, and three simple knives were now sheathed along his baldric—each long enough to look like it could gut me as easily as his beast's claws. His blond hair had been tied back from his face, revealing those pointed ears and that strange, beautiful mask. "Where are you going?" he said, gruffly enough that it almost sounded like a demand. *You*—I wondered if he even remembered my name.

It took a moment to will enough strength into my legs to rise from my half crouch. "Good morning," I said flatly. At least it was a better greeting than *You*. "You said my time was to be spent however I wanted. I didn't realize I was under house arrest."

His jaw tightened. "Of course you're not under house arrest." Even as he bit out the words, I couldn't ignore the sheer male beauty of that strong jaw, the richness of his golden-tan skin. He was probably handsome—if he ever took off that mask.

When he realized that I wasn't going to respond, he bared his teeth in what I supposed was an attempt at a smile and said, "Do you want a tour?"

"No, thank you," I managed to get out, conscious of every awkward motion of my body as I edged around him.

He stepped into my path—close enough that he conceded a step back. "I've been sitting inside all morning. I need some fresh air." *And you're insignificant enough that you wouldn't be a bother.*

"I'm fine," I said, casually dodging him. "You've . . . been generous enough." I tried to sound like I meant it.

A half smile, not so pleasant, no doubt unused to being denied. "Do you have some sort of problem with me?"

"No," I said quietly, and walked through the doors.

He let out a low snarl. "I'm not going to kill you, Feyre. I don't break my promises."

I almost stumbled down the garden steps as I glanced over my shoulder. He stood atop the stairs, as solid and ancient as the pale stones of the manor. "Kill—but not harm? Is that another loophole? One that Lucien might use against me—or anyone else here?"

"They're under orders not to even touch you."

"Yet I'm still trapped in your realm, for breaking a rule I didn't know existed. Why was your friend even in the woods that day? I thought the Treaty banned your kind from entering our lands."

He just stared at me. Perhaps I'd gone too far, questioned him too much. Perhaps he could tell why I'd really asked.

"That Treaty," he said quietly, "doesn't ban *us* from doing anything, except for enslaving you. The wall is an inconvenience. If we cared to, we could shatter it and march through to kill you all."

I might be forced to live in Prythian forever, but my family . . . I dared ask, "And do you care to destroy the wall?"

He looked me up and down, as if deciding whether I was worth the effort of explaining. "I have no interest in the mortal lands, though I can't speak for my kind."

But he still hadn't answered my question. "Then what was your friend doing there?"

Tamlin stilled. Such unearthly, primal grace, even to his breathing. "There is . . . a sickness in these lands. Across Prythian. There has been for almost fifty years now. It is why this house and these lands are so empty: most have left. The blight spreads slowly, but it has made magic act . . . strangely. My own powers are diminished due to it. These masks"—he tapped on his—"are the result of a surge of it that occurred during a masquerade forty-nine years ago. Even now, we can't remove them."

Stuck in masks—for nearly fifty years. I would have gone mad, would have peeled my skin off my face. "You didn't have a mask as a beast—and neither did your friend."

"The blight is cruel like that."

Either live as a beast, or live with the mask. "What—what sort of sickness is it?"

"It's not a disease—not a plague or illness. It's focused solely on magic, on those dwelling in Prythian. Andras was across the wall that day because I sent him to search for a cure."

"Can it hurt humans?" My stomach twisted. "Will it spread over the wall?"

"Yes," he said. "There is . . . a chance of it affecting mortals, and your territory. More than that, I don't know. It's slow-moving, and your kind is safe for now. We haven't had any progression in decades—magic seems to have stabilized, even though it's been weakened." That he'd even admitted so much spoke volumes about how he imagined my future: I was never going home, never going to encounter another human to whom I might spill this secret vulnerability.

"A mercenary told me she believed faeries might be thinking of attacking. Is it related?"

A hint of a smile, perhaps a bit surprised. "I don't know. Do you talk to mercenaries often?"

"I talk to whoever bothers to tell me anything useful."

He straightened, and it was only his promise not to kill me that kept me from cringing. Then he rolled his shoulders, as if shaking off his annoyance. "Was the trip wire you rigged in your room for me?"

I sucked on my teeth. "Can you blame me if it was?"

"I might take an animal form, but I am civilized, Feyre."

So he did remember my name, at least. But I looked pointedly at his hands, at the razor-sharp tips of those long, curved claws poking through his tanned skin.

Noticing my stare, he tucked his hands behind his back. He said sharply, "I'll see you at dinner."

It wasn't a request, but I still gave him a nod as I strode off between the hedges, not caring where I was going—only that he stayed far behind.

A sickness in their lands, affecting their magic, draining it from them . . . A magical blight that might one day spread to the human world. After so many centuries without magic, we'd be defenseless against it—against whatever it could do to humans.

I wondered if any of the High Fae would bother warning my kind.

It didn't take me long to know the answer.

CHAPTER 8

I pretended to meander through the exquisite and silent gardens, mentally marking the paths and clever places for hiding if I ever needed them. He'd taken my weapons, and I wasn't stupid enough to hope for an ash tree somewhere on the property with which to make my own. But his baldric had been laden with knives; there had to be an armory somewhere on the estate. And if not, I would find another weapon, then—steal it if I had to. Just in case.

Upon inspection the night before, I'd learned that there was no lock on my window. Sneaking out and rappelling down the wisteria vines wouldn't be difficult at all—I'd climbed enough trees to not mind the height. Not that I planned to escape, but . . . it was good to know, at least, how I might do so should I ever be desperate enough to risk it.

I didn't doubt Tamlin's claim that the rest of Prythian was deadly for a human—and if there was indeed some blight on these lands . . . I was better off here for the time being.

But not without trying to find someone who might plead my case to Tamlin.

Though Lucien—he could do with someone snapping at him, if you've the courage for it, Alis had said to me yesterday.

I chewed on my stubby nails as I walked, considering every possible plan and pitfall. I'd never been particularly good with words, had never learned the social warfare my sisters and mother had been so adept at, but . . . I'd been decent enough when selling hides at the village market.

So perhaps I'd seek out Tamlin's emissary, even if he detested me. He clearly had little interest in my living here—he'd suggested *killing me*. Perhaps he'd be eager to send me back, to persuade Tamlin to find some other way to fulfill the Treaty. If there even was one.

I approached a bench in an alcove blooming with foxglove when the sound of steps on shifting gravel filled the air. Two pairs of light, quick feet. I straightened, peering down the way I'd come, but the path was empty.

I lingered at the edge of an open field of lanky meadow buttercups. The vibrant green-and-yellow field was deserted. Behind me arose a gnarled crab apple tree in full, glorious bloom, the petals of its flowers littering the shaded bench on which I'd been about to sit. A breeze set the branches rustling, a waterfall of white petals flittering down like snow.

I scanned the garden, the field—carefully, carefully watching and listening for those two sets of feet.

There was nothing in the tree, or behind it.

A prickling sensation ran down my spine. I'd spent enough time in the woods to trust my instincts.

Someone stood behind me—perhaps two of them. A faint sniff and a quiet giggle issued from far too close. My heart leaped into my throat.

I cast a subtle glance over my shoulder. But only a shining silvery light flickered in the corner of my vision.

I had to turn around. I had to face it.

The gravel crunched, nearer now. The shimmering in the corner of my eye grew larger, separating into two small figures no taller than my waist. My hands clenched into fists.

"Feyre!" Alis's voice cut across the garden. I jumped out of my skin as she called me again. "Feyre, lunch!" she hollered. I whirled, a shout forming on my lips to alert her to whatever stood behind me, raising my fists, however futile it would be.

But the shining things had vanished, along with their sniffing and giggling, and I found myself facing a weathered statue of two merry, bounding lambs. I rubbed my neck.

Alis called me again, and I took a shuddering breath as I returned to the manor. But even as I strode through the hedges, carefully retracing my steps back to the house, I couldn't erase the creeping feeling that someone still watched me, curious and wanting to play.

+

I stole a knife from dinner that night. Just to have something—*anything*—to defend myself with.

It turned out that dinner was the only meal I was invited to attend, which was fine. Three meals a day with Tamlin and Lucien would have been torturous. I could endure an hour of sitting at their fancy table if it made them think I was docile and had no plans to change my fate.

While Lucien ranted to Tamlin about some malfunction of the magical, carved eye that indeed allowed him to see, I slipped my knife down the sleeve of my tunic. My heart beat so fast I thought they could hear it, but Lucien continued speaking, and Tamlin's focus remained on his courtier.

I supposed I should have pitied them for the masks they were forced to wear, for the blight that had infected their magic and people. But the less I interacted with them the better, especially when Lucien seemed to find everything I said to be hilariously human and uneducated. Snapping at him wouldn't help my plans. It would be an uphill battle to win his favor, if only for the fact that I was alive and his friend was not. I'd have to deal with him alone, or risk raising Tamlin's suspicions too soon.

Lucien's red hair shone in the firelight, the colors flickering with every movement he made, and the jewels in the hilt of his sword glinted—the ornate blade so unlike the baldric of knives still strapped across Tamlin's chest. But there was no one here to use a sword against. And while the sword was embedded with jewels and filigree, it was large enough to be more than decoration. Perhaps it had something to do with those invisible things in the garden. Maybe he'd lost his eye and earned that scar in battle. I fought against a shudder.

Alis had said the house was safe, but warned me to keep my wits about me. What might lurk beyond the house—or be able to use my human senses against me? Just how far would Tamlin's order not to harm me stretch? What kind of authority did he hold?

Lucien paused, and I found him smirking at me, making the scar even more brutal. "Were you admiring my sword, or just contemplating killing me, Feyre?"

"Of course not," I said softly, and glanced at Tamlin. The gold flecks in his eyes glowed, even from the other end of the table. My heart beat at a gallop. Had he somehow *heard* me take the knife, the whisper of metal on wood? I forced myself to look again at Lucien.

His lazy, vicious grin was still there. Act civilized, behave, possibly win him to my side . . . I could do that.

Tamlin broke the silence. "Feyre likes to hunt."

"I don't *like* to hunt." I should have probably used a more polite tone, but I went on. "I hunted out of necessity. And how did you know that?"

Tamlin's stare was bald, assessing. "Why else were you in the woods that day? You had a bow and arrows in your . . . house." I wondered whether he'd almost said *hovel*. "When I saw your father's hands, I knew he wasn't the one using them." He gestured to my scarred, callused hands. "You told him about the rations and money from pelts. Faeries might be many things, but we're not stupid. Unless your ridiculous legends claim that about us, too."

Ridiculous, *insignificant*.

I stared at the crumbs of bread and swirls of remaining sauce on my golden plate. Had I been at home, I would have licked my plate clean, desperate for any extra bit of nourishment. And the plates . . . I could have bought a team of horses, a plow, and a field for just one of them. Disgusting.

Lucien cleared his throat. "How old are you, anyway?"

"Nineteen." Pleasant, civilized . . .

Lucien tsked. "So young, and so grave. And a skilled killer already."

I tightened my hands into fists, the metal of the knife now warm against my skin. Docile, unthreatening, tame . . . I'd made my mother a promise, and I'd keep it. Tamlin's looking after my family wasn't the same as *my* looking after them. That wild, small dream could still come to pass: my sisters comfortably married off, and a lifetime with my father, with enough food for us both and enough time to maybe paint a little—or to maybe learn what *I* wanted. It could still happen—in a faraway land, perhaps—if I ever got out of this bargain. I could still cling to that scrap of a dream, though these High Fae would likely laugh at *how typically human* it was to think so small, to want so little.

Yet any bit of information might help, and if I showed interest in them, perhaps they would warm to me. What was this but another trap in the woods? So I said, "So is this what you do with your lives? Spare humans from the Treaty and have fine meals?" I gave a pointed glance toward Tamlin's baldric, the warrior's clothes, Lucien's sword.

Lucien smirked. "We also dance with the spirits under the full moon and snatch human babes from their cradles to replace them with changelings—"

"Didn't . . . ," Tamlin interrupted, his deep voice surprisingly gentle, "didn't your mother tell you anything about us?"

I prodded the table with my forefinger, digging my short nails into the wood. "My mother didn't have the time to tell me stories." I could reveal that part of my past, at least.

Lucien, for once, didn't laugh. After a rather stilted pause, Tamlin asked, "How did she die?" When I lifted my brows, he added a bit more softly, "I didn't see signs of an older woman in your house."

Predator or not, I didn't need his pity. But I said, "Typhus. When I was eight." I rose from my seat to leave.

"Feyre," Tamlin said, and I half turned. A muscle feathered in his cheek.

Lucien glanced between us, that metal eye roving, but kept silent. Then Tamlin shook his head, the movement more animal than anything, and murmured, "I'm sorry for your loss."

I tried to keep from grimacing as I turned on my heel and left. I didn't want or need his condolences—not for my mother, not when I hadn't missed her in years. Let Tamlin dismiss me as a rude, uncouth human not worth his careful watch.

I'd be better off persuading Lucien to speak to Tamlin on my behalf—and soon, before any of the others whom they'd mentioned appeared, or this blight of theirs grew. Tomorrow—I'd speak to Lucien then, test him out a bit.

In my room, I found a small satchel in the armoire and filled it with a spare set of clothes, along with my stolen knife. It was a pitiful blade, but a piece of cutlery was better than nothing. Just in case I was ever allowed to go—and had to leave at a moment's notice.

Just in case.

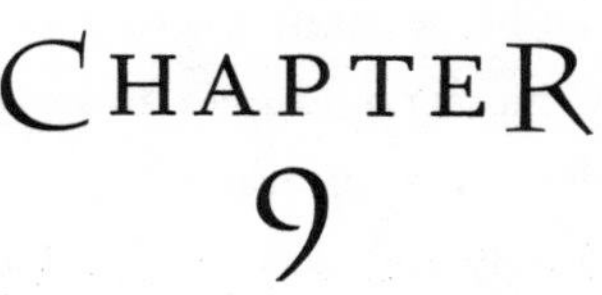

CHAPTER 9

The following morning, as Alis and the other servant woman prepared my bath, I contemplated my plan. Tamlin had mentioned that he and Lucien had various duties, and aside from running into him in the house yesterday, I'd seen neither of them around. So, locating Lucien—alone—would be the first order of business.

A casual question tossed in Alis's direction had her revealing that she believed Lucien was on border patrol today—and would be at the stables, preparing to leave.

I was halfway through the gardens, hurrying toward the outcropping of buildings I'd spied the day before, when Tamlin said from behind me, "No trip wires today?"

I froze midstep and looked over my shoulder. He was standing a few feet away.

How had he crept up so silently on the gravel? Faerie stealth, no doubt. I willed calm into my veins, my head. I said as politely as I could, "You said I was safe here. So I listened."

His eyes narrowed slightly, but he put on what I supposed was his attempt at a pleasant smile. "My morning work was postponed," he said.

Indeed, his usual tunic was off, the baldric gone, and the sleeves of his white shirt had been rolled up to the elbows to reveal tanned forearms corded with muscle. "If you want a ride across the grounds—if you're interested in your new . . . residence, I can take you."

Again, that effort to be accommodating, even when every word seemed to pain him. Maybe he could eventually be swayed by Lucien. And until then . . . how much could I get away with, if he was going to such lengths to make his people swear not to harm me, to shield me from the Treaty? I smiled blandly and said, "I'd prefer to spend today alone, I think. But thank you for the offer."

He tensed. "What about—"

"No, thank you," I interrupted, marveling a bit at my own audacity. But I had to catch Lucien alone, had to feel him out. He might already be gone.

Tamlin clenched his hands into fists, as if fighting against the claws itching to burst out. But he didn't reprimand me, didn't do anything other than prowl back into the house without another word.

Soon enough, if I was lucky, Tamlin wouldn't be my problem anymore. I hurried for the stables, tucking away the information. Maybe one day, if I was ever released, if there was an ocean and years between us, I would think back and wonder why he'd bothered.

I tried not to look too eager, too out of breath when I finally reached the pretty, painted stables. It didn't surprise me that the stableboys all wore horse masks. For them I felt a shred of pity at what the blight had done, the ridiculous masks they now had to wear until someone could figure out how to undo the magic binding them to their faces. But none of the stable hands even looked at me—either because I wasn't worth it or because they, too, resented me for the death of Andras. I didn't blame them.

Any attempt at casualness took a stumble when I finally found Lucien astride a black gelding, grinning down at me with too-white teeth.

"Morning, Feyre." I tried to hide the stiffening in my shoulders, tried to smile a bit. "Going for a ride, or merely reconsidering Tam's offer to live with us?" I tried to recall the words I'd come up with earlier, the words to win him, but he laughed—and not pleasantly. "Come now. I'm to patrol the southern woods today, and I'm curious about the . . . *abilities* you used to bring down my friend, whether accidental or not. It's been a while since I encountered a human, let alone a Fae-killer. Indulge me in a hunt."

Perfect—at least that part of this had gone well, even if it sounded as lovely as facing a bear in its den. So I stepped aside to let a stableboy pass. He moved with a fluid smoothness, like all of them here. And didn't look at me, either—no indication at all of what he thought of having a *Fae-killer* in his stable.

But my kind of hunting couldn't be done on horseback. Mine consisted of careful stalking and well-laid traps and snares. I didn't know how to give chase atop a horse. Lucien accepted a quiver of arrows from the returning stableboy with a nod of thanks. Lucien smiled in a way that didn't meet that metal eye—or the russet one. "No ash arrows today, unfortunately."

I clenched my jaw to keep a retort from slipping off my tongue. If he was forbidden from hurting me, I couldn't fathom why he would invite me along, save to mock me in whatever way he could. Perhaps he was truly that bored. Better for me.

So I shrugged, looking as bored as I could. "Well . . . I suppose I'm already dressed for a hunt."

"Perfect," Lucien said, his metal eye gleaming in the sunlight slanting in through the open stable doors. I prayed Tamlin wouldn't come prowling through them—prayed he wouldn't decide to go for a ride on his own and catch us here.

"Let's go, then," I said, and Lucien motioned for them to prepare a horse. I leaned against a wooden wall as I waited, keeping an eye on the doorway for signs of Tamlin, and offered my own bland replies to Lucien's remarks about the weather.

Mercifully, I was soon astride a white mare, riding with Lucien through the spring-shrouded woods beyond the gardens. I kept a healthy distance from the fox-masked faerie on the broad path, hoping that eye of his couldn't see through the back of his head.

The thought didn't sit well, and I shoved it away—along with the part of me that marveled at the way the sun illuminated the leaves, and the clusters of crocuses that grew like flashes of vibrant purple against the brown and green. Those were things that weren't necessary to my plans, useless details that only blocked out everything else: the shape and slope of the path, what trees were good for climbing, sounds of nearby water sources. *Those* things could help me survive if I ever needed to. But, like the rest of the grounds, the forest was utterly empty. No sign of faeries, nor any High Fae wandering around. Just as well.

"Well, you certainly have the *quiet* part of hunting down," Lucien said, falling back to ride beside me. Good—let him come to me, rather than me seeming too eager, too friendly.

I adjusted the weight of the quiver strap across my chest, then ran a finger along the smooth curve of the yew bow in my lap. The bow was larger than the one I used at home, the arrows heavier and heads thicker. I would probably miss whatever target I found until I adjusted to the weight and balance of the bow.

Five years ago I'd taken the very last of my father's coppers from our former fortune to purchase my bow and arrows. I'd since allotted a small sum every month for arrows and replacement strings.

"Well?" Lucien pressed. "No game good enough for you to slaughter? We've passed plenty of squirrels and birds." The canopy above cast shadows upon his fox mask—light and dark and gleaming metal.

"You seem to have enough food on your table that I don't need to add to it, especially when there's always plenty left over." I doubted squirrel would be good enough for their table.

Lucien snorted but didn't say anything else as we passed beneath a flowering lilac, its purple cones drooping low enough to graze my cheek like cool, velvety fingers. The sweet, crisp scent lingered in my nose even as we rode on. *Not useful*, I told myself. Although . . . the thick brush beyond it would be a good hiding spot, if I needed one.

"You said you were an emissary for Tamlin," I ventured. "Do emissaries usually patrol the grounds?" A casual, disinterested question.

Lucien clicked his tongue. "I'm Tamlin's emissary for formal uses, but this was Andras's shift. So someone needed to fill in. It's an honor to do it."

I swallowed hard. Andras had a place here, and *friends* here—he hadn't been just some nameless, faceless faerie. No doubt he was more missed than I was. "I'm . . . sorry," I said—and meant it. "I didn't know what—what he meant to you all."

Lucien shrugged. "Tamlin said as much, which was no doubt why he brought you here. Or maybe you looked so pathetic in those rags that he took pity on you."

"I wouldn't have joined you if I'd known you would use this ride as an excuse to insult me." Alis had mentioned that Lucien could use someone who snapped back at him. Easy enough.

Lucien smirked. "Apologies, Feyre."

I might have called him a liar for that apology had I not known he couldn't lie. Which made the apology . . . sincere? I couldn't sort it out.

"So," he said, "when are you going to start trying to persuade me to beseech Tamlin to find a way to free you from the Treaty's rules?"

I tried not to jolt. "What?"

"That's why you agreed to come out here, isn't it? Why you wound up at the stables exactly as I was leaving?" He shot me a sideways glance with that russet eye of his. "Honestly, I'm impressed—and flattered you think I have that kind of sway with Tamlin."

I wouldn't reveal my hand—not yet. "What are you talking—"

His cocked head was answer enough. He chuckled and said, "Before you waste one of your precious few human breaths, let me explain two things to you. One: if I had my way, you'd be gone, so it wouldn't take much convincing on your part. Two: I can't have my way, because there is no alternative to what the Treaty demands. There's no extra loophole."

"But—but there has to be something—"

"I admire your balls, Feyre—I really do. Or maybe it's stupidity. But since Tam won't gut you, which was *my* first choice, you're stuck here. Unless you want to rough it on your own in Prythian, which"—he looked me up and down—"I'd advise against."

No—no, I couldn't just . . . just *stay here*. Forever. Until I died. Maybe . . . maybe there was some other way, or someone else who could find a way out. I mastered my uneven breathing, shoving away the panicked, bleating thoughts.

"A valiant effort," Lucien said with a smirk.

I didn't bother hiding the glare I cut in his direction.

We rode on in silence, and aside from a few birds and squirrels, I saw nothing—heard nothing—unusual. After a few minutes I'd quieted my riotous thoughts enough to say, "Where is the rest of Tamlin's court? They all fled this blight on magic?"

"How'd you know about the court?" he asked so quickly that I realized he thought I meant something else.

I kept my face blank. "Do normal estates have emissaries? And servants chatter. Isn't that why you made them wear bird masks to that party?"

Lucien scowled, that scar stretching. "We each chose what to wear that night to honor Tamlin's shape-shifting gifts. The servants, too. But now, if we had the choice, we'd peel them off with our bare hands," he said, tugging on his own. It didn't move.

"What happened to the magic to make it act that way?"

Lucien let out a harsh laugh. "Something was sent from the shit-holes of Hell," he said, then glanced around and swore. "I shouldn't have said that. If word got back to her—"

"Who?"

The color had leeched from his sun-kissed skin. He dragged a hand through his hair. "Never mind. The less you know, the better. Tam might not find it troublesome to tell you about the blight, but I wouldn't put it past a human to sell the information to the highest bidder."

I bristled, but the few bits of information he'd released lay before me like glittering jewels. A *her* who scared Lucien enough to make him worry—to make him afraid someone might be listening, spying, monitoring his behavior. Even out here. I studied the shadows between the trees but found nothing.

Prythian was ruled by seven High Lords—perhaps this *she* was whoever governed this territory; if not a High Lord, then a High Lady. If that was even possible.

"How old are you?" I asked, hoping he'd keep divulging some more useful information. It was better than knowing nothing.

"Old," he said. He scanned the brush, but I had a feeling his darting eyes weren't looking for game. His shoulders were too tense.

"What sort of powers do you have? Can you shape-shift like Tamlin?"

He sighed, looking skyward before he studied me warily, that metal eye narrowing with unnerving focus. "Trying to figure out my weaknesses so you can—" I glowered at him. "Fine. No, I can't shape-shift. Only Tam can."

"But your friend—he appeared as a wolf. Unless that was his—"

"No, no. Andras was High Fae, too. Tam can shift us into other shapes if need be. He saves it for his sentries only, though. When Andras went across the wall, Tam changed him into a wolf so he wouldn't be spotted as a faerie. Though his size was probably indication enough."

A shudder went down my spine, violent enough that I didn't acknowledge the red-hot glare Lucien lobbed my way. I didn't have the nerve to ask if Tamlin could change me into another shape.

"Anyway," Lucien went on, "the High Fae don't have specific *powers* the way the lesser faeries do. I don't have a natural-born affinity, if that's what you're asking. I don't clean everything in sight or lure mortals to a watery death or grant you answers to whatever questions you might have if you trap me. We just exist—to rule."

I turned in the other direction so he couldn't see as I rolled my eyes. "I suppose if I were one of you, I'd be one of the faeries, not High Fae? A lesser faerie like Alis, waiting on you hand and foot?" He didn't reply, which amounted to a *yes*. With that arrogance, no wonder Lucien found my presence as a replacement for his friend to be abhorrent. And since he would probably loathe me forever, since he'd ended my scheming before it had even begun, I asked, "How'd you get that scar?"

"I didn't keep my mouth shut when I should have, and was punished for it."

"Tamlin did that to you?"

"Cauldron, no. He wasn't there. But he got me the replacement afterward."

More answers-that-weren't-answers. "So there are faeries who will actually answer any question if you trap them?" Maybe they'd know how to free me from the Treaty's terms.

"Yes," he said tightly. "The Suriel. But they're old and wicked, and not worth the danger of going out to find them. And if you're stupid enough to keep looking so intrigued, I'm going to become rather suspicious and tell Tam to put you under house arrest. Though I suppose you would deserve it if you were indeed stupid enough to seek one out."

They had to lurk nearby, then, if he was this concerned. Lucien whipped his head to the right, listening, his eye whirring softly. The hair on my neck stood, and I had my bow drawn in a heartbeat, pointing in the direction Lucien stared.

"Put your bow down," he whispered, his voice low and rough. "Put your damned bow down, human, and look straight ahead."

I did as he said, the hair on my arms rising as something rustled in the brush.

"Don't react," Lucien said, forcing his gaze ahead, too, the metal eye going still and silent. "No matter what you feel or see, don't react. *Don't look*. Just stare ahead."

I started trembling, gripping the reins in my sweaty hands. I might have wondered if this was some kind of horrible joke, but Lucien's face had gone so very, very pale. Our horses' ears flattened against their heads, but they continued walking, as if they'd also understood Lucien's command.

And then I felt it.

Chapter 10

My blood froze as a creeping, leeching cold lurched by. I couldn't see anything, just a vague shimmering in the corner of my vision, but my horse stiffened beneath me. I willed my face into blankness. Even the balmy spring woods seemed to recoil, to wither and freeze.

The cold thing whispered past, circling. I could see nothing, but I could *feel* it. And in the back of my mind, an ancient, hollow voice whispered:

I will grind your bones between my claws; I will drink your marrow; I will feast on your flesh. I am what you fear; I am what you dread . . . Look at me. Look at me.

I tried to swallow, but my throat had closed up. I kept my eyes on the trees, on the canopy, on anything but the cold mass circling us again and again.

Look at me.

I wanted to look—I needed to see what it was.

Look at me.

I stared at the coarse trunk of a distant elm, thinking of pleasant things. Like hot bread and full bellies—

I will fill my belly with you. I will devour you. Look at me.

A starry, unclouded night sky, peaceful and glittering and endless.

Summer sunrise. A refreshing bath in a forest pool. Meetings with Isaac, losing myself for an hour or two in his body, in our shared breaths.

It was all around us, so cold that my teeth chattered. *Look at me.*

I stared and stared at that ever-nearing tree trunk, not daring to blink. My eyes strained, filling with tears, and I let them fall, refusing to acknowledge the thing that lurked around us.

Look at me.

And just as I thought I would give in, when my eyes hurt so much from *not* looking, the cold disappeared into the brush, leaving a trail of still, recoiling plants behind it. Only after Lucien exhaled and our horses shook their heads did I dare sag in my seat. Even the crocuses seemed to straighten again.

"What was that?" I asked, brushing the tears from my face.

Lucien's face was still pale. "You don't want to know."

"Please. Was it that . . . Suriel you mentioned?"

Lucien's russet eye was dark as he answered hoarsely. "No. It was a creature that should not be in these lands. We call it the Bogge. You cannot hunt it, and you cannot kill it. Even with your beloved ash arrows."

"Why can't I look at it?"

"Because when you look at it—when you acknowledge it—that's when it becomes real. That's when it can kill you."

A shiver spider-walked down my spine. This was the Prythian I'd expected—the creatures that made humans speak of them in hushed tones even now. The reason I hadn't hesitated, not for a heartbeat, when I'd considered the possibility of that wolf being a faerie. "I heard its voice in my head. It told me to look."

Lucien rolled his shoulders. "Well, thank the Cauldron that you didn't. Cleaning up that mess would have ruined the rest of my day." He gave me a wan smile. I didn't return it.

I still heard the Bogge's voice whispering between the leaves, calling to me.

After an hour of meandering through the trees, hardly speaking to each other, I'd stopped trembling enough to turn to him.

"So you're old," I said. "And you carry around a sword, and go on border patrol. Did you fight in the War?" Fine—perhaps I hadn't quite let go of my curiosity about his eye.

He winced. "Shit, Feyre—I'm not that old."

"Are you a warrior, though?" *Would you be able to kill me if it ever came to that?*

Lucien huffed a laugh. "Not as good as Tam, but I know how to handle my weapons." He patted the hilt of his sword. "Would you like me to teach you how to wield a blade, or do you already know how, oh mighty mortal huntress? If you took down Andras, you probably don't need to learn anything. Only where to aim, right?" He tapped on his chest.

"I don't know how to use a sword. I only know how to hunt."

"Same thing, isn't it?"

"For me it's different."

Lucien fell silent, considering. "I suppose you humans are such hateful cowards that you would have wet yourself, curled up, and waited to die if you'd known beyond a doubt what Andras truly was." Insufferable. Lucien sighed as he looked me over. "Do you ever stop being *so* serious and dull?"

"Do you ever stop being such a prick?" I snapped back.

Dead—really, truly, I should have been dead for that.

But Lucien grinned at me. "Much better."

Alis, it seemed, had not been wrong.

⁜

Whatever tentative truce we built that afternoon vanished at the dinner table.

Tamlin was lounging in his usual seat, a long claw out and circling his goblet. It paused on the lip as soon as I entered, Lucien on my heels. His green eyes pinned me to the spot.

Right. I'd brushed him off that morning, claiming I wanted to be alone.

Tamlin slowly looked at Lucien, whose face had turned grave. "We went on a hunt," Lucien said.

"I heard," Tamlin said roughly, glancing between us as we took our seats. "And did you have fun?" Slowly, his claw sank back into his flesh.

Lucien didn't answer, leaving it to me. *Coward.* I cleared my throat. "Sort of," I said.

"Did you catch anything?" Every word was clipped out.

"No." Lucien gave me a pointed cough, as if urging me to say more.

But I had nothing to say. Tamlin stared at me for a long moment, then dug into his food, not all that interested in talking to me, either.

Then Lucien quietly said, "Tam."

Tamlin looked up, more animal than fae in those green eyes. A demand for whatever it was Lucien had to say.

Lucien's throat bobbed. "The Bogge was in the forest today."

The fork in Tamlin's hand folded in on itself. He said with lethal calm, "You ran into it?"

Lucien nodded. "It moved past but came close. It must have snuck through the border."

Metal groaned as Tamlin's claws punched out, obliterating the fork. He rose to his feet with a powerful, brutal movement. I tried not to tremble at the contained fury, at how his canines seemed to lengthen as he said, "Where in the forest?"

Lucien told him. Tamlin threw a glance in my direction before stalking out of the room and shutting the door behind him with unnerving gentleness.

Lucien loosed a breath, pushing away his half-eaten food and rubbing at his temples.

"Where is he going?" I asked, staring toward the door.

"To hunt the Bogge."

"You said it couldn't be killed—that you can't face it."

"Tam can."

My breath caught a bit. The gruff High Fae halfheartedly flattering me was capable of killing a thing like the Bogge. And yet he'd served me himself that first night, offered me life rather than death. I'd known he was lethal, that he was a warrior of sorts, but . . .

"So he went to hunt the Bogge where we were earlier today?"

Lucien shrugged. "If he's going to pick up a trail, it would be there."

I had no idea how anyone could face that immortal horror, but . . . it wasn't my problem.

And just because Lucien wasn't going to eat anymore didn't mean I wouldn't. Lucien, lost in thought, didn't even notice the feast I downed.

I returned to my room, and—awake and with nothing else to do—began monitoring the garden beyond for any signs of Tamlin's return. He didn't come back.

I sharpened the knife I'd hidden away on a bit of stone I'd taken from the garden. An hour passed—and still Tamlin didn't return.

The moon showed her face, casting the garden below in silver and shadow.

Ridiculous. Utterly ridiculous to watch for his return, to see if he could indeed survive against the Bogge. I turned from the window, about to drag myself into bed.

But something moved out in the garden.

I lunged for the curtains beside the window, not wanting to be caught waiting for him, and peered out.

Not Tamlin—but someone lurked by the hedges, facing the house. Looking toward *me*.

Male, hunched, and—

The breath went out of me as the faerie hobbled closer—just two steps into the light leaking from the house.

Not a faerie, but a man.

My father.

CHAPTER 11

I didn't give myself a chance to panic, to doubt, to do anything but wish I had stolen some food from my breakfast table as I layered on tunic after tunic and bundled myself in a cloak, stuffing the knife I'd stolen into my boot. The extra clothes in the satchel would just be a burden to carry.

My father. My father had come to take me—to save me. Whatever benefits Tamlin had given him upon my departure couldn't be too tempting, then. Maybe he had a ship prepared to take us far, far away—maybe he had somehow sold the cottage and gotten enough money to set us up in a new place, a new continent.

My father—my crippled, broken father had come.

A quick survey of the ground beneath my window revealed no one outside—and the silent house told me no one had spotted my father yet. He was still waiting by the hedge, now beckoning to me. At least Tamlin had not returned.

With a final glance at my room, listening for anyone approaching from the hall, I grasped the nearby trellis of wisteria and eased down the building.

I winced at the crunch of gravel beneath my boots, but my father was already moving toward the outer gates, limping along with his cane. How had he even *gotten* here? There had to be horses nearby, then. He was hardly wearing enough clothing for the winter that would await us once we crossed the wall. But I'd layered on so much that I could spare him some items if need be.

Keeping my movements light and silent, carefully avoiding the light of the moon, I hurried after my father. He moved with surprising swiftness toward the darkened hedges and the gate beyond.

Only a few hall candles were burning inside the house. I didn't dare breathe too loudly—didn't dare call for my father as he limped toward the gate. If we left now, if he indeed had horses, we could be halfway home by the time they realized I was gone. Then we'd flee—flee Tamlin, flee the blight that could soon invade our lands.

My father reached the gates. They were already open, the dark forest beyond beckoning. He must have hidden the horses deeper in. He turned toward me, that familiar face drawn and tight, those brown eyes clear for once, and beckoned. *Hurry, hurry*, every movement of his hand seemed to shout.

My heart was a raging beat in my chest, in my throat. Only a few feet now—to him, to freedom, to a new life—

A massive hand wrapped around my arm. "Going somewhere?"

Shit, shit, *shit*.

Tamlin's claws poked through my layers of clothing as I looked up at him in unabashed terror.

I didn't dare move, not as his lips thinned and the muscles in his jaw quivered. Not as he opened his mouth and I glimpsed fangs—long, throat-tearing fangs shining in the moonlight.

He was going to kill me—kill me right there, and then kill my father. No more loopholes, no more flattery, no more mercy. He didn't care anymore. I was as good as dead.

"Please," I breathed. "My father—"

"Your *father*?" He lifted his stare to the gates behind me, and his growl rumbled through me as he bared his teeth. "Why don't you look again?" He released me.

I staggered back a step, whirling, sucking in a breath to tell my father to *run*, but—

But he wasn't there. Only a pale bow and a quiver of pale arrows remained, propped up against the gates. Mountain ash. They hadn't been there moments before, hadn't—

They rippled, as if they were nothing but water—and then the bow and quiver became a large pack, laden with supplies. Another ripple—and there were my sisters, huddled together, weeping.

My knees buckled. "What is . . ." I didn't finish the question. My father now stood there, still hunched and beckoning. A flawless rendering.

"Weren't you warned to keep your wits about you?" Tamlin snapped. "That your human senses would betray you?" He stepped beyond me and let out a snarl so vicious that whatever the thing was by the gates shimmered with light and darted out as fast as lightning streaking through the dark.

"Fool," he said to me, turning. "If you're ever going to run away, at least do it in the daytime." He stared me down, and the fangs slowly retracted. The claws remained. "There are worse things than the Bogge prowling these woods at night. That thing at the gates isn't one of them—and it still would have taken a good, long while devouring you."

Somehow, my mouth began working again. And of all the things to say, I blurted, "Can you blame me? My crippled father appears beneath my window, and you think I'm not going to run for him? Did you actually think I'd gladly stay here *forever*, even if you'd taken care of my family, all for some Treaty that had nothing to do with me and allows *your kind* to slaughter humans as you see fit?"

He flexed his fingers as if trying to get the claws back in, but they remained out, ready to slice through flesh and bone. "What do you want, Feyre?"

"I want to go *home*!"

"Home to what, exactly? You'd prefer that miserable human existence to this?"

"I made a promise," I said, my breathing ragged. "To my mother, when she died. That I'd look after my family. That I'd take care of them. All I have done, every single day, every hour, has been for that vow. And just because I was hunting to *save* my family, to put food in their bellies, I'm now forced to break it."

He stalked toward the house, and I gave him a wide berth before falling into step behind him. His claws slowly, slowly retracted. He didn't look at me as he said, "You are not breaking your vow—you are fulfilling it, and then some, by staying here. Your family is better cared for now than they were when you were there."

Those chipped, miscolored paintings inside the cottage flashed in my vision. Perhaps they would forget who had even painted them in the first place. Insignificant—that's what all those years I'd given them would be, as insignificant as I was to these High Fae. And that dream I'd had, of one day living with my father, with enough food and money and paint . . . it had been my dream—no one else's.

I rubbed at my chest. "I can't just give up on it, on them. No matter what you say."

Even if I had been a fool—a stupid, human fool—to believe my father would ever actually come for me.

Tamlin eyed me sidelong. "You're not giving up on them."

"Living in luxury, stuffing myself with food? How is that not—"

"They are cared for—they are fed and comfortable."

Fed and comfortable. If he couldn't lie, if it was true, then . . . then it was beyond anything I'd ever dared hope for.

Then . . . my vow to my mother was fulfilled.

It stunned me enough that I didn't say anything for a moment as we walked.

My life was now owned by the Treaty, but . . . perhaps I'd been freed in another sort of way.

We neared the sweeping stairs that led into the manor, and I finally asked, "Lucien goes on border patrol, and you've mentioned other sentries—yet I've never seen one here. Where are they all?"

"At the border," he said, as if that were a suitable answer. Then he added, "We don't need sentries if I'm here."

Because he was deadly enough. I tried not to think about it, but still I asked, "Were you trained as a warrior, then?"

"Yes." When I didn't reply, he added, "I spent most of my life in my father's war-band on the borders, training as a warrior to one day serve him—or others. Running these lands . . . was not supposed to fall to me." The flatness with which he said it told me enough about how he felt about his current title, about why the presence of his silver-tongued friend was necessary.

But it was too personal, too demanding, to ask what had occurred to change his circumstances so greatly. So I cleared my throat and said, "What manner of faeries prowl the woods beyond this gate, if the Bogge isn't the worst of them? What *was* that thing?"

What I'd meant to ask was, *What would have tormented and then eaten me? Who are you to be so powerful that they pose no threat to you?*

He paused on the bottom step, waiting for me to catch up. "A puca. They use your own desires to lure you to some remote place. Then they eat you. Slowly. It probably smelled your human scent in the woods and followed it to the house." I shivered and didn't bother to hide it. Tamlin went on. "These lands used to be well guarded. The deadlier faeries were contained within the borders of their native territories, monitored by the local Fae lords, or driven into hiding. Creatures like the puca never would have dared set foot here. But now, the sickness that infected Prythian has weakened the wards that kept them out." A long pause, like the words were choked out of him. "Things are different now. It's not safe to travel alone at night—especially if you're human."

Because humans were defenseless as babes compared to natural-born predators like Lucien—and Tamlin, who didn't need weapons to hunt. I glanced at his hands but found no trace of the claws. Only tanned, callused skin.

"What else is different now?" I asked, trailing him up the marble front steps.

He didn't stop this time, didn't even look over his shoulder to see me as he said, "Everything."

✠

So I truly was to live there forever. As much as I longed to ensure that Tamlin's word about caring for my family was true, as much as his claim that I was taking better care of my family by staying away—even if I was truly fulfilling that vow to my mother by staying in Prythian . . . Without the weight of that promise, I was left hollow and empty.

Over the next three days, I found myself joining Lucien on Andras's old patrol while Tamlin hunted the grounds for the Bogge, unseen by us. Despite being an occasional bastard, Lucien didn't seem to mind my company, and he did most of the talking, which was fine; it left me to brood over the consequences of firing a single arrow.

An arrow. I never fired a single one during those three days we rode along the border. That very morning I'd spied a red doe in a glen and aimed out of instinct, my arrow poised to fly right into her eye as Lucien sneered that *she* was not a faerie, at least. But I'd stared at her—fat and healthy and content—and then slackened the bow, replaced the arrow in my quiver, and let the doe wander on.

I never saw Tamlin around the manor—off hunting the Bogge day and night, Lucien informed me. Even at dinner, he spoke little before leaving early—off to continue his hunt, night after night. I didn't mind his absence. It was a relief, if anything.

On the third night after my encounter with the puca, I'd scarcely sat down before Tamlin got up, giving an excuse about not wanting to waste hunting time.

Lucien and I stared after him for a moment.

What I could see of Lucien's face was pale and tight. "You worry about him," I said.

Lucien slumped in his seat, wholly undignified for a Fae lord. "Tamlin gets into . . . moods."

"He doesn't want your help hunting the Bogge?"

"He prefers being alone. And having the Bogge on our lands . . . I don't suppose you'd understand. The puca are minor enough not to bother him, but even after he's shredded the Bogge, he'll brood over it."

"And there's no one who can help him at all?"

"He would probably shred them for disobeying his order to stay away."

A brush of ice slithered across my nape. "He would be that brutal?"

Lucien studied the wine in his goblet. "You don't hold on to power by being everyone's friend. And among the faeries, lesser and High Fae alike, a firm hand is needed. We're too powerful, and too bored with immortality, to be checked by anything else."

It seemed like a cold, lonely position to have, especially when you didn't particularly want it. I wasn't sure why it bothered me so much.

The snow was falling, thick and merciless, already up to my knees as I pulled the bowstring back—farther and farther, until my arm trembled. Behind me, a shadow lurked—no, watched. *I didn't dare turn to look at it, to see who might be within that shadow, observing, not as the wolf stared at me across the clearing.*

Just staring. As if waiting, as if daring me to fire the ash arrow.

No—no, I didn't want to do it, not this time, not again, not—

But I had no control over my fingers, absolutely none, and he was still staring as I fired.

One shot—one shot straight through that golden eye.

A plume of blood splattering the snow, a thud of a heavy body, a sigh of wind. No.

It wasn't a wolf that hit the snow—no, it was a man, tall and well formed.

No—not a man. A High Fae, with those pointed ears.

I blinked, and then—then my hands were warm and sticky with blood, then his body was red and skinless, steaming in the cold, and it was his skin—his skin—*that I held in my hands, and—*

✠

I threw myself awake, sweat slipping down my back, and forced myself to breathe, to open my eyes and note each detail of the night-dark bedroom. Real—this was real.

But I could still see that High Fae male facedown in the snow, my arrow through his eye, red and bloody all over from where I'd cut and peeled off his skin.

Bile stung my throat.

Not real. Just a dream. Even if what I'd done to Andras, even as a wolf, was . . . was . . .

I scrubbed at my face. Perhaps it was the quiet, the hollowness, of the past few days—perhaps it was only that I no longer had to think hour to hour about how to keep my family alive, but . . . It was regret, and maybe shame, that coated my tongue, my bones.

I shuddered as if I could fling it off, and kicked back the sheets to rise from the bed.

CHAPTER 12

I couldn't entirely shake the horror, the gore of my dream as I walked down the dark halls of the manor, the servants and Lucien long since asleep. But I had to do something—*anything*—after that nightmare. If only to avoid sleeping. A bit of paper in one hand and a pen gripped in the other, I carefully traced my steps, noting the windows and doors and exits, occasionally jotting down vague sketches and *X*s on the parchment.

It was the best I could do, and to any literate human, my markings would have made no sense. But I couldn't write or read more than my basic letters, and my makeshift map was better than nothing. If I were to remain here, it was essential to know the best hiding places, the easiest way out, should things ever go badly for me. I couldn't entirely let go of the instinct.

It was too dim to admire any of the paintings lining the walls, and I didn't dare risk a candle. These past three days, there had been servants in the halls when I'd worked up the nerve to look at the art—and the part of me that spoke with Nesta's voice had laughed at the idea of an ignorant human trying to admire faerie art. *Some other time, then*, I'd told myself. I would find another day, a quiet hour when no one was around, to look at them. I had plenty of hours now—a whole lifetime in front of me. Perhaps . . . perhaps I'd figure out what I wished to do with it.

I crept down the main staircase, moonlight flooding the black-and-white tiles of the entrance hall. I reached the bottom, my bare feet silent on the cold tiles, and listened. Nothing—no one.

I set my little map on the foyer table and drew a few *X*s and circles to signify the doors, the windows, the marble stairs of the front hall. I would become so familiar with the house that I could navigate it even if someone blinded me.

A breeze announced his arrival—and I turned from the table toward the long hall, to the open glass doors to the garden.

I'd forgotten how huge he was in this form—forgotten the curled horns and lupine face, the bearlike body that moved with a feline fluidity. His green eyes glowed in the darkness, fixing on me, and as the doors snicked shut behind him, the clicking of claws on marble filled the hall. I stood still—not daring to flinch, to move a muscle.

He limped slightly. And in the moonlight, dark, shining stains were left in his wake.

He continued toward me, stealing the air from the entire hall. He was so big that the space felt cramped, like a cage. The scrape of claw, a huff of uneven breathing, the dripping of blood.

Between one step and the next, he changed forms, and I squeezed my eyes shut at the blinding flash. When at last my eyes adjusted to the returning darkness, he was standing in front of me.

Standing, but—not quite there. No sign of the baldric, or his knives. His clothes were in shreds—long, vicious slashes that made me wonder how he wasn't gutted and dead. But the muscled skin peering out beneath his shirt was smooth, unharmed.

"Did you kill the Bogge?" My voice was hardly more than a whisper.

"Yes." A dull, empty answer. As if he couldn't be bothered to remember to be pleasant. As if I were at the very, very bottom of a long list of priorities.

"You're hurt," I said even more quietly.

Indeed, his hand was covered in blood, even more splattering on the floor beneath him. He looked at it blankly—as if it took some monumental effort to remember that he even had a hand, and that it was injured. What effort of will and strength had it taken to kill the Bogge, to face that wretched menace? How deep had he had to dig inside himself—to whatever immortal power and animal that lived there—to kill it?

He glanced down at the map on the table, and his voice was void of anything—any emotion, any anger or amusement—as he said, "What is that?"

I snatched up the map. "I thought I should learn my surroundings."

Drip, drip, drip.

I opened my mouth to point out his hand again, but he said, "You can't write, can you."

I didn't answer. I didn't know what to say. *Ignorant, insignificant human.*

"No wonder you became so adept at other things."

I supposed he was so far gone in thinking about his encounter with the Bogge that he hadn't realized the compliment he'd given me. If it was a compliment.

Another splatter of blood on the marble. "Where can we clean up your hand?"

He lifted his head to look at me again. Still and silent and weary. Then he said, "There's a small infirmary."

I wanted to tell myself that it was probably the most useful thing I'd learned all night. But as I followed him there, avoiding the blood he trailed, I thought of what Lucien had told me about his isolation, that burden, thought of what Tamlin had mentioned about how these estates should not have been his, and felt . . . sorry for him.

✠

The infirmary was well stocked, but was more of a supply closet with a worktable than an actual place to host sick faeries. I supposed that was all they needed when they could heal themselves with their immortal powers. But this wound—this wound wasn't healing.

Tamlin slumped against the edge of the table, gripping his injured hand at the wrist as he watched me sort through the supplies in the cabinets and drawers. When I'd gathered what I needed, I tried not to balk at the thought of touching him, but . . . I didn't let myself give in to my dread as I took his hand, the heat of his skin like an inferno against my cool fingers.

I cleaned off his bloody, dirty hand, bracing for the first flash of those claws. But his claws remained retracted, and he kept silent as I bound and wrapped his hand—surprisingly enough, there were no more than a few vicious cuts, none of them requiring stitching.

I secured the bandage in place and stepped away, bringing the bowl of bloody water to the deep sink in the back of the room. His eyes were a brand upon me as I finished cleaning, and the room became too small, too hot. He'd killed the Bogge and walked away relatively unscathed. If Tamlin was that powerful, then the High Lords of Prythian must be near-gods. Every mortal instinct in my body bleated in panic at the thought.

I was almost at the open door, stifling the urge to bolt back to my room, when he said, "You can't write, yet you learned to hunt, to survive. How?"

I paused with my foot on the threshold. "That's what happens when you're responsible for lives other than your own, isn't it? You do what you have to do."

He was still sitting on the table, still straddling that inner line between the here and now and wherever he'd had to go in his mind to endure the fight with the Bogge. I met his feral and glowing stare.

"You aren't what I expected—for a human," he said.

I didn't reply. And he didn't say good-bye as I walked out.

The next morning, as I made my way down the grand staircase, I tried not to think too much about the clean-washed marble tiles on the floor below—no sign of the blood Tamlin had lost. I tried not to think too much at all about our encounter, actually.

When I found the front hall empty, I almost smiled—felt a ripple in that hollow emptiness that had been hounding me. Perhaps now, perhaps in this moment of quiet, I could at last look through the art on the walls, take time to observe it, learn it, admire it.

Heart racing at the thought, I was about to head toward a hall I had noted was nearly covered in painting after painting when low male voices floated out from the dining room.

I paused. The voices were tense enough that I made my steps silent as I slid into the shadows behind the open door. A cowardly, wretched thing to do—but what they were saying had me shoving aside any guilt.

"I just want to know what you think you're doing." It was Lucien—that familiar lazy viciousness coating each word.

"What are *you* doing?" Tamlin snapped. Through the space between the hinge and the door I could glimpse the two of them standing almost face-to-face. On Tamlin's nonbandaged hand, his claws shone in the morning light.

"Me?" Lucien put a hand on his chest. "By the Cauldron, Tam—there isn't much time, and you're just sulking and glowering. You're not even trying to fake it anymore."

My brows rose. Tamlin turned away but whirled back a moment later, his teeth bared. "It was a mistake from the start. I can't stomach it, not after what my father did to their kind, to their lands. I won't follow in his footsteps—won't be that sort of person. So *back off*."

"Back off? Back off while you seal our fates and ruin everything? I stayed with you out of hope, not to watch you stumble. For someone with a heart of stone, yours is certainly soft these days. The Bogge was on our lands—the *Bogge*, Tamlin! The barriers between courts have vanished, and even our woods are teeming with filth like the puca. Are you just going to start living out there, slaughtering every bit of vermin that slinks in?"

"Watch your mouth," Tamlin said.

Lucien stepped toward him, exposing his teeth as well. A pulsing kind of air hit me in the stomach, and a metallic stench filled my nose. But I couldn't *see* any magic—only feel it. I couldn't tell if that made it worse.

"Don't push me, Lucien." Tamlin's tone became dangerously quiet, and the hair on the back of my neck stood as he emitted a growl that was pure animal. "You think I don't know what's happening on my own lands? What I've got to lose? What's lost already?"

The blight. Perhaps it was contained, but it seemed it was still wreaking havoc—still a threat, and perhaps one they truly didn't want me knowing about, either from lack of trust or because . . . because I was no one and nothing to them. I leaned forward, but as I did, my finger slipped and softly thudded against the door. A human might not have heard, but both High Fae whirled. My heart stumbled.

I stepped toward the threshold, clearing my throat as I came up with a dozen excuses to shield myself. I looked at Lucien and forced myself to smile. His eyes widened, and I had to wonder if it was because of that smile, or because I looked truly guilty. "Are you going out for a ride?" I said, feeling a bit sick as I gestured behind me with a thumb. I hadn't planned on riding with him today, but it sounded like a decent excuse.

Lucien's russet eye was bright, though the smile he gave me didn't meet it. The face of Tamlin's emissary—more court-trained and calculating than I'd seen him yet. "I'm unavailable today," he said. He jerked his chin to Tamlin. "He'll go with you."

Tamlin shot his friend a look of disdain that he took few pains to hide. His usual baldric was armed with more knives than I'd seen before, and their ornate metal handles glinted as he turned to me, his shoulders tight.

"Whenever you want to go, just say so." The claws of his free hand slipped back under his skin.

No. I almost said it aloud as I turned pleading eyes to Lucien. Lucien merely patted my shoulder as he passed by. "Perhaps tomorrow, human."

Alone with Tamlin, I swallowed hard.

He stood there, waiting.

"I don't want to go for a hunt," I finally said quietly. True. "I hate hunting."

He cocked his head. "Then what do you want to do?"

✣

Tamlin led me down the halls. A soft breeze laced with the scent of roses slipped in through the open windows to caress my face.

"You've been going for hunts," Tamlin said at last, "but you really don't have any interest in hunting." He cast me a sidelong glance. "No wonder you two never catch anything."

No trace of the hollow, cold warrior of the night before, or of the angry Fae noble of minutes before. Just Tamlin right now, it seemed.

I'd be a fool to let my guard down around Tamlin, to think that his acting naturally meant anything, especially when something was so clearly amiss at his estate. He'd taken down the Bogge—and that made him the most dangerous creature I'd ever encountered. I didn't quite know what to make of him, and said somewhat stiltedly, "How's your hand?"

He flexed his bandaged hand, studying the white bindings, stark and clean against his sun-kissed skin. "I didn't thank you."

"You don't need to."

But he shook his head, and his golden hair caught and held the morning light as if it were spun from the sun itself. "The Bogge's bite was crafted to slow the healing of High Fae long enough to kill us. You have my gratitude." When I shrugged it off, he added, "How did you learn to bind wounds like this? I can still use the hand, even with the wrappings."

"Trial and error. I had to be able to pull a bowstring the next day."

He was quiet as we turned down another sun-drenched marble hallway, and I dared to look at him. I found him carefully studying me, his lips in a thin line. "Has anyone ever taken care of you?" he asked quietly.

"No." I'd long since stopped feeling sorry for myself about it.

"Did you learn to hunt in a similar manner—trial and error?"

"I spied on hunters when I could get away with it, and then practiced until I hit something. When I missed, we didn't eat. So learning how to aim was the first thing I figured out."

"I'm curious," he said casually. The amber in his green eyes was glowing. Perhaps not all traces of that beast-warrior were gone. "Are you ever going to use that knife you stole from my table?"

I stiffened. "How did you know?"

Beneath the mask, I could have sworn his brows were raised. "I was trained to notice those things. But I could smell the fear on you, more than anything."

I grumbled, "I thought no one noticed."

He gave me a crooked smile, more genuine than all the faked smiles and flattery he'd given me before. "Regardless of the Treaty, if you want to stand a chance at escaping my kind, you'll need to think more creatively than stealing dinner knives. But with your affinity for eavesdropping, maybe you'll someday learn something valuable."

My ears flared with heat. "I—I wasn't . . . Sorry," I mumbled. But I ran through what I'd overheard. There was no point in pretending I hadn't eavesdropped. "Lucien said you didn't have much time. What did he mean? Are more creatures like the Bogge going to come here thanks to the blight?"

Tamlin went rigid, scanning the hall around us, taking in every sight and sound and scent. Then he shrugged, too stiff to be genuine. "I'm an immortal. I have nothing *but* time, Feyre."

He said my name with such . . . intimacy. As if he weren't a creature capable of killing monsters made from nightmares. I opened my mouth to demand more of an answer, but he cut me off. "The force plaguing our lands and powers—that, too, will pass someday, if we're Cauldron-blessed. But yes—now that the Bogge entered these lands, I'd say it's fair to assume others might follow it, especially if the puca was already so bold."

If the borders between the courts were gone, though, as I'd heard Lucien say—if everything in Prythian was different, as Tamlin had claimed, thanks to this blight . . . Well, I didn't want to be caught up in some brutal war or revolution. I doubted I'd survive very long.

Tamlin strode ahead and opened a set of double doors at the end of the hall. The powerful muscles of his back shifted beneath his clothes. I'd never forget what he was—what he was capable of. What he'd been trained to do, apparently.

"As requested," he said, "the study."

I saw what lay beyond him and my stomach twisted.

CHAPTER 13

Tamlin waved his hand, and a hundred candles sprang to life. Whatever Lucien had said about magic being drained and off-kilter thanks to the blight clearly hadn't affected Tamlin as dramatically, or perhaps he'd been far more powerful to start with, if he could transform his sentries into wolves whenever he pleased. The tang of magic stung my senses, but I kept my chin high. That is, until I peered inside.

My palms began sweating as I took in the enormous, opulent study. Tomes lined each wall like the soldiers of a silent army, and couches, desks, and rich rugs were scattered throughout the room. But . . . it had been over a week since I left my family. Though my father had said never to return, though my vow to my mother was fulfilled, I could at least let them know I was safe—relatively safe. And warn them about the sickness sweeping across Prythian that might someday soon cross the wall.

There was only one method to convey it.

"Do you need anything else?" Tamlin asked, and I jerked. He still stood behind me.

"No," I said, striding into the study. I couldn't think about the casual power he'd just shown—the graceful carelessness with which he'd brought so many flames to life. I had to focus on the task at hand.

It wasn't entirely my fault that I was scarcely able to read. Before our downfall, my mother had sorely neglected our education, not bothering to hire a governess. And after poverty struck and my elder sisters, who could read and write, deemed the village school beneath us, they didn't bother to teach me. I could read enough to function—enough to form my letters, but so poorly that even signing my name was mortifying.

It was bad enough that Tamlin knew. I would think about *how* to get the letter to them once it was finished; perhaps I could beg a favor of him, or Lucien.

Asking them to write it would be too humiliating. I could hear their words: *typical ignorant human*. And since Lucien seemed convinced that I would turn spy the moment I could, he would no doubt burn the letter, and any I tried to write after. So I'd have to learn myself.

"I'll leave you to it, then," Tamlin said as our silence became too prolonged, too tense.

I didn't move until he'd closed the doors, shutting me inside. My heartbeat pulsed throughout my body as I approached a shelf.

I had to take a break for dinner and to sleep, but I was back in the study before the dawn had fully risen. I'd found a small writing desk in a corner and gathered papers and ink. My finger traced a line of text, and I whispered the words.

" '*She grab-bed . . . grabbed her shoe, sta . . . nd . . . standing from her pos . . . po . . .* ' " I sat back in my chair and pressed the heels of my palms into my eyes. When I felt less near to ripping out my hair, I took the quill and underlined the word: *position*.

With a shaking hand, I did my best to copy letter after letter onto the ever-growing list I kept beside the book. There were at least forty words on it, their letters malformed and barely legible. I would look up their pronunciations later.

I rose from the chair, needing to stretch my legs, my spine—or just to get away from that lengthy list of words I didn't know how to pronounce and the permanent heat that now warmed my face and neck.

I suppose the study was more of a library, as I couldn't see any of the walls thanks to the small labyrinths of stacks flanking the main area and a mezzanine dangling above, covered wall to wall in books. But *study* sounded less intimidating. I meandered through some of the stacks, following a trickle of sunlight to a bank of windows on the far side. I found myself overlooking a rose garden, filled with dozens of hues of crimson and pink and white and yellow.

I might have allowed myself a moment to take in the colors, gleaming with dew under the morning sun, had I not glimpsed the painting that stretched along the wall beside the windows.

Not a painting, I thought, blinking as I stepped back to view its massive expanse. No, it was . . . I searched for the word in that half-forgotten part of my mind. *Mural*. That's what it was.

At first I could do nothing but stare at its size, at the ambition of it, at the fact that this masterpiece was tucked back here for no one to ever see, as if it was nothing—absolutely nothing—to create something like this.

It told a story with the way colors and shapes and light flowed, the way the tone shifted across the mural. The story of . . . of Prythian.

It began with a cauldron.

A mighty black cauldron held by glowing, slender female hands in a starry, endless night. Those hands tipped it over, golden sparkling liquid pouring out over the lip. No—not sparkling, but . . . effervescent with small symbols, perhaps of some ancient faerie language. Whatever was written there, whatever it was, the contents of the cauldron were dumped into the void below, pooling on the earth to form our world . . .

The map spanned the entirety of our world—not just the land on which we stood, but also the seas and the larger continents beyond. Each territory was marked and colored, some with intricate, ornate depictions of the beings who had once ruled over lands that now belonged to humans. All of it, I remembered with a shudder, all of the world had once been theirs—at least as far as they believed, crafted for them by the bearer of the cauldron. There was no mention of humans—no sign of us here. I supposed we'd been as low as pigs to them.

It was hard to look at the next panel. It was so simple, yet so detailed that, for a moment, I stood there on that battlefield, feeling the texture of the bloodied mud beneath me, shoulder to shoulder with the thousands of other human soldiers lined up, facing the faerie hordes who charged at us. A moment of pause before the slaughter.

The humans' arrows and swords seemed so pointless against the High Fae in their glimmering armor, or the faeries bristling with claws and fangs. I knew—knew without another panel to explicitly show me—the humans hadn't survived that particular battle. The smear of black on the panel beside it, tinged with glimmers of red, said enough.

Then another map, of a much-reduced faerie realm. Northern territories had been cut up and divided to make room for the High Fae, who had lost their lands to the south of the wall. Everything north of the wall went to them; everything south was left as a blur of nothing. A decimated, forgotten world—as if the painter couldn't be bothered to render it.

I scanned the various lands and territories now given to the High Fae. Still so much territory—such monstrous power spread across the entire northern part of our world. I knew they were ruled by kings or queens or councils or empresses, but I'd never seen a representation of it, of how much they'd been forced to concede to the South, and how crammed their lands now were in comparison.

Our massive island had fared well for Prythian by comparison, with only the bottom tip given over to us miserable humans. The bulk of the sacrifice was borne by the southernmost of the seven territories: a territory painted with crocuses and lambs and roses. Spring lands.

I took a step closer, until I could see the dark, ugly smear that acted as the wall—another spiteful touch by the painter. No markers in the human realm, nothing to indicate any of the larger towns or centers, but . . . I found the rough area where our village was, and the woods that separated it from the wall. Those two days' journey seemed so small—too small—compared to the power lurking above us. I traced a line, my finger hovering over the paint, up over the wall, into these lands—the lands of the Spring Court. Again, no markers, but it was filled with touches of spring: trees in bloom, fickle storms, young animals . . . At least I was to live out my days in one of the more moderate courts, weather-wise. A small consolation.

I looked northward and stepped back again. The six other courts of Prythian occupied a patchwork of territories. Autumn, Summer, and Winter were easy enough to pick out. Then above them, two glowing courts: the southernmost one a softer, redder palate, the Dawn Court; above, in bright gold and yellow and blue, the Day Court. And above that, perched in a frozen mountainous spread of darkness and stars, the sprawling, massive territory of the Night Court.

There were things in the shadows between those mountains—little eyes, gleaming teeth. A land of lethal beauty. The hair on my arms rose.

I might have examined the other kingdoms across the seas that flanked our land, like the isolated faerie kingdom to the west that seemed to have gotten away with no territory loss and was still law unto itself, had I not looked to the heart of that beautiful, living map.

In the center of the land, as if it were the core around which everything else had spread, or perhaps the place where the cauldron's liquid had first touched, was a small, snowy mountain range. From it arose a mammoth, solitary peak. Bald of snow, bald of life—as if the elements refused to touch it. There were no more clues about what it might be; nothing to indicate its importance, and I supposed that the viewers were already supposed to know. This was not a mural for human eyes.

With that thought, I went back to my little table. At least I'd learned the layout of their lands—and I knew to never, ever go north.

I eased into my seat and found my place in the book, my face warming as I glanced at the illustrations scattered throughout. A children's book, and yet I could scarcely make it through its twenty or so pages. Why *did* Tamlin have children's books in his library? Were they from his own childhood, or in anticipation of children to come? It didn't matter. I couldn't even read them. I hated the smell of these books—the decaying rot of the pages, the mocking whisper of the paper, the rough skin of the binding. I looked at the piece of paper, at all those words I didn't know.

I bunched my list in my hand, crumpling the paper into a ball, and chucked it into the rubbish bin.

"I could help you write to them, if that's why you're in here."

I jerked back in my seat, almost knocking over the chair, and whirled to find Tamlin behind me, a stack of books in his arms. I pushed back against the heat rising in my cheeks and ears, the panic at the information he might be guessing I'd been trying to send. "Help? You mean a faerie is passing up the opportunity to mock an ignorant mortal?"

He set the books down on the table, his jaw tight. I couldn't read the titles glinting on the leather spines. "Why should I mock you for a shortcoming that isn't your fault? Let me help you. I owe you for the hand."

Shortcoming. It *was* a shortcoming.

Yet it was one thing to bandage his hand, to talk to him as if he wasn't a predator built to kill and destroy, but to reveal how little I truly knew, to let him see that part of me that was still a child, unfinished and raw . . . His face was unreadable. Though there had been no pity in his voice, I straightened. "I'm fine."

"You think I've got nothing better to do with my time than come up with elaborate ways to humiliate you?"

I thought of that smear of nothing that the painter had used to render the human lands, and didn't have an answer—at least, not one that was polite. I'd given enough already to them—to him.

Tamlin shook his head. "So you'll let Lucien take you on hunts and—"

"Lucien," I interrupted quietly but not softly, "doesn't pretend to be anything but what he is."

"What's that supposed to mean?" he growled, but his claws stayed retracted, even as he clenched his hands into fists at his sides.

I was definitely walking a dangerous line, but I didn't care. Even if he'd offered me sanctuary, I didn't have to fall at his feet. "It means," I said with that same cold quiet, "that I don't know you. I don't know who you are, or *what* you really are, or what you want."

"It means you don't trust me."

"How can I trust a faerie? Don't you delight in killing and tricking us?"

His snarl set the flames of the candles guttering. "You aren't what I had in mind for a *human*—believe me."

I could almost feel the wound deep in my chest as it ripped open and all those awful, silent words came pouring out. *Illiterate*, *ignorant*, *unremarkable*, *proud*, *cold*—all spoken from Nesta's mouth, all echoing in my head with her sneering voice.

I pinched my lips together.

He winced and lifted a hand slightly, as if about to reach for me. "Feyre," he began—softly enough that I just shook my head and left the room. He didn't stop me.

But that afternoon, when I went to retrieve my crumpled list from the wastebasket, it was gone. And my pile of books had been disturbed—the titles out of order. It had probably been a servant, I assured myself, calming the tightness in my chest. Just Alis or some other bird-masked faerie cleaning up. I hadn't written anything incriminating—there was no way he knew I'd been trying to warn my family. I doubted he would punish me for it, but . . . our conversation earlier had been bad enough.

Still, my hands were unsteady as I took my seat at the little desk and found my place in the book I'd used that morning. I knew it was shameful to mark the books with ink, but if Tamlin could afford gold plates, he could replace a book or two.

I stared at the book without seeing the jumble of letters.

Maybe I was a fool for not accepting his help, for not swallowing my pride and having him write the letter in a few moments. Not even a letter of warning, but just—just to let them know I was safe. If he had better things to do with his time than come up with ways to embarrass me, then surely he had better things to do than help me write letters to my family. And yet he'd offered.

A nearby clock chimed the hour.

Shortcoming—another one of my *shortcomings*. I rubbed my brows with my thumb and forefinger. I'd been equally foolish for feeling a shred of pity for him—for the lone, brooding faerie, for someone I had so *stupidly* thought would really care if he met someone who perhaps felt the same, perhaps understood—in my ignorant, insignificant human way—what it was like to bear the weight of caring for others. I should have let his hand bleed that night, should have known better than to think that maybe—maybe there would be someone, human or faerie or whatever, who could understand what my life—what *I*—had become these past few years.

A minute passed, then another.

Faeries might not be able to lie, but they could certainly withhold information; Tamlin, Lucien, and Alis had done their best not to answer my specific questions. Knowing more about the blight that threatened them—knowing *anything* about it, where it had come from, what else it could do, and especially what it could do to a *human*—was worth my time to learn.

And if there was a chance that they might also possess some knowledge about a forgotten loophole of that damned Treaty, if they knew some way to pay the debt I owed *and* return me to my family so I might warn them about the blight myself . . . I had to risk it.

Twenty minutes later I had tracked down Lucien in his bedroom. I'd marked on my little map where it was—in a separate wing on the second level, far from mine—and after searching in his usual haunts, it was the last place to look. I knocked on the white-painted double doors.

"Come in, human." He could probably detect me by my breathing patterns alone. Or maybe that eye of his could see through the door.

I eased open the door. The room was similar to mine in shape, but was bedecked in hues of orange and red and gold, with faint traces of green and brown. Like being in an autumn wood. But while my room was all softness and grace, his was marked with ruggedness. In lieu of a pretty breakfast table by the window, a worn worktable dominated the space, covered in various weapons. It was there he sat, wearing only a white shirt and trousers, his red hair unbound and gleaming like liquid fire. Tamlin's court-trained emissary, but a warrior in his own right.

"I haven't seen you around," I said, shutting the door and leaning against it.

"I had to go sort out some hotheads on the northern border—official emissary business," he said, setting down the hunting knife he'd been cleaning, a long, vicious blade. "I got back in time to hear your little spat with Tam, and decided I was safer up here. I'm glad to hear your human heart has warmed to me, though. At least I'm not on the top of your killing list."

I gave him a long look.

"Well," he went on, shrugging, "it seems that you managed to get under Tam's fur enough that he sought me out and nearly bit my head off. So I suppose I can thank you for ruining what should have been a peaceful lunch. Thankfully for me, there's been a disturbance out in the western forest, and my poor friend had to go deal with it in that way only he can. I'm surprised you didn't run into him on the stairs."

Thank the forgotten gods for some small mercies. "What sort of disturbance?"

Lucien shrugged, but the movement was too tense to be careless. "The usual sort: unwanted, nasty creatures raising hell."

Good—good that Tamlin was away and wouldn't be here to catch me in what I planned to do. Another bit of luck. "I'm impressed you answered me that much," I said as casually as I could, thinking through my words. "But it's too bad you're not like the Suriel, spouting any information I want if I'm clever enough to snare you."

For a moment, he blinked at me. Then his mouth twisted to the side, and that metal eye whizzed and narrowed on me. "I suppose you won't tell me what you want to know."

"You have your secrets, and I have mine," I said carefully. I couldn't tell whether he would try to convince me otherwise if I told him the truth. "But if you *were* a Suriel," I added with deliberate slowness, in case he hadn't caught my meaning, "how, exactly, would I trap you?"

Lucien set down the knife and picked at his nails. For a moment, I wondered if he would tell me anything at all. Wondered if he would go right to Tamlin and tattle.

But then he said, "I'd probably have a weakness for groves of young birch trees in the western woods, and freshly slaughtered chickens, and would probably be so greedy that I wouldn't notice the double-loop snare rigged around the grove to pin my legs in place."

"Hmm." I didn't dare ask why he had decided to be accommodating. There was still a good chance he wouldn't mind seeing me dead, but I would risk it. "I somehow prefer you as a High Fae."

He smirked, but the amusement was short-lived. "If I were insane and stupid enough to go after a Suriel, I'd also take a bow and quiver, and maybe a knife just like this one." He sheathed the knife he'd cleaned and set it down at the edge of the table—an offering. "And I'd be prepared to run like hell when I freed it—to the nearest running water, which they hate crossing."

"But you're not insane, so you'll be here, safe and sound?"

"I'll be conveniently hunting on the grounds, and with my superior hearing, I might be feeling generous enough to listen if someone screams from the western woods. But it's a good thing I had no role in telling you to go out today, since Tam would eviscerate anyone who told you how to trap a Suriel; and it's a good thing I had planned to hunt anyway, because if anyone caught me helping you, there would be trouble of a whole other hell awaiting us. I hope your secrets are worth it." He said it with his usual grin, but there was an edge to it—a warning I didn't miss.

Another riddle—and another bit of information. I said, "It's a good thing that while you have superior hearing, I possess superior abilities to keep my mouth shut."

He snorted as I took the knife from the table and turned to procure the bow from my room. "I think I'm starting to like you—for a murdering human."

CHAPTER 14

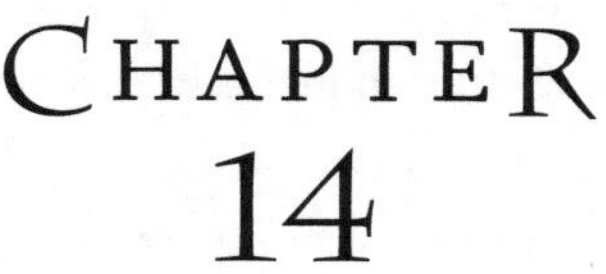

Western woods. Grove of young birch trees. Slaughtered chicken. Double-loop snare. Close to running water.

I repeated Lucien's instructions as I walked out of the manor, through the cultivated gardens, across the wild, rolling grassy hills beyond them, over clear streams, and into the spring woods beyond. No one had stopped me—no one had even been around to see me leave, bow and quiver across my back, Lucien's knife at my side. I lugged along a satchel stuffed with a freshly dead chicken courtesy of the baffled kitchen staff, and had tucked an extra blade into my boot.

The lands were as empty as the manor itself, though I occasionally glimpsed something shining in the corner of my eye. Every time I turned to look, the shimmering transformed into the sunlight dancing on a nearby stream, or the wind fluttering the leaves of a lone sycamore atop a knoll. As I passed a large pond nestled at the foot of a towering hill, I could have sworn I saw four shining female heads poking up from the bright water, watching me. I hurried my steps.

Only birds and the chittering and rustling of small animals sounded as I entered the still green western forest. I'd never ridden through these woods on my hunts with Lucien. There was no path here, nothing tame about it. Oaks, elms, and beeches intertwined in a thick weave, almost strangling the trickle of sunlight that crept in through the dense canopy. The moss-covered earth swallowed any sound I made.

Old—this forest was ancient. And alive, in a way that I couldn't describe but could only feel, deep in the marrow of my bones. Perhaps I was the first human in five hundred years to walk beneath those heavy, dark branches, to inhale the freshness of spring leaves masking the damp, thick rot.

Birch trees—running water. I made my way through the woods, breath tight in my throat. Night was the dangerous time, I reminded myself. I had only a few hours until sunset.

Even if the Bogge had stalked us in the daylight.

The Bogge was dead, and whatever horror Tamlin was now dealing with dwelled in another part of these lands. The Spring Court. I wondered in what ways Tamlin had to answer to its High Lord, or if it was his High Lord who had carved out Lucien's eye. Maybe it was the High Lord's consort—the *she* whom Lucien had mentioned—that instilled such fear in them. I pushed away the thought.

I kept my steps light, my eyes and ears open, and my heartbeat steady. Shortcomings or no, I could still hunt. And the answers I needed were worth it.

I found a glen of young, skinny birch trees, then stalked in ever-widening circles until I encountered the nearest stream. Not deep, but so wide that I'd have to take a running leap to cross it. Lucien had said to find running water, and this was close enough to make escape possible. If I needed to escape. Hopefully I wouldn't.

I traced and then retraced several different routes to the stream. And a few alternate routes, should my access to it somehow be blocked. And when I was sure of every root and rock and hollow in the surrounding area, I returned to the small clearing encircled by those white trees and laid my snare.

✢

From my spot up a nearby tree—a sturdy, dense oak whose vibrant leaves hid me entirely from anyone below—I waited. And waited. The afternoon sun crept overhead, hot enough even through the canopy that I had to shrug off my cloak and roll up the sleeves of my tunic. My stomach grumbled, and I pulled a hunk of cheese out of my rucksack. Eating it would be quieter than the apple I'd also swiped from the kitchen on my way out. When I finished it off, I swigged water from the canteen I'd brought, parched from the heat.

Did Tamlin or Lucien ever grow tired of day after day of eternal spring, or ever venture into the other territories, if only to experience a different season? I wouldn't have minded endless, mild spring while looking after my family—winter brought us dangerously close to death every year—but if I were immortal, I might want a little variation to pass the time. I'd probably want to do more than lurk about a manor house, too. Though I still hadn't worked up the nerve to make the request that had crept into the back of my mind when I saw the mural.

I moved about as much as I dared on the branch, only to keep the blood flowing to my limbs. I'd just settled in again when a ripple of silence came toward me. As if the wood thrushes and squirrels and moths held their breath while something passed by.

My bow was already strung. Quietly, I loosely nocked an arrow. Closer and closer the silence crept.

The trees seemed to lean in, their entwined branches locking tighter, a living cage keeping even the smallest of birds from soaring out of the canopy.

Maybe this had been a very bad idea. Maybe Lucien had overestimated my abilities. Or maybe he had been waiting for the chance to lead me to my doom.

My muscles strained from holding still atop the branch, but I kept my balance and listened. Then I heard it: a whisper, as if cloth were dragging over root and stone, a hungry, wheezing sniffing from the nearby clearing.

I'd laid my snares carefully, making the chicken look as if it had wandered too far and snapped its own neck as it sought to free itself from a fallen branch. I'd taken care to keep my own scent off the bird as much as possible. But these faeries had such keen senses, and even though I'd covered my tracks—

There was a snap, a whoosh, and a hollowed-out, wicked scream that made my bones and muscles and breath lock up.

Another enraged shriek pierced the forest, and my snares groaned as they held, and held, and held.

I climbed out of the tree and went to meet the Suriel.

✣

Lucien, I decided as I crept up to the faerie in the birch glen, really, truly wanted me dead.

I hadn't known what to expect as I entered the ring of white trees—tall and straight as pillars—but it was not the tall, thin veiled figure in dark tattered robes. Its hunched back facing me, I could count the hard knobs of its spine poking through the thin fabric. Spindly, scabby gray arms clawed at the snare with yellowed, cracked fingernails.

Run, some primal, intrinsically human part of me whispered. Begged. *Run and run and never look back*.

But I kept my arrow loosely nocked. I said quietly, "Are you one of the Suriel?"

The faerie went rigid. And sniffed. Once. Twice.

Then slowly, it turned to me, the dark veil draped over its bald head blowing in a phantom breeze.

A face that looked like it had been crafted from dried, weather-worn bone, its skin either forgotten or discarded, a lipless mouth and too-long teeth held by blackened gums, slitted holes for nostrils, and eyes . . . eyes that were nothing more than swirling pits of milky white—the white of death, the white of sickness, the white of clean-picked corpses.

Peeking above the ragged neck of its dark robes was a body of veins and bones, as dried and solid and horrific as the texture of its face. It let go of the snare, and its too-long fingers clicked against each other as it studied me.

"Human," it said, and its voice was at once one and many, old and young, beautiful and grotesque. My bowels turned watery. "Did you set this clever, wicked trap for me?"

"Are you one of the Suriel?" I asked again, my words scarcely more than a ragged breath.

"Indeed I am." *Click, click, click* went its fingers against each other, one for each word.

"Then the trap was for you," I managed. *Run, run, run.*

It remained sitting, its bare, gnarled feet caught in my snares. "I have not seen a human woman for an age. Come closer so I might look upon my captor."

I did no such thing.

It let out a huffing, awful laugh. "And which of my brethren betrayed my secrets to you?"

"None of them. My mother told me stories of you."

"Lies—I can smell the lies on your breath." It sniffed again, its fingers clacking together. It cocked its head to the side, an erratic, sharp movement, the dark veil snapping with it. "What would a human woman want from the Suriel?"

"You tell me," I said softly.

It let out another low laugh. "A test? A foolish and useless test, for if you dared to capture me, then you must want knowledge very badly." I said nothing, and it smiled with that lipless mouth, its grayed teeth horrifically large. "Ask me your questions, human, and then free me."

I swallowed hard. "Is there—is there truly no way for me to go home?"

"Not unless you seek to be killed, and your family with you. You must remain here."

Whatever last shred of hope I'd been clinging to, whatever foolish optimism, shriveled and died. This changed nothing. Before my fight with Tamlin that morning, I hadn't even entertained the idea, anyway. Perhaps I'd only come here out of spite. So, fine—if I was here, facing sure death, then I might as well learn something. "What do you know about Tamlin?"

"More specific, human. Be more specific. For I know a good many things about the High Lord of the Spring Court."

The earth tilted beneath me. "Tamlin is—Tamlin is a High Lord?"

Click, click, click. "You did not know. Interesting."

Not just some petty faerie lord of a manor, but . . . but a High Lord of one of the seven territories. A High Lord of Prythian.

"Did you also not know that this is the Spring Court, little human?"

"Yes—yes, I knew about that."

The Suriel settled on the ground. "Spring, Summer, Autumn, Winter, Dawn, Day, and Night," it mused, as if I hadn't even answered. "The seven Courts of Prythian, each ruled by a High Lord, all of them deadly in their own way. They are not merely powerful—they *are* Power." That was why Tamlin had been able to face the Bogge and live. High Lord.

I tucked away my fear. "Everyone at the Spring Court is stuck wearing a mask, and yet you aren't," I said cautiously. "Are you not a member of the Court?"

"I am a member of no Court. I am older than the High Lords, older than Prythian, older than the bones of this world."

Lucien had *definitely* overestimated my abilities. "And what can be done about this blight that has spread in Prythian, stealing and altering the magic? Where did it come from?"

"Stay with the High Lord, human," the Suriel said. "That's all you can do. You will be safe. Do not interfere; do not go looking for answers after today, or you will be devoured by the shadow over Prythian. He will shield you from it, so stay close to him, and all will be righted."

That wasn't exactly an answer. I repeated, "Where did the blight come from?"

Those milky eyes narrowed. "The High Lord does not know that you came here today, does he? He does not know that his human woman came to trap a Suriel, because he cannot give her the answers she seeks. But it is too late, human—for the High Lord, for you, perhaps for your realm as well . . ."

Despite all that it had said, despite its order to stop asking questions and stay with Tamlin, it was *his human woman* that echoed in my head. That made me clench my teeth.

But the Suriel went on. "Across the violent western sea, there is another faerie kingdom called Hybern, ruled by a wicked, powerful king. Yes, a king," he said when I raised a brow. "Not a High Lord—there, his territory is not divided into courts. There, he is law unto himself. Humans no longer exist in that realm—though his throne is made of their bones."

That large island I'd seen on the map, the one that hadn't yielded any lands to humans after the Treaty. And—a throne of bones. The cheese I'd eaten turned leaden in my stomach.

"For some time now, the King of Hybern has found himself unhappy with the Treaty the other ruling High Fae of the world made with you humans long ago. He resents that he was forced to sign it, to let his mortal slaves go and to remain confined to his damp green isle at the edge of the world. And so, a hundred years ago, he dispatched his most-trusted and loyal commanders, his deadliest warriors, remnants of the ancient armies that he once sailed to the continent to wage such a brutal war against you humans, all of them as hungry and vile as he. As spies and courtiers and lovers, they infiltrated the various High Fae courts and kingdoms and empires around the world for fifty years, and when they had gathered enough information, he made his plan. But nearly five decades ago, one of his commanders disobeyed him. The Deceiver. And—" The Suriel straightened. "We are not alone."

I drew my bow farther but kept it pointed at the ground as I scanned the trees. But everything had already gone silent in the presence of the Suriel.

"Human, you must free me and run," it said, those death-filled eyes widening. "Run for the High Lord's manor. Do not forget what I told you—*stay with the High Lord*, and live to see everything righted."

"What is it?" If I knew what came, I could stand a better chance of—

"The naga—faeries made of shadow and hate and rot. They heard my scream, and they smelled you. Free me, human. They will cage me if they catch me here. *Free me* and return to the High Lord's side."

Shit. *Shit*. I lunged for the snare, making to put away my bow and grab my knife.

But four shadowy figures slipped through the birch trees, so dark that they seemed made from a starless night.

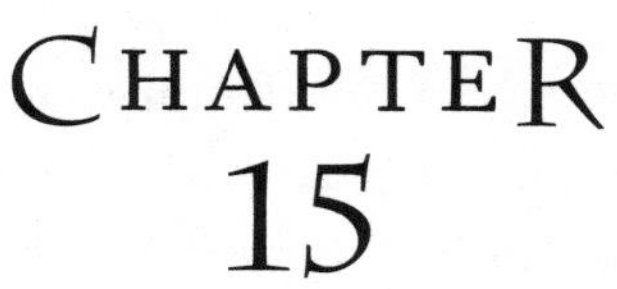

CHAPTER 15

The naga were sprung from a nightmare. Covered in dark scales and nothing more, they were a horrendous combination of serpentine features and male humanoid bodies whose powerful arms ended in polished black, flesh-shredding talons.

Here were the creatures of the blood-filled legends, the ones that slipped through the wall to torment and slaughter mortals. The ones I would have been glad to kill that day in the snowy woods. Their huge, almond-shaped eyes greedily took in the Suriel and me.

The four of them paused across the clearing, the Suriel between us, and I trained my arrow toward the one in the center.

The creature smiled, a row of razor-sharp teeth greeting me as a silvery forked tongue darted out.

"The Dark Mother has sent us a gift today, brothers," he said, gazing at the Suriel, who was clawing at the snare now. The naga's amber eyes shifted toward me again. "And a meal."

"Not much to eat," another one said, flexing its claws.

I began backing away—toward the stream, toward the manor below, keeping my arrow pointed at them. One scream from me would notify

Lucien—but my breath was thin. And he might not come at all, if he'd sent me here. I kept every sense fixed on my retreating steps.

"*Human*," the Suriel begged.

I had ten arrows—nine, once I fired the one nocked in my bow. None of them ash, but maybe they'd keep the naga down long enough for me to flee.

I backed away another step. The four naga crept closer, as if savoring the slowness of the hunt, as if they already knew how I tasted.

I had three heartbeats to make up my mind. Three heartbeats to execute my plan.

I drew my bowstring back farther, my arm trembling.

And then I screamed. Sharp and loud and with every bit of air in my too-tight lungs.

With the naga now focused entirely on me, I fired at the tether holding the Suriel in place.

The snare shattered. Like a shadow on the wind, the Suriel was off, a blast of dark that set the four naga staggering back.

The one closest to me surged toward the Suriel, the strong column of its scaly neck stretching out. No chance of my movements being considered an unprovoked attack anymore—not now that they'd seen my aim. They still wanted to kill me.

So I let my arrow fly.

The tip glittered like a shooting star through the gloom of the forest. I had all of a blink before it struck home and blood sprayed.

The naga toppled back just as the remaining three whirled to me. I didn't know if it was a killing shot. I was already gone.

I raced for the stream using the path I'd calculated earlier, not daring to look back. Lucien had said he'd be nearby—but I was deep in the woods, too far from the manor and help.

Branches and twigs snapped behind me—too close—and snarls that sounded like nothing I'd heard from Tamlin or Lucien or the wolf or any animal filled the still woods.

My only hope of getting away alive lay in outrunning them long enough to reach Lucien, and then only if he was there as he'd promised to be. I didn't let myself think of all the hills I would have to climb once I cleared the forest itself. Or what I would do if Lucien had changed his mind.

The crashing through the brush became louder, closer, and I veered to the right, leaping over the stream. Running water might have stopped the Suriel, but a hiss and a thud close behind told me it did nothing to hold the naga at bay.

I careened through a thicket, and thorns ripped at my cheeks. I barely felt their stinging kisses or the warm blood sliding down my face. I didn't even have time to wince, not as two dark figures flanked me, closing in to cut me off.

My knees groaned as I pushed myself harder, focusing on the growing brightness of the woods' end. But the naga to my right rushed at me, so fast that I could only leap aside to avoid the slashing talons.

I stumbled but stayed upright just as the naga on my left pounced.

I hurled myself into a stop, swinging my bow up in a wide arc. I nearly lost my grip as it connected with that serpentine face, and bone crunched with a horrific screech. I hurdled over his enormous fallen body, not pausing to look for the others.

I made it three feet before the third naga stepped in front of me.

I swung my bow at his head. He dodged it. The other two hissed as they came up behind me, and I gripped the bow harder.

Surrounded.

I turned in a slow circle, bow ready to strike.

One of them sniffed at me, those slitted nostrils flaring. "Scrawny human thing," he spat to the others, whose smiles grew sharper. "Do you know what you've cost us?"

I wouldn't go down without a fight, without taking some of them with me. "Go to Hell," I said, but it came out in a gasp.

They laughed, stepping nearer. I swung the bow at the closest. He dodged it, chuckling. "We'll have our sport—though you might not find it as amusing."

I gritted my teeth as I swung again. I would not be hunted down like a deer among wolves. I would find a way out of this; I would—

A black-clawed hand closed around the shaft of my bow, and a resounding *snap* echoed through the too-silent woods.

The air left my chest in a whoosh, and I only had time to half turn before one of them grabbed me by the throat and hurled me to the ground. He pounded my arm so hard against the earth that my bones groaned and my fingers splayed, dropping the remnants of my bow.

"When we're done ripping off your skin, you'll wish you hadn't crossed into Prythian," he breathed into my face, the reek of carrion shoving down my throat. I gagged. "We'll cut you up so fine there won't be much for the crows to pick at."

A white-hot flame went through me. Rage or terror or wild instinct, I don't know. I didn't think. I grabbed the knife in my boot and slammed it into his leathery neck.

Blood rained down onto my face, into my mouth as I bellowed my fury, my terror.

The naga slumped back. I scrambled up before the remaining two could pin me, but something rock hard hit my face. I tasted blood and soil and grass as I hit the earth. Stars danced in my vision, and I stumbled to my feet again out of instinct, grabbing for Lucien's hunting knife.

Not like this, not like this, not like this.

One of them lunged for me, and I dodged aside. His talons caught in my cloak and yanked, ripping it into ribbons just as his companion threw me to the ground, my arms tearing beneath those claws.

"You'll bleed," one of them panted, laughing under his breath at the knife I lifted. "We'll bleed you nice and slow." He wiggled his talons—perfect for deep, brutal cutting. He opened his mouth again, and a bone-shattering roar sounded through the clearing.

Only it hadn't come from the creature's throat.

The noise hadn't finished echoing before the naga went flying off me, crashing into a tree so hard that the wood cracked. I made out the gleaming gold of his mask and hair and the long, deadly claws before Tamlin tore into the creature.

The naga holding me shrieked and released his grip, leaping to his feet as Tamlin's claws shredded through his companion's neck. Flesh and blood ripped away.

I kept low to the ground, knife at the ready, waiting.

Tamlin let out another roar that made the marrow of my bones go cold and revealed those lengthened canines.

The remaining creature darted for the woods.

He got only a few steps away before Tamlin tackled him, pinning him to the earth. And disemboweled the naga in one deep, long swipe.

I remained where I lay, my face half buried in leaves and twigs and moss. I didn't try to raise myself. I was shaking so badly that I thought I would fall apart at the seams. It was all I could do to keep holding the knife.

Tamlin got to his feet, wrenching his claws out of the creature's abdomen. Blood and gore dripped from them, staining the deep green moss.

High Lord. High Lord. High Lord.

Feral rage still smoldered in his gaze, and I flinched as he knelt beside me. He reached for me again, but I jerked back, away from the bloody claws that were still out. I raised myself into a sitting position before the shaking resumed. I knew I couldn't get to my feet.

"Feyre," he said. The wrath faded from his eyes, and the claws slipped back under his skin, but the roar still sounded in my ears. There had been nothing in that sound but primal fury.

"How?" It was all I could manage to say, but he understood me.

"I was tracking a pack of them—these four escaped, and must have followed your scent through the woods. I heard you scream."

So he didn't know about the Suriel. And he—he'd come to help me.

He reached a hand toward me, and I shuddered as he ran cool, wet fingers down my stinging, aching cheek. Blood—that was blood on them.

And from the stickiness on my face, I knew there was already enough blood splattered on me that it wouldn't make a difference.

The pain in my face and my arm faded, then vanished. His eyes darkened a bit at the bruise I knew was already blossoming on my cheekbone, but the throbbing quickly lessened. The metallic scent of magic wrapped around me, then floated away on a light breeze.

"I found one dead half a mile away," he went on, his hands leaving my face as he unbuckled his baldric, then shucked off his tunic and handed it to me. The front of my own had been ripped and torn by the talons of the naga. "I saw one of my arrows in his throat, so I followed their tracks here."

I pulled on Tamlin's tunic over my own, ignoring how easily I could see the cut of his muscles beneath his white shirt, the way the blood soaking it made them stand out even more. A purebred predator, honed to kill without a second thought, without remorse. I shivered again and savored the warmth that leaked from the cloth. *High Lord*. I should have known, should have guessed. Maybe I hadn't wanted to—maybe I'd been afraid.

"Here," he said, rising to his feet and offering me a bloodstained hand. I didn't dare look at the slaughtered naga as I gripped his extended hand and he pulled me to my feet. My knees buckled, but I stayed upright.

I stared at our linked hands, both coated in blood that wasn't our own.

No, he hadn't been the only one to spill blood just now. And it wasn't just my blood that still coated my tongue. Perhaps that made me as much of a beast as him. But he'd saved me. Killed for me. I spat onto the grass, wishing I hadn't lost my canteen.

"Do I want to know what you were doing out here?" he asked.

No. Definitely not. Not after he'd warned me plenty of times already. "I thought I wasn't confined to the house and garden. I didn't realize I'd come so far."

He dropped my hand. "On the days that I'm called away to deal with . . . trouble, stay close to the house."

I nodded a bit numbly. "Thank you," I mumbled, fighting past the shaking racking my body, my mind. The naga's blood on me became nearly unbearable. I spat again. "Not—not just for this. For saving my life, I mean." I wanted to tell him how much that meant—that the High Lord of the Spring Court thought I was *worth* saving—but couldn't find the words.

His fangs vanished. "It was . . . the least I could do. They shouldn't have gotten this far onto my lands." He shook his head, more at himself, his shoulders slumping. "Let's go home," he said, sparing me the effort of explaining why I'd been out here in the first place. I couldn't bring myself to tell him that the manor wasn't my home—that I might not even have a home at all anymore.

We walked back in silence, both of us blood-drenched and pale. I could still sense the carnage we'd left behind—the blood-soaked ground and trees. The pieces of the naga.

Well, I'd learned something from the Suriel, at least. Even if it wasn't entirely what I'd wanted to hear—or know.

Stay with the High Lord. Fine—easy enough. But as for the history lesson it had been in the middle of giving me, about wicked kings and their commanders and however they tied into the High Lord at my side and the blight . . . I still didn't have enough specifics to be able to thoroughly warn my family. But the Suriel had told me not to go looking for further answers.

I had a feeling I would surely be a fool to ignore his advice. My family would have to make do with the bare bones of my knowledge, then. Hopefully it would be enough.

I didn't ask Tamlin anything more about the naga—about how many he'd killed before those four slipped away—didn't ask him anything at all, because I didn't detect a trace of triumph in him, but rather a deep, unending sort of shame and defeat.

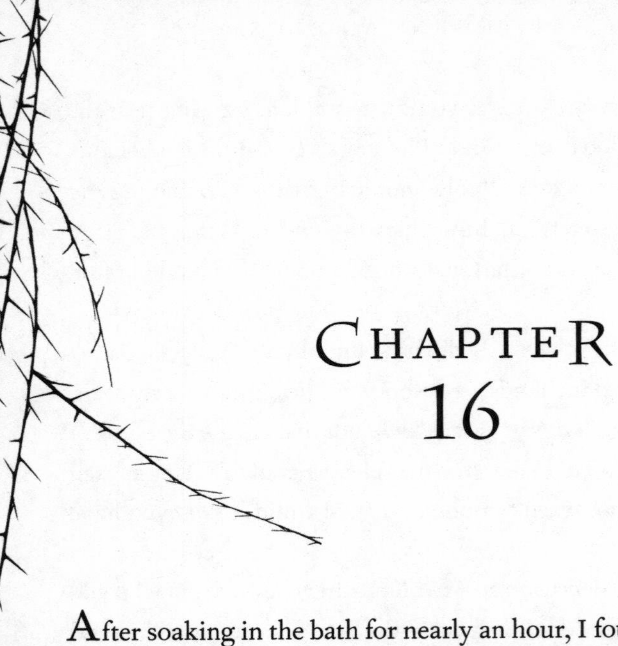

CHAPTER 16

After soaking in the bath for nearly an hour, I found myself sitting in a low-backed chair before my room's roaring fireplace, savoring the feel of Alis brushing out my damp hair. Though dinner was to be served soon, Alis had a cup of molten chocolate brought up and refused to do anything until I'd had a few sips.

It was the best thing I'd ever tasted. I drank from the thick mug as she brushed my hair, nearly purring at the feel of her thin fingers along my scalp.

But when the other maids had gone downstairs to help with the evening meal, I lowered my mug into my lap. "If more faeries keep crossing the court borders and attacking, is there going to be a war?" *Maybe we should just take a stand—maybe it's time to say* enough, Lucien had said to Tamlin that first night.

The brush stilled. "Don't ask such questions. You'll call down bad luck."

I twisted in my seat, glaring up into her masked face. "Why aren't the other High Lords keeping their subjects in line? Why are these awful creatures allowed to roam wherever they want?

Someone—someone began telling me a story about a king in Hybern—"

Alis grabbed my shoulder and pivoted me around. "It's none of your concern."

"Oh, I think it is." I turned around again, gripping the back of the wooden chair. "If this spills into the human world—if there's war, or this blight poisons our lands . . ." I pushed back against the crushing panic. I had to warn my family—*had* to write to them. Soon.

"The less you know, the better. Let Lord Tamlin deal with it—he's the only one who can." The Suriel had said as much. Alis's brown eyes were hard, unforgiving. "You think no one would tell me what you asked the kitchen to give you today, or realize what you went to trap? Foolish, stupid girl. Had the Suriel not been in a benevolent mood, you would have deserved the death it gave you. I don't know what's worse: this, or your idiocy with the puca."

"Would you have done anything else? If you had a family—"

"I do have a family."

I looked her up and down. There was no ring on her finger.

Alis noticed my stare and said, "My sister and her mate were murdered nigh on fifty years ago, leaving two younglings behind. Everything I do, everything I work for, is for those boys. So you don't get the right to give me that look and ask me if I would do anything different, girl."

"Where are they? Do they live here?" Perhaps that was why there were children's books in the study. Maybe those two small, shining figures in the garden . . . maybe that had been them.

"No, they don't live here," she said, too sharply. "They are somewhere else—far away."

I considered what she said, then cocked my head. "Do faerie children age differently?" If their parents had been killed almost fifty years ago, they could hardly be boys.

"Ah, some age like you and can breed as often as rabbits, but there are kinds—like me, like the High Fae—who are rarely able to produce younglings. The ones who are born age quite a bit slower. We all had a shock when my sister conceived the second one only five years later—and the eldest won't even reach adulthood until he's seventy-five. But they're so rare—all our young are—and more precious to us than jewels or gold." She clenched her jaw tightly enough that I knew that was all I would likely get from her.

"I didn't mean to question your dedication to them," I said quietly. When she didn't reply, I added, "I understand what you mean—about doing everything for them."

Alis's lips thinned, but she said, "The next time that fool Lucien gives you advice on how to trap the Suriel, you come to me. Dead chickens, my sagging ass. All you needed to do was offer it a new robe, and it would have groveled at your feet."

✠

By the time I entered the dining room I'd stopped shaking, and some semblance of warmth had returned to my veins. High Lord of Prythian or no, I wouldn't cower—not after what I'd been through today.

Lucien and Tamlin were already waiting for me at the table. "Good evening," I said, moving to my usual seat. Lucien cocked his head in a silent inquiry, and I gave him a subtle nod as I sat. His secret was still safe, though he deserved to be walloped for sending me so unprepared to the Suriel.

Lucien slouched a bit in his chair. "I heard you two had a rather exciting afternoon. I wish I could have been there to help."

A hidden, perhaps halfhearted apology, but I gave him another little nod.

He said with forced lightness, "Well, you still look lovely, regardless of your Hell-sent afternoon."

I snorted. I'd never looked lovely a day in my life. "I thought faeries couldn't lie."

Tamlin choked on his wine, but Lucien grinned, that scar stark and brutal. "Who told you that?"

"Everyone knows it," I said, piling food on my plate even as I began wondering about everything they'd said to me so far, every statement I'd accepted as pure truth.

Lucien leaned back in his chair, smiling with feline delight. "Of course we can lie. We find lying to be an art. And we lied when we told those ancient mortals that we couldn't speak an untruth. How else would we get them to trust us and do our bidding?"

My mouth became a thin, tight line. He was telling the truth—because if he was lying . . . The logic of it made my head spin. "Iron?" I managed to say.

"Doesn't do us a lick of harm. Only ash, as you well know."

My face warmed. I'd taken everything they said as truth. Perhaps the Suriel had been lying today, too, with that long-winded explanation about the politics of the faerie realms. About staying with the High Lord, and everything being fixed in the end.

I looked to Tamlin. *High Lord.* That wasn't a lie—I could feel its truth in my bones. Even though he didn't act like the High Lords of legend who had sacrificed virgins and slaughtered humans at will. No—Tamlin was . . . exactly as those fanatic, calf-eyed Children of the Blessed had depicted the bounties and comforts of Prythian.

"Even though Lucien revealed some of our closely guarded *secrets*," Tamlin said, throwing the last word at his companion with a growl, "we've never used your misinformation against you." His gaze met mine. "We never willingly lied to you."

I managed a nod and took a long sip of water. I ate in silence, so busy trying to decipher every word I'd overheard since arriving that I didn't realize when Lucien excused himself before dessert. I was left alone with the most dangerous being I'd ever encountered.

The walls of the room pressed in on me.

"Are you feeling . . . better?" Though he had his chin propped on a fist, concern—and perhaps surprise at that concern—shone in his eyes.

I swallowed hard. "If I never encounter a naga again, I'll consider myself fortunate."

"What were you doing out in the western woods?"

Truth or lie, lie or truth . . . both. "I heard a legend once about a creature who answers your questions, if you can catch it."

Tamlin flinched as his claws shot out, slicing his face. But the wounds closed as soon as they opened, leaving only a smear of blood running down his golden skin—which he wiped away with the back of his sleeve. "You went to catch the Suriel."

"I caught the Suriel," I corrected.

"And did it tell you what you wanted to know?" I wasn't sure he was breathing.

"We were interrupted by the naga before it could tell me anything worthwhile."

His mouth tightened. "I'd start shouting, but I think today was punishment enough." He shook his head. "You actually snared the Suriel. A human girl."

Despite myself, despite the afternoon, my lips twitched upward. "Is it supposed to be hard?"

He chuckled, then fished something out of his pocket. "Well, if I'm lucky, I won't have to trap the Suriel to learn what this is about." He lifted my crumpled list of words.

My heart dropped to my stomach. "It's . . ." I couldn't think of a suitable lie—everything was absurd.

"*Unusual*? *Queue*? *Slaying*? *Conflagration*?" He read the list. I wanted to curl up and die. Words I couldn't recognize from the books—words that now seemed so simple, so absurdly easy as he was saying them aloud. "Is this a poem about murdering me and then burning my body?"

My throat closed up, and I had to clench my hands into fists to keep from hiding my face behind them. "Good night," I said, barely more than a whisper, and stood on shaking knees.

I was nearly to the door when he spoke again. "You love them very much, don't you?"

I half turned to him. His green eyes met mine as he rose from his chair to walk to me. He stopped a respectable distance away.

The list of malformed words was still clutched in his hand. "I wonder if your family realizes it," he murmured. "That everything you've done wasn't about that promise to your mother, or for your sake, but for theirs." I said nothing, not trusting my voice to keep my shame hidden. "I know—I know that when I said it earlier, it didn't come out well, but I could help you write—"

"Leave me alone," I said. I was almost through the door when I ran into someone—into him. I stumbled back a step. I'd forgotten how fast he was.

"I'm not insulting you." His quiet voice made it all the worse.

"I don't need your help."

"Clearly not," he said with a half smile. But the smile faded. "A human who can take down a faerie in a wolf's skin, who ensnared the Suriel and killed two naga on her own . . ." He choked on a laugh, and shook his head. The firelight danced along his mask. "They're fools. Fools for not seeing it." He winced. But his eyes held no mischief. "Here," he said, extending the list of words.

I shoved it into my pocket. I turned, but he gently grabbed my arm. "You gave up so much for them." He lifted his other hand as if to brush my cheek. I braced myself for the touch, but he lowered it before making contact. "Do you even know how to laugh?"

I shook off his arm, unable to stop the angry words. High Lord be damned. "I don't want your pity."

His jade eyes were so bright I couldn't look away. "What about a friend?"

"Can faeries be friends with mortals?"

"Five hundred years ago, enough faeries were friends with mortals that they went to war on their behalf."

"What?" I'd never heard that before. And it hadn't been in that mural in the study.

"How do you think the human armies survived as long as they did, and did such damage that my kind even came to agree to a treaty? With ash weapons alone? There were faeries who fought and died at the humans' sides for their freedom, and who mourned when the only solution was to separate our peoples."

"Were you one of them?"

"I was a child at the time, too young to understand what was happening—or even to be told," he said. *A child*. Which meant he had to be over . . . "But had I been old enough, I would have. Against slavery, against tyranny, I would gladly go to my death, no matter whose freedom I was defending."

I wasn't sure if I would do the same. My priority would be to protect my family—and I would have picked whatever side could keep them safest. I hadn't thought of it as a weakness until now.

"For what it's worth," Tamlin said, "your family knows you're safe. They have no memory of a beast bursting into their cottage, and think a long-lost, very wealthy aunt called you away to aid her on her deathbed. They know you're alive, and fed, and cared for. But they also know that there have been rumors of a . . . threat in Prythian, and are prepared to run should any of the warning signs about the wall faltering occur."

"You—you altered their memories?" I took a step back. Faerie arrogance, such faerie arrogance to change our minds, to implant thoughts as if it wasn't a violation—

"Glamoured their memories—like putting a veil over them. I was afraid your father might come after you, or persuade some villagers to cross the wall with him and further violate the Treaty."

And they all would have died anyway, once they ran into things like the puca or the Bogge or the naga. A silence blanketed my mind, until I was so exhausted I could barely think, and couldn't stop myself from saying, "You don't know him. My father wouldn't have bothered to do either."

Tamlin looked at me for a long moment. "Yes, he would have."

But he wouldn't—not with that twisted knee. Not with it as an excuse. I'd realized that the moment the puca's illusion had been ripped away.

Fed, comfortable, and safe—they'd even been warned about the blight, whether they understood that warning or not. His eyes were open, honest. He had gone farther than I would have ever guessed toward assuaging my every concern. "You truly warned them about—the possible threat?"

A grave nod. "Not an outright warning, but . . . it's woven into the glamour on their memories—along with an order to run at the first sign of something being amiss."

Faerie arrogance, but . . . but he had done more than I could. My family might have ignored my letter entirely. Had I known he possessed those abilities, I might have even asked the High Lord to glamour their memories if he hadn't done it himself.

I truly had nothing to fret about, save for the fact that they'd probably forget me sooner than expected. I couldn't entirely blame them. My vow fulfilled, my task complete—what was left for me?

The firelight danced on his mask, warming the gold, setting the emeralds glinting. Such color and variation—colors I didn't know the names of, colors I wanted to catalog and weave together. Colors I had no reason not to explore now.

"Paint," I said, barely more than a breath. He cocked his head and I swallowed, squaring my shoulders. "If—if it's not too much to ask, I'd like some paint. And brushes."

Tamlin blinked. "You like—art? You like to paint?"

His stumbling words weren't unkind. It was enough for me to say, "Yes. I'm not—not any good, but if it's not too much trouble . . . I'll paint outside, so I don't make a mess, but—"

"Outside, inside, on the roof—paint wherever you want. I don't care," he said. "But if you need paint and brushes, you'll also need paper and canvas."

"I can work—help around the kitchen or in the gardens—to pay for it."

"You'd be more of a hindrance. It might take a few days to track them down, but the paint, the brushes, the canvas, and the space are yours. Work wherever you want. This house is too clean, anyway."

"Thank you—I mean it, truly. Thank you."

"Of course." I turned, but he spoke again. "Have you seen the gallery?"

I blurted, "There's a gallery in this house?"

He grinned—actually grinned, the High Lord of the Spring Court. "I had it closed off when I inherited this place." When he inherited a title he seemed to have little joy in holding. "It seemed like a waste of time to have the servants keep it cleaned."

Of course it would, to a trained warrior.

He went on. "I'm busy tomorrow, and the gallery needs to be cleaned up, so . . . the next day—let me show it to you the next day." He rubbed at his neck, faint color creeping into those cheeks of his—more alive and warm than I'd yet seen them. "Please—it would be my pleasure." And I believed him that it would.

I nodded dumbly. If the paintings along the halls were exquisite, then the ones selected for the gallery had to be beyond my human imaginings. "I would like that—very much."

He smiled at me still, broadly and without restraint or hesitation. Isaac had never smiled at me like that. Isaac had never made my breath catch, just a little bit.

The feeling was startling enough that I walked out, grasping the crumpled paper in my pocket as if doing so could somehow keep that answering smile from tugging on my lips.

Chapter 17

I jerked awake in the middle of the night, panting. My dreams had been filled with the clicking of the Suriel's bone-fingers, the grinning naga, and a pale, faceless woman dragging her bloodred nails across my throat, splitting me open bit by bit. She kept asking for my name, but every time I tried to speak, my blood bubbled out of the shallow wounds on my neck, choking me.

I ran my hands through my sweat-damp hair. As my panting eased, a different sound filled the air, creeping in from the front hall through the crack beneath the door. Shouts, and someone's screams.

I was out of my bed in a heartbeat. The shouts weren't aggressive, but rather commanding—organizing. But the screaming . . .

Every hair on my body stood upright as I flung open the door. I might have stayed and cowered, but I'd heard screams like that before, in the forest at home, when I didn't make a clean kill and the animals suffered. I couldn't stand it. And I had to know.

I reached the top of the grand staircase in time to see the front doors of the manor bang open and Tamlin rush in, a screaming faerie slung over his shoulder.

The faerie was almost as big as Tamlin, and yet the High Lord carried him as if he were no more than a sack of grain. Another species of the lesser faeries, with his blue skin, gangly limbs, pointed ears, and long onyx hair. But even from atop the stairs, I could see the blood gushing down the faerie's back—blood from the black stumps protruding from his shoulder blades. Blood that now soaked into Tamlin's green tunic in deep, shining splotches. One of the knives from his baldric was missing.

Lucien rushed into the foyer below just as Tamlin shouted, "The table—clear it off!" Lucien shoved the vase of flowers off the long table in the center of the hall. Either Tamlin wasn't thinking straight, or he'd been afraid to waste the extra minutes bringing the faerie to the infirmary. Shattering glass set my feet moving, and I was halfway down the stairs before Tamlin eased the shrieking faerie face-first onto the table. The faerie wasn't wearing a mask; there was nothing to hide the agony contorting his long, unearthly features.

"Scouts found him dumped just over the borderline," Tamlin explained to Lucien, but his eyes darted to me. They flashed with warning, but I took another step down. He said to Lucien, "He's Summer Court."

"By the Cauldron," Lucien said, surveying the damage.

"My wings," the faerie choked out, his glossy black eyes wide and staring at nothing. "She took my wings."

Again, that nameless *she* who haunted their lives. If she wasn't ruling the Spring Court, then perhaps she ruled another. Tamlin flicked a hand, and steaming water and bandages just *appeared* on the table. My mouth dried up, but I reached the bottom of the stairs and kept walking toward the table and the death that was surely hovering in this hall.

"She took my wings," said the faerie. "She took my wings," he repeated, clutching the edge of the table with spindly blue fingers.

Tamlin murmured a soft, wordless sound—gentle in a way I hadn't heard before—and picked up a rag to dunk in the water. I took up a spot across the table from Tamlin, and the breath whooshed from my chest as I beheld the damage.

Whoever *she* was, she hadn't just taken his wings. She'd ripped them off.

Blood oozed from the black velvety stumps on the faerie's back. The wounds were jagged—cartilage and tissue severed in what looked like uneven cuts. As if she'd sawed off his wings bit by bit.

"She took my wings," the faerie said again, his voice breaking. As he trembled, shock taking over, his skin shimmered with veins of pure gold—iridescent, like a blue butterfly.

"Keep still," Tamlin ordered, wringing the rag. "You'll bleed out faster."

"N-n-no," the faerie started, and began to twist onto his back, away from Tamlin, from the pain that was surely coming when that rag touched those raw stumps.

It was instinct, or mercy, or desperation, perhaps, to grab the faerie's upper arms and shove him down again, pinning him to the table as gently as I could. He thrashed, strong enough that I had to concentrate solely on holding him. His skin was velvet-smooth and slippery, a texture I would never be able to paint, not even if I had eternity to master it. But I pushed against him, gritting my teeth and willing him to stop. I looked to Lucien, but the color had blanched from his face, leaving a sickly white-green in its wake.

"Lucien," Tamlin said—a quiet command. But Lucien kept gaping at the faerie's ruined back, at the stumps, his metal eye narrowing and widening, narrowing and widening. He backed up a step. And another. And then vomited in a potted plant before sprinting from the room.

The faerie twisted again and I held tight, my arms shaking with the effort. His injuries must have weakened him greatly if I could keep him pinned. "Please," I breathed. "Please hold still."

"She took my wings," the faerie sobbed. "She took them."

"I know," I murmured, my fingers aching. "I know."

Tamlin touched the rag to one of the stumps, and the faerie screamed so loudly that my senses guttered, sending me staggering back. He tried to rise but his arms buckled, and he collapsed face-first onto the table again.

Blood gushed—so fast and bright that it took me a heartbeat to realize that a wound like this required a tourniquet—and that the faerie had lost far too much blood for it to even make a difference. It poured down his back and onto the table, where it ran to the edge and *drip-drip-drip*ped to the floor near my feet.

I found Tamlin's eyes on me. "The wounds aren't clotting," he said under his breath as the faerie panted.

"Can't you use your magic?" I asked, wishing I could rip that mask off his face and see his full expression.

Tamlin swallowed hard. "No. Not for major damage. Once, but not any longer."

The faerie on the table whimpered, his panting slowing. "She took my wings," he whispered. Tamlin's green eyes flickered, and I knew, right then, that the faerie was going to die. Death wasn't just hovering in this hall; it was counting down the faerie's remaining heartbeats.

I took one of the faerie's hands in mine. The skin there was almost leathery, and, perhaps more out of reflex than anything, his long fingers wrapped around mine, covering them completely. "She took my wings," he said again, his shaking subsiding a bit.

I brushed the long, damp hair from the faerie's half-turned face, revealing a pointed nose and a mouth full of sharp teeth. His dark eyes shifted to mine, beseeching, pleading.

"It will be all right," I said, and hoped he couldn't smell lies the way the Suriel was able to. I stroked his limp hair, its texture like liquid night—another I would never be able to paint but would try to, perhaps forever.

"It will be all right." The faerie closed his eyes, and I tightened my grip on his hand.

Something wet touched my feet, and I didn't need to look down to see that his blood had pooled around me. "My wings," the faerie whispered.

"You'll get them back."

The faerie struggled to open his eyes. "You swear?"

"Yes," I breathed. The faerie managed a slight smile and closed his eyes again. My mouth trembled. I wished for something else to say, something more to offer him than my empty promises. The first false vow I'd ever sworn. But Tamlin began speaking, and I glanced up to see him take the faerie's other hand.

"Cauldron save you," he said, reciting the words of a prayer that was probably older than the mortal realm. "Mother hold you. Pass through the gates, and smell that immortal land of milk and honey. Fear no evil. Feel no pain." Tamlin's voice wavered, but he finished. "Go, and enter eternity."

The faerie heaved one final sigh, and his hand went limp in mine. I didn't let go, though, and kept stroking his hair, even when Tamlin released him and took a few steps from the table.

I could feel Tamlin's eyes on me, but I wouldn't let go. I didn't know how long it took for a soul to fade from the body. I stood in the puddle of blood until it grew cold, holding the faerie's spindly hand and stroking his hair, wondering if he knew I'd lied when I'd sworn he would get his wings back, wondering if, wherever he had now gone, he *had* gotten them back.

A clock chimed somewhere in the house, and Tamlin gripped my shoulder. I hadn't realized how cold I'd become until the heat of his hand warmed me through my nightgown. "He's gone. Let him go."

I studied the faerie's face—so unearthly, so inhuman. Who could be so cruel to hurt him like that?

"Feyre," Tamlin said, squeezing my shoulder. I brushed the faerie's hair behind his long, pointed ear, wishing I'd known his name, and let go.

Tamlin led me up the stairs, neither of us caring about the bloody footprints I left behind or the freezing blood soaking the front of my nightgown. I paused at the top of the steps, though, twisting out of his grip, and gazed at the table in the foyer below.

"We can't leave him there," I said, making to step down. Tamlin caught my elbow.

"I know," he said, the words so drained and weary. "I was going to walk you upstairs first."

Before he buried him. "I want to go with you."

"It's too deadly at night for you to—"

"I can hold my—"

"No," he said, his green eyes flashing. I straightened, but he sighed, his shoulders curving inward. "I must do this. Alone."

His head was bowed. No claws, no fangs—there was nothing to be done against this enemy, this fate. No one for him to fight. So I nodded, because I would have wanted to do it alone, too, and turned toward my bedroom. Tamlin remained at the top of the stairs.

"Feyre," he said—softly enough that I faced him again. "Why?" He tilted his head to the side. "You dislike our kind on a good day. And after Andras . . ." Even in the darkened hallway, his usually bright eyes were shadowed. "So why?"

I took a step closer to him, my blood-covered feet sticking to the rug. I glanced down the stairs to where I could still see the prone form of the faerie and the stumps of his wings.

"Because I wouldn't want to die alone," I said, and my voice wobbled as I looked at Tamlin again, forcing myself to meet his stare. "Because I'd want someone to hold my hand until the end, and awhile after that. That's something everyone deserves, human or faerie." I swallowed hard, my throat painfully tight. "I regret what I did to Andras," I said, the words so strangled they were no more than a whisper. "I regret that there was . . . such hate in my heart. I wish I could undo it—and . . . I'm sorry. So very sorry."

I couldn't remember the last time—if ever—I'd spoken to anyone like that. But he just nodded and turned away, and I wondered if I should say more, if I should kneel and beg for his forgiveness. If he felt such grief, such guilt, over a stranger, then Andras . . . By the time I opened my mouth, he was already down the steps.

I watched him—watched every movement he made, the muscles of his body visible through that blood-soaked tunic, watched that invisible weight bearing down on his shoulders. He didn't look at me as he scooped up the broken body and carried it to the garden doors beyond my line of sight. I went to the window at the top of the stairs, watching as Tamlin carried the faerie through the moonlit garden and into the rolling fields beyond. He never once glanced back.

CHAPTER 18

The next day, the blood of the faerie had been cleaned up by the time I ate, washed, and dressed. I'd taken my time in the morning, and it was nearly noon as I stood atop the staircase, peering down at the entry hall below. Just to make sure it was gone.

I'd been set on finding Tamlin and explaining—truly explaining—how sorry I was about Andras. If I was supposed to stay here, stay with him, then I could at least attempt to repair what I'd ruined. I glanced to the large window behind me, the view so sweeping that I could see all the way to the reflecting pool beyond the garden.

The water was still enough that the vibrant sky and fat, puffy clouds above were flawlessly reflected. Asking about them seemed vulgar after last night, but maybe—maybe once those paints and brushes *did* arrive, I could venture to the pool to capture it.

I might have remained staring out toward that smear of color and light and texture had Tamlin and Lucien not emerged from another wing of the manor, discussing some border patrol or another. They fell silent as I came down the stairs, and Lucien strode right out the front door without so much as a good morning—just a casual wave. Not a vicious gesture, but he clearly had no intention of joining the conversation that Tamlin and I were about to have.

I glanced around, hoping for any sign of those paints, but Tam pointed to the open front doors through which Lucien had exited. Beyond them, I could see both of our horses, already saddled and waiting. Lucien was already climbing into the saddle of a third horse. I turned to Tamlin.

Stay with him; he will keep me safe, and things will get better. Fine. I could do that.

"Where are we going?" My words were half-mumbled.

"Your supplies won't arrive until tomorrow, and the gallery's being cleaned, and my . . . meeting was postponed." Was he *rambling*? "I thought we'd go for a ride—no killing involved. Or naga to worry about." Even as he finished with a half smile, sorrow flickered in his eyes. Indeed, I'd had enough death in the past two days. Enough of killing faeries. Killing anything. No weapons were sheathed at his side or on his baldric—but a knife hilt glinted at his boot.

Where had he buried that faerie? A High Lord digging a grave for a stranger. I might not have believed it if I'd been told, might not have believed it if he hadn't offered me sanctuary rather than death.

"Where to?" I asked. He only smiled.

✢

I couldn't come up with any words when we arrived—and knew that even if I had been able to paint it, nothing would have done it justice. It wasn't simply that it was the most beautiful place I'd ever been to, or that it filled me with both longing and mirth, but it just seemed . . . *right*. As if the colors and lights and patterns of the world had come together to form one perfect place—one true bit of beauty. After last night, it was exactly where I needed to be.

We sat atop a grassy knoll, overlooking a glade of oaks so wide and high they could have been the pillars and spires of an ancient castle. Shimmering tufts of dandelion fluff drifted by, and the floor of the clearing was carpeted with swaying crocuses and snowdrops and bluebells. It was an hour or two past noon by the time we arrived, but the light was thick and golden.

Though the three of us were alone, I could have sworn I heard singing. I hugged my knees and drank in the glen.

"We brought a blanket," Tamlin said, and I looked over my shoulder to see him jerk his chin to the purple blanket they'd laid out a few feet away. Lucien plopped down onto it and stretched his legs. Tamlin remained standing, waiting for my response.

I shook my head and faced forward, tracing my hand through the feather-soft grass, cataloging its color and texture. I'd never felt grass like it, and I certainly wasn't going to ruin the experience by sitting on a blanket.

Rushed whispers were exchanged behind me, and before I could turn around to investigate, Tamlin took a seat at my side. His jaw was clenched tight enough that I stared ahead. "What is this place?" I said, still running my fingers through the grass.

Out of the corner of my eye, Tamlin was no more than a glittering golden figure. "Just a glen." Behind us, Lucien snorted. "Do you like it?" Tamlin asked quickly. The green of his eyes matched the grass between my fingers, and the amber flecks were like the shafts of sunlight that streamed through the trees. Even his mask, odd and foreign, seemed to fit into the glen—as if this place had been fashioned for him alone. I could picture him here in his beast form, curled up in the grass, dozing.

"What?" I said. I'd forgotten his question.

"Do you like it?" he repeated, and his lips tugged into a smile.

I took an uneven breath and stared at the glen again. "Yes."

He chuckled. "That's it? '*Yes*'?"

"Would you like me to grovel with gratitude for bringing me here, High Lord?"

"Ah. The Suriel told you nothing important, did it?"

That smile of his sparked something bold in my chest. "He also said that you like being brushed, and if I'm a clever girl, I might train you with treats."

Tamlin tipped his head to the sky and roared with laughter. Despite myself, I let out a soft laugh.

"I might die of surprise," Lucien said behind me. "You made a joke, Feyre."

I turned to look at him with a cool smile. "You don't want to know what the Suriel said about *you*." I flicked my brows up, and Lucien lifted his hands in defeat.

"I'd pay good money to hear what the Suriel thinks of Lucien," Tamlin said.

A cork popped, followed by the sounds of Lucien chugging the bottle's contents and chuckling with a muttered "Brushed."

Tamlin's eyes were still bright with laughter as he put a hand at my elbow, pulling me to my feet. "Come on," he said, jerking his head down the hill to the little stream that ran along its base. "I want to show you something."

I got to my feet, but Lucien remained sitting on the blanket and lifted the bottle of wine in salute. He took a slug from it as he sprawled on his back and gazed at the green canopy.

Each of Tamlin's movements was precise and efficient, his powerfully muscled legs eating up the earth as we wove between the towering trees, hopped over tiny brooks, and clambered up steep knolls. We stopped atop a mound, and my hands slackened at my sides. There, in a clearing surrounded by towering trees, lay a sparkling silver pool. Even from a distance, I could tell that it wasn't water, but something more rare and infinitely more precious.

Tamlin grasped my wrist and tugged me down the hill, his callused fingers gently scraping against my skin. He let go of me to leap over the root of the tree in a single maneuver and prowled to the water's edge. I could only grind my teeth as I stumbled after him, heaving myself over the root.

He crouched by the pool and cupped his hand to fill it. He tilted his hand, letting the water fall. "Have a look."

The silvery sparkling water that dribbled from his hand set ripples dancing across the pool, each glimmering with various colors, and—"That looks like starlight," I breathed.

He huffed a laugh, filling and emptying his hand again. I gaped at the glittering water. "It *is* starlight."

"That's impossible," I said, fighting the urge to take a step toward the water.

"This is Prythian. According to your legends, nothing is impossible."

"How?" I asked, unable to take my eyes from the pool—the silver, but also the blue and red and pink and yellow glinting beneath, the lightness of it . . .

"I don't know—I never asked, and no one ever explained."

When I continued gaping at the pool, he laughed, drawing away my attention—only for me to find him unbuttoning his tunic. "Jump in," he said, the invitation dancing in his eyes.

A swim—unclothed, alone. With a High Lord. I shook my head, falling back a step. His fingers paused at the second button from his collar.

"Don't you want to know what it's like?"

I didn't know what he meant: swimming in starlight, or swimming with him. "I—no."

"All right." He left his tunic unbuttoned. There was only bare, muscled, golden skin beneath.

"Why this place?" I asked, tearing my eyes away from his chest.

"This was my favorite haunt as a boy."

"Which was when?" I couldn't stop the question from coming out.

He cut a glance in my direction. "A very long time ago." He said it so quietly that it made me shift on my feet. A very long time ago indeed, if he'd been a boy during the War.

Well, I'd started down that road, so I ventured to ask, "Is Lucien all right? After last night, I mean." He seemed back to his usual snide, irreverent self, but he'd vomited at the sight of that dying faerie. "He . . . didn't react well."

Tamlin shrugged, but his words were soft as he said, "Lucien . . . Lucien has endured things that make times like last night . . . difficult. Not just the scar and the eye—though I bet last night brought back memories of that, too."

Tamlin rubbed at his neck, then met my stare. Such an ancient heaviness in his eyes, in the set of his jaw. "Lucien is the youngest son of the High Lord of the Autumn Court." I straightened. "The youngest of seven brothers. The Autumn Court is . . . cutthroat. Beautiful, but his brothers see each other only as competition, since the strongest of them will inherit the title, not the eldest. It is the same throughout Prythian, at every court. Lucien never cared about it, never expected to be crowned High Lord, so he spent his youth doing everything a High Lord's son probably shouldn't: wandering the courts, making friends with the sons of other High Lords"—a faint gleam in Tamlin's eyes at that—"and being with females who were a far cry from the nobility of the Autumn Court." Tamlin paused for a moment, and I could almost feel the sorrow before he said, "Lucien fell in love with a faerie whom his father considered to be grossly inappropriate for someone of his bloodline. Lucien said he didn't care that she wasn't one of the High Fae, that he was certain the mating bond would snap into place soon and that he was going to marry her and leave his father's court to his scheming brothers." A tight sigh. "His father had her put down. Executed, in front of Lucien, as his two eldest brothers held him and made him watch."

My stomach turned, and I pushed a hand against my chest. I couldn't imagine, couldn't comprehend that sort of loss.

"Lucien left. He cursed his father, abandoned his title and the Autumn Court, and walked out. And without his title protecting him, his brothers thought to eliminate one more contender to the High Lord's crown. Three of them went out to kill him; one came back."

"Lucien . . . killed them?"

"He killed one," Tamlin said. "I killed the other, as they had crossed into my territory, and I was now High Lord and could do what I wanted with trespassers threatening the peace of my lands." A cold, brutal statement. "I claimed Lucien as my own—named him emissary, since he'd already made many friends across the courts and had always been good at talking to people, while I . . . can find it difficult. He's been here ever since."

"As emissary," I began, "has he ever had dealings with his father? Or his brothers?"

"Yes. His father has never apologized, and his brothers are too frightened of me to risk harming him." No arrogance in those words, just icy truth. "But he has never forgotten what they did to her, or what his brothers tried to do to him. Even if he pretends that he has."

It didn't quite excuse everything Lucien had said and done to me, but . . . I understood now. I could understand the walls and barriers he had no doubt constructed around himself. My chest was too tight, too small to fit the ache building in it. I looked at the pool of glittering starlight and let out a heavy breath. I needed to change the subject. "What would happen if I were to drink the water?"

Tamlin straightened a bit—then relaxed, as if glad to release that old sadness. "Legend claims you'd be happy until your last breath." He added, "Perhaps we both need a glass."

"I don't think that entire pool would be enough for me," I said, and he laughed.

"Two jokes in one day—a miracle sent from the Cauldron," he said.

I cracked a smile. He came a step closer, as if forcibly leaving behind the dark, sad stain of what had happened to Lucien, and the starlight danced in his eyes as he said, "What *would* be enough to make you happy?"

I blushed from my neck to the top of my head. "I—I don't know." It was true—I'd never given that sort of thing any thought beyond getting my sisters safely married off and having enough food for me and my father, and time to learn to paint.

"Hmm," he said, not stepping away. "What about the ringing of bluebells? Or a ribbon of sunshine? Or a garland of moonlight?" He grinned wickedly.

High Lord of Prythian indeed. High Lord of Foolery was more like it. And he knew—he knew I'd say no, that I'd squirm a bit from merely being alone with him.

No. I wouldn't let him have the satisfaction of embarrassing me. I'd had enough of that lately, enough of . . . of that girl encased in ice and bitterness. So I gave him a sweet smile, doing my best to pretend that my stomach wasn't flipping over itself. "A swim sounds delightful."

I didn't allow myself room for second-guessing. And I took no small amount of pride in the fact that my fingers didn't tremble once as I removed my boots, then unbuttoned my tunic and pants and shucked them onto the grass. My undergarments were modest enough that I wasn't showing much, but I still looked straight at him as I stood on the grassy bank. The air was warm and mild, and a soft breeze kissed its way across my bare stomach.

Slowly, so slowly, his eyes roved down, then up. As if he were studying every inch, every curve of me. And even though I wore my ivory underthings, that gaze alone stripped me bare.

His eyes met mine and he gave me a lazy smile before removing his clothes. Button by button. I could have sworn the gleam in his eyes turned hungry and feral—enough so that I had to look anywhere but at his face.

I let myself indulge in the glimpse of a broad chest, arms corded with muscle, and long, strong legs before I walked right into that pool. He wasn't built like Isaac, whose body had very much still been in that gangly place between boy and man. No—Tamlin's glorious body was honed by centuries of fighting and brutality.

The liquid was delightfully warm, and I strode in until it was deep enough to swim out a few strokes and casually tread in place. Not water, but something smoother, thicker. Not oil, but something purer, thinner. Like being wrapped in warm silk. I was so busy savoring the tug of my fingers through the silvery substance that I didn't notice him until he was treading beside me.

"Who taught you to swim?" he asked, and dunked his head under the surface. When he came up, he was grinning, sparkling streams of starlight running along the contours of his mask.

I didn't go under, didn't quite know if he'd been joking about the water making me mirthful if I drank it. "When I was twelve, I watched the village children swimming at a pond and figured it out myself."

It had been one of the most terrifying experiences of my life, and I'd swallowed half the pond in the process, but I'd gotten the gist of it, managed to conquer my blind panic and terror and trust myself. Knowing how to swim had seemed like a vital ability—one that might someday mean the difference between life and death. I'd never expected it would lead to *this*, though.

He went under again, and when he emerged, he ran a hand through his golden hair. "How did your father lose his fortune?"

"How'd you know about that?"

Tamlin snorted. "I don't think born peasants have your kind of diction."

Some part of me wanted to come up with a comment about snobbery, but . . . well, he was right, and I couldn't blame him for being a skilled observer.

"My father was called the Prince of Merchants," I said plainly, treading that silky, strange water. I hardly had to put any effort into it—the water was so warm, so *light*, that it felt as if I were floating in air, every ache in my body oozing away into nothing. "But that title, which he'd inherited from his father, and his father before that, was a lie. We were just a good name that masked three generations of bad debts. My father had been trying to find a way to ease those debts for years, and when he found an opportunity to pay them off, he took it, regardless of the risks." I swallowed. "Eight years ago, he amassed our wealth on three ships to sail to Bharat for invaluable spices and cloth."

Tamlin frowned. "Risky indeed. Those waters are a death trap, unless you go the long way."

"Well, he didn't go the long way. It would have taken too much time, and our creditors were breathing down his neck. So he risked sending the ships directly to Bharat. They never reached Bharat's shores." I tipped my hair back in the water, clearing the memory of my father's face the day that news arrived of the sinking. "When the ships sank, the creditors circled him like wolves. They ripped him apart until there was nothing left of him but a broken name and a few gold pieces to purchase that cottage. I was eleven. My father . . . he just stopped trying after that." I couldn't bring myself to mention that final, ugly moment when that other creditor had come with his cronies to wreck my father's leg.

"That's when you started hunting?"

"No; even though we moved to the cottage, it took almost three years for the money to entirely run out," I said. "I started hunting when I was fourteen."

His eyes twinkled—no trace of the warrior forced to accept a High Lord's burden. "And here you are. What else did you figure out for yourself?"

Maybe it was the enchanted pool, or maybe it was the genuine interest behind the question, but I smiled and told him about those years in the woods.

✠

Tired but surprisingly content from a few hours of swimming and eating and lounging in the glen, I eyed Lucien as we rode back to the manor that afternoon. We were crossing a broad meadow of new spring grass when he caught me glancing at him for the tenth time, and I braced myself as he fell back from Tamlin's side.

The metal eye narrowed on me while the other remained wary, unimpressed. "Yes?"

That was enough to persuade me not to say anything about his past. I would hate pity, too. And he didn't know me—not well enough to warrant anything but resentment if I brought it up, even if it weighed on *me* to know it, to grieve for him.

I waited until Tamlin was far enough ahead that even his High Fae hearing might not pick up on my words. "I never got to thank you for your advice with the Suriel."

Lucien tensed. "Oh?"

I looked ahead at the easy way Tamlin rode, the horse utterly unbothered by his mighty rider. "If you still want me dead," I said, "you might have to try a bit harder."

Lucien loosed a breath. "That's not what I intended." I gave him a long look. "I wouldn't shed any tears," he amended. I knew it was true. "But what happened to you—"

"I was joking," I said, and gave him a little smile.

"You can't possibly forgive me that easily for sending you into danger."

"No. And part of me would like nothing more than to wallop you for your lack of warning about the Suriel. But I understand: I'm a human who killed your friend, who now lives in your house, and you have to deal with me. I understand," I said again.

He was quiet for long enough that I thought he wouldn't reply. Just as I was about to move ahead, he spoke. "Tam told me that your first shot was to save the Suriel's life. Not your own."

"It seemed like the right thing to do."

The look he gave me was more contemplative than any he'd given me before. "I know far too many High Fae and lesser faeries who wouldn't have seen it that way—or bothered." He reached for something at his side and tossed it to me. I had to fight to stay in the saddle as I fumbled for it—a jeweled hunting knife.

"I heard you scream," he said as I examined the blade in my hands. I'd never held one so finely crafted, so perfectly balanced. "And I hesitated. Not long, but I hesitated before I came running. Even though Tam got there in time, I still broke my word in those seconds I waited." He jerked his chin at the knife. "It's yours. Don't bury it in my back, please."

CHAPTER 19

The next morning, my paint and supplies arrived from wherever Tamlin or the servants had dug them up, but before Tamlin let me see them, he brought me down hall after hall until we were in a wing of the house I'd never been to, even in my nocturnal exploring. I knew where we were going without his having to say. The marble floors shone so brightly that they had to have been freshly mopped, and that rose-scented breeze floated in through the opened windows. All this—he'd done this for me. As if I would have cared about cobwebs or dust.

When he paused before a set of wooden doors, the slight smile he gave me was enough to make me blurt, "Why do anything—anything this kind?"

The smile faltered. "It's been a long time since there was anyone here who appreciated these things. I like seeing them used again." Especially when there was such blood and death in every other part of his life.

He opened the gallery doors, and the breath was knocked from me.

The pale wooden floors gleamed in the clean, bright light pouring in from the windows. The room was empty save for a few large chairs and benches for viewing the . . . the . . .

I barely registered moving into the long gallery, one hand absentmindedly wrapping around my throat as I looked up at the paintings.

So many, so different, yet all arranged to flow together seamlessly . . . Such different views and snippets and angles of the world. Pastorals, portraits, still lifes . . . each a story and an experience, each a voice shouting or whispering or singing about what that moment, that feeling, had been like, each a cry into the void of time that they had been here, had existed. Some had been painted through eyes like mine, artists who saw in colors and shapes I understood. Some showcased colors I had not considered; these had a bend to the world that told me a different set of eyes had painted them. A portal into the mind of a creature so unlike me, and yet . . . and yet I looked at its work and understood, and felt, and cared.

"I never knew," Tamlin said from behind me, "that humans were capable of . . ." He trailed off as I turned, the hand I'd put on my throat sliding down to my chest, where my heart roared with a fierce sort of joy and grief and overwhelming humility—humility before that magnificent art.

He stood by the doors, head cocked in that animalistic way, the words still lost on his tongue.

I wiped at my damp cheeks. "It's . . ." *Perfect*, *wonderful*, *beyond my wildest imaginings* didn't cover it. I kept my hand over my heart. "Thank you," I said. It was all I could find to show him what these paintings—to be allowed into this room—meant.

"Come here whenever you want."

I smiled at him, hardly able to contain the brightness in my heart. His returning smile was tentative but shining, and then he left me to admire the gallery at my own leisure.

I stayed for hours—stayed until I was drunk on the art, until I was dizzy with hunger and wandered out to find food.

After lunch, Alis showed me to an empty room on the first floor with a table full of canvases of various sizes, brushes whose wooden handles gleamed in the perfect, clear light, and paints—so, so many paints, beyond the four basic ones I'd hoped for, that the breath was knocked from me again.

And when Alis was gone and the room was quiet and waiting and utterly mine . . .

Then I began to paint.

✢

Weeks passed, the days melting together. I painted and painted, most of it awful and useless.

I never let anyone see it, no matter how much Tamlin prodded and Lucien smirked at my paint-splattered clothes; I never felt satisfied that my work matched the images burning in my mind. Often I painted from dawn until dusk, sometimes in that room, sometimes out in the garden. Occasionally I'd take a break to explore the Spring lands with Tamlin as my guide, coming back with fresh ideas that had me leaping out of bed the next morning to sketch or scribble down the scenes or colors as I'd glimpsed them.

But there were the days when Tamlin was called away to face the latest threat to his borders, and even painting couldn't distract me until he returned, covered in blood that wasn't his own, sometimes in his beast form, sometimes as the High Lord. He never gave me details, and I didn't presume to ask about them; his safe return was enough.

Around the manor itself, there was no sign of creatures like the naga or the Bogge, but I stayed well away from the western woods, even though I painted them often enough from memory. And though my dreams continued to be plagued by the deaths I'd witnessed, the deaths I'd caused, and that horrible pale woman ripping me to shreds—all watched over by a shadow I could never quite glimpse—I slowly stopped being so afraid. *Stay with the High Lord. You will be safe.* So I did.

The Spring Court was a land of rolling green hills and lush forests and clear, bottomless lakes. Magic didn't just abound in the bumps and the hollows—it *grew* there. Try as I might to paint it, I could never capture it—the feel of it. So sometimes I dared to paint the High Lord, who rode at my side when we wandered his grounds on lazy days—the High Lord, whom I was happy to talk to or spend hours in comfortable silence with.

It was probably the lulling of magic that clouded my thoughts, and I didn't think of my family until I passed the outer hedge wall one morning, scouting for a new spot to paint. A breeze from the south ruffled my hair—fresh and warm. Spring was now dawning on the mortal world.

My family, glamoured, cared for, safe, still had no idea where I was. The mortal world . . . it had moved on without me, as if I had never existed. A whisper of a miserable life—gone, unremembered by anyone whom I'd known or cared for.

I didn't paint, nor did I go riding with Tamlin that day. Instead, I sat before a blank canvas, no colors at all in my mind.

No one would remember me back home—I was as good as dead to them. And Tamlin had *let* me forget them. Maybe the paints had even been a distraction—a way to get me to stop complaining, to stop being a pain in his ass about wanting to see my family. Or maybe they were a distraction from whatever was happening with the blight and Prythian. I'd stopped asking, just as the Suriel had ordered—like a stupid, useless, obedient human.

It was an effort of stubborn will to make it through dinner. Tamlin and Lucien noticed my mood and kept conversation between themselves. It didn't do much for my growing rage, and when I had eaten my fill, I stalked into the moonlit garden and lost myself in its labyrinth of hedges and flower beds.

I didn't care where I was going. After a while, I paused in the rose garden. The moonlight stained the red petals a deep purple and cast a silvery sheen on the white blooms.

"My father had this garden planted for my mother," Tamlin said from behind me. I didn't bother to face him. I dug my nails into my palms as he stopped by my side. "It was a mating present."

I stared at the flowers without seeing anything. The flowers I'd painted on the table at home were probably crumbling or gone by now. Nesta might have even scraped them off.

My nails pricked the skin of my palms. Tamlin providing for them or no, glamouring their memories or no, I'd been . . . erased from their lives. Forgotten. I'd let him erase me. He'd offered me paints and the space and time to practice; he'd shown me pools of starlight; he'd saved my life like some kind of feral knight in a legend, and I'd gulped it down like faerie wine. I was no better than those zealot Children of the Blessed.

His mask was bronze in the darkness, and the emeralds glittered. "You seem . . . upset."

I stalked to the nearest rosebush and ripped off a rose, my fingers tearing on the thorns. I ignored the pain, the warmth of the blood that trickled down. I could never paint it accurately—never render it the way those artists had in the gallery pieces. I would never be able to paint Elain's little garden outside the cottage the way I remembered it, even if my family didn't remember me.

He didn't reprimand me for taking one of his parents' roses—parents who were as absent as my own, but who had probably loved each other and loved him better than mine cared for me. A family that would have offered to go in his place if someone had come to steal him away.

My fingers stung and ached, but I still held on to the rose as I said, "I don't know why I feel so tremendously ashamed of myself for leaving them. Why it feels so selfish and horrible to paint. I shouldn't—shouldn't feel that way, should I? I know I shouldn't, but I can't help it." The rose hung limply from my fingers. "All those years, what I did for them . . . And they didn't try to stop you from taking me." There it was, the giant pain that cracked me in two if I thought about it too long. "I don't know why I expected them to—why I believed that the puca's illusion was real that night. I don't know why I bother still thinking about it. Or still caring." He was silent long enough that I added, "Compared to you—to your borders and magic being weakened—I suppose my self-pity is absurd."

"If it grieves you," he said, the words caressing my bones, "then I don't think it's absurd at all."

"Why?" A flat question, and I chucked the rose into the bushes.

He took my hands. His callused fingers, strong and sturdy, were gentle as he lifted my bleeding hand to his mouth and kissed my palm. As if that were answer enough.

His lips were smooth against my skin, his breath warm, and my knees buckled as he lifted my other hand to his mouth and kissed it, too. Kissed it carefully—in a way that made heat begin pounding in my core, between my legs.

When he withdrew, my blood shone on his mouth. I glanced at my hands, which he still held, and found the wounds gone. I looked at his face again, at his gilded mask, the tanness of his skin, the red of his blood-covered lips as he murmured, "Don't feel bad for one moment about doing what brings you joy." He stepped closer, releasing one of my hands to tuck the rose I'd plucked behind my ear. I didn't know how it had gotten into his hand, or where the thorns had gone.

I couldn't stop myself from pushing. "Why—why do any of this?"

He leaned in closer, so close that I had to tip my head back to see him. "Because your human joy fascinates me—the way you experience things, in your life span, so wildly and deeply and all at once, is . . . entrancing. I'm drawn to it, even when I know I shouldn't be, even when I try not to be."

Because I was human, and I would grow old and—I didn't let myself get that far as he came closer still. Slowly, as if giving me time to pull away, he brushed his lips against my cheek. Soft and warm and heartbreakingly gentle. It was hardly more than a caress before he straightened. I hadn't moved from the moment his mouth had met my skin.

"One day—one day there will be answers for everything," he said, releasing my hand and stepping away. "But not until the time is right. Until it's safe." In the dark, his tone was enough to know that his eyes were flecked with bitterness.

He left me, and I took a gasping breath, not realizing I'd been holding it.

Not realizing that I craved his warmth, his nearness, until he was gone.

✠

Lingering mortification over what I'd admitted, what had . . . *changed* between us had me skulking out of the manor after breakfast, fleeing for the sanctuary of the woods for some fresh air—and to study the light and colors. I brought my bow and arrows, along with the jeweled hunting knife that Lucien had given me. Better to be armed than caught empty-handed.

I crept through the trees and brush for no more than an hour before I felt a presence behind me—coming ever closer, sending the animals running for cover. I smiled to myself, and twenty minutes later, I settled in the crook of a towering elm and waited.

Brush rustled—hardly more than a breeze's passing, but I knew what to expect, knew the signs.

A snap and roar of fury echoed across the lands, scattering the birds.

When I climbed out of the tree and walked into the little clearing, I merely crossed my arms and looked up at the High Lord, dangling by his legs from the snare I'd laid.

Even upside down, he smiled lazily at me as I approached. "Cruel human."

"That's what you get for stalking someone."

He chuckled, and I came close enough to dare stroke a finger along the silken golden hair dangling just above my face, admiring the many colors within it—the hues of yellow and brown and wheat. My heart thundered, and I knew he could probably hear it. But he leaned his head toward me, a silent invitation, and I ran my fingers through his hair—gently, carefully. He purred, the sound rumbling through my fingers, arms, legs, and core. I wondered how that sound would feel if he were fully pressed up against me, skin-to-skin. I stepped back.

He curled upward in a smooth, powerful motion and swiped with a single claw at the creeping vine I'd used for rope. I took a breath to shout, but he flipped as he fell, landing smoothly on his feet. It would be impossible for me to ever forget what he was, and what he was capable of. He took a step closer to me, the laughter still dancing on his face. "Feeling better today?"

I mumbled some noncommittal response.

"Good," he said, either ignoring or hiding his amusement. "But just in case, I wanted to give you this," he added, pulling some papers from his tunic and extending them to me.

I bit the inside of my cheek as I stared down at the three pieces of paper. It was a series of five-lined . . . *poems*. There were five of them altogether, and I began sweating at words I didn't recognize. It would take me an entire day just to figure out what these words meant.

"Before you bolt or start yelling . . . ," he said, coming around to peer over my shoulder. If I'd dared, I could have leaned back into his chest. His breath warmed my neck, the shell of my ear.

He cleared his throat and read the first poem.

There once was a lady most beautiful
Spirited, if a little unusual
Her friends were few
But how the men did queue
But to all she gave a refusal.

My brows rose so high I thought they'd touch my hairline, and I turned, blinking at him, our breath mingling as he finished the poem with a smile.

Without waiting for my response, Tamlin took the papers and stepped a pace away to read the second poem, which wasn't nearly as polite as the first. By the time he read the third poem, my face was burning. Tamlin paused before he read the fourth, then handed me back the papers.

"Final word in the second and fourth line of each poem," he said, jerking his chin toward the papers in my hands.

Unusual. Queue. I looked at the second poem. *Slaying. Conflagration.*

"These are—" I started.

"Your list of words was too interesting to pass up. And not good for love poems at all." When I lifted my brow in silent inquiry, he said, "We had contests to see who could write the dirtiest limericks while I was living with my father's war-band by the border. I don't particularly enjoy losing, so I took it upon myself to become good at them."

I didn't know how he'd remembered that long list I'd compiled—I didn't want to. Sensing I wasn't about to draw an arrow and shoot him, Tamlin took the papers and read the fifth poem, the dirtiest and foulest of them all.

When he finished, I tipped back my head and howled, my laughter like sunshine shattering age-hardened ice.

✠

I was still smiling when we walked out of the park and toward the rolling hills, meandering back to the manor. "You said—that night in the rose garden . . ." I sucked on my teeth for a moment. "You said that your father had it planted for your parents upon their mating—not wedding?"

"High Fae mostly marry," he said, his golden skin flushing a bit. "But if they're blessed, they'll find their mate—their equal, their match in every way. High Fae wed without the mating bond, but if you find your mate, the bond is so deep that marriage is . . . insignificant in comparison."

I didn't have the nerve to ask if faeries had ever had mating bonds with humans, but instead dared to say, "Where are your parents? What happened to them?"

A muscle feathered in his jaw, and I regretted the question, if only for the pain that flickered in his eyes. "My father . . ." His claws gleamed at his knuckles but didn't go out any farther. I'd definitely asked the wrong question. "My father was as bad as Lucien's. Worse. My two older brothers were just like him. They kept slaves—all of them. And my brothers . . . I was young when the Treaty was forged, but I still remember what my brothers used to . . ." He trailed off. "It left a mark—enough of a mark that when I saw you, your house, I couldn't—wouldn't let myself be like them. Wouldn't bring harm to your family, or you, or subject you to faerie whims."

Slaves—there had been slaves *here*. I didn't want to know—had never looked for traces of them, even five hundred years later. I was still little better than chattel to most of his people, his world. That was why—why he'd offered the loophole, why he'd offered me the freedom to live wherever I wished in Prythian.

"Thank you," I said. He shrugged, as if that would dismiss his kindness, the weight of the guilt that still bore down on him. "What about your mother?"

Tamlin loosed a breath. "My mother—she loved my father deeply. Too deeply, but they were mated, and . . . Even if she saw what a tyrant he was, she wouldn't say an ill word against him. I never expected—never wanted—my father's title. My brothers would have never let me live to adolescence if they had suspected that I did. So the moment I was old enough, I joined my father's war-band and trained so that I might someday serve my father, or whichever of my brothers inherited his title." He flexed his hands, as if imagining the claws beneath. "I'd realized from an early age that fighting and killing were about the only things I was good at."

"I doubt that," I said.

He gave me a wry smile. "Oh, I can play a mean fiddle, but High Lords' sons don't become traveling minstrels. So I trained and fought for my father against whomever he told me to fight, and I would have been happy to leave the scheming to my brothers. But my power kept growing, and I couldn't hide it—not among our kind." He shook his head. "Fortunately or unfortunately, they were all killed by the High Lord of an enemy court. I was spared for whatever reason or Cauldron-granted luck. My mother, I mourned. The others . . ." A too-tight shrug. "My brothers would not have tried to save me from a fate like yours."

I looked up at him. Such a brutal, harsh world—with families killing each other for power, for revenge, for spite and control. Perhaps his generosity, his kindness, was a reaction to that—perhaps he'd seen me and found it to be like gazing into a mirror of sorts. "I'm sorry about your mother," I said, and it was all I could offer—all he'd once been able to offer me. He gave me a small smile. "So that's how you became High Lord."

"Most High Lords are trained from birth in manners and laws and court warfare. When the title fell to me, it was a . . . rough transition. Many of my father's courtiers defected to other courts rather than have a warrior-beast snarling at them."

A half-wild beast, Nesta had once called me. It was an effort to not take his hand, to not reach out to him and tell him that I understood. But I just said, "Then they're idiots. You've kept these lands protected from the blight, when it seems that others haven't fared so well. They're idiots," I said again.

But darkness flickered in Tamlin's eyes, and his shoulders seemed to curve inward ever so slightly. Before I could ask about it, we cleared the little wood, a spread of hills and knolls laid out ahead. In the distance, there were masked faeries atop many of them, building what seemed to be unlit fires. "What are those?" I asked, halting.

"They're setting up bonfires—for *Calanmai*. It's in two days."

"For what?"

"Fire Night?"

I shook my head. "We don't celebrate holidays in the human realm. Not after you—your people left. In some places, it's forbidden. We don't even remember the names of your gods. What does Cala—Fire Night celebrate?"

He rubbed his neck. "It's just a spring ceremony. We light bonfires, and . . . the magic that we create helps regenerate the land for the year ahead."

"How do you create the magic?"

"There's a ritual. But it's . . . very faerie." He clenched his jaw and continued walking, away from the unlit fires. "You might see more faeries around than usual—faeries from this court, and from other territories, who are free to wander across the borders that night."

"I thought the blight had scared many of them away."

"It has—but there will be a number of them. Just . . . stay away from them all. You'll be safe in the house, but if you run into one before we light the fires at sundown in two days, ignore them."

"And I'm not invited to your ceremony?"

"No. You're not." He clenched and loosened his fingers, again and again, as if trying to keep the claws contained.

Though I tried to ignore it, my chest caved a bit.

We walked back in the sort of tense silence we hadn't endured in weeks.

Tamlin went rigid the moment we entered the gardens. Not from me or our awkward conversation—it was quiet with that horrible stillness that usually meant one of the nastier faeries was around. Tamlin bared his teeth in a low snarl. "Stay hidden, and no matter what you overhear, don't come out."

Then he was gone.

Alone, I looked to either side of the gravel path, like some gawking idiot. If there was indeed something here, I'd be caught in the open. Perhaps it was shameful not to go to his aid, but—he was a High Lord. I would just get in the way.

I had just ducked behind a hedge when I heard Tamlin and Lucien approaching. I silently swore and froze. Maybe I could sneak across the fields to the stables. If there was something amiss, the stables not only had shelter but also a horse for me to flee on. I was about to make for the high grasses mere steps beyond the edge of the gardens when Tamlin's snarl rippled through the air on the other side of the hedge.

I turned—just enough to spy them through the dense leaves. *Stay hidden*, he'd said. If I moved now, I would surely be noticed.

"I know what day it is," Tamlin said—but not to Lucien. Rather, the two of them faced . . . nothing. Someone who wasn't *there*. Someone invisible. I would have thought they were playing a prank on me had I not heard a low, disembodied voice reply.

"Your continued behavior is garnering a lot of interest at court," the voice said, deep and sibilant. I shivered, despite the warmth of the day. "She has begun wondering—wondering why you haven't given up yet. And why four naga wound up dead not too long ago."

"Tamlin's not like the other fools," Lucien snapped, his shoulders pushed back to raise himself to his full height, more warrior-like than I'd yet seen him. No wonder he had all those weapons in his room. "If she expected bowed heads, then she's more of an idiot than I thought."

The voice hissed, and my blood went cold at the noise. "Speak you so ill of she who holds your fate in her hands? With one word, she could destroy this pathetic estate. She wasn't pleased when she heard of you dispatching your warriors." The voice now seemed turned toward Tamlin. "But, as nothing has come of it, she has chosen to ignore it."

There was a deep-throated growl from the High Lord, but his words were calm as he said, "Tell her I'm getting sick of cleaning up the trash she dumps on my borders."

The voice chuckled, the sound like sand shifting. "She sets them loose as gifts—and reminders of what will happen if she catches you trying to break the terms of—"

"He's not," Lucien snarled. "Now, *get out*. We have enough of your ilk swarming on the borders—we don't need you defiling our home, too. For that matter, stay the hell out of the cave. It's not some common road for filth like you to travel through as they please."

Tamlin loosed a growl of agreement.

The invisible thing laughed again, such a horrible, vicious sound. "Though you have a heart of stone, Tamlin," it said, and Tamlin went rigid, "you certainly keep a host of fear inside it." The voice sank into a croon. "Don't worry, *High Lord*." It spat the title like a joke. "All will be right as rain soon enough."

"Burn in Hell," Lucien replied for Tamlin, and the thing laughed again before a flap of leathery wings boomed, a foul wind bit my face, and everything went silent.

They breathed deeply after another moment. I closed my eyes, needing a steadying breath as well, but massive hands clamped onto my shoulders, and I yelped.

"It's gone," Tamlin said, releasing me. It was all I could do not to sag against the hedges.

"What did you hear?" Lucien demanded, coming around the corner and crossing his arms. I shifted my gaze to Tamlin's face, but found it to be so white with anger—anger at that *thing*—that I had to look again at Lucien.

"Nothing—I . . . well, nothing I understood," I said, and meant it. None of it made any sense. I couldn't stop shaking. Something about that voice had ripped away the warmth from me. "Who—*what* was that?"

Tamlin began pacing, the gravel churning beneath his boots.

"There are certain faeries in Prythian who inspired the legends that you humans are so afraid of. Some, like that one, are myth given flesh."

Inside that hissing voice I'd heard the screaming of human victims, the pleading of young maidens whose chests had been split open on sacrificial altars. Mentions of "court," seemingly different from Tamlin's own—was that *she* the one who had killed Tamlin's parents? A High Lady, perhaps, in lieu of a Lord. Considering how ruthless the High Fae were to their families, they had to be nightmarish to their enemies. And if there was to be warring between the courts, if the blight had left Tamlin already weakened . . .

"If the Attor saw her—" Lucien said, glancing around.

"It didn't," Tamlin said.

"Are you certain it—"

"*It didn't*," Tamlin growled over his shoulder, then looked at me, his face still pale with fury, lips tight. "I'll see you at dinner."

Understanding a dismissal, and craving the locked door of my bedroom, I trudged back to the house, contemplating who this *she* was to make Tamlin and Lucien so nervous and to command that *thing* as her messenger.

The spring breeze whispered that I didn't want to know.

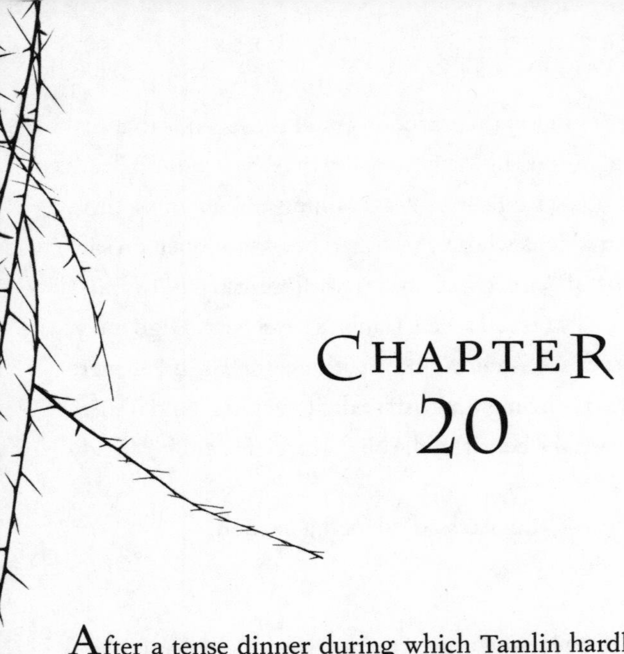

Chapter 20

After a tense dinner during which Tamlin hardly spoke to Lucien or me, I lit all the candles in my room to chase away the shadows.

I didn't go outside the following day, and when I sat down to paint, what emerged on my canvas was a tall, skeletally thin gray creature with bat ears and giant, membranous wings. Its snout was open in a roar, revealing row after row of fangs as it leaped into flight. As I painted it, I could have sworn that I could smell breath that reeked of carrion, that the air beneath its wings whispered promises of death.

The finished product was chilling enough that I had to set aside the painting in the back of the room and go try to persuade Alis to let me help with the Fire Night food preparations in the kitchen. Anything to avoid going into the garden, where the Attor might appear.

The day of Fire Night—*Calanmai*, Tamlin had called it—dawned, and I didn't see Tamlin or Lucien all day. As the afternoon shifted into dusk, I found myself again at the main crossroads of the house. None of the bird-faced servants were to be found. The kitchen was empty of staff and the food they'd been preparing for two days. The sound of drums issued.

The drumbeats came from far away—beyond the garden, past the game park, into the forest that lay beyond. They were deep, probing. A single beat, echoed by two responding calls. Summoning.

I stood by the doors to the garden, staring out over the property as the sky became awash in hues of orange and red. In the distance, upon the sloping hills that led into the woods, a few fires flickered, plumes of dark smoke marring the ruby sky—the unlit bonfires I'd spotted two days ago. Not invited, I reminded myself. Not invited to whatever party had all the kitchen faeries tittering and laughing among one another.

The drums turned faster—louder. Though I'd grown accustomed to the smell of magic, my nose pricked with the rising tang of metal, stronger than I'd yet sensed it. I took a step forward, then halted on the threshold. I should go back in. Behind me, the setting sun stained the black-and-white tiles of the hall floor a shimmering shade of tangerine, and my long shadow seemed to pulse to the beat of the drums.

Even the garden, usually buzzing with the orchestra of its denizens, had quieted to hear the drums. There was a string—a string tied to my gut that pulled me toward those hills, commanding me to go, to hear the faerie drums . . .

I might have done just that had Tamlin not appeared from down the hall.

He was shirtless, with only the baldric across his muscled chest. The pommel of his sword glinted golden in the dying sunlight, and the feathered tops of arrows were stained red as they poked above his broad shoulder. I stared at him, and he watched me back. The warrior incarnate.

"Where are you going?" I managed to get out.

"It's *Calanmai*," he said flatly. "I have to go." He jerked his chin to the fires and drums.

"To do what?" I asked, glancing at the bow in his hand. My heart echoed the drums outside, building into a wilder beat.

His green eyes were shadowed beneath the gilded mask. "As a High Lord, I have to partake in the Great Rite."

"What's the Great—"

"Go to your chamber," he snarled, and glanced toward the fires. "Lock your doors, set up a snare, whatever you do."

"Why?" I demanded. The Attor's voice snaked through my memory. Tamlin had said something about a very faerie ritual—what the hell was it? From the weapons, it had to be brutal and violent—especially if Tamlin's beast form wasn't weapon enough.

"Just do it." His canines began to lengthen. My heart leaped into a gallop. "Don't come out until morning."

Stronger, faster, the drums beat, and the muscles in Tamlin's neck quivered, as if standing still were somehow painful to him.

"Are you going into battle?" I whispered, and he let out a breathy laugh.

He lifted a hand as if to touch my arm. But he lowered it before his fingers could graze the fabric of my tunic. "Stay in your chamber, Feyre."

"But I—"

"Please." Before I could ask him to reconsider bringing me along, he took off running. The muscles in his back shifted as he leaped down the short flight of stairs and bounded into the garden, as spry and swift as a stag. Within seconds he was gone.

✠

I did as he commanded, though I soon realized that I'd locked myself in my room without having eaten dinner. And with the incessant drumming and dozens of bonfires that popped up along the far hills, I couldn't stop pacing up and down my room, gazing out toward the fires burning in the distance.

Stay in your chamber.

But a wild, wicked voice weaving in between the drumbeats whispered otherwise. *Go*, that voice said, tugging at me. *Go see.*

By ten o'clock, I could no longer stand it. I followed the drums.

The stables were empty, but Tamlin had taught me how to ride bareback these past few weeks, and my white mare was soon trotting along. I didn't need to guide her—she, too, followed the lure of the drums, and ascended the first of the foothills.

Smoke and magic hung thick in the air. Concealed in my hooded cloak, I gaped as I approached the first giant bonfire atop the hill. There were hundreds of High Fae milling about, but I couldn't discern any of their features beyond the various masks they wore. Where had they come from—where did they live, if they belonged to the Spring Court but did not dwell in the manor? When I tried to focus on a specific feature of their faces, it became a blur of color. They were more solid when I viewed them from the side of my vision, but if I turned to face them, I was met with shadows and swirling colors.

It was magic—some kind of glamour put on *me*, meant to prevent my viewing them properly, just as my family had been glamoured. I would have been furious, would have considered going back to the manor had the drums not echoed through my bones and that wild voice not beckoned to me.

I dismounted my mare but kept close to her as I made my way through the crowd, my telltale human features hidden in the shadows of my hood. I prayed that the smoke and countless scents of various High Fae and faeries were enough to cover my human smell, but I checked to ensure that my two knives were still at my sides anyway as I moved deeper into the celebration.

Though a cluster of drummers played on one side of the fire, the faeries flocked to a trench between two nearby hills. I left my horse tied to a solitary sycamore crowning a knoll and followed them, savoring the pulsing beat of the drums as it resonated through the earth and into the soles of my feet. No one looked twice in my direction.

I almost slid down the steep bank as I entered the hollow. At one end, a cave mouth opened into a soft hillside. Its exterior had been adorned with flowers and branches and leaves, and I could make out the beginnings of a pelt-covered floor just past the cave mouth. What lay inside was hidden from view as the chamber veered away from the entrance, but firelight danced upon the walls.

Whatever was occurring inside the cave—or whatever was about to happen—was the focus of the shadowy faeries as they lined either side of a long path leading to it. The path wended between the trenches among the hills, and the High Fae swayed in place, moving to the rhythm of the drumming, whose beats sounded in my stomach.

I watched them sway, then shifted on my feet. I'd been banned from *this*? I scanned the firelit area, trying to peer through the veil of night and smoke. I found nothing of interest, and none of the masked faeries paid me any heed. They remained along the path, more and more of them coming each minute. Something was definitely going to happen—whatever this Great Rite was.

I made my way back up the hillside and stood along the edge of a bonfire near the trees, watching the faeries. I was about to work up the courage to ask a lesser faerie who passed by—a bird-masked servant, like Alis—what sort of ritual was going to happen when someone grasped my arm and whirled me around.

I blinked at the three strangers, dumbfounded as I beheld their sharp-featured faces—free of masks. They looked like High Fae, but there was something slightly different about them, something taller and leaner than Tamlin or Lucien—something crueler in their pitch-black, depthless eyes. Faeries, then.

The one grasping my arm smiled down at me, revealing slightly pointed teeth. "Human woman," he murmured, running an eye over me. "We've not seen one of you for a while."

I tried yanking my arm back, but he held my elbow firm. "What do you want?" I demanded, keeping my voice steady and cold.

The two faeries who flanked him smiled at me, and one grabbed my other arm—just as I went for my knife. "Just some Fire Night fun," one of them said, reaching out a pale, too-long hand to brush back a lock of my hair. I twisted my head away and tried to step out of his touch, but he held firm. None of the faeries near the bonfire reacted—no one bothered to look.

If I cried for help, would someone answer? Would Tamlin answer? I couldn't be that lucky again; I'd probably used up my allotted portion of luck with the naga.

I yanked my arms in earnest. Their grip tightened until it hurt, and they kept my hands well away from my knives. The three of them stepped closer, sealing me off from the others. I glanced around, looking for any ally. There were more nonmasked faeries here now. The three faeries chuckled, a low hissing noise that ran along my body. I hadn't realized how far I stood from everyone else—how close I'd come to the forest's edge. "Leave me alone," I said, louder and angrier than I'd expected, given the shaking that was starting in my knees.

"Bold statement from a human on *Calanmai*," said the one holding my left arm. The fires didn't reflect in his eyes. It was as if they gobbled up the light. I thought of the naga, whose horrible exteriors matched their rotten hearts. Somehow, these beautiful, ethereal faeries were far worse. "Once the Rite's performed, we'll have some fun, won't we? A treat—such a treat—to find a human woman here."

I bared my teeth at him. "Get your hands off me," I said, loud enough for anyone to hear.

One of them ran a hand down my side, its bony fingers digging into my ribs, my hips. I jerked back, only to slam into the third one, who wove his long fingers through my hair and pressed close. No one looked; no one noticed.

"Stop it," I said, but the words came out in a strangled gasp as they began herding me toward the line of trees, toward the darkness. I pushed and thrashed against them; they only hissed. One of them shoved me and I staggered, falling out of their grasp. The ground welled up beneath me, and I reached for my knives, but sturdy hands grasped me under the shoulders before I could draw them or hit the grass.

They were strong hands—warm and broad. Not at all like the prodding, bony fingers of the three faeries who went utterly still as whoever caught me gently set me upright.

"There you are. I've been looking for you," said a deep, sensual male voice I'd never heard. But I kept my eyes on the three faeries, bracing myself for flight as the male behind me stepped to my side and slipped a casual arm around my shoulders.

The three lesser faeries paled, their dark eyes wide.

"Thank you for finding her for me," my savior said to them, smooth and polished. "Enjoy the Rite." There was enough of a bite beneath his last words that the faeries stiffened. Without further comment, they scuttled back to the bonfires.

I stepped out of the shelter of my savior's arm and turned to thank him.

Standing before me was the most beautiful man I'd ever seen.

CHAPTER 21

Everything about the stranger radiated sensual grace and ease. High Fae, no doubt. His short black hair gleamed like a raven's feathers, offsetting his pale skin and blue eyes so deep they were violet, even in the firelight. They twinkled with amusement as he beheld me.

For a moment, we said nothing. *Thank you* didn't seem to cover what he'd done for me, but something about the way he stood with absolute stillness, the night seeming to press in closer around him, made me hesitate to speak—made me want to run in the other direction.

He, too, wasn't wearing a mask. From another court, then.

A half smile played on his lips. "What's a mortal woman doing here on Fire Night?" His voice was a lover's purr that sent shivers through me, caressing every muscle and bone and nerve.

I took a step back. "My friends brought me."

The drumming was increasing in tempo, building to a climax I didn't understand. It had been so long since I'd seen a bare face that looked even vaguely human. His clothes—all black, all finely made—were cut close enough to his body that I could see how magnificent he was. As if he'd been molded from the night itself.

"And who are your friends?" He was still smiling at me—a predator sizing up prey.

"Two ladies," I lied again.

"Their names?" He prowled closer, slipping his hands into his pockets. I retreated a little more and kept my mouth shut. Had I just traded three monsters for something far worse?

When it became apparent I wouldn't answer, he chuckled. "You're welcome," he said. "For saving you."

I bristled at his arrogance but retreated another step. I was close enough to the bonfire, to that little hollow where the faeries were all gathered, that I could make it if I sprinted. Maybe someone would take pity on me—maybe Lucien or Alis were there.

"Strange for a mortal to be friends with two faeries," he mused, and began circling me. I could have sworn tendrils of star-kissed night trailed in his wake. "Aren't humans usually terrified of us? And aren't you, for that matter, supposed to keep to your side of the wall?"

I was terrified of *him*, but I wasn't about to let him know. "I've known them my whole life. I've never had anything to fear from them."

He paused his circling. He now stood between me and the bonfire—and my escape route. "And yet they brought you to the Great Rite and abandoned you."

"They went to get refreshments," I said, and his smile grew. Whatever I'd just said had given me away. I'd spotted the servants hauling off the food, but—maybe it wasn't here.

He smiled for a heartbeat longer. I had never seen anyone so handsome—and never had so many warning bells pealed in my head because of it.

"I'm afraid the refreshments are a long way off," he said, coming closer now. "It might be a while before they return. May I escort you somewhere in the meantime?" He removed a hand from his pocket to offer his arm.

He'd been able to scare off those faeries without lifting a finger. "No," I said, my tongue thick and heavy.

He waved his hand toward the hollow—toward the drums. "Enjoy the Rite, then. Try to stay out of trouble." His eyes gleamed in a way that suggested staying out of trouble meant staying far, far away from him.

Though it might have been the biggest risk I'd ever taken, I blurted, "So you're not a part of the Spring Court?"

He returned to me, every movement exquisite and laced with lethal power, but I held my ground as he gave me a lazy smile. "Do I look like I'm part of the Spring Court?" The words were tinged with an arrogance that only an immortal could achieve. He laughed under his breath. "No, I'm not a part of the noble Spring Court. And glad of it." He gestured to his face, where a mask might go.

I should have walked away, should have shut my mouth. "Why are you here, then?"

The man's remarkable eyes seemed to glow—with enough of a deadly edge that I backed up a step. "Because all the monsters have been let out of their cages tonight, no matter what court they belong to. So I may roam wherever I wish until the dawn."

More riddles and questions to be answered. But I'd had enough—especially as his smile turned cold and cruel. "Enjoy the Rite," I repeated as blandly as I could.

I hurried back to the hollow, too aware of the fact that I was putting my back to him. I was grateful to lose myself in the crowd milling along the path to the cave, still waiting for some moment to occur.

When I stopped shaking, I looked around at the gathered faeries. Most of them still wore masks, but there were some, like that lethal stranger and those three horrible faeries, who wore no masks at all—either faeries with no allegiance or members of other courts. I couldn't tell them apart. As I scanned the crowd, my eyes met with those of a masked faerie across the path. One was russet and shone as brightly as his red hair. The other was—metal. I blinked at the same moment he did, and then his eyes went wide. He vanished into nothing, and a second later, someone grabbed my elbow and yanked me out of the crowd.

"Have you lost your senses?" Lucien shouted above the drums. His face was ghostly pale. "What are you doing here?"

None of the faeries noticed us—they were all staring intensely down the path, away from the cave. "I wanted to—" I started, but Lucien cursed violently.

"Idiot!" he yelled at me, then glanced behind him toward where the other faeries stared. "Useless human fool." Without further word, he slung me over his shoulder as if I were a sack of potatoes.

Despite my wriggling and shouts of protest, despite my demands that he get my horse, he held firm, and when I looked up, I found that he was running—fast. Faster than anything should be able to move. It made me so nauseated that I shut my eyes. He didn't stop until the air was cooler and calmer, and the drumming was distant.

Lucien dropped me on the floor of the manor hallway, and when I steadied myself, I found his face just as pale as before. "You stupid mortal," he snapped. "Didn't he tell you to stay in your room?" Lucien looked over his shoulder, toward the hills, where the drumming became so loud and fast that it was like a rainstorm.

"That was hardly anything—"

"That wasn't even the ceremony!" It was only then that I saw the sweat on his face and the panicked gleam in his eyes. "By the Cauldron, if Tam found you there . . ."

"So what?" I said, shouting as well. I hated feeling like a disobedient child.

"It's the *Great Rite*, Cauldron boil me! Didn't anyone tell you what it is?" My silence was answer enough. I could almost see the drumbeats pulsing against his skin, beckoning him to rejoin the crowd. "Fire Night signals the official start of spring—in Prythian, as well as in the mortal world," Lucien said. While his words were calm, they trembled slightly. I leaned against the wall of the hallway, forcing myself into a casualness I didn't feel. "Here, our crops depend upon the magic we regenerate on *Calanmai*—tonight."

I stuffed my hands into the pockets of my pants. Tamlin had said something similar two days ago. Lucien shuddered, as if shaking off an invisible touch. "We do this by conducting the Great Rite. Each of the seven High Lords of Prythian performs this every year, since their magic comes from the earth and returns to it at the end—it's a give-and-take."

"But what is it?" I asked, and he clicked his tongue.

"Tonight, Tam will allow . . . great and terrible magic to enter his body," Lucien said, staring at the distant fires. "The magic will seize control of his mind, his body, his soul, and turn him into the Hunter. It will fill him with his sole purpose: to find the Maiden. From their coupling, magic will be released and spread to the earth, where it will regenerate life for the year to come."

My face became hot, and I fought the urge to fidget.

"Tonight, Tam won't be the faerie you know," Lucien said. "He won't even know his name. The magic will consume everything in him but that one basic command—and need."

"Who . . . who's the Maiden?" I got out.

Lucien snorted. "No one knows until it's time. After Tam hunts down the white stag and kills it for the sacrificial offering, he'll make his way to that sacred cave, where he'll find the path lined with faerie females waiting to be chosen as his mate for tonight."

"What?"

Lucien laughed. "Yes—all those female faeries around you were females for Tamlin to pick. It's an honor to be chosen, but it's his instincts that select her."

"But you were there—and other male faeries." My face burned so hot that I began sweating. That was why those three horrible faeries had been there—and they'd thought that just by my presence, I was happy to comply with their plans.

"Ah." Lucien chuckled. "Well, Tam's not the only one who gets to perform the rite tonight. Once he makes his choice, we're free to mingle. Though it's not the Great Rite, our own dalliances tonight will help the land, too." He shrugged off that invisible hand a second time, and his eyes fell upon the hills. "You're lucky I found you when I did, though," he said. "Because he would have smelled you, and claimed you, but it wouldn't have been Tamlin who brought you into that cave." His eyes met mine, and a chill went over me. "And I don't think you would have liked it. Tonight is not for lovemaking."

I swallowed my nausea.

"I should go," Lucien said, gazing at the hills. "I need to return before he arrives at the cave—at least to *try* to control him when he smells you and can't find you in the crowd."

It made me sick—the thought of Tamlin forcing me, that magic could strip away any sense of self, of right or wrong. But hearing that . . . that some feral part of him *wanted* me . . . My breath was painful.

"Stay in your room tonight, Feyre," Lucien said, walking to the garden doors. "No matter who comes knocking, keep the door locked. Don't come out until morning."

✣

At some point, I dozed off while sitting at my vanity. I awoke the moment the drums stopped. A shuddering silence went through the house, and the hair on my arms arose as magic swept past me, rippling outward.

Though I tried not to, I thought about the probable source and blushed, even as my chest tightened. I glanced at the clock. It was past two in the morning.

Well, he'd certainly taken his time with the ritual, which meant the girl was probably beautiful and charming, and appealed to his *instincts*.

I wondered whether she was glad to be chosen. Probably. She'd come to the hill of her own free will. And after all, Tamlin was a High Lord, and it was a great honor. And I supposed Tamlin was handsome. Terribly handsome. Even though I couldn't see the upper part of his face, his eyes were fine, and his mouth beautifully curved and full. And then there was his body, which was . . . was . . . I hissed and stood.

I stared at my door, at the snare I'd rigged. How utterly absurd—as if bits of rope and wood could protect me from the demons in this land.

Needing to do something with my hands, I carefully disassembled the snare. Then I unlocked the door and strode into the hallway. What a ridiculous holiday. Absurd. It was good that humans had cast them aside.

I made it to the empty kitchen, gobbled down half a loaf of bread, an apple, and a lemon tart. I nibbled on a chocolate cookie as I walked to my little painting room. I needed to get some of the furious images out of my mind, even if I had to paint by candlelight.

I was about to turn down the hallway when a tall male figure appeared before me. The moonlight from the open window turned his mask silver, and his golden hair—unbound and crowned with laurel leaves—gleamed.

"Going somewhere?" Tamlin asked. His voice was not entirely of this world.

I suppressed a shudder. "Midnight snack," I said, and I was keenly aware of every movement, every breath I took as I neared him.

His bare chest was painted with whorls of dark blue woad, and from the smudges in the paint, I knew exactly where he'd been touched. I tried not to notice that they descended past his muscled midriff.

I was about to pass him when he grabbed me, so fast that I didn't see anything until he had me pinned against the wall. The cookie dropped from my hand as he grasped my wrists. "I smelled you," he breathed, his painted chest rising and falling so close to mine. "I searched for you, and you weren't there."

He reeked of magic. When I looked into his eyes, remnants of power flickered there. No kindness, none of the wry humor and gentle reprimands. The Tamlin I knew was gone.

"Let go," I said as evenly as I could, but his claws punched out, imbedding in the wood above my hands. Still riding the magic, he was half-wild.

"You drove me mad," he growled, and the sound trembled down my neck, along my breasts until they ached. "I searched for you, and you weren't there. When I didn't find you," he said, bringing his face closer to mine, until we shared breath, "it made me pick another."

I couldn't escape. I wasn't entirely sure that I wanted to.

"She asked me not to be gentle with her, either," he snarled, his teeth bright in the moonlight. He brought his lips to my ear. "I would have been gentle with you, though." I shuddered as I closed my eyes. Every inch of my body went taut as his words echoed through me. "I would have had you moaning my name throughout it all. And I would have taken a very, very long time, Feyre." He said my name like a caress, and his hot breath tickled my ear. My back arched slightly.

He ripped his claws free from the wall, and my knees buckled as he let go. I grasped the wall to keep from sinking to the floor, to keep from grabbing him—to strike or caress, I didn't know. I opened my eyes. He still smiled—smiled like an animal.

"Why should I want someone's leftovers?" I said, making to push him away. He grabbed my hands again and bit my neck.

I cried out as his teeth clamped onto the tender spot where my neck met my shoulder. I couldn't move—couldn't think, and my world narrowed to the feeling of his lips and teeth against my skin. He didn't pierce my flesh, but rather bit to keep me pinned. The push of his body against mine, the hard and the soft, made me see red—see lightning, made me grind my hips against his. I should hate him—hate him for his stupid ritual, for the female he'd been with tonight . . .

His bite lightened, and his tongue caressed the places his teeth had been. He didn't move—he just remained in that spot, kissing my neck. Intently, territorially, lazily. Heat pounded between my legs, and as he ground his body against me, against every aching spot, a moan slipped past my lips.

He jerked away. The air was bitingly cold against my freed skin, and I panted as he stared at me. "Don't ever disobey me again," he said, his voice a deep purr that ricocheted through me, awakening everything and lulling it into complicity.

Then I reconsidered his words and straightened. He grinned at me in that wild way, and my hand connected with his face.

"Don't tell me what to do," I breathed, my palm stinging. "And don't bite me like some enraged beast."

He chuckled bitterly. The moonlight turned his eyes to the color of leaves in shadow. More—I wanted the hardness of his body crushing against mine; I wanted his mouth and teeth and tongue on my bare skin, on my breasts, between my legs. Everywhere—I wanted him *everywhere*. I was drowning in that need.

His nostrils flared as he scented me—scented every burning, raging thought that was pounding through my body, my senses. The breath rushed from him in a mighty whoosh.

He growled once, low and frustrated and vicious, before prowling away.

CHAPTER 22

I awoke when the sun was high, after tossing and turning all night, empty and aching.

The servants were sleeping in after their night of celebrating, so I made myself a bath and took a good, long soak. Try as I might to forget the feel of Tamlin's lips on my neck, I had an enormous bruise where he'd bitten me. After bathing, I dressed and sat at the vanity to braid my hair.

I opened the drawers of the vanity, searching for a scarf or something to cover the bruise peeking over the collar of my blue tunic, but then paused and glared at myself in the mirror. He'd acted like a brute and a savage, and if he'd come to his senses by this morning, then seeing what he'd done would be minimal punishment.

Sniffing, I opened the collar of my tunic farther and tucked stray strands of my golden-brown hair behind my ears so there would be no concealing it. I was beyond cowering.

Humming to myself and swinging my hands, I strode downstairs and followed my nose to the dining room, where I knew lunch was usually served for Tamlin and Lucien. When I flung open the doors, I found them both sprawled in their chairs. I could have sworn that Lucien was sleeping upright, fork in hand.

"Good afternoon," I said cheerfully, with an especially saccharine smile for the High Lord. He blinked at me, and both of the faerie men murmured their greetings as I took a seat across from Lucien, not my usual place facing Tamlin.

I drank deeply from my goblet of water before piling food on my plate. I savored the tense silence as I consumed the meal before me.

"You look . . . refreshed," Lucien observed with a glance at Tamlin. I shrugged. "Sleep well?"

"Like a babe." I smiled at him and took another bite of food, and felt Lucien's eyes travel inexorably to my neck.

"What is that bruise?" Lucien demanded.

I pointed with my fork to Tamlin. "Ask him. He did it."

Lucien looked from Tamlin to me and then back again. "Why does Feyre have a bruise on her neck from you?" he asked with no small amount of amusement.

"I bit her," Tamlin said, not pausing as he cut his steak. "We ran into each other in the hall after the Rite."

I straightened in my chair.

"She seems to have a death wish," he went on, cutting his meat. The claws stayed retracted but pushed against the skin above his knuckles. My throat closed up. Oh, he was mad—furious at my foolishness for leaving my room—but somehow managed to keep his anger on a tight, tight leash. "So, if Feyre can't be bothered to listen to orders, then I can't be held accountable for the consequences."

"Accountable?" I sputtered, placing my hands flat on the table. "You cornered me in the hall like a wolf with a rabbit!"

Lucien propped an arm on the table and covered his mouth with his hand, his russet eye bright.

"While I might not have been myself, Lucien *and* I both told you to stay in your room," Tamlin said, so calmly that I wanted to rip out my hair.

I couldn't help it. Didn't even try to fight the red-hot temper that razed my senses. "Faerie pig!" I yelled, and Lucien howled, almost tipping back in his chair. At the sight of Tamlin's growing smile, I left.

It took me a couple of hours to stop painting little portraits of Tamlin and Lucien with pigs' features. But as I finished the last one—*Two faerie pigs wallowing in their own filth*, I would call it—I smiled into the clear, bright light of my private painting room. The Tamlin I knew had returned.

And it made me . . . happy.

⁜

We apologized at dinner. He even brought me a bouquet of white roses from his parents' garden, and while I dismissed them as nothing, I made certain that Alis took good care of them when I returned to my room. She gave me only a wry nod before promising to set them in my painting room. I fell asleep with a smile still on my lips.

For the first time in a long, long while, I slept peacefully.

⁜

"Don't know if I should be pleased or worried," Alis said the next night as she slid the golden underdress over my upraised arms, then tugged it down.

I smiled a bit, marveling at the intricate metallic lace that clung to my arms and torso like a second skin before falling loosely to the rug. "It's just a dress," I said, lifting my arms again as she brought over the gossamer turquoise overgown. It was sheer enough to see the gleaming gold mesh beneath, and light and airy and full of movement, as if it flowed on an invisible current.

Alis just chuckled to herself and guided me over to the vanity to work on my hair. I didn't have the courage to look at the mirror as she fussed over me.

"Does this mean you'll be wearing gowns from now on?" she asked, separating sections of my hair for whatever wonders she was doing to it.

"No," I said quickly. "I mean—I'll be wearing my usual clothes during the day, but I thought it might be nice to . . . try it out, at least for tonight."

"I see. Good that you aren't losing your common sense entirely, then."

I twisted my mouth to the side. "Who taught you how to do hair like this?"

Her fingers stilled, then continued their work. "My mother taught me and my sister, and her mother taught her before that."

"Have you always been at the Spring Court?"

"No," she said, pinning my hair in various, subtle places. "No, we were originally from the Summer Court—that's where my kin still dwells."

"How'd you wind up here?"

Alis met my eyes in the mirror, her lips a tight line. "I made a choice to come here—and my kin thought me mad. But my sister and her mate had been killed, and for her boys . . ." She coughed, as if choking on the words. "I came here to do what I could." She patted my shoulder. "Have a look."

I dared a glimpse at my reflection.

I hurried from the room before I could lose my nerve.

✣

I had to keep my hands clenched at my sides to avoid wiping my sweaty palms on the skirts of my gown as I reached the dining room, and immediately contemplated bolting upstairs and changing into a tunic and pants. But I knew they'd already heard me, or smelled me, or used whatever heightened senses they had to detect my presence, and since fleeing would only make it worse, I found it in myself to push open the double doors.

Whatever discussion Tamlin and Lucien had been having stopped, and I tried not to look at their wide eyes as I strode to my usual place at the end of the table.

"Well, I'm late for something incredibly important," Lucien said, and before I could call him on his outright lie or beg him to stay, the fox-masked faerie vanished.

I could feel the full weight of Tamlin's undivided attention on me—on every breath and movement I took. I studied the candelabras atop the mantel beside the table. I had nothing to say that didn't sound absurd—yet for some reason, my mouth decided to start moving.

"You're so far away." I gestured to the expanse of table between us. "It's like you're in another room."

The quarters of the table vanished, leaving Tamlin not two feet away, sitting at an infinitely more intimate table. I yelped and almost tipped over in my chair. He laughed as I gaped at the small table that now stood between us. "Better?" he asked.

I ignored the metallic tang of magic as I said, "How . . . how did you *do* that? Where did it go?"

He cocked his head. "Between. Think of it as . . . a broom closet tucked between pockets of the world." He flexed his hands and rolled his neck, as if shaking off some pain.

"Does it tax you?" Sweat seemed to gleam on the strong column of his neck.

He stopped flexing his hands and set them flat on the table. "Once, it was as easy as breathing. But now . . . it requires concentration."

Because of the blight on Prythian and the toll it had taken on him. "You could have just taken a closer seat," I said.

Tamlin gave me a lazy grin. "And miss a chance to show off to a beautiful woman? Never." I smiled down at my plate.

"You do look beautiful," he said quietly. "I mean it," he added when my mouth twisted to the side. "Didn't you look in the mirror?"

Though his bruise still marred my neck, I *had* looked pretty.

Feminine. I wouldn't go so far as to call myself a beauty, but . . . I hadn't cringed. A few months here had done wonders for the awkward sharpness and angles of my face. And I dared say that some kind of light had crept into my eyes—*my* eyes, not my mother's eyes or Nesta's eyes. *Mine*.

"Thank you," I said, and was grateful to avoid saying anything else as he served me and then himself. When my stomach was full to bursting, I dared to look at him—really *look* at him—again.

Tamlin leaned back in his chair, yet his shoulders were tight, his mouth a thin line. He hadn't been called to the border in a few days—hadn't come back weary and covered in blood since before Fire Night. And yet . . . He'd grieved for that nameless Summer Court faerie with the hacked-off wings. What grief and burdens did he bear for whoever else had been lost in this conflict—lost to the blight, or to the attacks on the borders? High Lord—a position he hadn't wanted or expected, yet he'd been forced to bear its weight as best he could.

"Come," I said, rising from my chair and tugging on his hand. The calluses scraped against mine, but his fingers tightened as he looked up at me. "I have something for you."

"For me," he repeated carefully, but rose. I led him out of the dining room. When I went to drop his hand, he didn't let go. It was enough to keep me walking quickly, as if I could outrun my thundering heart or the sheer immortal presence of him at my side. I brought him down hall after hall until we got to my little painting room, and he finally released my hand as I reached for the key. Cold air bit into my skin without the warmth of his hand around mine.

"I knew you'd asked Alis for a key, but I didn't think you actually locked the room," he said behind me.

I gave him a narrowed glance over my shoulder as I pushed open the door. "Everyone snoops in this house. I didn't want you or Lucien coming in here until I was ready."

I stepped into the darkened room and cleared my throat, a silent request for him to light the candles. It took him longer than I'd seen him need before, and I wondered if shortening the table had somehow drained him more than he'd let on. The Suriel had said the High Lords *were* Power—and yet . . . yet something had to be truly, thoroughly wrong if this was all he could manage. The room gradually flared with light, and I pushed my worry aside as I stepped farther into the room. I took a deep breath and gestured to the easel and the painting I'd put there. I hoped he wouldn't notice the paintings I'd leaned against the walls.

He turned in place, staring around him at the room.

"I know they're strange," I said, my hands sweating again. I tucked them behind my back. "And I know they're not like—not as good as the ones you have here, but . . ." I walked to the painting on the easel. It was an impression, not a lifelike rendering. "I wanted you to see this one," I said, pointing to the smear of green and gold and silver and blue. "It's for you. A gift. For everything you've done."

Heat flared in my cheeks, my neck, my ears, as he silently approached the painting.

"It's the glen—with the pool of starlight," I said quickly.

"I know what it is," he murmured, studying the painting. I backed away a step, unable to bear watching him look at it, wishing I hadn't brought him in here, blaming it on the wine I'd had at dinner, on the stupid dress. He examined the painting for a miserable eternity, then looked away—to the nearest painting leaning against the wall.

My gut tightened. A hazy landscape of snow and skeletal trees and nothing else. It looked like . . . like nothing, I supposed, to anyone but me. I opened my mouth to explain, wishing I'd turned the others away from view, but he spoke.

"That was your forest. Where you hunted." He came closer to the painting, gazing at the bleak, empty cold, the white and gray and brown and black. "This was your life," he clarified.

I was too mortified, too stunned, to reply. He walked to the next painting I'd left against the wall. Darkness and dense brown, flickers of ruby red and orange squeezing out between them. "Your cottage at night."

I tried to move, to tell him to stop looking at those ones and look at the others I'd laid out, but I couldn't—couldn't even breathe properly as he moved to the next painting. A tanned, sturdy male hand fisted in the hay, the pale pieces of it entwined among strands of brown coated with gold—my hair. My gut twisted. "The man you used to see—in your village." He cocked his head again as he studied the picture, and a low growl slipped out. "While you made love." He stepped back, looking at the row of pictures. "This is the only one with any brightness."

Was that . . . jealousy? "It was the only escape I had." Truth. I wouldn't apologize for Isaac. Not when Tamlin had just been in the Great Rite. I didn't hold that against him—but if he was going to be jealous of *Isaac*—

Tamlin must have realized it, too, for he loosed a long, controlled breath before moving to the next painting. Tall shadows of men, bright red dripping off their fists, off their wooden clubs, hovering and filling the edges of the painting as they towered over the curled figure on the floor, the blood leaking from him, the leg at a wrong angle.

Tamlin swore. "You were there when they wrecked your father's leg."

"Someone had to beg them to stop."

Tamlin threw a too-knowing glance in my direction and turned to look at the rest of the paintings. There they were, all the wounds I'd slowly been leeching these few months. I blinked. A few months. Did my family believe that I would be forever away with this so-called dying aunt?

At last, Tamlin looked at the painting of the glen and the starlight. He nodded in appreciation. But he pointed to the painting of the snow-veiled woods. "That one. I want that one."

"It's cold and melancholy," I said, hiding my wince. "It doesn't suit this place at all."

He went up to it, and the smile he gave me was more beautiful than any enchanted meadow or pool of stars. "I want it nonetheless," he said softly.

I'd never yearned for anything more than to remove his mask and see the face beneath, to find out whether it matched how I'd dreamed he looked.

"Tell me there's some way to help you," I breathed. "With the masks, with whatever threat has taken so much of your power. Tell me—just tell me what I can do to help you."

"A human wishes to help a faerie?"

"Don't tease me," I said. "Please—just . . . tell me."

"There's nothing I want you to do, nothing you *can* do—or anyone. It's my burden to bear."

"You don't have to—"

"I do. What I have to face, what I endure, Feyre . . . you would not survive."

"So I'm to live here forever, in ignorance of the true scope of what's happening? If you don't want me to understand what's going on . . . would you rather . . ." I swallowed hard. "Rather I found someplace else to live? Where I'm not a distraction?"

"Didn't *Calanmai* teach you anything?"

"Only that magic makes you into a brute."

He laughed, though not entirely with amusement. When I remained silent, he sighed. "No, I don't want you to live somewhere else. I want you here, where I can look after you—where I can come home and know you're here, painting and safe."

I couldn't look away from him. "I thought about sending you away at first," he murmured. "Part of me still thinks I should have found somewhere else for you to live. But maybe I was selfish. Even when you made it so clear that you were more interested in ignoring the Treaty or finding a way out of it, I couldn't bring myself to let you go—to find someplace in Prythian where you'd be comfortable enough to not attempt to flee."

"Why?"

He picked up the small painting of the frozen forest and examined it again. "I've had many lovers," he admitted. "Females of noble birth, warriors, princesses . . ." Rage hit me, low and deep in the gut at the thought of them—rage at their titles, their undoubtedly good looks, at their closeness to him. "But they never understood. What it was like, what it *is* like, for me to care for my people, my lands. What scars are still there, what the bad days feel like." That wrathful jealousy faded away like morning dew as he smiled at my painting. "This reminds me of it."

"Of what?" I breathed.

He lowered the painting, looking right at me, right into me. "That I'm not alone."

I didn't lock my bedroom door that night.

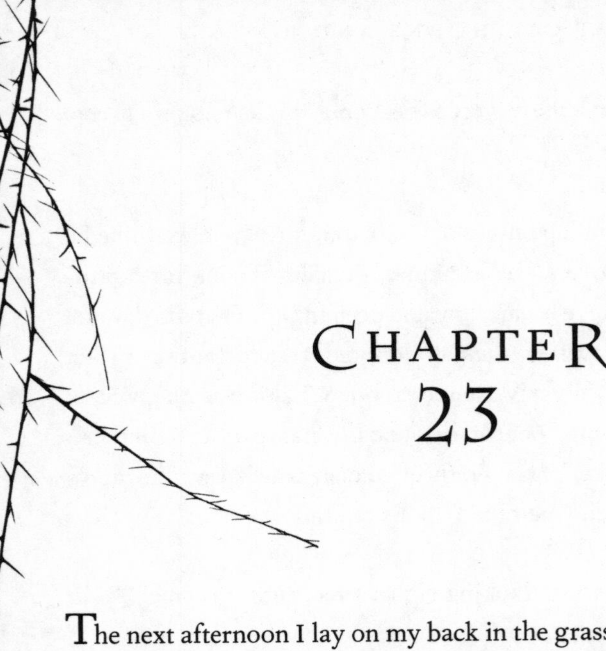

Chapter 23

The next afternoon I lay on my back in the grass, savoring the warmth of the sunshine filtering through the canopy of leaves, noting how I might incorporate it into my next painting. Lucien, claiming that he had miserable emissary business to attend to, had left Tamlin and me to our own devices, and the High Lord had taken me to yet another beautiful spot in his enchanted forest.

But there were no enchantments here—no pools of starlight, no rainbow waterfalls. It was just a grassy glen watched over by a weeping willow, with a clear brook running through it. We lounged in comfortable silence, and I glanced at Tamlin, who dozed beside me. His golden hair and mask glistened bright against the emerald carpet. The delicate arch of his pointed ears made me pause.

He opened an eye and smiled lazily at me. "That willow's singing always puts me to sleep."

"The what of what?" I said, propping myself on my elbows to stare at the tree above us.

Tamlin pointed toward the willow. The branches sighed as they moved in the breeze. "It sings."

"I suppose it sings war-camp limericks, too?"

He smiled and half sat up, twisting to look at me. "You're human," he said, and I rolled my eyes. "Your senses are still sealed off from everything."

I made a face. "Just another of my many shortcomings." But the word—*shortcomings*—had somehow stopped finding its mark.

He plucked a strand of grass from my hair. Heat radiated from my face as his fingers grazed my cheek. "I could make you able to see it," he said. His fingers lingered at the end of my braid, twirling the curl of hair around. "See my world—hear it, smell it." My breathing became shallow as he sat up. "Taste it." His eyes flicked to the fading bruise on my neck.

"How?" I asked, heat blooming as he crouched before me.

"Every gift comes with a price." I frowned, and he grinned. "A kiss."

"Absolutely not!" But my blood raced, and I had to clench my hands in the grass to keep from touching him. "Don't you think it puts me at a disadvantage to not be able to see all this?"

"I'm one of the High Fae—we don't give anything without gaining something from it."

To my own surprise, I said, "Fine."

He blinked, probably expecting me to have fought a little harder. I hid my smile and sat up so that I faced him, our knees touching as we knelt in the grass. I licked my lips, my heart fluttering so quickly it felt as if I had a hummingbird inside my chest.

"Close your eyes," he said, and I obeyed, my fingers grappling onto the grass. The birds chattered, and the willow branches sighed. The grass crunched as Tamlin rose up on his knees. I braced myself at the brush of his mouth on one of my eyelids, then on the other. He pulled away, and I was left breathless, the kisses still lingering on my skin.

The singing of birds became an orchestra—a symphony of gossip and mirth. I'd never heard so many layers of music, never heard the variations and themes that wove between their arpeggios. And beyond the birdsong, there was an ethereal melody—a woman, melancholy and weary . . . the willow. Gasping, I opened my eyes.

The world had become richer, clearer. The brook was a near-invisible rainbow of water that flowed over stones as invitingly smooth as silk. The trees were clothed in a faint shimmer that radiated from their centers and danced along the edges of their leaves. There was no tangy metallic stench—no, the smell of magic had become like jasmine, like lilac, like roses. I would never be able to paint it, the richness, the feel . . . Maybe fractions of it, but not the whole thing.

Magic—*everything* was magic, and it broke my heart.

I looked to Tamlin, and my heart cracked entirely.

It was Tamlin, but not. Rather, it was the Tamlin I'd dreamed of. His skin gleamed with a golden sheen, and around his head glowed a circlet of sunshine. And his eyes—

Not merely green and gold, but every hue and variation that could be imagined, as though every leaf in the forest had bled into one shade. *This* was a High Lord of Prythian—devastatingly handsome, captivating, powerful beyond belief.

My breath caught in my throat as I touched the contours of his mask. The cool metal bit into my fingertips, and the emeralds slipped against my callused skin. I lifted my other hand and gently grasped either side of the mask. I pulled lightly.

It wouldn't move.

He began smiling as I pulled again, and I blinked, dropping my hands. Instantly, the golden, glowing Tamlin vanished, and the one I knew returned. I could still hear the singing of the willow and the birds, but . . .

"Why can't I see you anymore?"

"Because I willed my glamour back into place."

"Glamour for what?"

"To look normal. Or as normal as I can look with this damned thing," he added, gesturing to the mask. "Being a High Lord, even one with . . . limited powers, comes with physical markers, too. It's why I couldn't hide what I was becoming from my brothers—from anyone. It's still easier to blend in."

"But the mask truly can't come off—I mean, are you sure there's no one who knows how to fix what the magic did that night? Even someone in another court?" I don't know why the mask bothered me so greatly. I didn't need to see his entire face to know him.

"I'm sorry to disappoint you."

"I just . . . just want to know what you look like." I wondered when I'd grown so shallow.

"What do you think I look like?"

I tilted my head to the side. "A strong, straight nose," I said, drawing from what I'd once tried to paint. "High cheekbones that bring out your eyes. Slightly . . . slightly arched brows," I finished, blushing. He was grinning so broadly that I could almost see all of his teeth—those fangs nowhere in sight. I tried to think up an excuse for my forwardness, but a yawn crept from me as a sudden weight pressed on my eyes.

"What about your part of the bargain?"

"What?"

He leaned closer, his smile turning wicked. "What about my kiss?"

I grabbed his fingers. "Here," I said, and slammed my mouth against the back of his hand. "There's your kiss."

Tamlin roared with laughter, but the world blurred, lulling me to sleep. The willow beckoned me to lie down, and I obliged. From far off, I heard Tamlin curse. "Feyre?"

Sleep. I wanted sleep. And there was no better place to sleep than right here, listening to the willow and the birds and the brook. I curled on my side, using my arm for a pillow.

"I should bring you home," he murmured, but he didn't move to drag me to my feet. Instead, I felt a slight thud in the earth, and the spring rain and new grass scent of him cloyed in my nose as he lay beside me. I tingled with pleasure as he stroked my hair.

This was such a lovely dream. I'd never slept so wonderfully before. So warm, nestled beside him. Calm. Faintly, echoing into my world of slumber, he spoke again, his breath caressing my ear. "You're exactly as I dreamed you'd be, too." Darkness swallowed everything.

CHAPTER 24

It wasn't the dawn that awoke me, but rather a buzzing noise. I groaned as I sat up in bed and squinted at the squat woman with skin made from tree bark who fussed with my breakfast dishes.

"Where's Alis?" I asked, rubbing the sleep from my eyes. Tamlin must have carried me up here—must have carried me the whole way home.

"What?" She turned toward me. Her bird mask was familiar. But I would have remembered a faerie with skin like that. Would have painted it already.

"Is Alis unwell?" I said, sliding from the bed. This *was* my room, wasn't it? A quick glance told me yes.

"Are you out of your right mind?" the faerie said. I bit my lip. "I *am* Alis," she clucked, and with a shake of her head, she strode into the bathing room to start my bath.

It was impossible. The Alis I knew was fair and plump and looked like a High Fae.

I rubbed my eyes with my thumb and forefinger. A glamour—that's what Tamlin had said he wore. His faerie sight had stripped away the glamours I'd been seeing. But why bother to glamour everything?

Because I'd been a cowering human, that's why. Because Tamlin knew

I would have locked myself in this room and never come out if I'd seen them all for their true selves.

Things only got worse when I made my way downstairs to find the High Lord. The hallways were bustling with masked faeries I'd never seen before. Some were tall and humanoid—High Fae like Tamlin—others were . . . not. Faeries. I tried to avoid looking at those ones, as they seemed the most surprised to notice my attention.

I was almost shaking by the time I reached the dining room. Lucien, mercifully, appeared like Lucien. I didn't ask whether that was because Tamlin had informed him to put up a better glamour or because he didn't bother trying to be something he wasn't.

Tamlin lounged in his usual chair but straightened as I lingered in the doorway. "What's wrong?"

"There are . . . a lot of people—faeries—around. When did they arrive?"

I'd almost yelped when I looked out my bedroom window and spotted all the faeries in the garden. Many of them—all with insect masks—pruned the hedges and tended the flowers. Those faeries had been the strangest of all, with their iridescent, buzzing wings sprouting from their backs. And, of course, then there was the green-and-brown skin, and their unnaturally long limbs, and—

Tamlin bit his lip as if to keep from smiling. "They've been here all along."

"But . . . but I didn't *hear* anything."

"Of course you didn't," Lucien drawled, and twirled one of his daggers between his hands. "We made sure you couldn't see or hear anyone but those who were necessary."

I adjusted the lapels of my tunic. "So you mean that . . . that when I ran after the puca that night—"

"You had an audience," Lucien finished for me. I thought I'd been so stealthy. Meanwhile, I'd been tiptoeing past faeries who had probably laughed their heads off at the blind human following an illusion.

Fighting against my rising mortification, I turned to Tamlin. His lips twitched and he clamped them tightly together, but the amusement still danced in his eyes as he nodded. "It *was* a valiant effort."

"But I *could* see the naga—and the puca, and the Suriel. And—and that faerie whose wings were . . . ripped off," I said, wincing inwardly. "Why didn't the glamour apply to them?"

His eyes darkened. "They're not members of my court," Tamlin said, "so my glamour didn't keep a hold on them. The puca belongs to the wind and weather and everything that changes. And the naga . . . they belong to someone else."

"I see," I lied, not quite seeing at all. Lucien chuckled, sensing it, and I glared sidelong at him. "You've been noticeably absent again."

He used the dagger to clean his nails. "I've been busy. So have you, I take it."

"What's that supposed to mean?" I demanded.

"If I offer you the moon on a string, will you give me a kiss, too?"

"Don't be an ass," Tamlin said to him with a soft snarl, but Lucien continued laughing, and was still laughing when he left the room.

Alone with Tamlin, I shifted on my feet. "So if I were to encounter the Attor again," I said, mostly to avoid the heavy silence, "would I actually see it?"

"Yes, and it wouldn't be pleasant."

"You said it didn't see me that time, and it certainly doesn't seem like a member of your court," I ventured. "Why?"

"Because I threw a glamour over you when we entered the garden," he said simply. "The Attor couldn't see, hear, or smell you." His gaze went to the window beyond me, and he ran a hand through his hair. "I've done all I can to keep you invisible to creatures like the Attor—and worse. The blight is acting up again—and more of these creatures are being freed from their tethers."

My stomach turned over. "If you spot one," Tamlin continued, "even if it looks harmless but makes you feel uncomfortable, pretend you don't see it. Don't talk to it. If it hurts you, I . . . the results wouldn't be pleasant for it, or for me. You remember what happened with the naga."

This was for my own safety, not his amusement. He didn't want me hurt—he didn't want to punish them for hurting *me*. Even if the naga hadn't been part of his court, had it hurt him to kill them?

Realizing he waited for my answer, I nodded. "The . . . the blight is growing again?"

"So far, only in other territories. You're safe here."

"It's not my safety I'm worried about."

Tamlin's eyes softened, but his lips became a thin line as he said, "It'll be fine."

"Is it possible that the surge will be temporary?" A fool's hope.

Tamlin didn't reply, which was answer enough. If the blight was becoming active again . . . I didn't bother to offer my aid. I already knew he wouldn't allow me to help with whatever this conflict was.

But I thought of that painting I'd given him, and what he'd said about it . . . and wished he would let me in anyway.

✣

The next morning, I found a head in the garden.

A bleeding male High Fae head—spiked atop a fountain statue of a great heron flapping its wings. The stone was soaked in enough blood to suggest that the head had been fresh when someone had impaled it on the heron's upraised bill.

I had been hauling my paints and easel out to the garden to paint one of the beds of irises when I stumbled across it. My tins and brushes had clattered to the gravel.

I didn't know where I went as I stared at that still-screaming head, the brown eyes bulging, the teeth broken and bloody. No mask—so he wasn't a part of the Spring Court. Anything else about him, I couldn't discern.

His blood was so bright on the gray stone—his mouth open so vulgarly. I backed away a step—and slammed into something warm and hard.

I whirled, hands rising out of instinct, but Tamlin's voice said, "It's me," and I stopped cold. Lucien stood beside him, pale and grim.

"Not Autumn Court," Lucien said. "I don't recognize him at all."

Tamlin's hands clamped on my shoulders as I turned back toward the head. "Neither do I." A soft, vicious growl laced his words, but no claws pricked my skin as he kept gripping me. His hands tightened, though, while Lucien stepped into the small pool in which the statue stood—striding through the red water until he peered up at the anguished face.

"They branded him behind the ear with a sigil," Lucien said, swearing. "A mountain with three stars—"

"Night Court," Tamlin said too quietly.

The Night Court—the northernmost bit of Prythian, if I recalled the mural's map correctly. A land of darkness and starlight. "Why . . . why would they do this?" I breathed.

Tamlin let go, coming to stand at my side as Lucien climbed the statue to remove the head. I looked toward a blossoming crab apple tree instead.

"The Night Court does what it wants," Tamlin said. "They live by their own codes, their own corrupt morals."

"They're all sadistic killers," Lucien said. I dared a glance at him; he was now perched on the heron's stone wing. I looked away again. "They delight in torture of every kind—and would find this sort of stunt to be amusing."

"Amusing, but not a message?" I scanned the garden.

"Oh, it's a message," Lucien said, and I cringed at the thick, wet sounds of flesh and bone on stone as he yanked the head off. I'd skinned enough animals, but this . . . Tamlin put another hand on my shoulder. "To get in and out of our defenses, to possibly commit the crime nearby, with the blood this fresh . . ." A splash as Lucien landed in the water again. "It's exactly what the High Lord of the Night Court would find amusing. The bastard."

I gauged the distance between the pool and the house. Sixty, maybe seventy feet. That's how close they'd come to us. Tamlin brushed a thumb against my shoulder. "You're still safe here. This was just their idea of a prank."

"This isn't connected to the blight?" I asked.

"Only in that they know the blight is again awakening—and want us to know they're circling the Spring Court like vultures, should our wards fall further." I must have looked as sick as I felt, because Tamlin added, "I won't let that happen."

I didn't have the heart to say that their masks made it fairly clear that nothing could be done against the blight.

Lucien splashed out of the fountain, but I couldn't look at him, not with the head he bore, the blood surely on his hands and clothes. "They'll get what's coming to them soon enough. Hopefully the blight will wreck them, too." Tamlin growled at Lucien to take care of the head, and the gravel crunched as Lucien departed.

I crouched to pick up my paints and brushes, my hands shaking as I fumbled for a large brush. Tamlin knelt next to me, but his hands closed around mine, squeezing.

"You're still safe," he said again. The Suriel's command echoed through my mind. *Stay with the High Lord, human. You will be safe.*

I nodded.

"It's court posturing," he said. "The Night Court is deadly, but this was only their lord's idea of a joke. Attacking anyone here—attacking you—would cause more trouble than it's worth for him. If the blight truly does harm these lands, and the Night Court enters our borders, we'll be ready."

My knees shook as I rose. Faerie politics, faerie courts . . . "Their idea of jokes must have been even more horrible when we were enslaved to you all." They must have tortured us whenever they liked—must have done such unspeakable, awful things to their human pets.

A shadow flickered in his eyes. "Some days, I'm very glad I was still a child when my father sent his slaves south of the wall. What I witnessed then was bad enough."

I didn't want to imagine. Even now, I still hadn't looked to see if any hints of those long-ago humans had been left behind. I did not think five centuries would be enough to cleanse the stain of the horrors that my people had endured. I should have let it go—should have, but couldn't. "Do you remember if they were happy to leave?"

Tamlin shrugged. "Yes. Yet they had never known freedom, or known the seasons as you do. They didn't know what to do in the mortal world. But yes—most of them were very, very happy to leave." Each word was more ground out than the next. "I was happy to see them go, even if my father wasn't." Despite the stillness with which he stood, his claws poked out from above his knuckles.

No wonder he'd been so awkward with me, had no idea what to do with me, when I'd first arrived. But I said quietly, "You're not your father, Tamlin. Or your brothers." He glanced away, and I added, "You never made me feel like a prisoner—never made me feel like little more than chattel."

The shadows that flickered in his eyes as he nodded his thanks told me there was more—still more that he had yet to tell me about his family, his life before they'd been killed and this title had been thrust upon him. I wouldn't ask, not with the blight pressing down on him—not until he was ready. He'd given me space and respect; I could offer him no less.

Still, I couldn't bring myself to paint that day.

CHAPTER 25

Tamlin was called away to one of the borders hours after I found that head—where and why, he wouldn't tell me. But I sensed enough from what he didn't say: the blight was indeed crawling from other courts, directly toward ours.

He stayed the night—the first he'd ever spent away—but sent Lucien to inform me that he was alive. Lucien had emphasized that last word enough that I slept terribly, even as a small part of me marveled that Tamlin had bothered to let me know about his well-being. I knew—I knew I was headed down a path that would likely end in my mortal heart being left in pieces, and yet . . . And yet I couldn't stop myself. I hadn't been able to since that day with the naga. But seeing that head . . . the games these courts played, with people's lives as tokens on a board . . . it was an effort to keep food down whenever I thought about it.

Yet despite the creeping malice, I awoke the next day to the sound of merry fiddling, and when I looked out the window I found the garden bedecked in ribbons and streamers. On the distant hills, I spied the makings of fires and maypoles being raised. When I asked Alis—whose people, I'd learned, were called the *urisk*—she simply said, "Summer Solstice. The main celebration used to be at the Summer Court, but . . . things are different. So now we have one here, too. You're going."

Summer—in the weeks that I'd been painting and dining with Tamlin and wandering the court lands at his side, summer had come. Did my family still truly believe me to be visiting some long-lost aunt? What were they doing with themselves? If it was the solstice, then there would be a small gathering in the village center—nothing religious, of course, though the Children of the Blessed might wander in to try to convert the young people; just some shared food, donated ale from the solitary tavern, and maybe some line dances. The only thing to celebrate was a day's break from the long summer days of planting and tilling. From the decorations around the estate, I could tell this would be something far grander—far more spirited.

Tamlin remained gone for most of the day. Worry gnawed at me even as I painted a quick, loose rendering of the streamers and ribbons in the garden. Perhaps it was petty and selfish, given the returning blight, but I also quietly hoped that the solstice didn't require the same rites as Fire Night. I didn't let myself think too much about what I would do if Tamlin had a flock of beautiful faeries lining up for him.

It wasn't until late afternoon that I heard Tamlin's deep voice and Lucien's braying laugh echo through the halls all the way to my painting room. Relief sent my chest caving in, but as I rushed to find them, Alis yanked me upstairs. She stripped off my paint-splattered clothes and insisted I change into a flowing, cornflower-blue chiffon gown. She left my hair unbound but wove a garland of pink, white, and blue wildflowers around the crown of my head.

I might have felt childish with it on, but in the months I'd been there, my sharp bones and skeletal form had filled out. A woman's body. I ran my hands over the sweeping, soft curves of my waist and hips. I had never thought I would feel anything but muscle and bone.

"Cauldron boil me," Lucien whistled as I came down the stairs. "She looks positively Fae."

I was too busy looking Tamlin over—scanning for any injury, any sign of blood or mark that the blight might have left—to thank Lucien for the compliment. But Tamlin was clean, almost glowing, completely unarmed—and smiling at me. Whatever he'd gone to deal with had left him unscathed. "You look lovely," Tamlin murmured, and something in his soft tone made me want to purr.

I squared my shoulders, disinclined to let him see how much his words or voice or sheer well-being impacted me. Not yet. "I'm surprised I'm even allowed to participate tonight."

"Unfortunately for you and your neck," Lucien countered, "tonight's just a party."

"Do you lie awake at night to come up with all your witty replies for the following day?"

Lucien winked at me, and Tamlin laughed and offered me his arm. "He's right," the High Lord said. I was aware of every inch where we touched, of the hard muscles beneath his green tunic. He led me into the garden, and Lucien followed. "Solstice celebrates when the sun outshines the night. As the longest day of the year, it's a time when everyone can take down their hair and simply enjoy being a faerie—not High Fae or faerie, just *us*, and nothing else."

"So there's singing and dancing and excessive drinking," Lucien chimed in, falling into step beside me. "And dallying," he added with a wicked grin.

Indeed, every brush of Tamlin's body against mine made it harder to avoid the urge to lean into him entirely, to smell him and touch him and taste him. Whether he noticed the heat singeing my neck and face, or heard my uneven heartbeat, he revealed nothing, holding my arm tighter as we walked out of the garden and into the fields beyond.

The sun was beginning its final descent when we reached the plateau on which the festivities were to be held. I tried not to gawk at the faeries gathered, even as I was in turn gawked at by them. I'd never seen so many in one place before, at least not without the glamour hiding them from me. Now that my eyes were open to the sight, the exquisite dresses and lithe forms that were shaped and colored and built so strangely and differently were a marvel to behold. Yet what little novelty my own presence by the High Lord's side offered soon wore off—helped by a low, warning growl from Tamlin that sent the others scattering to mind their own business.

Table after table of food had been lined up along the far edge of the plateau, and I lost Tamlin while I waited in line to fill a plate, leaving me to try my best not to look like I was some human plaything of his. Music started near the giant, smoking bonfire—fiddles and drums and merry instruments that had me tapping my feet in the grass. Light and joyous and open, the mirthful sister to the bloodthirsty Fire Night.

Lucien, of course, excelled at disappearing when I needed him, and so I ate my fill of strawberry shortcake, apple tart, and blueberry pie—no different from summer treats in the mortal realm—alone beneath a sycamore covered with silken lanterns and sparkling ribbons.

I didn't mind the solitude—not when I was busy contemplating the way the lanterns and ribbons shone, the shadows they cast; perhaps it would be my next painting. Or maybe I would paint the ethereal faeries beginning to dance. Such angles and colors to them. I wondered if any of them had been the subjects of the painters whose work was displayed in the gallery.

I moved only to get myself something to drink. The plateau became more crowded as the sun sank toward the horizon. Across the hills, other bonfires and parties began, their music filtering through the occasional pause in ours. I was pouring myself a goblet of golden sparkling wine when Lucien finally appeared behind me, peering over my shoulder. "I wouldn't drink that if I were you."

"Oh?" I said, frowning at the fizzing liquid.

"Faerie wine at the solstice," Lucien hinted.

"Hmm," I said, taking a sniff. It didn't reek of alcohol. In fact, it smelled like summers spent lying in the grass and bathing in cool pools. I'd never smelled anything so fantastic.

"I'm serious," Lucien said as I lifted the glass to my lips, my brows raised. "Remember the last time you ignored my warning?" He poked me in the neck, and I batted his hand away.

"I also remember you telling me how witchberries were harmless, and the next thing I knew, I was half-delirious and falling all over myself," I said, recalling the afternoon from a few weeks ago. I'd had hallucinations for hours afterward, and Lucien had laughed himself sick—enough so that Tamlin had chucked him into the reflection pool. I shook away the thought. Today—just for today—I would indeed let my hair down. Today, let caution be damned. Forget the blight hovering at the edges of the court, threatening my High Lord and his lands. Where *was* Tamlin, anyway? If there had been some threat, surely Lucien would have known—surely they would have called off the celebration.

"Well, I mean it this time," Lucien said, and I shifted my goblet out of his reach. "Tam would gut me if he caught you drinking that."

"Always looking after your best interests," I said, and pointedly chugged the contents of the glass.

It was like a million fireworks exploding inside me, filling my veins with starlight. I laughed aloud, and Lucien groaned.

"Human fool," he hissed. But his glamour had been ripped away. His auburn hair burned like hot metal, and his russet eye smoldered like a bottomless forge. *That* was what I would capture next.

"I'm going to paint you," I said, and giggled—actually *giggled*—as the words popped out.

"Cauldron boil and fry me," he muttered, and I laughed again. Before he could stop me, I'd downed another glass of faerie wine. It was the most glorious thing I'd ever tasted. It liberated me from bonds I hadn't known existed.

The music became a siren song. The melody was my lodestone, and

I was powerless against its lure. With each step, I savored the dampness of the grass beneath my bare feet. I didn't remember when I'd lost my shoes.

The sky was an eddy of molten amethyst, sapphire, and ruby, all bleeding into a final pool of onyx. I wanted to swim in it, wanted to bathe in its colors and feel the stars twinkling between my fingers.

I stumbled, blinking, and found myself standing at the edge of the ring of dancing. A cluster of musicians played their faerie instruments, and I swayed on my feet as I watched the faeries dancing, circling the bonfire. Not formal dancing. It was like they were as loose as I was. Free. I loved them for it.

"Damn it, Feyre," Lucien said, gripping my elbow. "Do you want me to kill myself trying to keep you from impaling your mortal hide on another rock?"

"What?" I said, turning to him. The whole world spun with me, delightful and entrancing.

"Idiot," he said when he looked at my face. "Drunken idiot."

The tempo increased. I wanted to be in the music, wanted to ride its speed and weave between its notes. I could *feel* the music around me, like a living, breathing thing of wonder and joy and beauty.

"Feyre, stop," Lucien said, and grabbed me again. I'd been dancing away, and my body was still swaying toward the pull of the sound.

"*You* stop. Stop being so serious," I said, shaking him off. I wanted to hear the music, wanted to hear it hot off the instruments. Lucien swore as I burst into movement.

I skipped between the dancers, twirling my skirts. The seated, masked musicians didn't look up at me as I leaped before them, dancing in place. No chains, no boundaries—just me and the music, dancing and dancing. I wasn't faerie, but I was a part of this earth, and the earth was a part of me, and I would be content to dance upon it for the rest of my life.

One of the musicians looked up from his fiddling, and I halted.

Sweat gleamed on the strong column of his neck as he rested his chin upon the dark wood of the fiddle. He'd rolled up the sleeves of his shirt, revealing the cords of muscle along his forearms. He had once mentioned that he would have liked to be a traveling minstrel if not a warrior or a High Lord—now, hearing him play, I knew he could have made a fortune from it.

"I'm sorry, Tam," Lucien panted, appearing from nowhere. "I left her alone for a little at one of the food tables, and when I caught up to her, she was drinking the wine, and—"

Tamlin didn't pause in his playing. His golden hair damp with sweat, he looked marvelously handsome—even though I couldn't see most of his face. He gave me a feral smile as I began to dance in place before him. "I'll look after her," Tamlin murmured above the music, and I glowed, my dancing becoming faster. "Go enjoy yourself." Lucien fled.

I shouted over the music, "I don't need a keeper!" I wanted to spin and spin and spin.

"No, you don't," Tamlin said, never once stumbling over his playing. How his bow did dance upon the strings, his fingers sturdy and strong, no signs of those claws that I had come to stop fearing . . . "Dance, Feyre," he whispered.

So I did.

I was loosened, a top whirling around and around, and I didn't know who I danced with or what they looked like, only that I had become the music and the fire and the night, and there was nothing that could slow me down.

Through it all, Tamlin and his musicians played such joyous music that I didn't think the world could contain it all. I sashayed over to him, my faerie lord, my protector and warrior, my friend, and danced before him. He grinned at me, and I didn't break my dancing as he rose from his seat and knelt before me in the grass, offering up a solo on his fiddle to me.

Music just for me—a gift. He played on, his fingers fast and hard upon the strings of his fiddle. My body slithering like a snake, I tipped my head back to the heavens and let Tamlin's music fill all of me.

There was a pressure at my waist, and I was swept away in someone's arms as they whisked me back into the ring of dancing. I laughed so hard I thought I'd combust, and when I opened my eyes, I found Tamlin there, spinning me round and round.

Everything became a blur of color and sound, and he was the only object in it, tethering me to sanity, to my body, which glowed and burned in every place he touched.

I was filled with sunshine. It was like I'd never experienced summer before, like I'd never known who was waiting to emerge from that forest of ice and snow. I didn't want it to end—I never wanted to leave this hilltop.

The music came to a close, and, gasping for breath, I glanced at the moon—it was near setting. Sweat slid down every part of my body.

Tamlin, panting as well, took my hand. "Time goes faster when you're drunk on faerie wine."

"I'm not drunk," I said, snorting. He only chuckled and led me from the dancing. I dug my heels into the ground as we neared the edge of the firelight. "They're starting again," I said, pointing to the dancers gathering before the refreshed musicians.

He leaned close, his breath caressing the shell of my ear as he whispered, "I want to show you something better."

I stopped objecting.

He led me off the hill, navigating his way by moonlight. Whatever path he chose, he did so out of consideration for my bare feet, for only soft grass cushioned my steps. Soon, even the music faded away, replaced by the sighing of trees in the night breeze.

"Here," Tamlin said, pausing at the edge of a vast meadow. His hand lingered on my shoulder as we looked out.

The high grasses moved like water as the last of the moonlight danced upon them.

"What is it?" I breathed, but he put a finger to his lips and beckoned me to look.

For a few minutes, there was nothing. Then, from the opposite side of the meadow, dozens of shimmering shapes floated out across the grass, little more than mirages of moonlight. That was when the singing began.

It was a collective voice, but in it existed both male and female—two sides of the same coin, singing to each other in a call and response. I raised a hand to my throat as their music rose and they danced. Ghostly and ethereal, they waltzed across the field, no more than slender slants of moonlight.

"What are they?"

"Will-o'-the-wisps—spirits of air and light," he said softly. "Come to celebrate the solstice."

"They're beautiful."

His lips grazed my neck as he murmured against my skin, "Dance with me, Feyre."

"Really?" I turned and found my face mere inches from his.

He cracked a lazy smile. "Really." As though I were nothing but air myself, he pulled me into a sweeping dance. I barely remembered any of the steps I'd learned in childhood, but he compensated for it with his feral grace, never faltering, always sensing any stumble before I made it as we danced across the spirit-riddled field.

I was as unburdened as a piece of dandelion fluff, and he was the wind that stirred me about the world.

He smiled at me, and I found myself smiling back. I didn't need to pretend, didn't need to be anything but what I was right then, being twirled about the meadow, the will-o'-the-wisps dancing around us like dozens of moons.

Our dancing slowed and we stood there, holding each other as we swayed to the songs of the spirits. He rested his chin upon my head and stroked my hair, his fingers grazing the bare skin of my neck.

"Feyre," he whispered onto my head. He made my name sound beautiful. "Feyre," he whispered again—not in question, but simply as if he enjoyed saying it.

As quickly as they'd appeared, the spirits vanished, taking their music with them. I blinked. The stars were fading, and the sky had turned grayish purple.

Tamlin's face was inches from my own. "It's almost dawn."

I nodded, mesmerized by the sight of him, the smell and feel of him holding me. I reached up to touch his mask. It was so cold, despite how flushed his skin was just beyond it. My hand shook, and my breathing became shallow as I grazed the skin of his jaw. It was smooth—and hot.

He wet his lips, his breathing as uneven as my own. His fingers contracted against the plane of my lower back, and I let him tug me closer to him—until our bodies were touching, and the warmth of him seeped into me.

I had to tilt my head back to see his face. His mouth was caught somewhere between a smile and a wince.

"What?" I asked, and put a hand on his chest, preparing to shove myself back. But his other hand slipped under my hair, resting at the base of my neck.

"I'm thinking I might kiss you," he said quietly, intently.

"Then do it." I blushed at my own boldness.

But Tamlin only gave that breathy laugh, and leaned in.

His lips brushed mine—testing, soft and warm. He pulled back a little. He was still staring at me, and I stared right back as he kissed me again, harder, but nothing like the way he'd kissed my neck. He withdrew more fully this time and watched me.

"That's it?" I demanded, and he laughed and kissed me fiercely.

My hands went around his neck, pulling him closer, crushing myself against him. His hands roved my back, playing in my hair, grasping my waist, as if he couldn't touch enough of me at once.

He let out a low groan. "Come," he said, kissing my brow. "We'll miss it if we don't go now."

"Better than will-o'-the-wisps?" I asked, but he kissed my cheeks, my neck, and finally my lips. I followed him into the trees, through the ever-lightening world. His hand was solid and unmovable around mine as we passed through the low-lying mists, and he helped me up a bare hill slick with dew.

We sat atop its crest, and I hid my smile as Tamlin put an arm around my shoulders, tucking me in close. I rested my head against his chest while he toyed with the flowers in my garland.

In silence, we stared out over the rolling green expanse.

The sky shifted into periwinkle, and the clouds filled with pink light. Then, like a shimmering disk too rich and clear to be described, the sun slipped over the horizon and lined everything with gold. It was like seeing the world being born, and we were the sole witnesses.

Tamlin's arm tightened around me, and he kissed the top of my head. I pulled back, looking up at him.

The gold in his eyes, bright with the rising sun, flickered. "What?"

"My father once told me that I should let my sisters imagine a better life—a better world. And I told him that there was no such thing." I ran my thumb over his mouth, marveling, and shook my head. "I never understood—because I couldn't . . . couldn't believe that it was even possible." I swallowed, lowering my hand. "Until now."

His throat bobbed. His kiss that time was deep and thorough, unhurried and intent.

I let the dawn creep inside me, let it grow with each movement of his lips and brush of his tongue against mine. Tears pricked beneath my closed eyes.

It was the happiest moment of my life.

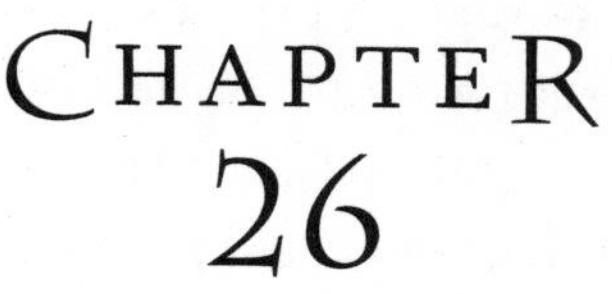

CHAPTER 26

The next day, Lucien joined us for lunch—which was breakfast for all of us. Ever since I'd complained about the unnecessary size of the table, we'd taken to dining at a much-reduced version. Lucien kept rubbing at his temples as he ate, unusually silent, and I hid my smile as I asked him, "And where were you last night?"

Lucien's metal eye narrowed on me. "I'll have you know that while you two were dancing with the spirits, I was stuck on border patrol." Tamlin gave a pointed cough, and Lucien added, "With some company." He gave me a sly grin. "Rumor has it you two didn't come back until after dawn."

I glanced at Tamlin, biting my lip. I'd practically floated into my bedroom that morning. But Tamlin's gaze now roved my face as if searching for any tinge of regret, of fear. Ridiculous.

"You bit my neck on Fire Night," I said under my breath. "If I can face you after that, a few kisses are nothing."

He braced his forearms on the table as he leaned closer to me. "Nothing?" His eyes flicked to my lips. Lucien shifted in his seat, muttering to the Cauldron to spare him, but I ignored him.

"Nothing," I repeated a bit distantly, watching Tamlin's mouth move, so keenly aware of every movement he made, resenting the table between us. I could almost feel the warmth of his breath.

"Are you sure?" he murmured, intent and hungry enough that I was glad I was sitting. He could have had me right there, on top of that table. I wanted his broad hands running over my bare skin, wanted his teeth scraping against my neck, wanted his mouth all over me.

"I'm trying to eat," Lucien said, and I blinked, the air whooshing out of me. "But now that I have your attention, *Tamlin*," he snapped, though the High Lord was looking at me again—devouring me with his eyes. I could hardly sit still, could hardly stand the clothes scratching my too-hot skin. With some effort, Tamlin glanced back at his emissary.

Lucien shifted in his seat. "Not to be the bearer of truly bad tidings, but my contact at the Winter Court managed to get a letter to me." Lucien took a steadying breath, and I wondered—wondered if being emissary also meant being spymaster. And wondered why he was bothering to say this in my presence at all. The smile instantly faded from Tamlin's face. "The blight," Lucien said tightly, softly. "It took out two dozen of their younglings. *Two dozen*, all gone." He swallowed. "It just . . . burned through their magic, then broke apart their minds. No one in the Winter Court could do anything—no one could stop it once it turned its attention toward them. Their grief is . . . unfathomable. My contact says other courts are being hit hard—though the Night Court, of course, manages to remain unscathed. But the blight seems to be sending its wickedness this way—farther south with every attack."

All the warmth, all the sparkling joy, drained from me like blood down a drain. "The blight can . . . can truly kill people?" I managed to say. Younglings. It had killed children, like some storm of darkness and death. And if offspring were as rare as Alis had claimed, the loss of so many would be more devastating than I could imagine.

Tamlin's eyes were shadowed, and he slowly shook his head—as if trying to clear the grief and shock of those deaths from him. "The blight is capable of hurting us in ways you—" He shot to his feet so quickly that his chair flipped over. He unsheathed his claws and snarled at the open doorway, canines long and gleaming.

The house, usually full of the whispering skirts and chatter of servants, had gone silent.

Not the pregnant silence of Fire Night, but rather a trembling quiet that made me want to scramble under the table. Or just start running. Lucien swore and drew his sword.

"Get Feyre to the window—by the curtains," Tamlin growled to Lucien, not taking his eyes off the open doors. Lucien's hand gripped my elbow, dragging me out of my chair.

"What's—" I started, but Tamlin growled again, the sound echoing through the room. I snatched one of the knives off the table and let Lucien lead me to the window, where he pushed me against the velvet drapes. I wanted to ask why he didn't bother hiding me behind them, but the fox-masked faerie just pressed his back into me, pinning me between him and the wall.

The tang of magic shoved itself up my nostrils. Though his sword was pointed at the floor, Lucien's grip tightened on it until his knuckles turned white. Magic—a glamour. To conceal me, to make me a part of Lucien—invisible, hidden by the faerie's magic and scent. I peered over his shoulder at Tamlin, who took a long breath and sheathed his claws and fangs, his baldric of knives appearing from thin air across his chest. But he didn't draw any of the knives as he righted his chair and slouched in it, picking at his nails. As if nothing were happening.

But someone was coming, someone awful enough to frighten them—someone who would want to hurt me if they knew I was here.

The hissing voice of the Attor slithered through my memory. There were worse creatures than it, Tamlin had told me. Worse than the naga, and the Suriel, and the Bogge, too.

Footsteps sounded from the hall. Even, strolling, casual.

Tamlin continued cleaning his nails, and in front of me, Lucien assumed a position of appearing to be looking out the window. The footsteps grew louder—the scuff of boots on marble tiles.

And then he appeared.

No mask. He, like the Attor, belonged to something else. Some*one* else.

And worse . . . I'd met him before. He'd saved me from those three faeries on Fire Night.

With steps that were too graceful, too feline, he approached the dining table and stopped a few yards from the High Lord. He was exactly as I remembered him, with his fine, rich clothing cloaked in tendrils of night: an ebony tunic brocaded with gold and silver, dark pants, and black boots that went to his knees. I'd never dared to paint him—and now knew I would never have the nerve to.

"High Lord," the stranger crooned, inclining his head slightly. Not a bow.

Tamlin remained seated. With his back to me, I couldn't see his face, but Tamlin's voice was laced with the promise of violence as he said, "What do you want, Rhysand?"

Rhysand smiled—heartbreaking in its beauty—and put a hand on his chest. "Rhysand? Come now, Tamlin. I don't see you for forty-nine years, and you start calling me Rhysand? Only my prisoners and my enemies call me that." His grin widened as he finished, and something in his countenance turned feral and deadly, more so than I'd ever seen Tamlin look. Rhysand turned, and I held my breath as he ran an eye over Lucien. "A fox mask. Appropriate for you, Lucien."

"Go to Hell, Rhys," Lucien snapped.

"Always a pleasure dealing with the rabble," Rhysand said, and faced Tamlin again. I still didn't breathe. "I hope I wasn't interrupting."

"We were in the middle of lunch," Tamlin said—his voice void of the warmth to which I'd become accustomed. The voice of the High Lord. It turned my insides cold.

"Stimulating," Rhysand purred.

"What are you doing here, Rhys?" Tamlin demanded, still in his seat.

"I wanted to check up on you. I wanted to see how you were faring. If you got my little present."

"Your *present* was unnecessary."

"But a nice reminder of the fun days, wasn't it?" Rhysand clicked his tongue and surveyed the room. "Almost half a century holed up in a country estate. I don't know how you managed it. But," he said, facing Tamlin again, "you're such a stubborn bastard that this must have seemed like a paradise compared to Under the Mountain. I suppose it is. I'm surprised, though: forty-nine years, and no attempts to save yourself or your lands. Even now that things are getting interesting again."

"There's nothing to be done," conceded Tamlin, his voice low.

Rhysand approached Tamlin, each movement smooth as silk. His voice dropped into a whisper—an erotic caress of sound that brought heat to my cheeks. "What a pity that you must endure the brunt of it, Tamlin—and an even greater pity that you're so resigned to your fate. You might be stubborn, but this is pathetic. How different the High Lord is from the brutal war-band leader of centuries ago."

Lucien interrupted, "What do you know about anything? You're just Amarantha's whore."

"Her whore I might be, but not without my reasons." I flinched as his voice whetted itself into an edge. "At least I haven't bided my time among the hedges and flowers while the world has gone to Hell."

Lucien's sword rose slightly. "If you think that's all I've been doing, you'll soon learn otherwise."

"Little Lucien. You certainly gave them something to talk about when you switched to Spring. Such a sad thing, to see your lovely mother in perpetual mourning over losing you."

Lucien pointed his sword at Rhysand. "Watch your filthy mouth."

Rhysand laughed—a lover's laugh, low and soft and intimate. "Is that any way to speak to a High Lord of Prythian?"

My heart stopped dead. That was why those faeries had run off on Fire Night. To cross him would have been suicide. And from the way darkness seemed to ripple from him, from those violet eyes that burned like stars . . .

"Come now, Tamlin," Rhysand said. "Shouldn't you reprimand your lackey for speaking to me like that?"

"I don't enforce rank in my court," Tamlin said.

"Still?" Rhysand crossed his arms. "But it's so entertaining when they grovel. I suppose your father never bothered to show you."

"This isn't the Night Court," Lucien hissed. "And you have no power here—so clear out. Amarantha's bed is growing cold."

I tried not to breathe too loudly. Rhysand—*he'd* been the one to send that head. As a *gift*. I flinched. Was the Night Court where this woman—this Amarantha—was located, too?

Rhysand snickered, but then he was upon Lucien, too fast for me to follow with my human eyes, growling in his face. Lucien pressed me into the wall with his back, hard enough that I stifled a cry as I was squished against the wood.

"I was slaughtering on the battlefield before you were even born," Rhysand snarled. Then, as quickly as he had come, he withdrew, casual and careless. No, I would never dare to paint that dark, immortal grace—not in a hundred years. "Besides," he said, stuffing his hands into his pockets, "who do you think taught your beloved Tamlin the finer aspects of swords and females? You can't truly believe he learned everything in his father's little war-camps."

Tamlin rubbed his temples. "Save it for another time, Rhys. You'll see me soon enough."

Rhysand meandered toward the door. "She's already preparing for you. Given your current state, I think I can safely report that you've already been broken and will reconsider her offer." Lucien's breath hitched as Rhysand passed the table. The High Lord of the Night Court ran a finger along the back of my chair—a casual gesture. "I'm looking forward to seeing your face when you—"

Rhysand studied the table.

Lucien went stick-straight, pressing me harder against the wall. The table was still set for three, my half-eaten plate of food sitting right before him.

"Where's your guest?" Rhysand asked, lifting my goblet and sniffing it before setting it down again.

"I sent them off when I sensed your arrival," Tamlin lied coolly.

Rhysand now faced the High Lord, and his perfect face was void of emotion before his brows rose. A flicker of excitement—perhaps even disbelief—flashed across his features, but he whipped his head to Lucien. Magic seared my nostrils, and I stared at Rhysand in undiluted terror as his face contorted with rage.

"You *dare* glamour *me*?" he growled, his violet eyes burning as they bore into my own. Lucien just pressed me harder into the wall.

Tamlin's chair groaned as it was shoved back. He rose, claws at the ready, deadlier than any of the knives strapped to him.

Rhysand's face became a mask of calm fury as he stared and stared at me. "I remember you," he purred. "It seems like you ignored my warning to stay out of trouble." He turned to Tamlin. "Who, pray tell, is your guest?"

"My betrothed," Lucien answered.

"Oh? Here I was, thinking you still mourned your commoner lover after all these centuries," Rhysand said, stalking toward me. The sunlight didn't gleam on the metallic threads of his tunic, as if it balked from the darkness pulsing from him.

Lucien spat at Rhysand's feet and shoved his sword between us.

Rhysand's venom-coated smile grew. "You draw blood from me, Lucien, and you'll learn how quickly Amarantha's whore can make the entire Autumn Court bleed. Especially its darling Lady."

The color leeched from Lucien's face, but he held his ground. It was Tamlin who answered. "Put your sword down, Lucien."

Rhysand ran an eye over me. "I knew you liked to stoop low with your lovers, Lucien, but I never thought you'd actually dabble with mortal trash." My face burned. Lucien was trembling—with rage or fear or sorrow, I couldn't tell. "The Lady of the Autumn Court will be grieved indeed when she hears of her youngest son. If I were you, I'd keep your new pet well away from your father."

"Leave, Rhys," Tamlin commanded, standing a few feet behind the High Lord of the Night Court. And yet he didn't make a move to attack, despite the claws, despite Rhysand still approaching me. Perhaps a battle between two High Lords could tear this manor to its foundations—and leave only dust in its wake. Or perhaps, if Rhysand was indeed this woman's lover, the retaliation from hurting him would be too great. Especially with the added burden of facing the blight.

Rhysand brushed Lucien aside as if he were a curtain.

There was nothing between us now, and the air was sharp and cold. But Tamlin remained where he was, and Lucien didn't so much as blink as Rhysand, with horrific gentleness, pried the knife from my hands and sent it scattering across the room.

"That won't do you any good, anyway," Rhysand said to me. "If you were wise, you would be screaming and running from this place, from these people. It's a wonder that you're still here, actually." My confusion must have been written across my face, for Rhysand laughed loudly. "Oh, she doesn't know, does she?"

I trembled, unable to find words or courage.

"You have seconds, Rhys," Tamlin warned. "Seconds to get out."

"If I were you, I wouldn't speak to me like that."

Against my volition, my body straightened, every muscle going taut, my bones straining. Magic, but deeper than that. Power that seized everything inside me and took control: even my blood flowed where he willed it.

I couldn't move. An invisible, talon-tipped hand scraped against my mind. And I knew—one push, one swipe of those mental claws, and who I was would cease to exist.

"Let her go," Tamlin said, bristling, but didn't advance forward. A kind of panic had entered his eyes, and he glanced from me to Rhysand. *"Enough."*

"I'd forgotten that human minds are as easy to shatter as eggshells," Rhysand said, and ran a finger across the base of my throat. I shuddered, my eyes burning. "Look at how delightful she is—look how she's trying not to cry out in terror. It would be quick, I promise."

Had I retained any semblance of control over my body, I might have vomited.

"She has the most delicious thoughts about you, Tamlin," he said. "She's wondered about the feeling of your fingers on her thighs—between them, too." He chuckled. Even as he said my most private thoughts, even as I burned with outrage and shame, I trembled at the grip still on my mind. Rhysand turned to the High Lord. "I'm curious: Why did she wonder if it would feel good to have you bite her breast the way you bit her neck?"

"Let. Her. Go." Tamlin's face was twisted with such feral rage that it struck a different, deeper chord of terror in me.

"If it's any consolation," Rhysand confided to him, "she would have been the one for you—and you might have gotten away with it. A bit late, though. She's more stubborn than you are."

Those invisible claws lazily caressed my mind again—then vanished. I sank to the floor, curling over my knees as I reeled in everything that I was, as I tried to keep from sobbing, from screaming, from emptying my stomach onto the floor.

"Amarantha will enjoy breaking her," Rhysand observed to Tamlin. "Almost as much as she'll enjoy watching *you* as she shatters her bit by bit."

Tamlin was frozen, his arms—his claws—hanging limply at his side. I'd never seen him look like that. "Please" was all that Tamlin said.

"Please *what?*" Rhysand said—gently, coaxingly. Like a lover.

"Don't tell Amarantha about her," Tamlin said, his voice strained.

"And why not? As her *whore*," he said with a glance tossed in Lucien's direction, "I should tell her everything."

"Please," Tamlin managed, as if it were difficult to breathe.

Rhysand pointed at the ground, and his smile became vicious. "Beg, and I'll consider not telling Amarantha."

Tamlin dropped to his knees and bowed his head.

"Lower."

Tamlin pressed his forehead to the floor, his hands sliding along the floor toward Rhysand's boots. I could have wept with rage at the sight of Tamlin being forced to bow to someone, at the sight of my High Lord being put so low. Rhysand pointed at Lucien. "You too, fox-boy."

Lucien's face was dark, but he lowered himself to his knees, then touched his head to the ground. I wished for the knife Rhysand had chucked away, for anything with which to kill him.

I stopped shaking long enough to hear Rhys speak again. "Are you doing this for your sake, or for hers?" he pondered, then shrugged, as if he weren't forcing a High Lord of Prythian to grovel. "You're far too desperate, Tamlin. It's off-putting. Becoming High Lord made you so boring."

"Are you going to tell Amarantha?" Tamlin said, keeping his face on the floor.

Rhysand smirked. "Perhaps I'll tell her, perhaps I won't."

In a flash of motion too fast for me to detect, Tamlin was on his feet, fangs dangerously close to Rhysand's face.

"None of that," Rhysand said, clicking his tongue and lightly shoving Tamlin away with a single hand. "Not with a lady present." His eyes shifted to my face. "What's your name, love?"

Giving him my name—and my family name—would lead only to more pain and suffering. He might very well find my family and drag them into Prythian to torment, just to amuse himself. But he could steal my name from my mind if I hesitated for too long. Keeping my mind blank and calm, I blurted the first name that came to mind, a village friend of my sisters' whom I'd never spoken to and whose face I couldn't recall. "Clare Beddor." My voice was nothing more than a gasp.

Rhysand turned back to Tamlin, unfazed by the High Lord's proximity. "Well, this was entertaining. The most fun I've had in ages, actually. I'm looking forward to seeing you three Under the Mountain. I'll give Amarantha your regards."

Then Rhysand vanished into nothing—as if he'd stepped through a rip in the world—leaving us alone in horrible, trembling silence.

CHAPTER 27

I lay in bed, watching the pools of moonlight shift on the floor. It was an effort not to dwell on Tamlin's face as he ordered me and Lucien to leave and shut the door to the dining room. Had I not been so bent on piecing myself together, I might have stayed. Might have even asked Lucien about it—about everything. But, like the coward I was, I bolted to my room, where Alis was waiting with a cup of molten chocolate. It was even more of an effort not to recall the roaring that rattled the chandelier or the cracking of shattering furniture that echoed through the house.

I didn't go to dinner. I didn't want to know if there was a dining room to eat in. And I couldn't bring myself to paint.

The house had been quiet for some time now, but the ripples of Tamlin's rage echoed through it, reverberating in the wood and stone and glass.

I didn't want to think about all that Rhysand had said—didn't want to think about the looming storm of the blight, or Under the Mountain—whatever it was called—and why I might be forced to go there. And Amarantha—at last a name to go with the female presence that stalked their lives. I shuddered each time I considered how deadly she must be to command the High Lords of Prythian. To hold Rhysand's leash and to make Tamlin beg to keep me hidden from her.

The door creaked, and I jerked upright. Moonlight glimmered on gold, but my heart didn't ease as Tamlin shut the door and approached my bed. His steps were slow and heavy—and he didn't speak until he'd taken a seat on the edge of the mattress.

"I'm sorry," he said. His voice was hoarse and empty.

"It's fine," I lied, clenching the sheets in my hands. If I thought too long about it, I could still feel the claw-tipped caresses of Rhysand's power scraping against my mind.

"It's not fine," he growled, and grabbed one of my hands, wrenching my fingers from the sheets. "It's . . ." He hung his head, sighing deeply as his hand tightened on mine. "Feyre . . . I wish . . ." He shook his head and cleared his throat. "I'm sending you home, Feyre."

Something inside me splintered. "What?"

"I'm sending you home," he repeated, and though his words were stronger—louder—they trembled a bit.

"What about the terms of the Treaty—"

"I have taken on your life-debt. Should someone come inquiring after the broken laws, I'll take responsibility for Andras's death."

"But you once said that there was no other loophole. The Suriel said there was no—"

A snarl. "If they have a problem with it, they can tell me." And wind up in ribbons.

My chest caved in. Leaving—*free*. "Did I do something wrong—"

He lifted my hand to press it to his lower cheek. He was so invitingly warm. "You did nothing wrong." He turned his face to kiss my palm. "You were perfect," he murmured onto my skin, then lowered my hand.

"Then why do I have to go?" I yanked my hand away.

"Because there are . . . there are people who would hurt you, Feyre. Hurt you because of what you are to me. I thought I would be able to handle them, to shield you from it, but after today . . . I can't. So you need to go home—far from here. You'll be safe there."

"I can hold my own, and—"

"You *can't*," he said, and his voice wobbled. "Because *I* can't." He seized my face in both hands. "I can't even protect myself against them, against what's happening in Prythian." I felt every word as it passed from his mouth and onto my lips, a rush of hot, frantic air. "Even if we stood against the blight . . . they would hunt you down—she would find a way to kill you."

"Amarantha." He bristled at the name but nodded. "Who is—"

"When you get home," he cut in, "don't tell anyone the truth about where you were; let them believe the glamour. Don't tell them who I am; don't tell them where you stayed. Her spies will be looking for you."

"I don't understand." I grabbed his forearm and squeezed it tight. "*Tell me*—"

"You have to go *home*, Feyre."

Home. It wasn't my home—it was Hell. "I want to stay with you," I whispered, my voice breaking. "Treaty or no treaty, blight or no blight."

He ran a hand over his face. His fingers contracted when they met with his mask. "I know."

"So let me—"

"There's no debate," he snarled, and I glared at him. "Don't you understand?" He shot to his feet. "Rhys was the start of it. Do you want to be here when the Attor returns? Do you want to know what kind of creatures the Attor answers to? Things like the Bogge—and worse."

"Let me help you—"

"*No*." He paced before the bed. "Didn't you read between the lines today?"

I hadn't, but I lifted my chin and crossed my arms. "So you're sending me away because I'm useless in a fight?"

"I'm sending you away because it makes me *sick* thinking about you in their hands!"

Silence fell, filled only by the sounds of his heavy breathing. He sank onto the bed and pressed the heels of his palms into his eyes.

His words echoed through me, melting my anger, turning everything inside me watery and frail. "How . . . how long do I have to go away for?"

He didn't reply.

"A week?" No answer. "A month?" He shook his head slowly. My upper lip curled, but I forced myself into neutrality. "A year?" That much time away from him . . .

"I don't know."

"But not forever, right?" Even if the blight spread to the Spring Court again, even if it could shred me apart . . . I would come back. He brushed the hair from my face. I shook him off. "I suppose it'll be easier if I'm gone," I said, looking away from him. "Who wants someone around who's so covered in thorns?"

"Thorns?"

"Thorny. Prickly. Sour. Contrary."

He leaned forward and kissed me lightly. "Not forever," he said onto my mouth.

And though I knew it was a lie, I put my arms around his neck and kissed him.

He pulled me onto his lap, holding me tightly against him as his lips parted mine. I became aware of every pore in my body when his tongue entered my mouth.

Though the horror of Rhysand's magic still tore at me, I pushed Tamlin onto the bed, straddling him, pinning him as if it would somehow keep me from leaving, as if it would make time stop entirely.

His hands rested on my hips, and their heat singed me through the thin silk of my nightgown. My hair fell around our faces like a curtain. I couldn't kiss him fast enough, hard enough to express the rushing need within me. He growled softly and deftly flipped us over, spreading me beneath him as he wrenched his lips from my mouth and made a trail of kisses down my neck.

My entire world constricted to the touch of his lips on my skin. Everything beyond them, beyond him, was a void of darkness and moonlight. My back arched as he reached the spot he'd once bitten, and I dragged my hands through his hair, savoring the silken smoothness.

He traced the arc of my hipbones, lingering at the edge of my undergarments. My nightgown had become hitched around my waist, but I didn't care. I hooked my bare legs around his, running my feet down the hard muscles of his calves.

He breathed my name onto my chest, one of his hands exploring the plane of my torso, rising up to the slope of my breast. I trembled, anticipating the feel of his hand there, and his mouth found mine again as his fingers stopped just below.

His kissing was slower this time—gentler. The fingertips of his other hand slipped beneath the waist of my undergarment, and I sucked in a breath.

He hesitated at the sound, pulling back slightly. But I bit his lip in a silent command that had him growling into my mouth. With one long claw, he shredded through silk and lace, and my undergarment fell away in pieces. The claw retracted, and his kiss deepened as his fingers slid between my legs, coaxing and teasing. I ground against his hand, yielding completely to the writhing wildness that had roared alive inside me, and breathed his name onto his skin.

He paused again—his fingers retracting—but I grabbed him, pulling him farther on top of me. I wanted him *now*—I wanted the barriers of our clothing to vanish, I wanted to taste his sweat, wanted to become full of him. "Don't stop," I gasped out.

"I—" he said thickly, resting his brow between my breasts as he shuddered. "If we keep going, I won't be able to stop at all."

I sat up and he watched me, hardly breathing. But I kept my eyes on his, my own breathing becoming steady as I raised my nightgown over my head and tossed it to the floor. Utterly naked before him, I watched his gaze travel to my bare breasts, peaked against the chill night, to my abdomen, to between my thighs. A ravenous, unyielding sort of hunger passed over his face. I bent a leg and slid it to the side, a silent invitation. He let out a low growl—and slowly, with predatory intent, raised his gaze to mine again.

The full force of that wild, unrelenting High Lord's power focused solely on me—and I felt the storm contained beneath his skin, so capable of sweeping away everything I was, even in its lessened state. But I could trust him, trust myself to weather that mighty power. I could throw all that I was at him and he wouldn't balk. "Give me everything," I breathed.

He lunged, a beast freed of its tether.

We were a tangle of limbs and teeth, and I tore at his clothes until they were on the floor, then tore at his skin until I marked him down his back, his arms. His claws were out, but devastatingly gentle on my hips as he slid down between my thighs and feasted on me, stopping only after I shuddered and fractured. I was moaning his name when he sheathed himself inside me in a powerful, slow thrust that had me splintering around him.

We moved together, unending and wild and burning, and when I went over the edge the next time, he roared and went with me.

✣

I fell asleep in his arms, and when I awoke a few hours later, we made love again, lazily and intently, a slow-burning smolder to the wildfire of earlier. Once we were both spent, panting and sweat-slicked, we lay in silence for a time, and I breathed in the smell of him, earthy and crisp. I would never be able to capture that—never be able to paint the *feel* and taste of him, no matter how many times I tried, no matter how many colors I used.

Tamlin traced idle circles on the plane of my stomach and murmured, "We should sleep. You have a long journey tomorrow."

"Tomorrow?" I sat upright, not at all minding my nakedness, not after he'd seen everything, tasted everything.

His mouth was a hard line. "At dawn."

"But it's—"

He sat up in a smooth motion. "Please, Feyre."

Please. Tamlin had *bowed* before Rhysand. For my sake. He shifted toward the edge of the bed. "Where are you going?"

He looked over his shoulder at me. "If I stay, you won't get any sleep."

"Stay," I said. "I promise to keep my hands to myself." Lie—such an outright lie.

He gave me a half smile that told me he knew it, too, but nestled down, tugging me into his arms. I wrapped an arm around his waist and rested my head in the hollow of his shoulder.

He idly stroked my hair. I didn't want to sleep—didn't want to lose a minute with him—but an immense exhaustion was pulling me away from consciousness, until all I knew was the touch of his fingers in my hair and the sounds of his breathing.

I was leaving. Just when this place had become more than a sanctuary, when the command of the Suriel had become a blessing and Tamlin far, far more than a savior or friend, I was leaving. It could be years until I saw this house again, years until I smelled his rose garden, until I saw those gold-flecked eyes. Home—this was home.

As consciousness left me at last, I thought I heard him speak, his mouth close to my ear.

"I love you," he whispered, and kissed my brow. "Thorns and all."

He was gone when I awoke, and I was certain I had dreamed it.

Chapter 28

There wasn't much to my packing and farewells. I was somewhat surprised when Alis clothed me in an outfit very unlike my usual garb—frilly and confining and binding in all the wrong places. Some mortal fashion among the wealthy, no doubt. The dress was made up of layers of pale pink silk, accented with white and blue lace. Alis placed a short, lightweight jacket of white linen on me, and atop my head she angled an absurd little ivory hat, clearly for decoration. I half expected a parasol to go with it.

I said as much to Alis, who clicked her tongue. "Shouldn't you be giving me a weepy farewell?"

I tugged at the lace gloves—useless and flimsy. "I don't like goodbyes. If I could, I'd just walk out and not say anything."

Alis gave me a long look. "I don't like them, either."

I went to the door, but despite myself, I said, "I hope you get to be with your nephews again soon."

"Make the most of your freedom" was all she said.

Downstairs, Lucien snorted at the sight of me. "Those clothes are enough to convince me I never want to enter the human realm."

"I'm not sure the human realm would know what to do with you," I said.

Lucien's smile was edged, his shoulders tight as he gave a sharp look behind me to where Tam was waiting in front of a gilded carriage. When he turned back, that metal eye narrowed. "I thought you were smarter than this."

"Good-bye to you, too," I said. Friend indeed. It wasn't my choice, or my fault that they'd kept the bulk of their conflict from me. Even if I could do nothing against the blight, or against the creatures, or against Amarantha—whoever she was.

Lucien shook his head, his scar stark in the bright sun, and stalked toward Tamlin, despite the High Lord's warning growl. "You're not even going to give her a few more days? Just a few—before you send her back to that human cesspit?" Lucien demanded.

"This isn't up for debate," Tamlin snapped, pointing at the house. "I'll see you at lunch."

Lucien stared him down for a moment, spat on the ground, and stormed up the stairs. Tamlin didn't reprimand him.

I might have thought more on Lucien's words, might have shouted a retort after him, but . . . My chest hollowed out as I faced Tamlin in front of the gilded carriage, my hands sweaty within the gloves.

"Remember what I told you," he said. I nodded, too busy memorizing the lines of his face to reply. Had he meant what I thought he'd said last night—that he loved me? I shifted, already aching in the little white pumps into which Alis had stuffed my poor feet. "The mortal realm remains safe—for you, for your family." I nodded, wondering whether he might have tried to persuade me to leave our territory, to sail south, but understood that I would have refused to be so far from the wall, from him. That going back to my family was as far as I would allow to be sent from his side.

"My paintings—they're yours," I said, unable to come up with anything better to express how I felt, what it did to me to be sent away, and how terrified I was of the carriage looming behind me.

He lifted my chin with a finger. "I will see you again."

He kissed me, and pulled away too quickly. I swallowed hard, fighting the burning in my eyes. *I love you, Feyre.*

I turned before my vision blurred, but he was immediately there to help me into the opulent carriage. He watched me take my seat through the open door, his face a mask of calm. "Ready?"

No, no, I wasn't ready, not after last night, not after all these months. But I nodded. If Rhysand came back, if this Amarantha person was indeed such a threat that I would only be another body for Tamlin to defend . . . I needed to go.

He shut the door, sealing me inside with a click that sounded through me. He leaned through the open window to caress my cheek—and I could have sworn that I felt my heart crack. The footman snapped the whip.

Tamlin's fingers brushed my mouth. The carriage jolted as the six white horses started into a walk. I bit my lip to keep it from wobbling.

Tamlin smiled at me one last time. "I love you," he said, and stepped away.

I should say it—I should say those words, but they got stuck in my throat, because . . . because of what he had to face, because he might not find me again despite his promise, because . . . because beneath it all, he was an immortal, and I would grow old and die. And maybe he meant it now, and perhaps last night had been as altering for him as it had been for me, but . . . I would not become a burden to him. I would not become another weight pressing upon his shoulders.

So I said nothing as the carriage moved. And I did not look back as we passed through the manor gates and into the forest beyond.

✢

Almost as soon as the carriage entered the woods, the sparkle of magic stuffed itself up my nose and I was dragged into a deep sleep. I was furious when I jerked awake, wondering why it had been at all necessary, but the air was full of the thunderous clopping of hooves against a flagstone path. Rubbing my eyes, I peered out the window to see a sloping drive lined with conical hedges and irises. I had never been here before.

I took in as many details as I could as the carriage came to a stop before a chateau of white marble and emerald roofs—nearly as large as Tamlin's manor.

The faces of the approaching servants were unfamiliar, and I kept my face blank as I gripped the footman's hand and stepped out of the carriage.

Human. He was utterly human, with his rounded ears, his ruddy face, his clothes.

The other servants were human, too—all of them restless, not at all like the utter stillness with which the High Fae held themselves. Unfinished, graceless creatures of earth and blood.

The servants were eyeing me but keeping back—shrinking away. Did I look so grand, then? I straightened at the flurry of motion and color that burst from the front doors.

I recognized my sisters before they saw me. They approached, smoothing their fine dresses, their brows rising at the gilded carriage.

That cracking, caved-in feeling in my chest worsened. Tamlin had said he'd taken care of my family, but *this* . . .

Nesta spoke first, curtsying low. Elain followed suit. "Welcome to our home," Nesta said a bit flatly, her eyes on the ground. "Lady . . ."

I let out a stark laugh. "Nesta," I said, and she went rigid. I laughed again. "Nesta, don't you recognize your own sister?"

Elain gasped. "Feyre?" She reached for me, but paused. "What of Aunt Ripleigh, then? Is she . . . dead?"

That was the story, I remembered—that I'd gone to care for a long-lost, wealthy aunt. I nodded slowly. Nesta took in my clothes and carriage, the pearls that were woven into her gold-brown hair gleaming in the sunlight. "She left you her fortune," Nesta stated flatly. It wasn't a question.

"Feyre, you should have told us!" Elain said, still gaping. "Oh, how awful—and you had to endure losing her all on your own, you poor thing. Father will be devastated that he didn't get to pay his respects."

Such . . . such simple things: relatives dying and fortunes being left and paying respect to the dead. And yet—yet . . . a weight I hadn't realized I'd still been carrying eased. These were the only things that worried them now.

"Why are you being so quiet?" Nesta said, keeping her distance.

I'd forgotten how cunning her eyes were, how cold. She'd been made differently, from something harder and stronger than bone and blood. She was as different from the humans around us as I had become.

"I'm . . . glad to see how well your own fortunes have improved," I managed. "What happened?" The driver—glamoured to look human, no mask in sight—began unloading trunks for the footmen. I hadn't known Tamlin had sent me off with belongings.

Elain beamed. "Didn't you get our letters?" She didn't remember—or maybe she'd never actually known, then, that I wouldn't have been able to read them, anyway. When I shook my head, she complained about the uselessness of the post and then said, "Oh, you'll never believe it! Almost a week after you went to care for Aunt Ripleigh, some stranger appeared at our door and asked Father to invest his money for him! Father was hesitant because the offer was so good, but the stranger insisted, so Father did it. He gave us a trunk of gold just for agreeing! Within a month, he'd doubled the man's investment, and then money started pouring in. And you know what? All those ships we lost were found in Bharat, complete with Father's profits!"

Tamlin—Tamlin had done that for them. I ignored the growing hollowness in my chest.

"Feyre, you look as dumbfounded as we were," Elain said, hooking elbows with me. "Come inside. We'll show you the house! We don't have a room decorated for you, because we thought you'd be with poor old Aunt Ripleigh for months yet, but we have so many bedrooms that you can sleep in a different one each night if you wish!"

I glanced over my shoulder at Nesta, who watched me with a carefully blank face. So she hadn't married Tomas Mandray after all.

"Father will likely faint when he sees you," Elain babbled on, patting my hand as she escorted me toward the main door. "Oh, maybe he'll throw a ball in your honor, too!"

Nesta fell into step behind us, a quiet, stalking presence. I didn't want to know what she was thinking. I wasn't certain whether I should be furious or relieved that they'd gotten on so well without me—and whether Nesta was wondering the same.

Horseshoes clopped, and the carriage began ambling down the driveway—away from me, back to my true home, back to Tamlin. It took all my will to keep from running after it.

He had said he loved me, and I'd felt the truth of it with our lovemaking, and he'd sent me away to keep me safe; he'd freed me from the Treaty to keep me safe. Because whatever storm was about to break in Prythian was brutal enough that even a High Lord couldn't stand against it.

I had to stay; it was wise to stay here. But I couldn't fight the sensation, like a darkening shadow within me, that I'd made a very, very big mistake in leaving, no matter Tamlin's orders. *Stay with the High Lord*, the Suriel had said. Its only command.

I shoved the thought from my mind as my father wept at the sight of me and did indeed order a ball in my honor. And though I knew that the promise I had once made to my mother was fulfilled—though I knew that I truly was free of it, and that my family was forever cared for . . . that growing, lengthening shadow blanketed my heart.

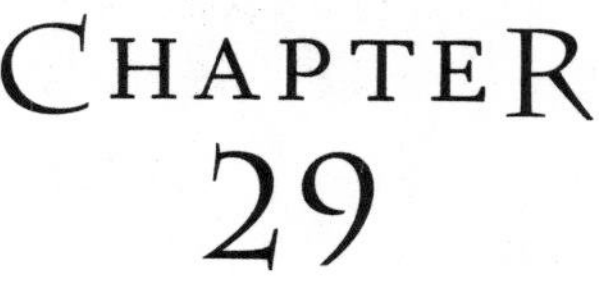

CHAPTER 29

Inventing stories about my time with Aunt Ripleigh required minimal effort: I read to her daily, she instructed me on deportment from her bedside, and I nursed her until she died in her sleep two weeks ago, leaving her fortune to me.

And what a tremendous fortune it was: the trunks that accompanied me hadn't contained just clothing—several of them had been filled with gold and jewels. Not cut jewels, either, but enormous, raw jewels that would pay for a thousand estates.

My father was currently taking inventory of those jewels; he'd holed himself up in the office that overlooked the garden in which I was sitting beside Elain in the grass. Through the window, I spied my father hunched over his desk, a little scale before him as he weighed an uncut ruby the size of a duck's egg. He was clear-eyed again, and moved with a sense of purpose, of vibrancy, that I hadn't seen since before the downfall. Even his limp was improved—made miraculously better by some tonic and a salve a strange, passing healer had given him for free. I would have been forever grateful to Tamlin for that kindness alone.

Gone were his hunched shoulders and downcast, misty eyes. My father smiled freely, laughed readily, and doted on Elain, who in turn doted on him. Nesta, though, had been quiet and watchful, only giving Elain answers not longer than a word or two.

"These bulbs," Elain said, pointing with a gloved hand to a cluster of purple-and-white flowers, "came all the way from the tulip fields of the continent. Father promised that next spring he'll take me to see them. He claims that for mile after mile, there's nothing but these flowers." She patted the rich, dark soil. The little garden beneath the window was hers: every bloom and shrub had been picked and planted by her hand; she would allow no one else to care for it. Even the weeding and watering she did on her own.

Though the servants *did* help her carry over the heavy watering cans, she admitted. She would have marveled—likely wept—at the gardens I'd become so accustomed to, at the flowers in perpetual bloom at the Spring Court.

"You should come with me," Elain went on. "Nesta won't go, because she says she doesn't want to risk the sea crossing, but you and I . . . Oh, we'd have fun, wouldn't we?"

I glanced sidelong at her. My sister was beaming, content—prettier than I'd ever seen her, even in her simple muslin gardening dress. Her cheeks were flushed beneath her large, floppy hat. "I think—I think I'd like to see the continent," I said.

And it was true, I realized. There was so much of the world that I hadn't seen, hadn't ever thought about visiting. Hadn't ever been *able* to dream of visiting.

"I'm surprised you're so eager to go next spring," I said. "Isn't that right in the middle of the season?" The socialite season, which had ended a few weeks ago, apparently, full of parties and balls and luncheons and gossip, gossip, gossip. Elain had told me all about it at dinner the night before, hardly noticing that it was an effort for me to get down my food. So much of it was the same—the meat, the bread, the vegetables, and yet . . . it was ash in my mouth compared to what I'd consumed in Prythian. "And I'm surprised you don't have a line of suitors out the door, begging for your hand."

Elain flushed but plunged her little shovel into the ground to dig out a weed. "Yes, well—there will always be other seasons. Nesta won't tell you, but this season was somewhat . . . strange."

"In what way?"

She shrugged her slim shoulders. "People acted as if we'd all just been ill for eight years, or had gone away to some distant country—not that we'd been a few villages over in that cottage. You'd think we dreamed it all up, what happened to us over those years. No one said a word about it."

"Did you think they would?" If we were as rich as this house suggested, there were surely plenty of families willing to overlook the stain of our poverty.

"No—but it made me . . . made me wish for those years again, even with the hunger and cold. This house feels so big sometimes, and father is always busy, and Nesta . . ." She looked over her shoulder to where my eldest sister stood by a gnarled mulberry tree, looking out over the flat expanse of our lands. She'd barely spoken to me the night before, and not at all during breakfast. I'd been surprised when she joined us outside, even if she'd stayed by the tree this whole time. "Nesta didn't finish the season. She wouldn't tell me why. She began refusing every invitation. She hardly talks to anyone, and I feel wretched when my friends pay a visit, because she makes them so uncomfortable when she stares at them in that way of hers . . ." Elain sighed. "Maybe you could talk to her."

I contemplated telling Elain that Nesta and I hadn't had a civil conversation in years, but then Elain added, "She went to see you, you know."

I blinked, my blood going a bit cold. "What?"

"Well, she was gone for only about a week, and she said that her carriage broke down not halfway there, and it was easier to come back. But you wouldn't know, since you never got any of our letters."

I looked over at Nesta, standing so still under the branches, the summer breeze rustling the skirts of her dress. Had she gone to see me, only to be turned back by whatever glamour magic Tamlin had cast on her?

I turned back to the garden and caught Elain staring at me. "What?"

Elain shook her head and went back to weeding. "You just look so . . . different. You sound so different, too."

Indeed, I hadn't quite believed my eyes when I'd passed a hall mirror last night. My face was still the same, but there was a . . . *glow* about me, a kind of shimmering light that was nearly undetectable. I knew without a doubt that it was because of my time in Prythian, that all that magic had somehow rubbed off on me. I dreaded the day it would forever fade.

"Did something happen at Aunt Ripleigh's house?" Elain asked. "Did you . . . meet someone?"

I shrugged and yanked at a weed nearby. "Just good food and rest."

✠

Days passed. The shadow within me didn't lighten, and even the thought of painting was abhorrent. Instead I spent most of my time with Elain in her little garden. I was content to listen to her talk about every bud and bloom, about her plans to start another garden by the greenhouse, perhaps a vegetable garden, if she could learn enough about it over the next few months.

She had come alive here, and her joy was infectious. There wasn't a servant or gardener who didn't smile at her, and even the brusque head cook found excuses to bring her plates of cookies and tarts at various points in the day. I marveled at it, actually—that those years of poverty hadn't stripped away that light from Elain. Perhaps buried it a bit, but she was generous, loving, and kind—a woman I found myself proud to know, to call sister.

My father finished counting my jewels and gold; I was an extraordinarily wealthy woman. I invested a small percentage of it in his business, and when I looked at the remaining behemoth sum, I had him draw me up several bags of money and set out.

The manor was only three miles from our rundown cottage, and the road was familiar. I didn't mind when my hem became coated in mud from the sodden path. I savored hearing the wind in the trees and the sighing of the high grasses. If I drifted far enough into my memories, I could imagine myself walking alongside Tamlin through his woods.

I had no reason to believe that I would see him anytime soon, but I went to bed each night praying that I'd awaken to find myself in his manor, or that I'd receive a message summoning me to his side. Even worse than my disappointment that no such thing had happened was the creeping, nagging fear that he was in danger—that Amarantha, whoever she was, would somehow hurt him.

"*I love you.*" I could almost hear the words—almost hear him saying them, could almost see the sunlight glinting in his golden hair and the dazzling green of his eyes. I could almost feel his body pressed against mine, his fingers playing along my skin.

I reached a bend in the road that I could have navigated in the dark, and there it was.

So small—the cottage had been so small. Elain's old flower garden was a wild tangle of weeds and blooms, and the ward-markings were still etched on the stone threshold. The front door—shattered and broken the last time I'd seen it—had been replaced, but one of the circular windowpanes had become cracked. The interior was dark, the land undisturbed.

I traced the invisible path I'd taken across the tall grass every morning from our front door, over the road, and then across the rolling field, all the way to that line of trees. The forest—my forest.

It had seemed so terrifying once—so lethal and hungry and brutal. And now it just seemed . . . plain. Ordinary.

I gazed again at that sad, dark house—the place that had been a prison. Elain had said she missed it, and I wondered what she saw when she looked at the cottage. If she beheld not a prison but a shelter—a shelter from a world that had possessed so little good, but she tried to find it anyway, even if it had seemed foolish and useless to me.

She had looked at that cottage with hope; I had looked at it with nothing but hatred. And I knew which one of us had been stronger.

CHAPTER 30

I had one task left to do before I returned to my father's manor. The villagers who had once sneered at or ignored me instead gaped now, and a few stepped into my path to ask about my aunt, my fortune, on and on. I firmly but politely refused to fall into conversation with them, to give them anything to gossip over. But it still took me so long to reach the poor part of our village that I was fully drained by the time I knocked on the first dilapidated door.

The impoverished of our village didn't ask questions when I handed them the little bags of silver and gold. They tried to refuse, some of them not even recognizing me, but I left the money anyway. It was the least I could do.

As I walked back to my father's manor, I passed Tomas Mandray and his cronies lurking by the village fountain, chatting about some house that had burned down with its family trapped inside a week before and whether there was anything to loot from it. He gave me a too-long look, his eyes roving freely over my body, with a half smile I'd seen him give to the village girls a hundred times before. Why had Nesta changed her mind? I just stared him down and continued along.

I was almost out of town when a woman's laugh flitted over the stones, and I turned a corner to come face-to-face with Isaac Hale—and a pretty, plump young woman who could only be his new wife. They were arm in arm, both smiling—both lit up from within.

His smile faltered as he beheld me.

Human—he seemed so *human*, with his gangly limbs, his simple handsomeness, but that smile he'd had moments before had transformed him into something more.

His wife looked between us, perhaps a bit nervously. As if whatever she felt for him—the love I'd already seen shining—was so new, so unexpected, that she was still worried it would vanish. Carefully, Isaac inclined his head to me in greeting. He'd been a boy when I left, and yet this person who now approached me . . . whatever had blossomed with his wife, whatever was between them, it had made him into a man.

Nothing—there was nothing in my chest, my soul, for him beyond a vague sense of gratitude.

A few more steps had us passing each other. I smiled broadly at him, at them both, and bowed my head, wishing them well with my entire heart.

✢

The ball my father was throwing in my honor was in two days, and the house was already a flurry of activity. Such money being thrown away on things we'd never dreamed of having again, even for a moment. I would have begged him not to host it, but Elain had taken charge of planning *and* finding me a last-minute dress, and . . . it would only be for an evening. An evening of enduring the people who had shunned us and let us starve for years.

The sun was near to setting as I stopped my work for the day: digging out a new square of earth for Elain's next garden. The gardeners had been slightly horrified that another one of us had taken up the activity—as if we'd soon be doing all their work ourselves and would get rid of them. I reassured them I had no green thumb and just wanted something to do with my day.

But I hadn't yet figured out what I would be doing with my week, or my month, or anything after that. If there was indeed a surge in the blight happening over the wall, if that Amarantha woman was sending out creatures to take advantage of it . . . It was hard not to dwell on that shadow in my heart, the shadow that trailed my every step. I hadn't felt like painting since I'd arrived—and that place inside me where all those colors and shapes and lights had come from had become still and quiet and dull. Soon, I told myself. Soon I would purchase some paints and start again.

I slid the shovel into the ground and set my foot atop it, resting for a moment. Perhaps the gardeners had just been horrified by the tunic and pants I'd scrounged up. One of them had even gone running to fetch me one of those big, floppy hats that Elain wore. I wore it for their sake; my skin had already become tan and freckled from months roaming the Spring Court lands.

I glanced at my hands, clutching the top of the shovel. Callused and flecked with scars, arcs of dirt under my nails. They'd surely be horrified when they beheld me splattered with paint.

"Even if you washed them, there'd be no hiding it," Nesta said behind me, coming over from that tree she liked to sit by. "To fit in, you'd have to wear gloves and never take them off."

She wore a simple, pale lavender muslin gown, her hair half-up and billowing behind her in a sheet of gold-brown. Beautiful, imperious, still as one of the High Fae.

"Maybe I don't want to fit in with your social circles," I said, turning back to the shovel.

"Then why are you bothering to stay here?" A sharp, cold question.

I plunged the shovel deeper, my arms and back straining as I heaved up a pile of dark soil and grass. "It's my home, isn't it?"

"No, it's not," she said flatly. I slammed the shovel back into the earth. "I think your home is somewhere very far away."

I paused.

I left the shovel in the ground and slowly turned to face her. "Aunt Ripleigh's house—"

"There is no Aunt Ripleigh." Nesta reached into her pocket and tossed something onto the churned-up earth.

It was a chunk of wood, as if it had been ripped from something. Painted on its smooth surface was a pretty tangle of vines and—foxglove. Foxglove painted in the wrong shade of blue.

My breath hitched. All this time, all these months . . .

"Your beast's little trick didn't work on me," she said with quiet steel. "Apparently, an iron will is all it takes to keep a glamour from digging in. So I had to watch as Father and Elain went from sobbing hysterics into *nothing*. I had to listen to them talk about how lucky it was for you to be taken to some made-up aunt's house, how some winter wind had shattered our door. And I thought I'd gone mad—but every time I did, I would look at that painted part of the table, then at the claw marks farther down, and know it wasn't in my head."

I'd never heard of a glamour not working. But Nesta's mind was so entirely her own; she had put up such strong walls—of steel and iron and ash wood—that even a High Lord's magic couldn't pierce them.

"Elain said—said you went to visit me, though. That you tried."

Nesta snorted, her face grave and full of that long-simmering anger that she could never master. "He stole you away into the night, claiming some nonsense about the Treaty. And then everything went on as if it had never happened. It wasn't right. None of it was right."

My hands slackened at my sides. "You went after me," I said. "You went after me—to Prythian."

"I got to the wall. I couldn't find a way through."

I raised a shaking hand to my throat. "You trekked two days there and two days back—through the winter woods?"

She shrugged, looking at the sliver she'd pried from the table. "I hired that mercenary from town to bring me a week after you were taken. With the money from your pelt. She was the only one who seemed like she would believe me."

"You did that—for me?"

Nesta's eyes—my eyes, our mother's eyes—met mine. "It wasn't right," she said again. Tamlin had been wrong when we'd discussed whether my father would have ever come after me—he didn't possess the courage, the anger. If anything, he would have hired someone to do it for him. But Nesta had gone with that mercenary. My hateful, cold sister had been willing to brave Prythian to rescue me.

"What happened to Tomas Mandray?" I asked, the words strangled.

"I realized he wouldn't have gone with me to save you from Prythian."

And for her, with that raging, unrelenting heart, it would have been a line in the sand.

I looked at my sister, really *looked* at her, at this woman who couldn't stomach the sycophants who now surrounded her, who had never spent a day in the forest but had gone into wolf territory . . . Who had shrouded the loss of our mother, then our downfall, in icy rage and bitterness, because the anger had been a lifeline, the cruelty a release. But she *had* cared—beneath it, she had cared, and perhaps loved more fiercely than I could comprehend, more deeply and loyally. "Tomas never deserved you anyway," I said softly.

My sister didn't smile, but a light shone in her blue-gray eyes. "Tell me everything that happened," she said—an order, not a request.

So I did.

And when I finished my story, Nesta merely stared at me for a long while before asking me to teach her how to paint.

✠

Teaching Nesta to paint was about as pleasant as I had expected it to be, but at least it provided an excuse for us to avoid the busier parts of the house, which became more and more chaotic as my ball drew near. Supplies were easy enough to come by, but explaining how I painted, convincing Nesta to express what was in her mind, her heart . . . At the very least, she repeated my brushstrokes with a precise and solid hand.

When we emerged from the quiet room we'd commandeered, both of us splattered in paint and smeared with charcoal, the chateau was finishing up its preparations. Colored glass lanterns lined the long drive, and inside, wreaths and garlands of every flower and color decorated every rail, every surface, every archway. Beautiful. Elain had selected each flower herself and instructed the staff where to put them.

Nesta and I slipped up the stairs, but as we reached the landing, my father and Elain appeared below, arm in arm.

Nesta's face tightened. My father murmured his praises to Elain, who beamed at him and rested her head on his shoulder. And I was happy for them—for the comfort and ease of their lifestyle, for the contentment on both my father's and my sister's faces. Yes, they had their small sorrows, but both of them seemed so . . . relaxed.

Nesta walked down the hall, and I followed her. "There are days," Nesta said as she paused in front of the door to her room, across from mine, "when I want to ask him if he remembers the years he almost let us starve to death."

"You spent every copper I could get, too," I reminded her.

"I knew you could always get more. And if you couldn't, then I wanted to see if he would ever try to do it himself, instead of carving those bits of wood. If he would actually go out and fight for us. I couldn't take care of us, not the way you did. I hated you for that. But I hated him more. I still do."

"Does he know?"

"He's always known I hate him, even before we became poor. He let Mother die—he had a fleet of ships at his disposal to sail across the world for a cure, or he could have hired men to go into Prythian and beg them for help. But he let her waste away."

"He loved her—he grieved for her." I didn't know what the truth was—perhaps both.

"He let her die. You would have gone to the ends of the earth to save your High Lord."

My chest hollowed out again, but I merely said, "Yes, I would have," and slipped inside my room to get ready.

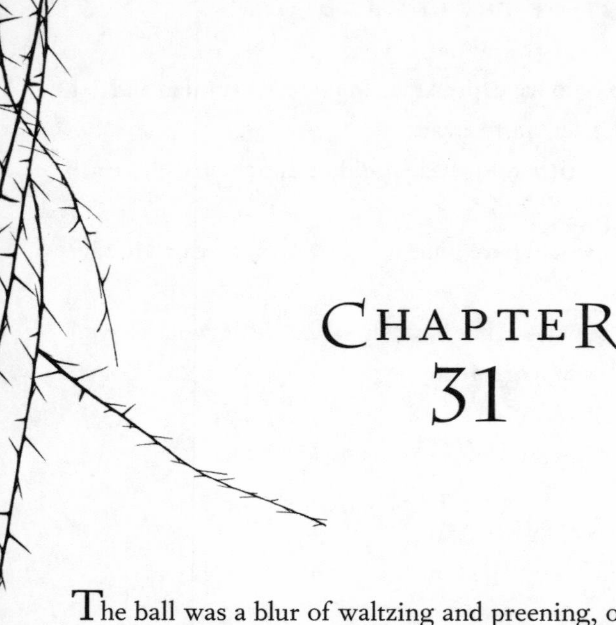

CHAPTER 31

The ball was a blur of waltzing and preening, of bejeweled aristos, of wine and toasts in my honor. I lingered at Nesta's side, because she seemed to do a good job of scaring off the too-curious suitors who wanted to know more about my fortune. But I tried to smile, if only for Elain, who flitted about the room, personally greeting each guest and dancing with all their important sons.

But I kept thinking about what Nesta had said—about saving Tamlin.

I'd known something was wrong. I'd known he was in trouble—not just with the blight on Prythian, but also that the forces gathering to destroy him were deadly, and yet . . . and yet I'd stopped looking for answers, stopped fighting it, glad—so selfishly *glad*—to be able to set down that savage, wild part of me that had only survived hour to hour. I'd let him send me home. I hadn't tried harder to piece together the information I'd gathered about the blight or Amarantha; I hadn't tried to save him. I hadn't even told him I loved him. And Lucien . . . Lucien had known it, too—and shown it in his bitter words on my last day, his disappointment in me.

Two in the morning, and yet the party was showing no signs of slowing. My father held court with several other merchants and aristo men to whom I had been introduced but whose names I'd instantly forgotten. Elain was laughing among a circle of beautiful friends, flushed and brilliant. Nesta had silently left at midnight, and I didn't bother to say good-bye as I finally slipped upstairs.

The following afternoon, bleary-eyed and quiet, we all gathered at the lunch table. I thanked my sister and father for the party, and dodged my father's inquiries regarding whether any of his friends' sons had caught my eye.

The summer heat had arrived, and I propped my chin on a fist as I fanned myself. I'd slept fitfully in the heat last night. It was never too hot or too cold at Tamlin's estate.

"I'm thinking of buying the Beddor land," my father was saying to Elain, who was the only one of us listening to him. "I heard a rumor it'll go up for sale soon, since none of the family survived, and it would be a good investment property. Perhaps one of you girls might build a house on it when you're ready."

Elain nodded interestedly, but I blinked. "What happened to the Beddors?"

"Oh, it was awful," Elain said. "Their house burned down, and everyone died. Well, they couldn't find Clare's body, but . . ." She looked down at her plate. "It happened in the dead of night—the family, their servants, everyone. The day before you came home to us, actually."

"Clare Beddor," I said slowly.

"Our friend, remember?" Elain said.

I nodded, feeling Nesta's eyes on me.

No—no, it couldn't be possible. It had to be a coincidence—*had* to be a coincidence, because the alternative . . .

I had given that name to Rhysand.

And he had not forgotten it.

My stomach turned over, and I fought against the nausea that roiled within me.

"Feyre?" my father asked.

I put a shaking hand over my eyes, breathing in. What had happened? Not just at the Beddors', but at home, in Prythian?

"Feyre," my father said again, and Nesta hissed at him, "Quiet."

I pushed back against the guilt, the disgust and terror. I had to get answers—had to know if it had been a coincidence, or if I might yet be able to save Clare. And if something had happened here, in the mortal realm, then the Spring Court . . . then those creatures Tamlin had been so frightened of . . . the blight that had infected magic, their lands . . .

Faeries. They had come over the wall and left no trace behind.

I lowered my hand and looked at Nesta. "You must listen very carefully," I said to her, swallowing hard. "Everything I have told you must remain a secret. You do not come looking for me. You do not speak my name again to anyone."

"What are you talking about, Feyre?" My father gaped at me from the end of the table. Elain glanced between us, shifting in her seat.

But Nesta held my gaze. Unflinching.

"I think something very bad might be happening in Prythian," I said softly. I'd never learned what warning signs Tamlin had instilled in their glamours to prod my family to run, but I wasn't going to risk relying solely on them. Not when Clare had been taken, her family murdered . . . because of me. Bile burned my throat.

"Prythian!" my father and Elain blurted. But Nesta held up a hand to silence them.

I went on, "If you won't leave, then hire guards—hire scouts to watch the wall, the forest. The village, too." I rose from my seat. "The first sign of danger, the first rumor you hear of the wall being breached or even something being *strange*, you get on a ship and go. You sail far away, as far south as you can get, to someplace the faeries would never desire."

My father and Elain began blinking, as if clearing some fog from their minds—as if emerging from a deep sleep. But Nesta followed me into the hall, up the stairs.

"The Beddors," she said. "That was meant to be us. But you gave them a fake name—those wicked faeries who threatened your High Lord." I nodded. I could see the plans calculating in her eyes. "Is there going to be an invasion?"

"I don't know. I don't know what's happening. I was told that there was a kind of sickness that had made their powers weaken or go wild, a blight on the land that had damaged the safety of their borders and could kill people if it struck badly enough. They—they said it was surging again . . . on the move. The last I heard, it wasn't near enough to harm our lands. But if the Spring Court is about to fall, then the blight has to be getting close, and Tamlin . . . Tamlin was one of the last bastions keeping the other courts in check—the deadly courts. And I think he's in danger."

I entered my room and began peeling off my gown. My sister helped me, then opened the wardrobe to pull out a heavy tunic and pants and boots. I slipped into them and was braiding back my hair when she said, "We don't need you here, Feyre. Do not look back."

I tugged on my boots and went for the hunting knives I'd discreetly acquired while here.

"Father once told you to never come back," Nesta said, "and I'm telling you now. We can take care of ourselves."

Once I might have thought it was an insult, but now I understood—understood what a gift she was offering me. I sheathed the knives at my side and slung a quiver of arrows across my back—none of them ash—before scooping up my bow. "They *can* lie," I said, giving her information I hoped she would never need. "Faeries can lie, and iron doesn't bother them one bit. But ash wood—that seems to work. Take my money and buy a damned grove of it for Elain to tend."

Nesta shook her head, clutching her wrist, the bracelet of iron still there. "What do you think you can even do to help? He's a High Lord—you're just a human." That wasn't an insult, either. A question from a coolly calculating mind.

"I don't care," I admitted, at the door now, which I flung open. "But I've got to try."

Nesta remained in my room. She would not say good-bye—she hated farewells as much as I did.

But I turned to my sister and said, "There is a better world, Nesta. There is a better world out there, waiting for you to find it. And if I ever get the chance, if things are ever better, safer . . . I will find you again."

It was all I could offer her.

But Nesta squared her shoulders. "Don't bother. I don't think I'd be particularly fond of faeries." I raised a brow. She went on with a slight shrug. "Try to send word once it's safe. And if it ever is . . . Father and Elain can have this place. I think I'd like to see what else is out there, what a woman might do with a fortune and a good name."

No limits, I thought. There were no limits to what Nesta might do, what she might make of herself once she found a place to call her own. I prayed I would be lucky enough to someday see it.

✢

Elain, to my surprise, had a horse, a satchel of food, and supplies ready when I hurried down the stairs. My father was nowhere in sight. But Elain threw her arms around me, and, holding tightly, said, "I remember—I remember all of it now."

I wrapped my arms around her. "Be on your guard. All of you."

She nodded, tears in her eyes. "I would have liked to see the continent with you, Feyre."

I smiled at my sister, memorizing her lovely face, and wiped her tears away. "Maybe someday," I said. Another promise that I'd be lucky to keep.

Elain was still crying as I spurred my horse and galloped down the drive. I didn't have it in me to say good-bye to my father once more.

I rode all day and stopped only when it was too dark for me to see. Due north—that's where I would start and go until I hit the wall. I had to get back—had to see what had happened, had to tell Tamlin everything that was in my heart before it was too late.

I rode all of the second day, slept fitfully, and was off before first light.

On and on, through the summer forest, lush and dense and humming.

Until an absolute silence fell. I slowed my horse to a careful walk and scanned the brush and trees ahead for any sign, any ripple. There was nothing. Nothing, and then—

My horse bucked and shook her head, and it was all I could do to stay in the saddle as she refused to go forward. But still, there was nothing—no marker. Yet when I dismounted, hardly breathing as I put a hand out, I found that I could not pass.

There, cleaving through the forest, was an invisible wall.

But the faeries came and went through it—through holes, rumor claimed. So I led my horse down the line, tapping the wall every so often to make sure I hadn't veered away.

It took me two days—and the night between them was more terrifying than any I'd experienced at the Spring Court. Two days, before I spied the mossy stones placed across from each other, a faint whorl carved into them both. A gate.

This time, when I mounted my horse and steered her between them, she obeyed.

Magic stung my nostrils, zapping until my horse bucked again, but we were through.

I knew these trees.

I rode in silence, an arrow nocked and ready, the threats lurking in the forest far greater than those in the woods I'd just left.

Tamlin might be furious—he might command me to turn around and go home. But I would tell him that I was going to help, tell him that I loved him and would fight for him however I could, even if I had to tie him down to make him listen.

I became so intent on contemplating how I might convince him not to start roaring that I didn't immediately notice the quiet—how the birds didn't sing, even as I drew closer to the manor itself, how the hedges of the estate looked in need of a trim.

By the time I reached the gates, my mouth had gone dry. The gates were open, but the iron had been bent out of shape, as if mighty hands had wrenched them apart.

Every step of the horse's hooves was too loud on the gravel path, and my stomach dropped further when I beheld the wide-open front doors. One of them hung at an angle, ripped off its top hinge.

I dismounted, arrow still at the ready. But there was no need. Empty—it was utterly empty here. Like a tomb.

"Tam?" I called. I bounded up the front steps and into the house. I rushed inside, swearing as I slid on a piece of broken porcelain—the remnants of a vase. Slowly, I turned in the front hall.

It looked as if an army had marched through. Tapestries hung in shreds, the marble banister was fractured, and the chandeliers lay broken on the ground, reduced to mounds of shattered crystal.

"Tamlin?" I shouted. Nothing.

The windows had all been blown out. "Lucien?"

No one answered.

"Tam?" My voice echoed through the house, mocking me.

Alone in the wreckage of the manor, I sank to my knees.

He was gone.

CHAPTER 32

I gave myself a minute—just one minute—to kneel in the remnants of the entry hall.

Then I eased to my feet, careful not to disturb any of the shattered glass or wood or—blood. There were splatters of it everywhere, along with small puddles and smears down the gouged walls.

Another forest, I told myself. Another set of tracks.

Slowly, I moved across the floor, tracing the information left. It had been a vicious fight—and from the blood patterns, most of the damage to the house had been done during the fight, not afterward. The crushed glass and footprints came and went from the front and back of the house, as if the whole place had been surrounded. The intruders had needed to force their way in though the front door; they'd just completely shattered the doors to the garden.

No bodies, I kept repeating to myself. There were no bodies, and not much gore. They had to be alive. Tamlin *had* to be alive.

Because if he were dead . . .

I rubbed my face, taking a shuddering breath. I wouldn't let myself get that far. My hands shook as I paused before the dining room doors, both barely hanging on their hinges.

I couldn't tell if the damage was from his lashing out after Rhysand's arrival the day before my departure or if someone else had caused it. The giant table was in pieces, the windows smashed, the curtains in shreds. But no blood—there was no blood here. And from the prints in the shards of glass . . .

I studied the trail across the floor. It had been disturbed, but I could make out two sets—large and side by side—leading from where the table had been. As if Tamlin and Lucien had been sitting in here as the attack happened, and walked out without a fight.

If I was right . . . then they were alive. I traced the steps to the doorway, squatting for a moment to work through the churned-up shards, dirt, and blood. They'd been met here—by multiple sets of prints. And headed toward the garden—

Debris crunched from down the hall. I drew my hunting knife and ducked farther into the dining room, scanning for a place to hide. But everything was in pieces. With no other option, I lunged behind the open door. I pressed a hand over my mouth to keep from breathing too loudly and peered through the crack between the door and the wall.

Something limped into the room and sniffed. I could only see its back—cloaked in a plain cape, medium height . . . All it had to do to find me was shut the door. Perhaps if it came far enough into the dining room, I could slip out—but that would require leaving my hiding spot. Perhaps it would just look around and then leave.

The figure sniffed again, and my stomach clenched. It could smell me. I dared a better glance at it, hoping to find a weakness, a spot for my knife, if things came down to it.

The figure turned slightly toward me.

I cried out, and the figure screeched as I shoved away the door. *"Alis."*

She gaped at me, a hand on her heart, her usual brown dress torn and dirty, her apron gone entirely. Not bloodied, though—nothing save for the slight limp that favored her right ankle as she rushed for me, her tree-bark skin bleaching birch white. "You can't be here." She took in my knife, the bow and quiver. "You were told to stay away."

"Is he alive?"

"Yes, but—"

My knees buckled at the onslaught of relief. "And Lucien?"

"Alive as well. But—."

"Tell me what happened—tell me *everything*." I kept an eye on the window, listening to the manor and grounds around us. Not a sound.

Alis grasped my arm and pulled me from the room. She didn't speak as we hurried through the empty, too-quiet halls—all of them wrecked and bloodied, but . . . no bodies. Either they'd been hauled away, or—I didn't let myself consider it as we entered the kitchen.

A fire had scorched the giant room, and it was little more than cinders and blackened stone. After sniffing about and listening for any signs of danger, Alis released me. "What are you doing here?"

"I had to come back. I thought something had gone wrong—I couldn't stay away. I had to help."

"He told you not to come back," Alis snapped.

"Where is he?"

Alis covered her face with her long, bony hands, her fingertips grappling into the upper edge of her mask as if trying to tear it from her face. But the mask remained, and Alis sighed as she lowered her tree-bark hands. "She took him," she said, and my blood went cold. "She took him to her court Under the Mountain."

"Who?" But I already knew the answer.

"Amarantha," Alis whispered, and glanced again around the kitchen as if fearful that speaking her name would summon her.

"Why? And who is she—*what* is she? Please, *please* just tell me—just give me the truth."

Alis shuddered. "You want the truth, girl? Then here it is: she took him for the curse—because the seven times seven years were over, and he hadn't shattered her curse. She's summoned all the High Lords to her court this time—to make them watch her break him."

"What is she—*wh-what curse?*" A curse—the curse *she* had put on this place. A curse that I had failed to even see.

"Amarantha is High Queen of this land. The High Queen of Prythian," Alis breathed, her eyes wide with some memory of horror.

"But the seven High Lords rule Prythian—equally. There's no High Queen."

"That's how it used to be—how it's always been. Until a hundred years ago, when she appeared in these lands as an emissary from Hybern." Alis grabbed a large satchel that she must have left by the door. It was already half full of what looked like clothes and supplies.

As she began sifting through the ruined kitchen, gathering up knives and any food that had survived, I wondered at the information the Suriel had given me—of a wicked faerie king who had spent centuries resenting the Treaty he'd been forced to sign, and who had sent out his deadliest commanders to infiltrate the other faerie kingdoms and courts to see if they felt as he did—to see if they might consider reclaiming the human lands for themselves. I leaned against one of the soot-stained walls.

"She went from court to court," Alis went on, turning an apple over in her hands as she inspected it, deemed it good enough, and stuffed it into the bag, "charming the High Lords with talk of more trade between Hybern and Prythian, more communication, more sharing of assets. The Never-Fading Flower, they called her. And for fifty years, she lived here as a courtier bound to no court, making amends, she claimed, for her own actions and the actions of Hybern during the War."

"She fought in the War against mortals?"

Alis paused her gathering. "Her story is legend among our kind—legend, and nightmare. She was the King of Hybern's most lethal general—she fought on the front lines, slaughtering humans and any High Fae and faeries who dared defend them. But she had a younger sister,

Clythia, who fought at her side, as vicious and wretched as she . . . until Clythia fell in love with a mortal warrior. Jurian." Alis loosed a shaking sigh. "Jurian commanded mighty human armies, but Clythia still secretly sought him out, still loved him with an unrelenting madness. She was too blind to realize that Jurian was using her for information about Amarantha's forces. Amarantha suspected, but could not persuade Clythia to leave him—and could not bring herself to kill him, not when it would cause her sister such pain." Alis clicked her tongue and began opening the cabinets, scanning their ravaged insides. "Amarantha delighted in torture and killing, and yet she loved her sister enough to stay her hand."

"What happened?" I breathed.

"Oh, Jurian betrayed Clythia. After months of stomaching being her lover, he got the information he needed, then tortured and butchered her, crucifying her with ash wood so she couldn't move while he did it. He left the pieces of her for Amarantha to find. They say Amarantha's wrath could have brought down the skies themselves, had her king not ordered her to stand down. But she and Jurian had their final confrontation later—and since then, Amarantha has hated humans with a rage you cannot imagine." Alis found what looked to be a jar of preserves and added it to the satchel.

"After the two sides made the Treaty," Alis said, now going through the drawers, "she butchered her own slaves, rather than free them." I blanched. "But centuries later, the High Lords believed her when she told them that the death of her sister had changed her—especially when she opened trade lines between our two territories. The High Lords never knew that those same ships that brought over Hybernian goods also brought over her own personal forces. The King of Hybern didn't know, either. But we all soon learned that, in those fifty years she was here, she had decided she wanted Prythian for her own, to begin amassing power and use our lands as a launching point to one day destroy your world once and for all, with or without her king's blessing. So forty-nine years ago, she struck.

"She knew—knew that even with her personal army, she could never conquer the seven High Lords by numbers or power alone. But she was also cunning and cruel, and she waited until they absolutely trusted her, until they gathered at a ball in her honor, and that night she slipped a potion stolen from the King of Hybern's unholy spell book into their wine. Once they drank, the High Lords were prone, their magic laid bare—and she stole their powers from where they originated inside their bodies—plucked them out as if she were taking an apple from its branch, leaving them with only the basest elements of their magic. Your Tamlin—what you saw of him here was a shade of what he used to be, the power that he used to command. And with the High Lords' power so greatly decreased, Amarantha wrested control of Prythian from them in a matter of days. For forty-nine years, we have been her slaves. For forty-nine years, she has been biding her time, waiting for the right moment to break the Treaty and take your lands—and all human territories beyond it."

I wished there were a stool, a bench, a chair for me to slump into. Alis slammed shut the final drawer and limped for the pantry.

"Now they call her the Deceiver—she who trapped the seven High Lords and built her palace beneath the sacred Mountain in the heart of our land." Alis paused before the pantry door and covered her face again, taking a few steadying breaths.

The sacred mountain—that bald, monstrous peak I'd spotted in the mural in the library all those months ago. "But . . . the sickness in the lands . . . Tamlin said that the blight took their power—"

"*She* is the sickness in these lands," Alis snapped, lowering her hands and entering the pantry. "There is no blight but her. The borders were collapsing because she laid them to rubble. She found it amusing to send her creatures to attack our lands, to test whatever strength Tamlin had left."

If the blight was Amarantha, then the threat to the human realm . . . *She* was the threat to the human realm.

Alis emerged from the pantry, her arms full of various root vegetables. "You could have been the one to stop her." Her eyes were hard upon me, and she bared her teeth. They were alarmingly sharp. She shoved the turnips and beets into the bag. "You could have been the one to free him and his power, had you not been so blind to your own heart. Humans," she spat.

"I—I . . ." I lifted my hands, exposing my palms to her. "I didn't know."

"You couldn't know," Alis said bitterly, her laugh harsh as she entered the pantry again. "It was part of Tamlin's curse."

My head swam, and I pressed myself further against the wall. "What was?" I fought the rising hitch in my voice. "What was his curse? What did she do to him?"

Alis yanked remaining spice jars off the pantry shelf. "Tamlin and Amarantha knew each other before—his family had long been tied to Hybern. During the War, the Spring Court allied with Hybern to keep the humans enslaved. So his father—his father, who was a fickle and vicious Lord—was very close with the King of Hybern, to Amarantha. Tamlin as a child often accompanied him on trips to Hybern. And he met Amarantha in the process."

Tamlin had once said to me that he would fight to *protect* someone's freedom—that he would never allow slavery. Had it been solely because of shame for his own legacy, or because he . . . he'd come to somehow know what it was to be enslaved?

"Amarantha eventually grew to desire Tamlin—to lust for him with her entire wicked heart. But he'd heard the stories from others about the War, and knew what Amarantha and his father and the Hybern king had done to faeries and humans alike. What she did to Jurian as punishment for her sister's death. He was wary of her when she came here, despite her attempts to lure him into her bed—and kept his distance, right up until she stole his powers. Lucien . . . Lucien was sent to her as Tamlin's emissary, to try to treat for peace between them."

Bile rose in my throat.

"She refused, and . . . Lucien told her to go back to the shit-hole she'd crawled out of. She took his eye as punishment. Carved it out with her own fingernail, then scarred his face. She sent him back so bloody that Tamlin . . . The High Lord vomited when he saw his friend."

I couldn't let myself imagine what state Lucien had been in, then, if it had made Tamlin sick.

Alis tapped on her mask, the metal pinging beneath her nails. "After that, she hosted a masquerade Under the Mountain for herself. All the courts were present. A party, she said—to make amends for what she'd done to Lucien, and a masquerade so he didn't have to reveal the horrible scarring on his face. The entire Spring Court was to attend, even the servants, and to wear masks—to honor Tamlin's shape-shifting powers, she said. He was willing to try to end the conflict without slaughter, and he agreed to go—to bring all of us."

I pressed my hands against the stone wall behind me, savoring its coolness, its steadiness.

Pausing in the center of the kitchen, Alis set down her satchel, now full of food and supplies. "When all were assembled, she claimed that peace could be had—if Tamlin joined her as her lover and consort. But when she tried to touch him, he refused to let her near. Not after what she'd done to Lucien. He said—in front of everyone that night—that he would sooner take a human to his bed, sooner *marry* a human, than ever touch her. She might have let it go, had he not then said that her own sister had preferred a human's company to hers, that her own sister had chosen Jurian over her."

I winced, already knowing what Alis would say as she braced her hands on her hips and went on. "You can guess how well that went over with Amarantha. But she told Tamlin that she was in a generous mood—told him she'd give him a chance to break the spell she'd put upon him to steal his power.

"He spat in her face, and she laughed. She said he had seven times seven years before she claimed him, before he *had* to join her Under the Mountain. If he wanted to break her curse, he need only find a human girl willing to marry him. But not any girl—a human with ice in her heart, with hatred for our kind. A human girl willing to kill a faerie." The ground rocked beneath me, and I was grateful for the wall I leaned against. "Worse, the faerie she killed had to be one of *his* men, sent across the wall by him like lambs to slaughter. The girl could only be brought here to be courted if she killed one of his men in an unprovoked attack—killed him for hatred alone, just as Jurian had done to Clythia . . . So he could understand her sister's pain."

"The Treaty—"

"That was all a lie. There was no provision for that in the Treaty. You can kill as many innocent faeries as you want and never suffer the consequences. You just killed Andras, sent out by Tamlin as that day's sacrifice." *Andras was looking for a cure*, Tamlin had said. Not for some magical blight—but a cure to save Prythian from Amarantha, a cure for this curse.

The wolf—Andras had just . . . stared at me before I killed him. *Let* me kill him. So it could begin this chain of events, so that Tamlin might stand a chance of breaking the spell. And if Tamlin had sent Andras across the wall, knowing he might very well die . . . *Oh, Tamlin.*

Alis stooped to gather up a butter knife, twisted and bent, and carefully straightened out the blade. "It was all a cruel joke, a clever punishment, to Amarantha. You humans loathe and fear faeries so much it would be impossible—impossible for the same girl who slaughtered a faerie in cold blood to then fall in love with one. But the spell on Tamlin could only be broken if she did just that before the forty-nine years were over—if that girl said to his face that she loved him, and meant it with her entire heart. Amarantha knows humans are preoccupied with beauty, and thus bound the masks to all our faces, to his face, so it would be more difficult to find a girl willing to look beyond the mask, beyond his faerie nature, and to the soul beneath. Then she bound us so we couldn't say a word about the curse. Not a single word. We could hardly tell you a thing about our world, about our fate. He couldn't tell you—none of us properly could. The lies about the blight—that was the best he could do, the best we could all do. That I can tell you now . . . it means the game is over, to her." She pocketed the knife.

"When she first cursed him, Tamlin sent one of his men across the wall every day. To the woods, to farms, all disguised as wolves to make it more likely for one of your kind to want to kill them. If they came back, it was with stories of human girls who ran and screamed and begged, who didn't even lift a hand. When they didn't come back—Tamlin's bond with them as their Lord and master told him they'd been killed by others. Human hunters, older women, perhaps. For two years he sent them out, day after day, having to pick who crossed the wall. When all but a dozen of them were left, it broke him so badly he stopped. Called it all off. And since then, Tamlin has been here, defending his borders as chaos and disorder ruled in the other courts under Amarantha's thumb. The other High Lords fought back, too. Forty years ago, she executed three of them and most of their families for banding together against her."

"Open rebellion? What courts?" I straightened, taking a step away from the wall. Perhaps I might find allies among them to help me save Tamlin.

"The Day Court, Summer Court, and Winter Court. And no—it didn't even get far enough to be considered an open rebellion. She used the High Lords' powers to bind us to the land. So the rebel lords tried calling for aid from the other Fae territories using as messengers whatever humans were foolish enough to enter our lands—most of them young women who worshipped us like gods." The Children of the Blessed. They had indeed made it over the wall—but not to be brides. I was too battered by what I'd heard to grieve for them, rage for them.

"But Amarantha caught them all before they left these shores, and . . . you can imagine how it ended for those girls. Afterward, once Amarantha also butchered the rebellious High Lords, their successors were too terrified to tempt her wrath again."

"And where are they now? Are they allowed to live on their lands, like Tamlin was?"

"No. She keeps them and their entire courts Under the Mountain, where she can torment them as she pleases. Others—others, if they swear allegiance, if they grovel and serve her, she allows them a bit more freedom to come and go Under the Mountain as they will. Our court was only allowed to remain here until Tamlin's curse ran out, but . . ." Alis shivered.

"That's why you keep your nephews in hiding—to keep them away from this," I said, glancing at the full satchel at her feet.

Alis nodded, and as she went to right the overturned worktable, I moved to help her, both of us grunting at the weight. "My sister and I served in the Summer Court—and she and her mate were among those put down for spite when Amarantha first invaded. I took the boys and ran before Amarantha had everyone dragged Under the Mountain. I came here because it was the only place to go, and asked Tamlin to hide my boys. He did—and when I begged him to let me help, in whatever small way, he gave me a position here, days before the masque that put this wretched thing on my face. So I've been here for nearly fifty years, watching as Amarantha's noose grew tighter around his neck."

We set the table upright again, and both of us panted a bit as we slumped against it.

"He tried," Alis said. "Even with her spies, he tried finding ways to break the curse, to do anything against it, against having to send his men out again to be slaughtered by humans. He thought that if the human girl loved true, then bringing her here to free him was another form of slavery. And he thought that if he did indeed fall in love with her, Amarantha would do everything she could to destroy her, as her sister had been destroyed. So he spent decades refusing to do it, to even risk it. But this winter, with months to go, he just . . . snapped. He sent the last of his men out, one by one. And they were willing—they had begged him to go, all these years. Tamlin was desperate to save his people, desperate enough to risk the lives of his men, risk that human girl's life to save us. Three days in, Andras finally ran into a human girl in a clearing—and you killed him with hate in your heart."

But I had failed them. And in so doing, I'd damned them all.

I had damned each and every person on this estate, damned Prythian itself.

I was glad I was leaning against the table's edge—or else I might have slid to the floor.

"You could have broken it," Alis snarled, those sharp teeth mere inches from my face. "All you had to do was say that you loved him—say that you loved him and mean it with your whole useless human heart, and his power would have been freed. You stupid, *stupid* girl."

No wonder Lucien had resented me and yet still tolerated my presence—no wonder he'd been so bitterly disappointed when I left, had argued with Tamlin to let me stay longer. "I'm sorry," I said, my eyes burning.

Alis snorted. "Tell that to Tamlin. He had only three days after you left before the forty-nine years were over. *Three days*, and he let you go. She came here with her cronies at the exact moment the seven times seven years were over and seized him, along with most of the court, and brought them Under the Mountain to be her subjects. Creatures like me are too *lowly* for her—though she's not above murdering us for sport."

I tried not to visualize it. "But what of the King of Hybern—if she's conquered Prythian for herself and stolen his spells, then does he see her as insubordinate or as an ally?"

"If they are on bad terms, he has made no move to punish her. For forty-nine years now, she's held these lands in her grip. Worse, after the High Lords fell, all the wicked ones in our lands—the ones too awful even for the Night Court—flocked to her. They still do. She's offered them sanctuary. But we know—we know she's building her army, biding her time before launching an attack on your world, armed with the most lethal and vicious faeries in Prythian and Hybern."

"Like the Attor," I said, horror and dread twisting in my gut, and Alis nodded. "In the human territory," I said, "rumor claims more and more faeries have been sneaking over the wall to attack humans. And if no faeries can cross the wall without her permission, then that has to mean she's been sanctioning those attacks."

And if I was right about what had happened to Clare Beddor and her family, then Amarantha had given the order for that, too.

Alis swiped some dirt I couldn't see from the table we leaned against. "I would not be surprised if she has sent her minions into the human realm to investigate your strengths and weaknesses in anticipation of the destruction she one day hopes to cause."

This was worse—so much worse than I had thought when I warned Nesta and my family to stay on alert and leave at the slightest sign of trouble. I felt sick to think of what kind of company Tamlin was keeping—sick at the thought of him being so desperate, so stricken by guilt and grief over having to sacrifice his sentries and never being able to tell me . . . And he'd let me go. Let all their sacrifices, let Andras's sacrifice, be in vain.

He'd known that if I remained, I would be at risk of Amarantha's wrath, even if I freed him.

"I can't even protect myself against them, against what's happening in Prythian . . . Even if we stood against the blight, they would hunt you down—she would find a way to kill you."

I remembered that pathetic effort to flatter me upon my arrival—and then he'd given up on it, on any attempt to win me when I'd seemed so desperate to get away, to never talk to him. But he'd fallen in love with me despite all that—known I'd loved him, and let me go with days to spare. He had put me before his entire court, before all of Prythian.

"If Tamlin were freed—if he had his full powers," I said, staring at a blackened bit of wall, "would he be able to destroy Amarantha?"

"I don't know. She tricked the High Lords through cunning, not force. Magic's a specific kind of thing—it likes rules, and she manipulated them too well. She keeps their powers locked up inside herself, as if she can't use them, or can access very little of them, at least. She has her own deadly powers, yes, so if it came down to a fight—"

"But is he stronger?" I started wringing my hands.

"He's a High Lord," Alis replied, as if that were answer enough. "But none of that matters now. He's to be her slave, and we're all to wear these masks until he agrees to become her lover—even then, he'll never regain his full powers. And she'll never let those Under the Mountain go."

I pushed off the table and squared my shoulders. "How do I get Under the Mountain?"

She clicked her tongue. "You can't go Under the Mountain. No human who goes in ever comes out."

I squeezed my fists so hard that my nails bit into my flesh. "How. Do. I. Get. There."

"It's suicide—she'll kill you, even if you get close enough to see her."

Amarantha had tricked him—she had hurt him so badly. Hurt them all so badly.

"You're a human," Alis went on, standing as well. "Your flesh is paper-thin."

Amarantha must also have taken Lucien—she had carved out Lucien's eye and scarred him like that. Did his mother grieve for him?

"You were too blind to see Tamlin's curse," Alis continued. "How do you expect to face Amarantha? You'll make things worse."

Amarantha had taken everything I wanted, everything I finally dared desire. "Show me the way," I said, my voice trembling, but not with tears.

"No." Alis slung her satchel over a shoulder. "Go home. I'll take you as far as the wall. There's naught to be done now. Tamlin will remain her slave forever, and Prythian will stay under her rule. That's what Fate dealt, that was what the Eddies of the Cauldron decided."

"I don't believe in Fate. Nor do I believe in some ridiculous *Cauldron*."

She shook her head again, her wild brown hair like glistening mud in the dim light.

"Take me to her," I insisted.

If Amarantha ripped out my throat, at least I would die doing something for him—at least I would die trying to fix the destruction I hadn't prevented, trying to save the people I'd doomed. At least Tamlin would know it was for him, and that I loved him.

Alis studied me for a moment before her eyes softened. "As you wish."

Chapter 33

I might have been going to my death, but I wouldn't arrive unarmed.

I tightened the strap of the quiver across my chest and then grazed my fingers over the arrow feathers peeking over my shoulder. Of course, there were no ash arrows. But I would make do with what I'd found scattered throughout the manor. I could have taken more, but weapons would only weigh me down, and I didn't know how to use most of them anyway. So I wore a full quiver, two daggers at my waist, and a bow slung over a shoulder. Better than nothing, even if I was up against faeries who'd been born knowing how to kill.

Alis led me through the silent woods and foothills, pausing every so often to listen, to alter our course. I didn't want to know what she heard or smelled out there, not when such stillness blanketed the lands. *Stay with the High Lord*, the Suriel had said. Stay with him, fall in love with him, and all would be righted. If I had stayed, if I had admitted what I'd felt . . . None of this would have happened.

The world steadily filled with night, and my legs ached from the steep slopes of the hills, but Alis pressed on—never once looking back to see that I followed.

I was beginning to wonder whether I should have brought more than a day's worth of food when she stopped in the hollow between two hills. The air was cold—far colder than the air at the top of the hill, and I shivered as my eyes fell upon a slender cave mouth. There was no way this was the entrance—not when that mural had painted Under the Mountain to be in the center of Prythian. It was weeks of travel away.

"All dark and miserable roads lead Under the Mountain," Alis said so quietly that her voice was nothing more than the rustling of leaves. She pointed to the cave. "It's an ancient shortcut—once considered sacred, but no more."

This was the cave Lucien had ordered the Attor not to use that day. I tried to master my trembling. I loved Tamlin, and I would go to the ends of the earth to make it right, to save him, but if Amarantha was worse than the Attor . . . if the Attor wasn't the wickedest of her cronies . . . if even Tamlin had been scared of her . . .

"I reckon you're regretting your hotheadedness right now."

I straightened. "I *will* free him."

"You'll be lucky if she gives you a clean death. You'll be lucky if you even get brought before her." I must have turned pale, because she pursed her lips and patted me on the shoulder. "A few rules to remember, girl," she said, and we both stared at the cave mouth. The darkness reeked from its maw to poison the fresh night air. "Don't drink the wine—it's not like what we had at the Solstice, and will do more harm than good. Don't make deals with anyone unless your life depends on it—and even then, consider whether it's worth it. And most of all: don't trust a soul in there—not even your Tamlin. Your senses are your greatest enemies; they will be waiting to betray you."

I fought the urge to touch one of my daggers and nodded my thanks instead.

"Do you have a plan?"

"No," I admitted.

"Don't expect that steel to do you any good," she said with a glance at my weapons.

"I don't." I faced her, biting the inside of my lip.

"There was one part of the curse. One part we can't tell you. Even now, my bones are crying out just for mentioning it. One part you have to figure out . . . on your own, one part she . . . she . . ." She swallowed loudly. "That she still doesn't want you to know, if I can't say it," she gasped out. "But keep—keep your ears open, girl. *Listen* to what you hear."

I touched her arm. "I will. Thank you for bringing me." For wasting precious hours, when that satchel of supplies—for herself, for her boys—said enough about where she was going.

"It's a rare day indeed when someone thanks you for bringing them to their death." If I thought about the danger too long, I might lose my nerve, Tamlin or no. She wasn't helping. "I'll wish you luck nonetheless," Alis added.

"Once you retrieve them, if you and your nephews need somewhere to flee," I said, "cross the wall. Go to my family's house." I told her the location. "Ask for Nesta—my eldest sister. She knows who you are, knows everything. She will shelter you in any way she can."

Nesta would do it, too, I knew now, even if Alis and her boys terrified her. She would keep them safe. Alis patted my hand. "Stay alive," she said.

I looked at her one last time, then at the night sky that was unfurling above us, and at the deep green of the hills. The color of Tamlin's eyes.

I walked into the cave.

✣

The only sounds were my shallow breathing and the crunch of my boots on stone. Stumbling through the frigid dark, I inched onward. I kept close to the wall, and my hand soon turned numb as the cold, wet stone bit into my skin. I took small steps, fearful of some invisible pit that might send me tumbling to my doom.

After what felt like an eternity, a crack of orange light cleaved through the dark. And then came the voices.

Hissing and braying, eloquent and guttural—a cacophony bursting the silence like a firecracker. I pressed myself against the cave wall, but the sounds passed and faded.

I crept toward the light, blinking back my blindness when I found the source: a slight fissure in the rock. It opened onto a crudely carved, fire-lit subterranean passageway. I lingered in the shadows, my heart wild in my chest. The crack in the cave wall was large enough for one person to squeeze through—so jagged and rough that it was obviously not often used. A glance at the dirt revealed no tracks, no sign of anyone else using this entrance. The hallway beyond was clear, but it veered off, obscuring my view.

The passage was deathly quiet, but I remembered Alis's warning and didn't trust my ears, not when faeries could be silent as cats.

Still, I had to leave this cave. Tamlin had been here for weeks already. I had to find where Amarantha kept him. And hopefully not run into anyone in the process. Killing animals and the naga had been one thing, but killing any others . . .

I took several deep breaths, bracing myself. It was the same as hunting. Only this time the animals were faeries. Faeries who could torture me endlessly—torture me until I begged for death. Torture me the way they tormented that Summer Court faerie whose wings had been ripped off.

I didn't let myself think about those bleeding stumps as I eased toward the tiny opening, sucking in my stomach to squeeze through. My weapons scraped against the stone, and I winced at the hiss of falling pebbles. *Keep moving, keep moving.* Hurrying across the open hallway, I pressed into an alcove in the opposite wall. It didn't provide much cover.

I slunk along the wall, pausing at the bend in the hall. This was a mistake—only an idiot would come here. I could be anywhere in

Amarantha's court. Alis should have given me more information. I should have been smart enough to ask. Or smart enough to think of another way—*any* way but this.

I risked a glance around the corner and almost sobbed in frustration. Another hallway carved out of the mountain's pale stone, lined on either side by torches. No shadowy spots for concealment, and at its other end, my view was yet again obscured by a sharp turn. It was wide open. I was as good as a starving doe, ripping bark off a tree in a clearing.

But the halls were silent—the voices I'd heard earlier were gone. And if I heard anyone, I could sprint back to that cave mouth. I could do reconnaissance for a time, gather information, find out where Tamlin was—

No. A second opportunity might not arise for a while. I had to act *now*. If I stopped for too long, I'd never work up the nerve again. I made to slip around the corner.

Long, bony fingers wrapped around my arm, and I went rigid.

A pointed, leathery gray face came into view, and its silver fangs glistened as it smiled at me. "Hello," it hissed. "What's something like you doing here?"

I knew that voice. It still haunted my nightmares.

So it was all I could do to keep from screaming as its bat-like ears cocked, and I realized that I stood before the Attor.

CHAPTER 34

The Attor kept its icy grip on my upper arm as it half dragged me to the throne room. It didn't bother to strip me of my weapons. We both knew they were of little use.

Tamlin. Alis and her boys. My sisters. Lucien. I silently chanted their names again and again as the Attor loomed above me, a demon of malice. Its leathery wings rustled occasionally—and had I been able to speak without screaming, I might have asked why it hadn't killed me outright. The Attor just tugged me onward with that slithering gait, its clawed feet making leisurely scratches on the cave floor. It looked unnervingly identical to how I had painted it.

Leering faces—cruel and harsh—watched me go by, none of them looking remotely concerned or disturbed that I was in the claws of the Attor. Faeries—lots of them—but few High Fae to be seen.

We strode through two ancient, enormous stone doors—taller than Tamlin's manor—and into a vast chamber carved from pale rock, upheld by countless carved pillars. That small part of me that had again become trivial and useless noted that the carvings weren't just ornate designs, but actually depicted faeries and High Fae and animals in various environments and states of movement. Countless stories of Prythian were etched on them. Chandeliers of jewels hung between the pillars, staining the red marble floor with color. Here—here were the High Fae.

An assembled crowd took up most of the space, some of them dancing to strange, off-kilter music, some milling about chatting—a party of sorts. I thought I spied some glittering masks among the attendees, but everything was a blur of sharp teeth and fine clothing. The Attor hurled me forward, and the world spun.

The cold marble floor was unyielding as I slammed into it, my bones groaning and barking. I pushed myself up, sparks dancing in my eyes, but stayed on the ground, kept low, as I beheld the dais before me. A few steps led onto the platform. I lifted my head higher.

There, lounging on a black throne, was Amarantha.

Though lovely, she wasn't as devastatingly beautiful as I had imagined, wasn't some goddess of darkness and spite. It made her all the more petrifying. Her red-gold hair was neatly braided and woven through her golden crown, the deep color enriching her snow-white skin, which, in turn, set off her ruby lips. But while her ebony eyes shone, there was . . . *something* that sucked at her beauty, some kind of permanent sneer to her features that made her allure seem contrived and cold. To paint her would have driven me to madness.

The highest commander of the King of Hybern. She'd slaughtered human armies centuries ago, had murdered her slaves rather than free them. And she'd captured all of Prythian in a matter of days.

Then I looked to the black rock throne beside her, and my arms buckled beneath me.

He was still wearing that golden mask, still wearing his warrior's clothes, that baldric—even though there were no knives sheathed along it, not a single weapon anywhere on him. His eyes didn't widen; his mouth didn't tighten. No claws, no fangs. He just stared at me, unfeeling—unmoved. Unimpressed.

"What's this?" Amarantha said, her voice lilting despite the adder's smile she gave me. From her slender, creamy neck hung a long, thin chain—and from it dangled a single, age-worn bone the size of a finger. I didn't want to consider whom it might have belonged to as I remained on the floor. If I shifted my arm, I could draw my dagger—

"Just a human thing I found downstairs," the Attor hissed, and a forked tongue darted out between its razor-sharp teeth. It flapped its wings once, blasting foul-smelling air at me, and then neatly tucked them behind its skeletal body.

"Obviously," Amarantha purred. I avoided meeting her eyes, focusing on Tamlin's brown boots. He was ten feet from me—ten feet, and not saying a word, not even looking horrified or angry. "But why should I bother with her?"

The Attor chuckled, the sound like sizzling water on a griddle, and a taloned foot jabbed my side. "Tell Her Majesty why you were sneaking around the catacombs—why you came out of the old cave that leads to the Spring Court."

Would it be better to kill the Attor, or to try to make it to Amarantha? The Attor kicked me again, and I winced as its claws bit into my ribs. "Tell Her Majesty, you human filth."

I needed time—I needed to figure out my surroundings. If Tamlin was under some kind of spell, then I would have to worry about grabbing him. I eased to my feet, keeping my hands within casual reach of my daggers. I stared at Amarantha's glittering golden gown rather than meet her eyes.

"I came to claim the one I love," I said quietly. Perhaps the curse could still be broken. Again I looked at him, and the sight of those emerald eyes was a balm.

"Oh?" Amarantha said, leaning forward.

"I've come to claim Tamlin, High Lord of the Spring Court."

A gasp rippled through the assembled court. But Amarantha tipped back her head and laughed—a raven's caw.

The High Queen turned to Tamlin, and her lips pulled back in a wicked smile. "You certainly were busy all those years. Developed a taste for human beasts, did you?"

He said nothing, his face impassive. What had she done? He didn't move—her curse had worked, then. I was too late. I'd failed him, damned him.

"But," Amarantha said slowly. I could sense the Attor and the entire court looming behind me. "It makes me wonder—if only *one* human girl could be taken once she killed your sentinel . . ." Her eyes sparked. "Oh, you are *delicious*. You let me torture that innocent girl to keep *this* one safe? You lovely thing! You actually made a human worm love you. Marvelous." She clapped her hands, and Tamlin merely looked away from her, the only reaction I'd seen from him.

Tortured. She'd tortured—

"Let him go," I said, trying to keep my voice steady.

Amarantha laughed again. "Give me one reason why I shouldn't destroy you where you stand, human." Her teeth were so straight and white—almost glowing.

My blood pounded in my veins, but I kept my chin high as I said, "You tricked him—he is bound unfairly." Tamlin had gone very, very still.

Amarantha clicked her tongue and looked at one of her slender white hands—at the ring on her index finger. A ring, I noticed as she lowered her hand again, set with what looked like . . . like a human eye encased in crystal. I could have sworn it swiveled inside. "You human beasts are so uncreative. We spent years teaching you poetry and fine speech, and *that* is all you can come up with? I should rip out your tongue for letting it go to waste."

I clamped my teeth together.

"But I'm curious: What eloquence will pour from your lips when you behold what you should have been?" My brows narrowed as Amarantha pointed behind me, that hideous eye ring indeed looking with her, and I turned.

There, nailed high on the wall of the enormous cavern, was the mangled corpse of a young woman. Her skin was burned in places, her fingers were bent at odd angles, and garish red lines crisscrossed her naked body. I could hardly hear Amarantha over the roar in my ears.

"Perhaps I should have listened when she said she'd never seen Tamlin before," Amarantha mused. "Or when she insisted she'd never killed a faerie, never hunted a day in her life. Though her screaming was delightful. I haven't heard such lovely music in ages." Her next words were directed at me. "I should thank you for giving Rhysand her name instead of yours."

Clare Beddor.

This was where they'd taken her, what they'd done to her after they burned her family alive in their house. This was what *I'd* done to her, by giving Rhysand her name to protect my family.

My insides twisted; it was a concentrated effort not to empty my stomach onto the stones.

The Attor's talons dug into my shoulders as it shoved me around to face Amarantha, who was still giving me that snake's smile. I had as good as killed Clare. I'd saved my own life and damned her. That rotting body on the wall should be mine. Mine.

Mine.

"Come now, precious," Amarantha said. "What have you to say to that?"

I wanted to spit that she deserved to burn in Hell for eternity, but I could only see Clare's body nailed there, even as I stared blankly at Tamlin. He'd *let* them kill Clare like that—to keep them from knowing that I was alive. My eyes stung as bile burned my throat.

"Do you still wish to claim someone who would do that to an innocent?" Amarantha said softly—consolingly.

I snapped my gaze to her. I wouldn't let Clare's death be in vain. I wasn't going down without a fight. "Yes," I said. "Yes, I do."

Her lip curled back, revealing too-sharp canines. And as I stared into her black eyes, I realized I was going to die.

But Amarantha leaned back in her throne and crossed her legs. "Well, Tamlin," she said, putting a proprietary hand on his arm, "I don't suppose you ever expected *this* to occur." She waved a hand in my general direction. A murmur of laughter from those assembled echoed around me, hitting me like stones. "What do *you* have to say, High Lord?"

I looked at the face I loved so dearly, and his next words almost sent me to my knees. "I've never seen her before. Someone must have glamoured her as a joke. Probably Rhysand." Still trying to protect me, even now, even here.

"Oh, that's not even a halfway decent lie." Amarantha angled her head. "Could it be—could it be that *you*, despite your words so many years ago, return the human's feelings? A girl with hate in her heart for our kind has managed to fall in love with a faerie. And a faerie whose father once slaughtered the human masses by my side has actually fallen in love with her, too?" She let out that crow's laugh again. "Oh, this is too good—this is too fun." She fingered the bone hanging from her necklace and looked at the encased eye upon her hand. "I suppose if anyone can appreciate the moment," she said to the ring, "it would be you, Jurian." She smiled prettily. "A pity your human whore on the side never bothered to save you, though."

Jurian—that was *his* eye, his finger bone. Horror coiled in my gut. Through whatever evil, whatever power, she somehow held his soul, his consciousness, to the ring, the bone.

Tamlin still looked at me without recognition, without a flicker of feeling. Perhaps she had used that same power to glamour him; perhaps she'd taken all his memories.

The queen picked at her nails. "Things have been awfully boring since Clare decided to die on me. Killing you outright, human, would be dull." She flicked her gaze to me, then back to her nails—to the ring on her finger. "But Fate stirs the Cauldron in strange ways. Perhaps my darling Clare had to die in order for me to have some true amusement with you."

My bowels turned watery—I couldn't help it.

"You came to claim Tamlin?" Amarantha said—it wasn't a question, but a challenge. "Well, as it happens, I'm bored to tears of his sullen silence. I was worried when he didn't flinch while I played with darling Clare, when he didn't even show those lovely claws . . .

"But I'll make a bargain with you, human," she said, and warning bells pealed in my mind. *Unless your life depends on it*, Alis had said. "You complete three tasks of my choosing—three tasks to prove how deep that human sense of loyalty and love runs, and Tamlin is yours. Just three little challenges to prove your dedication, to prove to me, to darling Jurian, that your kind can indeed love true, and you can have your High Lord." She turned to Tamlin. "Consider it a favor, High Lord—these human dogs can make our kind so lust-blind that we lose all common sense. Better for you to see her true nature now."

"I want his curse broken, too," I blurted. She raised a brow, her smile growing, revealing far too many of those white teeth. "I complete all three of your tasks, and his curse is broken, and we—and all his court—can leave here. And remain free forever," I added. Magic was specific, Alis had said—that was how Amarantha had tricked them. I wouldn't let loopholes be my downfall.

"Of course," Amarantha purred. "I'll throw in another element, if you don't mind—just to see if you're worthy of one of our kind, if you're smart enough to deserve him." Jurian's eye swiveled wildly, and she clicked her tongue at it. The eye stopped moving. "I'll give you a way out, girl," she went on. "You'll complete all the tasks—*or*, when you can't stand it anymore, all you have to do is answer one question." I could barely hear her above the blood pounding in my ears. "A riddle. You solve the riddle, and his curse will be broken. *Instantaneously*. I won't even need to lift my finger and he'll be free. Say the right answer, and he's yours.

You can answer it at any time—but if you answer incorrectly . . ." She pointed, and I didn't need to turn to know she gestured to Clare.

I turned her words over, looking for traps and loopholes within her phrasing. But it all sounded right. "And what if I fail your tasks?"

Her smile became almost grotesque, and she rubbed a thumb across the dome of her ring. "If you fail a task, there won't be anything left of you for me to play with."

A chill slithered down my spine. Alis had warned me—warned me against bargains. But Amarantha would kill me in an instant if I said no. "What is the nature of my tasks?"

"Oh, revealing that would take all the fun out of it. But I'll tell you that you'll have one task every month—at the full moon."

"And in the meantime?" I dared a glance at Tamlin. The gold in his eyes was brighter than I remembered.

"In the meantime," Amarantha said a bit sharply, "you shall either remain in your cell or do whatever additional work I require."

"If you run me ragged, won't that put me at a disadvantage?" I knew she was losing interest—that she hadn't expected me to question her so much. But I had to try to gain some kind of edge.

"Nothing beyond basic housework. It's only fair for you to earn your keep." I could have strangled her for that, but I nodded. "Then we are agreed."

I knew she waited for me to echo her response, but I had to make sure. "If I complete your three tasks or solve your riddle, you'll do as I request?"

"Of course," Amarantha said. "Is it agreed?"

His face ghastly white, Tamlin's eyes met with mine, and they almost imperceptibly widened. *No*.

But it was either this or death—death like Clare's, slow and brutal. The Attor hissed behind me, a warning to reply. I didn't believe in Fate or the Cauldron—and I had no other choice.

Because when I looked into Tamlin's eyes, even now, seated beside

Amarantha as her slave or worse, I loved him with a fierceness that swept up my whole heart. Because when he had widened his eyes, I'd known he still loved me.

I had nothing left but that, but the shred of fool's hope that I might win—that I might outwit and defeat a Faerie Queen as ancient as the stone beneath me.

"Well?" Amarantha demanded. Behind me, I sensed the Attor preparing to pounce, to beat the answer from me, if need be. She'd tricked them all, but I hadn't survived poverty and years in the woods for naught. My best chance lay in revealing nothing about myself, or what I knew. What was her court but another forest, another hunting ground?

I glanced at Tamlin one last time before I said "Agreed."

Amarantha gave me a small, horrible smile, and magic sizzled in the air between us as she snapped her fingers. She nestled back in her throne. "Give her a greeting worthy of my hall," she said to someone behind me.

The Attor's hiss was my only warning as something rock-hard collided with my jaw.

I was thrown sideways, stunned from the pain, but another brutal blow to my face awaited. Bones crunched—*my* bones. My legs twisted beneath me, and the Attor's leathery skin grated against my cheek as it punched me again. I ricocheted away, but met with the fist of another—a twisted, lesser faerie whose face I didn't glimpse. It was like being slugged with a brick. *Crunch, crack*. I think there were three of them, and I became their punching bag—passed off from blow to blow, my bones screaming in agony. Maybe I was screaming in agony, too.

Blood sprayed from my mouth, and its metallic tang coated my tongue before I knew no more.

CHAPTER 35

My senses slowly returned to me, each one more painful than the last. The sound of dripping water first, then the fading echo of heavy footsteps. A lingering coppery taste coated my mouth—blood. Above the wheezing of what had to be my clogged nostrils, the tang of mold and the reek of mildew scented the damp, cold air. Sharp bits of hay jabbed my cheek. My tongue probed the makings of a split lip, and the movement set my face on fire. Wincing, I opened my eyes, but could only manage to widen them a little—swelling. What I beheld through my undoubtedly black eyes didn't do much for my spirits.

I was in a prison cell. My weapons were gone, and my only sources of light were the torches beyond the door. Amarantha had said a cell was to be where I would spend my time, but even as I sat up—my head so dizzy I almost blacked out again—my heartbeat quickened. A dungeon. I examined the slants of light that crept in through the cracks between the door and the wall, then gingerly touched my face.

It ached—ached worse than anything I'd ever endured. I bit down on a cry as my fingers grazed my nose, flakes of blood crumbling from my nostrils. It was broken. Broken. I would have clenched my teeth had my jaw not been a throbbing mess of agony, too.

I couldn't panic. No, I had to keep my tears in check, had to keep my wits together. I had to survey the damage as best I could, then figure out what to do. Maybe my shirt could be used for bandages—maybe they would give me water at some point to wash out the injuries. Taking a breath that was all too shallow, I explored the rest of my face. My jaw wasn't broken, and though my eyes were swollen and my lip was split, the worst damage was to my nose.

I curled my knees to my chest, grasping them tightly as I reined in my breathing. I'd violated one of Alis's rules. I'd had no choice, though. Seeing Tamlin seated beside Amarantha . . .

My jaw protested, but I ground my teeth anyway. The full moon—it had been a half moon when I left my father's home. How long had I been unconscious down here? I wasn't foolish enough to believe that any amount of time would prepare me for Amarantha's first task.

I didn't allow myself to imagine what she had in mind for me. It was enough to know that she expected me to die—that there wouldn't be enough *left of me* for her to torture.

I gripped my legs harder to keep my hands from shaking. Somewhere—not too far off—screaming began. A high-pitched, pleading bleat, accentuated with crescendos of shrieking that made bile sting in my throat. I might sound like that when faced with Amarantha's first task.

A whip cracked, and the screaming built, hardly pausing for a breath. Clare had probably cried similarly. I had as good as tortured her myself. What had she made of all this—all these faeries lusting after her blood and misery? I deserved this—deserved whatever pain and suffering was in store—if only for what she had endured. But . . . but I would make it right. Somehow.

I must have drifted off at some point, because I awoke to the scrape of my cell door against stone. Forgetting the cascading pain in my face, I scrambled to duck into the shadows of the nearest corner. Someone slipped into my cell and swiftly shut the door—leaving it just a bit ajar.

"Feyre?"

I tried to stand, but my legs shook so badly that I couldn't move. "Lucien?" I breathed, and the hay crunched as he dropped to the ground before me.

"By the Cauldron, are you all right?"

"My face—"

A small light flared by his head, and as his eyes swam into view, the metal one narrowed. He hissed. "Have you lost your mind? What are you doing here?"

I fought the tears—they were pointless, anyway. "I went back to the manor . . . Alis told me . . . told me about the curse, and I couldn't let Amarantha—"

"You shouldn't have come, Feyre," he said sharply. "You weren't meant to be here. Don't you understand what he sacrificed in getting you out? How could you be so foolish?"

"Well, I'm here now!" I said, louder than was wise. "I'm here, and there's nothing that can be done about it, so don't bother telling me about my weak human flesh and my stupidity! I know all that, and I . . ." I wanted to cover my face in my hands, but it hurt too much. "I just . . . I had to tell him that I love him. To see if it wasn't too late."

Lucien sat back on his heels. "So you know everything, then." I managed to nod without blacking out from the pain. My agony must have shown, because he winced. "Well, at least we don't have to lie to you anymore. Let's clean you up a bit."

"I think my nose is broken. But nothing else." As I said it, I looked around him for any signs of water or bandages—and found none. It would be magic, then.

Lucien glanced over his shoulder, checking the door. "The guards are drunk, but their replacements will be here soon," he said, and then studied my nose. I braced myself as I allowed him to gently touch it.

Even the graze of his fingertips sent flashes of burning pain through me. "I'm going to have to set it before I can heal it."

I clamped down on my blind panic. "Do it. Right now." Before I could wallow in my cowardice and tell him to forget about it. He hesitated. "*Now*," I panted.

Too swift for me to follow, his fingers latched onto my nose. Pain lanced through me, and a *crack* burst through my ears, my head, before I fainted.

When I came to, I could open both eyes fully, and my nose—my nose was clear, and didn't throb or send agony splintering through my face. Lucien was crouched over me, frowning. "I couldn't heal you completely—they would know someone helped you. The bruises are there, along with a hideous black eye, but . . . all the swelling's gone."

"And my nose?" I said, feeling it before he answered.

"Fixed—as pert and pretty as before." He smirked at me. The familiar gesture made my chest tighten to the point of pain.

"I thought she'd taken most of your power," I managed to say. I'd barely seen him handle magic at all while at the estate.

He nodded to the little light bobbing over his shoulder. "She gave me back a fraction—to entice Tamlin to accept her offer. But he still refuses her." He jerked his chin to my healed face. "I knew some good would come of being down here."

"So you're trapped Under the Mountain, too?"

A grim nod. "She's summoned all the High Lords to her now—and even those who swore obedience are now forbidden to leave until . . . until your trials are over."

Until I was dead was probably what he truly meant. "That ring," I said. "Is it—is it actually Jurian's eye?"

Lucien cringed. "Indeed. So you really know everything, then?"

"Alis didn't say what happened after Jurian and Amarantha faced each other."

"They wrecked an entire battlefield, using their soldiers as shields, until their forces were nearly all dead. Jurian had been gifted some protection against her, but once they entered into single combat . . . It didn't take her long to render him prone. Then she dragged him back to her camp and took weeks—*weeks*—to torture and kill him. She refused orders to march to the King of Hybern's aid—cost him armies and the War; she refused to do anything until she'd finished Jurian's demise. All that she kept was his finger bone and his eye. Clythia promised him that he would never die—and so long as Amarantha keeps that eye of his preserved through her magic, keeps his soul and consciousness bound to it, he'll remain trapped, watching through it. A fitting punishment for what he did, but"—Lucien tapped his own missing eye—"I'm glad she didn't do the same to me. She seems to have an obsession with that sort of thing."

I shuddered. A huntress—she was little more than an immortal, cruel huntress, collecting trophies from her kills and conquests to gloat over through the ages. The rage and despair and horror Jurian must endure every day, for eternity . . . Deserved, perhaps, but worse than anything I could imagine. I shook the thought from me. "Is Tamlin—"

"He's—" But Lucien shot to his feet at a sound my human ears couldn't hear. "The guards are about to change rotations and are headed this way. Try not to die, will you? I already have a long list of faeries to kill—I don't need to add more to it, if only for Tamlin's sake."

Which was no doubt why he'd even come down here.

Lucien vanished—just *vanished* into the dim light. A moment later, a yellowish eye tinged with red appeared at the peephole in the door, glared at me, and continued onward.

✠

I dozed on and off for what could have been hours or days. They gave me three miserable meals of stale bread and water at no regular interval that I could detect. All I knew when the door to my cell swung open was that my relentless hunger no longer mattered, and it would be wise not to struggle when the two squat, red-skinned faeries half dragged me to the throne room. I marked the path, picking out details in the hall—interesting cracks in the walls, features in the tapestries, an odd bend—anything to remind me of the way out of the dungeons.

I observed more of Amarantha's throne room this time, too, noting the exits. No windows, as we were underground. And the mountain I'd seen depicted on that map at the manor was in the heart of the land—far from the Spring Court, even farther from the wall. If I were to escape with Tamlin, my best chance would be to run for that cave in the belly of the mountain.

A crowd of faeries stood along a far wall. Over their heads, I could make out the arch of a doorway. I tried not to look up at Clare's rotting body as we passed, and instead focused on the assembled court. Everyone was clad in rich, colorful clothing—all of them seeming clean and fed. Dispersed among them were faeries with masks. The Spring Court. If I had any chance of finding allies, it would be with them.

I scanned the crowd for Lucien but didn't find him before I was thrown at the foot of the dais. Amarantha wore a gown of rubies, drawing attention to her red-gold hair and to her lips, which spread in a serpentine smile as I looked up at her.

The Faerie Queen clicked her tongue. "You look positively dreadful." She turned to Tamlin, still at her side. His expression remained distant. "Wouldn't you say she's taken a turn for the worse?"

He didn't reply; he didn't even meet my gaze.

"You know," Amarantha mused, leaning against an arm of her throne, "I couldn't sleep last night, and I realized why this morning." She ran an eye over me. "I don't know your name. If you and I are going to be such close friends for the next three months, I should know your name, shouldn't I?"

I prevented myself from nodding. There was something charming and inviting about her—a part of me began to understand why the High Lords had fallen under her thrall, believed in her lies. I hated her for it.

When I didn't reply, Amarantha frowned. "Come, now, pet. You know my name—isn't it fair that I know yours?" There was movement to my right, and I tensed as the Attor appeared through the parted crowd, grinning at me with row after row of teeth. "After all"—Amarantha waved an elegant hand to the space behind me, the crystal casing around Jurian's eye catching the light—"you've already learned the consequences of giving false names." A black cloud wrapped around me as I sensed Clare's nailed form on the wall behind me. Still, I kept my mouth shut.

"Rhysand," Amarantha said—not needing to raise her voice to summon him. My heart became a leaden weight as those casual, strolling steps sounded from behind. They stopped when they were beside me—far too close for my liking.

From the corner of my eye, I studied the High Lord of the Night Court as he bowed at the waist. Night still seemed to ripple off him, like some near-invisible cloak.

Amarantha lifted her brows. "Is this the girl you saw at Tamlin's estate?"

He brushed some invisible fleck of dust off his black tunic before he surveyed me. His violet eyes held boredom—and disdain. "I suppose."

"But did you or did you *not* tell me *that girl*," Amarantha said, her tone sharpening as she pointed to Clare, "was the one you saw?"

He stuffed his hands into his pockets. "Humans all look alike to me."

Amarantha gave him a saccharine smile. "And what about faeries?"

Rhysand bowed again—so smooth it looked like a dance. "Among a sea of mundane faces, yours is a work of art."

Had I not been straddling the line between life and death, I might have snorted.

Humans all look alike . . . I didn't believe him for a second. Rhysand knew exactly how I looked—he'd recognized me that day at the manor.

I willed my features into neutrality as Amarantha's attention again returned to me.

"What's her name?" she demanded of Rhysand.

"How would I know? She lied to me." Either toying with Amarantha was a joke to him—as much of a joke as impaling a head in Tamlin's garden—or . . . it was just more court scheming.

I braced myself for the scrape of those talons against my mind, braced myself for the order I was sure she was to give next.

Still, I kept my lips sealed. I prayed Nesta had hired those scouts and guards—prayed she'd persuaded my father to take the precautions.

"If you're inclined to play games, girl, then I suppose we can do this the fun way," Amarantha said. She snapped her fingers at the Attor, who reached into the crowd and grabbed someone. Red hair glinted, and I jolted a step as the Attor yanked Lucien forward by the collar of his green tunic. No. *No.*

Lucien thrashed against the Attor but could do nothing against those needlelike nails as it forced him to his knees. The Attor smiled, releasing his tunic, but kept close.

Amarantha flicked a finger in Rhysand's direction. The High Lord of the Night Court lifted a groomed brow. "Hold his mind," she commanded.

My heart dropped to the floor. Lucien went utterly still, sweat gleaming on his neck as Rhysand bowed his head to the queen and faced him.

Behind them, pressing to the front of the crowd, came four tall, red-haired High Fae. Toned and muscled, some of them looking like warriors about to set foot on a battlefield, some like pretty courtiers, they all stared at Lucien—and grinned. The four remaining sons of the High Lord of the Autumn Court.

"Her name, Emissary?" Amarantha asked of Lucien. But Lucien only glanced at Tamlin before closing his eyes and squaring his shoulders. Rhysand began smiling faintly, and I shuddered at the memory of what those invisible claws had felt like as they gripped my mind. How easy it would have been for him to crush it.

Lucien's brothers lurked on the edges of the crowd—no remorse, no fear on their handsome faces.

Amarantha sighed. "I thought you would have learned your lesson, Lucien. Though this time your silence will damn you as much as your tongue." Lucien kept his eyes shut. Ready—he was ready for Rhysand to wipe out everything he was, to turn his mind, his self, into dust.

"Her name?" she asked Tamlin, who didn't reply. His eyes were fixed on Lucien's brothers, as if marking who was smiling the broadest.

Amarantha ran a nail down the arm of her throne. "I don't suppose your handsome brothers know, Lucien," she purred.

"If we did, Lady, we would be the first to tell you," said the tallest. He was lean, well dressed, every inch of him a court-trained bastard. Probably the eldest, given the way even the ones who looked like born warriors stared at him with deference and calculation—and fear.

Amarantha gave him a considering smile and lifted her hand. Rhysand cocked his head, his eyes narrowing slightly on Lucien.

Lucien stiffened. A groan slipped out of him, and—

"Feyre!" I shouted. "My name is Feyre."

It was all I could do to keep from sinking to my knees as Amarantha nodded and Rhysand stepped back. He hadn't even removed his hands from his pockets.

She must have allowed him more power than the others, then, if he could still inflict such harm while leashed to her. Or else his power before she'd stolen it had been . . . extraordinary, for *this* to be considered the basest remnants.

Lucien sagged on the ground, trembling. His brothers frowned—the eldest going so far as to bare his teeth at me in a silent snarl. I ignored him.

"Feyre," Amarantha said, testing my name, the taste of the two syllables on her tongue. "An old name—from our earlier dialects. Well, *Feyre*," she said. I could have wept with relief when she didn't ask for my family name. "I promised you a riddle."

Everything became thick and murky. Why did Tamlin do nothing, say nothing? What had Lucien been about to say before he'd fled my cell?

"Solve this, Feyre, and you and your High Lord, and all his court, may immediately leave with my blessing. Let's see if you are indeed clever enough to deserve one of our kind." Her dark eyes shone, and I cleared my mind as best I could as she spoke.

There are those who seek me a lifetime but never we meet,
And those I kiss but who trample me beneath ungrateful feet.

At times I seem to favor the clever and the fair,
But I bless all those who are brave enough to dare.

By large, my ministrations are soft-handed and sweet,
But scorned, I become a difficult beast to defeat.

For though each of my strikes lands a powerful blow,
When I kill, I do it slow . . .

I blinked, and she repeated herself, smiling when she finished, smug as a cat. My mind was void, a blank mass of uselessness. Could it be some sort of disease? My mother had died of typhus, and her cousin had died of malaria after going to Bharat . . . But none of those symptoms seemed to match the riddle. Maybe it was a person?

A ripple of laughter spread across those assembled behind us, the loudest from Lucien's brothers. Rhysand was watching me, wreathed in night and smiling faintly.

The answer was so close—one little answer and we could all be free.

Immediately, she'd said—as opposed to . . . wait, had the conditions of my trials been different from those of the riddle? She'd emphasized *immediately* only when talking about solving the riddle. No, I couldn't think about that right now. I had to solve this riddle. We could all be free. *Free.*

But I couldn't do it—I couldn't even come up with a possibility. I'd be better off slitting my own throat and ending my suffering there, before she could rip me to shreds. I was a fool—a common human idiot. I looked to Tamlin. The gold in his eyes flickered, but his face betrayed nothing.

"Think on it," Amarantha said consolingly, and flicked a grin down at her ring—at the eye swiveling within. "When it comes to you, I'll be waiting."

I gazed at Tamlin even as I was pulled away to the dungeons, my vacant mind reeling.

As they locked me in my cell once more, I knew I was going to lose.

✣

I spent two days in that cell, or at least I figured it was two days, based on the meal pattern I'd begun to work out. I ate the decent parts of the half-moldy food, and though I hoped for it, Lucien never came to see me. I knew better than to wish for Tamlin.

I had little to do other than ponder Amarantha's riddle. The more I thought about it, the less sense it made. I dwelled on various kinds of poisons and venomous animals—and that yielded nothing beyond my growing sense of stupidity. Not to mention the nagging feeling that she might have wound up tricking me with this bargain when she'd emphasized *immediately* regarding the riddle. Maybe she meant she would *not* free us immediately after I finished her trials. That she could take however long she wanted. No—no, I was just being paranoid. I was overthinking it. But the riddle could free us all—instantaneously. I had to solve it.

While I'd sworn not to think too long on what tasks awaited me, I didn't doubt Amarantha's imagination, and I often awoke sweating and panting from my restless dreams—dreams in which *I* was trapped within a crystal ring, forever silent and forced to witness their bloodthirsty, cruel world, cleaved from everything I'd ever loved. Amarantha had claimed there wouldn't be enough left of me to play with if I failed a trial—and I prayed that she hadn't lied. Better to be obliterated than to endure Jurian's fate.

Still, fear like nothing I had ever known swallowed me whole when my cell door opened and the red-skinned guards told me that the full moon had arisen.

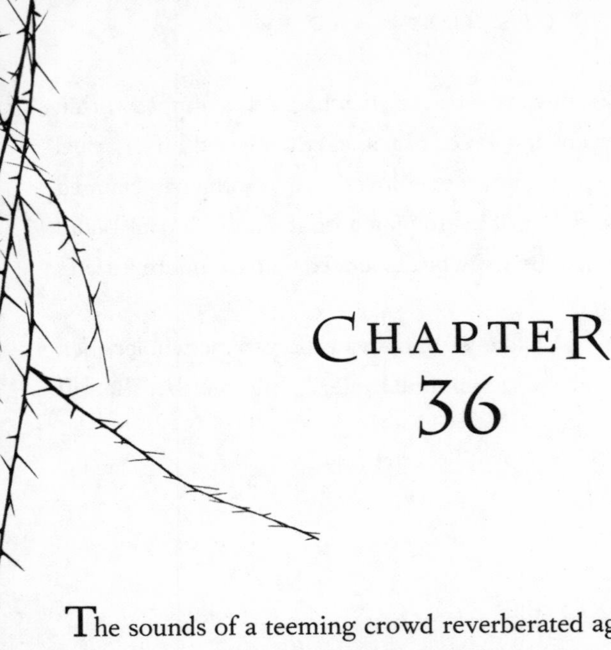

CHAPTER 36

The sounds of a teeming crowd reverberated against the passageway. My armed escort didn't bother with drawn weapons as they tugged me forward. I wasn't even shackled. Someone or something would catch me before I moved three feet and gut me where I stood.

The cacophony of laughter, shouting, and unearthly howls worsened when the hall opened into what had to be a massive arena. There had been no attempts to decorate the torch-lit cavern—and I couldn't tell if it had been hewn from the rock or if it was formed by nature. The floor was slick and muddy, and I struggled to keep my footing as we walked.

But it was the enormous, riotous crowd that turned my insides cold as they stared at me. I couldn't decipher what they were shouting, but I had a good-enough idea. Their cruel, ethereal faces and wide grins told me everything I needed to know. Not just lesser faeries but High Fae, too, their excitement making their faces almost as feral as their more unearthly brethren.

I was hauled toward a wooden platform erected above the crowd. Atop it sat Amarantha and Tamlin, and before it . . .

I did my best to keep my chin high as I beheld the exposed labyrinth of tunnels and trenches running along the floor. The crowd stood along the banks, blocking my view of what lay within as I was thrown to my knees before Amarantha's platform. The half-frozen mud seeped into my pants.

I rose on trembling legs. Around the platform stood a group of six males, secluded from the main crowd. From their cold, beautiful faces, from that echo of power still about them, I knew they were the other High Lords of Prythian. I ignored Rhysand as soon as I noticed his feline smile, the corona of darkness around him.

Amarantha had only to raise a hand and the roaring crowd silenced.

It became so quiet that I could almost hear my heart beating. "Well, Feyre," the Faerie Queen said. I tried not to look at the hand she rested on Tamlin's knee, that ring as vulgar as the gesture itself. "Your first task is here. Let us see how deep that human affection of yours runs."

I ground my teeth and almost exposed them to her. Tamlin's face remained blank.

"I took the liberty of learning a few things about you," Amarantha drawled. "It was only fair, you know."

Every instinct, every bit of me that was intrinsically human, screamed to run, but I kept my feet planted, locking my knees to avoid them giving out.

"I think you'll like this task," she said. She waved a hand, and the Attor stepped forward to part the crowd, clearing the way to the lip of a trench. "Go ahead. Look."

I obeyed. The trenches, probably twenty feet deep, were slick with mud—in fact, they seemed to have been dug from mud. I fought to keep my footing as I peered in farther. The trenches ran in a maze along the entire floor of the chamber, and their path made little sense. It was full of pits and holes, which undoubtedly led to underground tunnels, and—

Hands slammed into my back, and I cried out as I had the sickening feeling of falling before being suddenly jerked up by a bone-hard grip—up, up into the air. Laughter echoed through the chamber as I dangled from the Attor's claws, its powerful wing-beats booming across the arena. It swooped down into the trench and dropped me on my feet.

Mud squelched, and I swung my arms as I teetered and slipped. More laughter, even as I remained upright.

The mud smelled atrocious, but I swallowed my gag. I turned to find Amarantha's platform now floating to the lip of the trench. She looked down at me, smiling that serpent's grin.

"Rhysand tells me you're a huntress," she said, and my heartbeat faltered.

He must have read my thoughts again, or . . . or maybe he'd found my family, and—

Amarantha flicked her fingers in my direction. "Hunt this."

The faeries cheered, and I saw gold flash between spindly, multihued palms. Betting on my life—on how long I would last once this started.

I raised my eyes to Tamlin. His emerald gaze was frozen, and I memorized the lines of his face, the shape of his mask, the shade of his hair, one last time.

"Release it," Amarantha called. I trembled to the marrow of my bones as a grate groaned, and then a slithering, swift-moving noise filled the chamber.

My shoulders rose toward my ears. The crowd quieted to a murmur, silent enough to hear a guttural kind of grumble, so I could feel the vibrations in the ground as whatever it was rushed at me.

Amarantha clicked her tongue, and I whipped my head to her. Her brows rose. "Run," she whispered.

Then it appeared.

I ran.

It was a giant worm, or what might have once been a worm had its front end not become an enormous mouth filled with ring after ring of razor-sharp teeth. It barreled toward me, its pinkish brown body surging and twisting with horrific ease. These trenches were its lair.

And I was dinner.

Sliding and slipping on the reeking mud, I hurtled down the length of the trench, wishing I'd memorized more of the layout in the few moments I'd had, knowing full well that my path could lead to a dead end, where I would surely—

The crowd roared, drowning out the slurping and gnashing noises of the worm, but I didn't dare a glance over my shoulder. The ever-nearing stench of it told me enough about how close it was. I didn't have the breath for a sob of relief as I found a fork in the pathway and veered sharply left.

I had to get as much distance between us as possible; I had to find a spot where I could make a plan, a spot where I could find an advantage.

Another fork—I veered left again. Perhaps if I took as many lefts as I could, I could make a circle, and somehow come up behind the creature, and—

No, that was absurd. I'd have to be thrice as fast as the worm, and right now, I could barely keep ahead of it. I slid into a wall as I made another left and slammed into the slick muck. Cold, reeking, smothering. I wiped it from my eyes to find the leering faces of faeries floating above me, laughing. I ran for my life.

I reached a straight, flat stretch of trench and threw my strength to my legs as I bolted down its course. I finally dared a look over my shoulder, and my fear became wild and thrashing as the worm surged into the path, hot on my trail.

I almost missed a slender opening in the side of the trench thanks to that look, and I gave up valuable steps as I skidded to a halt to squeeze myself through the gap. It was too small for the worm, but the creature could probably shatter through the mud. If not, its teeth could do the trick. But it was worth the risk.

As I made to pull myself through, a force grabbed me back. No—not a force, but the walls. The crack was too small, and I'd so frantically thrown myself through it that I'd become wedged between it. My back to the worm, and too far between the walls to be able to turn, I couldn't see as it approached. The smell, though—the smell was growing worse.

I pushed and pulled, but the mud was too slick, and held fast.

The trenches reverberated with the thunderous movements of the worm. I could almost feel its reeking breath upon my half-exposed body, could hear those teeth slashing through the air, closer and closer. Not like this. It couldn't end like this.

I clawed at the mud, twisting, tearing at anything to pull me through. The worm neared with each of my heartbeats, the smell nearly overpowering my senses.

I ripped away mud, wriggling, kicking, and pushing, sobbing through my gritted teeth. *Not like this.*

The ground shook. A stench wrapped right around me, and hot air slammed into my body. Its teeth clicked together.

Grabbing onto the wall, I pulled and pulled. There was a squelch, and a sudden release of pressure around my middle, and I fell through the crack, sprawling in the mud.

The crowd sighed. I didn't have time for tears of relief as I found myself in another passageway, and I launched farther into the labyrinth. From the continuing quieted roars, I knew the worm had overshot me.

But that made no sense—the passage offered no place to hide. It would have seen me stuck there. Unless it couldn't break through and was now taking some alternate route, and would spring upon me.

I didn't check my speed, though I knew I wasted momentum by smashing into wall after wall as I made each sharp turn. The worm also had to lose its speed making these bends—a creature that big couldn't take the turns without slowing, no matter how dexterous it might be.

I risked a look at the crowd. Their faces were tight with

disappointment, and turned away entirely from me, toward the other end of the chamber. That was where the worm had to be—that was where that passage had ended. It hadn't seen where I went. It hadn't seen me.

It was blind.

I was so surprised that I didn't notice the enormous pit that opened before me, hidden by a slight rise, and it was all I could do to not scream as I tumbled in. Air, empty air, and—

I slammed into ankle-deep mud, and the crowd cried out. The mud softened the landing, but my teeth still sang with the impact. But nothing was broken, nothing hurt.

A few faeries peered in, leering from high above the gaping mouth of the pit. I whirled around, scanning my surroundings, trying to find the fastest way out. The pit itself opened into a small, dark tunnel, but there was no way to climb up—the wall was too steep.

I was trapped. Gasping for breath, I fumbled a few steps into the blackness of the tunnel. I bit down on my shriek as something beneath my foot crunched hard. I staggered back, and my tailbone wailed in pain. I kept scrambling away, but my hand connected with something smooth and hard, and I lifted it to see a gleam of white.

Through my muddy fingers, I knew that texture all too well. Bone.

Twisting onto my hands and knees, I patted the ground, moving farther into the darkness. Bones, bones, bones, of every shape and size, and I swallowed my scream as I realized what this place was. It was only when my hand landed on the smooth dome of a skull that I jumped to my feet.

I had to get out. *Now.*

"Feyre," I heard Amarantha's distant call. "You're ruining everyone's fun!" She said it as if I were a lousy shuttlecock partner. "Come out!"

I certainly would not, but she told me what I needed to know. The worm didn't know where I was; it couldn't smell me. I had precious seconds to get out.

As my sight adjusted to the darkness of the worm's den, mounds and mounds of bones gleamed, piles rolling away into the gloom. The chalkiness of the mud had to be from endless layers of them decomposing. I had to get out *now*, had to find a place to hide that wasn't a death trap. I stumbled out of the den, bones clattering away.

Once more in the open air of the pit, I groped one of its steep walls. Several green-faced faeries barked curses at me, but I ignored them as I tried to scale the wall, made it an inch, and slid to the floor. I couldn't get out without a rope or a ladder, and plunging farther into the worm's lair to see if there was another way out wasn't an option. Of course, there was a back door. Every animal's den had two exits, but I wasn't about to risk the darkness—effectively blinding myself—and completely eliminate my small edge.

I needed a way *up*. I tried scaling the wall again. The faeries were still murmuring their discontent; as long as they remained that way, I was fine. I again latched onto the muddy wall, digging into the pliable dirt. All I got was freezing mud digging beneath my nails as I slid to the ground yet again.

The stench of the place invaded every part of me. I bit down on my nausea as I tried again and again. The faeries were laughing now. "A mouse in a trap," one of them said. "Need a stepping stool?" another crowed.

A stepping stool.

I whirled toward the piles of bones, then pushed my hand hard against the wall. It felt firm. The entire place was made of packed mud, and if this creature was anything like its smaller, harmless brethren, I could assume that the stench—and therefore the mud itself—was the remnant of whatever had passed through its system after it sucked the bones clean.

Disregarding that wretched fact, I seized the spark of hope and grabbed the two biggest, strongest bones I could quickly find. Both were longer than my leg and heavy—so heavy as I jammed them into the wall. I didn't know what the creature usually ate, but it must have been at least cattle-sized.

"What's it doing? What's it planning?" one of the faeries hissed.

I grabbed a third bone and impaled it deep into the wall, as high as I could reach. I grabbed a fourth, slightly smaller bone and set it into my belt, strapping it across my back. Testing the three bones with a few sharp tugs, I sucked in my breath, ignored the twittering faeries, and began climbing my ladder. My stepping stool.

The first bone held firm, and I grunted as I grabbed the second bone-step and pulled myself up. I was putting my foot on the step when another idea flashed, and I paused.

The faeries—not too far off—began to shout again.

But it could work. It could work, if I played it right. It could work, because it *had* to work. I dropped back to the mud, and the faeries watching me murmured their confusion. I drew the bone from my belt, and with a sharp intake of breath, I snapped it across my knee.

My own bones burned with pain, but the shaft broke, leaving me with two sharp-ended spikes. It was going to work.

If Amarantha wanted me to hunt, I would hunt.

I walked to the middle of the pit opening, calculated the distance, and plunged the two bones into the ground. I returned back to the mound of bones and made quick work of whatever I could find that was sturdy and sharp. When my knee became too tender to use as a breaking point, I snapped the bones with my foot. One by one, I stuck them into the muddy floor beneath the pit opening until the whole area, save for one small spot, was filled with white lances.

I didn't double-check my work—it would succeed, or I would wind up among those bones on the floor. Just one chance. That was all I had. Better than no chances at all.

I dashed to my bone ladder and ignored the sting of the splinters in my fingers as I climbed to the third rung, where I balanced before embedding a fourth bone in the wall.

And just like that, I heaved myself out of the pit mouth, and almost wept to be exposed to the open air once more.

I secured the three bones I'd taken in my belt, their weight a comforting presence, and rushed to the nearest wall. I grabbed a fistful of the reeking mud and smeared it across my face. The faeries hissed as I grabbed more, this time coating my hair, then my neck. Already accustomed to the staggering reek, my eyes watered only a little as I made swift work of painting myself. I even paused to roll on the ground. Every inch of me had to be covered. Every damn inch.

If the creature was blind, then it relied on smell—and my smell would be my greatest weakness.

I rubbed mud on me until I was certain I was nothing more than a pair of blue-gray eyes. I doused myself a final time, my hands so slick that I could barely maintain a grasp on one of the sharp-ended bones as I drew it from my belt.

"What's it doing?" the green-faced faerie whined again.

A deep, elegant voice replied this time. "She's building a trap." Rhysand.

"But the Middengard—"

"Relies on its scent to see," Rhysand answered, and I gave a special glower for him as I glanced at the rim of the trench and found him smiling at me. "And Feyre just became invisible."

His violet eyes twinkled. I made an obscene gesture before I broke into a run, heading straight for the worm.

✢

I placed the remaining bones at especially tight corners, knowing well enough that I couldn't turn at the speed I hoped I would be running. It didn't take much to find the worm, as a crowd of faeries had gathered to taunt it, but I had to get to the right spot—I had to pick my battleground.

I slowed to a stalking pace and flattened my back against a wall as I heard the slithering and grunting of the worm. The crunching.

The faeries watching the worm—ten of them, with frosty blue skin and almond-shaped black eyes—giggled. I could only assume they'd grown bored of me and decided to watch something else die.

Which was wonderful, but only if the worm was still hungry—only if it would respond to the lure I offered. The crowd murmured and grumbled.

I eased around a bend, craning my neck. Too covered in its scent to smell me, the worm continued feasting, stretching its bulbous form upward as one of the faeries dangled what looked like a hairy arm. The worm gnashed its teeth, and the blue faeries cackled as they dropped the arm into its waiting mouth.

I recoiled around the bend and raised the bone-sword I'd made. I reminded myself of the path I'd taken, of the turns I'd counted.

Still, my heart lodged in my throat as I drew the jagged edge of the bone across my palm, splitting open my flesh. Blood welled, bright and shining as rubies. I let it build before clenching my hand into a fist. The worm would smell that soon enough.

It was only then that I realized the crowd had gone silent.

Almost dropping the bone, I leaned around the bend again to see the worm.

It was gone.

The blue faeries grinned at me.

Then, shattering the silence like a shooting star, a voice—*Lucien's*—bellowed across the chamber. "*TO YOUR LEFT!*"

I bolted, getting a few feet before the wall behind me exploded, mud spraying as the worm burst through, a mass of shredding teeth just inches away.

I was already running, so fast that the trenches were a blur of reddish brown. I needed a bit of distance or else it'd fall right on top of me.

But I also needed it close, so it couldn't check itself, so it was in a frenzy of hunger.

I took the first sharp turn, and grabbed onto the bone-rail I'd embedded in the corner wall. I used it to swing around, not breaking my speed, propelling me faster, giving me a few more seconds on the worm.

Then a left. My breath was a flame ravaging my throat. The second hairpin turn came upon me, and I again used the bit of bone to hurtle around the bend.

My knees and ankles groaned as I fought to keep from slipping in the mud. Only one more turn, then a straight run . . .

I flipped around the final turn, and the roar of the faeries became different than it had been earlier. The worm was a raging, crashing force behind me, but my steps were steady as I flew down the last passage.

The mouth of the pit loomed, and with a final prayer, I leaped.

There was only open black air, reaching up to swallow me.

I swung my arms as I careened down, aiming for the spot I'd planned. Pain barked through my bones, my head, as I collided with the muddy ground and rolled. I flipped over myself and screamed as something hit my arm, biting through flesh.

But I didn't have time to think, to even look at it, as I scrambled out of the way, as far into the darkness of the worm's den as I could get. I grabbed another bone and whirled when the worm plummeted into the pit.

It hit the earth and lashed its massive body to the side, anticipating the strike to kill me, but a wet, crunching noise filled the air instead.

And the worm didn't move.

I squatted there, gulping down burning air, staring into the abyss of its flesh-shredding mouth, still open wide to devour me. It took me a few heartbeats to realize the worm wasn't going to swallow me whole, and a few more heartbeats to understand that it was truly impaled on the bone spikes. Dead.

I didn't entirely hear the gasps, then the cheering—didn't quite think or feel very much of anything as I edged around the worm and slowly climbed out of the pit, still holding the bone-sword in my hand.

Silently, still beyond words, I stumbled back through the labyrinth, my left arm throbbing, but my body tingled so much I didn't notice.

But the moment I beheld Amarantha on her platform at the edge of the trench, I clenched my free hand. *Prove my love*. Pain shot through my arm, but I embraced it. I had won.

I looked up at her from beneath lowered brows and didn't check myself as I exposed my teeth. Her lips were thin, and she no longer grasped Tamlin's knee.

Tamlin. *My* Tamlin.

I tightened my grip on the long bone in my hand. I was shaking—shaking all over. But not with fear. Oh, no. It wasn't fear at all. I'd proved my love—and then some.

"Well," Amarantha said with a little smirk. "I suppose anyone could have done that."

I took a few running steps and hurled the bone at her with all my remaining strength.

It embedded itself in the mud at her feet, splattering filth onto her white gown, and remained there, quivering.

The faeries gasped again, and Amarantha stared at the wobbling bone before touching the mud on her bodice. She smiled slowly. "Naughty," she tsked.

Had there not been an insurmountable trench between us, I would have ripped her throat out. Someday—if I lived through this—I would skin her alive.

"I suppose you'll be happy to learn most of my court lost a good deal of money tonight," she said, picking up a piece of parchment. I looked at Tamlin as she scanned the paper. His green eyes were bright, and though his face was deathly pale, I could have sworn there was a ghost of triumph on his face. "Let's see," Amarantha went on, reading the paper as she toyed with Jurian's finger bone at the end of her necklace. "Yes, I'd say almost my entire court bet on you dying within the first minute; some said you'd last five, and"—she turned over the paper—"and just one person said you would win."

Insulting, but not surprising. I didn't fight as the Attor hauled me out of the trenches, dumping me at the foot of the platform before flying off. My arm burned at the impact.

Amarantha frowned at her list, and she waved a hand. "Take her away. I tire of her mundane face." She clenched the arms of her throne hard enough that the whites of her knuckles showed. "Rhysand, come here."

I didn't stay long enough to see the High Lord prowl forward. Red hands grabbed me, holding tightly to keep from sliding off. I'd forgotten the mud caked on me like a second skin. As they yanked me away, a shooting pain shot along my arm, and agony blanketed my senses.

I looked at my left forearm then, and my stomach rose at the trickling blood and ripped tendons, at the lips of my skin pulled back to accommodate the shaft of a bone shard protruding clean through it.

I couldn't even glance back at Tamlin, couldn't find Lucien to say thank you before pain consumed me whole, and I could barely manage to walk back to my cell.

CHAPTER 37

No one, not even Lucien, came to fix my arm in the days following my victory. The pain overwhelmed me to the point of screaming whenever I prodded the embedded bit of bone, and I had no other option but to sit there, letting the wound gnaw on my strength, trying my best not to think about the constant throbbing that shot sparks of poisoned lightning through me.

But worse than that was the growing panic—panic that the wound hadn't stopped bleeding. I knew what it meant when blood continued to flow. I kept one eye on the wound, either out of hope that I'd find the blood clotting, or the terror that I'd spy the first signs of infection.

I couldn't eat the rotten food they gave me. The sight of it aroused such nausea that a corner of my cell now reeked of vomit. It didn't help that I was still covered in mud, and the dungeon was perpetually freezing.

I was sitting against the far wall of my cell, savoring the coolness of the stone beneath my back. I'd awoken from a fitful sleep and found myself burning hot. A kind of fire that made everything a bit muddled. My injured arm dangled at my side as I gazed dully at the cell door. It seemed to sway, its lines rippling.

This heat in my face was some kind of small cold—not a fever from infection. I put a hand on my chest, and dried mud crumbled into my lap. Each of my breaths was like swallowing broken glass. Not a fever. Not a fever. Not a fever.

My eyelids were heavy, stinging. I couldn't go to sleep. I had to make sure the wound wasn't infected, I had to . . . to . . .

The door actually did move then—no, not the door, but rather the darkness around it, which seemed to ripple. Real fear coiled in my stomach as a male figure formed out of that darkness, as if he'd slipped in from the cracks between the door and the wall, hardly more than a shadow.

Rhysand was fully corporeal now, and his violet eyes glowed in the dim light. He slowly smiled from where he stood by the door. "What a sorry state for Tamlin's champion."

"Go to Hell," I snapped, but the words were little more than a wheeze. My head was light and heavy all at once. If I tried to stand, I would topple over.

He stalked closer with that feline grace and dropped into an easy crouch before me. He sniffed, grimacing at the corner splattered with my vomit. I tried to bring my feet into a position more inclined for scrambling away or kicking him in the face, but they were full of lead.

Rhysand cocked his head. His pale skin seemed to radiate alabaster light. I blinked away the haze, but couldn't even turn aside my face as his cold fingers grazed my brow. "What would Tamlin say," he murmured, "if he knew his beloved was rotting away down here, burning up with fever? Not that he can even come here, not when his every move is watched."

I kept my arm hidden in the shadows. The last thing I needed them to know was how weak I was. "Get away," I said, and my eyes stung as the words burned my throat. I had difficulty swallowing.

He raised an eyebrow. "I come here to offer you help, and you have the nerve to tell me to leave?"

"Get away," I repeated. My eyes were so sore that it hurt to keep them open.

"You made me a lot of money, you know. I figured I would repay the favor."

I leaned my head against the wall. Everything was spinning—spinning like a top, spinning like . . . I kept my nausea down.

"Let me see your arm," he said too quietly.

I kept my arm in the shadows—if only because it was too heavy to lift.

"Let me see it." A growl rippled from him. Without waiting for my reaction, he grabbed my elbow and forced my arm into the dim light of the cell.

I bit my lip to keep from crying out—bit it hard enough to draw blood as rivers of fire exploded inside me, as my head swam, and all my senses narrowed down to the piece of bone sticking through my arm. They couldn't know—couldn't know how bad it was, because then they would use it against me.

Rhysand examined the wound, a smile appearing on his sensuous lips. "Oh, that's wonderfully gruesome." I swore at him, and he chuckled. "Such words from a lady."

"Get out," I wheezed. My frail voice was as terrifying as the wound.

"Don't you want me to heal your arm?" His fingers tightened around my elbow.

"At what cost?" I shot back, but kept my head against the stone, needing its damp strength.

"Ah, *that*. Living among faeries has taught you some of our ways."

I focused on the feeling of my good hand on my knee—focused on the dry mud beneath my fingernails.

"I'll make a trade with you," he said casually, and gently set my arm down. As it met with the floor, I had to close my eyes to brace against the flow of that poisoned lightning. "I'll heal your arm in exchange for *you*. For two weeks every month, two weeks of my choosing, you'll live with me at the Night Court. Starting after this messy three-trials business."

My eyes flew open. "No." I'd already made one fool's bargain.

"No?" He braced his hands on his knees and leaned closer. "Really?"

Everything was starting to dance. "Get out," I breathed.

"You'd turn down my offer—and for what?" I didn't reply, so he went on. "You must be holding out for one of your friends—for Lucien, correct? After all, he healed you before, didn't he? Oh, don't look so innocent. The Attor and his cronies broke your nose. So unless you have some kind of magic you're not telling us about, I don't think human bones heal that quickly." His eyes sparkled, and he stood, pacing a bit. "The way I see things, Feyre, you have two options. The first, and the smartest, would be to accept my offer."

I spat at his feet, but he kept pacing, only giving me a disapproving look.

"The second option—and the one only a fool would take—would be for you to refuse my offer and place your life, and thus Tamlin's, in the hands of chance."

He stopped pacing and stared hard at me. Though the world spun and danced in my vision, something primal inside me went still and cold beneath that gaze.

"Let's say I walk out of here. Perhaps Lucien will come to your aid within five minutes of my leaving. Perhaps he'll come in five days. Perhaps he won't come at all. Between you and me, he's been keeping a low profile after his rather embarrassing outburst at your trial. Amarantha's not exactly pleased with him. Tamlin even broke his delightful brooding to beg for him to be spared—such a noble warrior, your High Lord. She listened, of course—but only after she made Tamlin bestow Lucien's punishment. Twenty lashes."

I started shaking, sick all over again to think about what it had to have been like for my High Lord to be the one to punish his friend.

Rhysand shrugged, a beautiful, easy gesture. "So, it's really a question of how much you're willing to trust Lucien—and how much you're willing to risk for it. Already you're wondering if that fever of yours is the first sign of infection. Perhaps they're unconnected, perhaps not. Maybe it's fine. Maybe that worm's mud isn't full of festering filth. And maybe Amarantha will send a healer, and by that time, you'll either be dead, or they'll find your arm so infected that you'll be lucky to keep anything above the elbow."

My stomach tightened into a painful ball.

"I don't need to invade your thoughts to know these things. I already know what you've slowly been realizing." He again crouched in front of me. "You're dying."

My eyes stung, and I sucked my lips into my mouth.

"How much are you willing to risk on the hope that another form of help will come?"

I stared at him, sending as much hate as I could into my gaze. He'd been the one who'd caused all this. He'd told Amarantha about Clare; he'd made Tamlin beg.

"Well?"

I bared my teeth. "Go. To. Hell."

Swift as lightning, he lashed out, grabbing the shard of bone in my arm and twisting. A scream shattered out of me, ravaging my aching throat. The world flashed black and white and red. I thrashed and writhed, but he kept his grip, twisting the bone a final time before releasing my arm.

Panting, half sobbing as the pain reverberated through my body, I found him smirking at me again. I spat in his face.

He only laughed as he stood, wiping his cheek with the dark sleeve of his tunic.

"This is the last time I'll extend my assistance," he said, pausing by the cell door. "Once I leave this cell, my offer is dead." I spat again, and he shook his head. "I bet you'll be spitting on Death's face when she comes to claim you, too."

He began to ripple with darkness, his edges blurring into endless night.

He could be bluffing, trying to trick me into accepting his offer. Or he might be right—I might be dying. My life depended on it. *More* than my life depended on my choice. And if Lucien was indeed unable to come . . . or if he came too late . . .

I *was* dying. I'd known it for some time now. And Lucien had underestimated my abilities in the past—had never quite grasped my limitations as a human. He'd sent me to hunt the Suriel with a few knives and a bow. He'd even admitted to hesitating that day, when I had screamed for help. And he might not even know how bad off I was. Might not understand the gravity of an infection like this. He might come a day, an hour, a minute too late.

Rhysand's moon-white skin began to darken into nothing but shadow.

"Wait."

The darkness consuming him paused. For Tamlin . . . for Tamlin, I would sell my soul; I would give up everything I had for him to be free.

"Wait," I repeated.

The darkness vanished, leaving Rhysand in his solid form as he grinned. "Yes?"

I raised my chin as high as I could manage. "Just two weeks?"

"Just two weeks," he purred, and knelt before me. "Two teensy, tiny weeks with me every month is all I ask."

"Why? And what are to . . . to be the terms?" I said, fighting past the dizziness.

"Ah," he said, adjusting the lapel of his obsidian tunic. "If I told you those things, there'd be no fun in it, would there?"

I looked at my ruined arm. Lucien might never come, might decide I wasn't worth risking his life any further, not now that he'd been punished for it. And if Amarantha's healers cut off my arm . . .

Nesta would have done the same for me, for Elain. And Tamlin had done so much for me, for my family; even if he had lied about the Treaty, about sparing me from its terms, he'd still saved my life that day against the naga, and saved it again by sending me away from the manor.

I couldn't think entirely of the enormity of what I was about to give—or else I might refuse again. I met Rhysand's gaze. "Five days."

"You're going to bargain?" Rhysand laughed under his breath. "Ten days."

I held his stare with all my strength. "A week."

Rhysand was silent for a long moment, his eyes traveling across my body and my face before he murmured: "A week it is."

"Then it's a deal," I said. A metallic taste filled my mouth as magic stirred between us.

His smile became a bit wild, and before I could brace myself, he grabbed my arm. There was a blinding, quick pain, and my scream sounded in my ears as bone and flesh were shattered, blood rushed out of me, and then—

Rhysand was still grinning when I opened my eyes. I hadn't any idea how long I'd been unconscious, but my fever was gone, and my head was clear as I sat up. In fact, the mud was gone, too; I felt as if I'd just bathed.

But then I lifted my left arm.

"What have you done to me?"

Rhysand stood, running a hand through his short, dark hair. "It's custom in my court for bargains to be permanently marked upon flesh."

I rubbed my left forearm and hand, the entirety of which was now covered in swirls and whorls of black ink. Even my fingers weren't spared, and a large eye was tattooed in the center of my palm. It was feline, and its slitted pupil stared right back at me.

"Make it go away," I said, and he laughed.

"You humans are truly grateful creatures, aren't you?"

From a distance, the tattoo looked like an elbow-length lace glove, but when I held it close to my face, I could detect the intricate depictions of flowers and curves that flowed throughout to make up a larger pattern. Permanent. Forever.

"You didn't tell me this would happen."

"You didn't ask. So how am I to blame?" He walked to the door but lingered, even as pure night wafted off his shoulders. "Unless this lack of gratitude and appreciation is because you fear a certain High Lord's reaction."

Tamlin. I could already see his face going pale, his lips becoming thin as the claws came out. I could almost hear the growl he'd emit when he asked me what I had been thinking.

"I think I'll wait to tell him until the moment's right, though," Rhysand said. The gleam in his eyes told me enough. Rhysand hadn't done any of this to save me, but rather to hurt Tamlin. And I'd fallen into his trap—fallen into it worse than the worm had fallen into mine.

"Rest up, Feyre," Rhysand said. He turned into nothing more than living shadow and vanished through a crack in the door.

CHAPTER 38

I tried not to look at my left arm as I scrubbed at the floors of the hallway. The ink—which, in the light, was actually a blue so dark it appeared black—was a cloud upon my thoughts, and those were bleak enough even without knowing I'd sold myself to Rhysand. I couldn't look at the eye on my palm. I had an absurd, creeping feeling that it watched me.

I dunked the large brush into the bucket the red-skinned guards had thrown into my arms. I could barely comprehend them through their mouths full of long yellow teeth, but when they gave me the brush and bucket and shoved me into a long hallway of white marble, I understood.

"If it's not washed and shining by supper," one of them had said, its teeth clicking as it grinned, "we're to tie you to the spit and give you a few good turns over the fire."

With that, they left. I had no idea when supper was, and so I frantically began washing. My back already ached like fire, and I hadn't been scrubbing the marble hall for more than thirty minutes. But the water they'd given me was filthy, and the more I scrubbed the floor, the dirtier it became. When I went to the door to ask for a bucket of clean water, I found it locked. There would be no help.

An impossible task—a task to torment me. The spit—perhaps that was the source of the constant screaming in the dungeons. Would a few turns on the spit melt all the flesh from me, or just burn me badly enough to force me into another bargain with Rhysand? I cursed as I scrubbed harder, the coarse bristles of the brush crinkling and whispering against the tiles. A rainbow of brown was left in their wake, and I growled as I dunked the brush again. Filthy water came out with it, dripping all over the floor.

A trail of brown muck grew with each sweep. Breathing quickly, I hurled the brush to the ground and covered my face with my wet hands. I lowered my left hand when I realized the eye was pressed against my cheek.

I gulped down steadying gasps of air. There had to be a rational way to do this; there had to be some old wives' trick. The spit—tied to a spit like a roast pig.

I grabbed the brush from where it had bounced away and scrubbed at the floor until my hands throbbed. It looked like someone had spilled mud all over the place. The dirt was *actually* turning into mud the harder I scrubbed it. I'd probably wail and beg for mercy when they rotated me on that spit. There had been red lines covering Clare's naked body—what instrument of torture had they come from? My hands trembled, and I set down the brush. I could take down a giant worm, but washing a floor—*that* was the impossible task.

A door clicked open somewhere down the hall, and I shot to my feet. An auburn head peered at me. I sagged with relief. Lucien—

Not Lucien. The face that turned toward me was female—and unmasked.

She looked perhaps a bit older than Amarantha, but her porcelain skin was exquisitely colored, graced with the faintest blush of rose along her cheeks. Had the red hair not been indication enough, when her russet eyes met mine, I knew who she was.

I bowed my head to the Lady of the Autumn Court, and she inclined her chin slightly. I supposed that was honor enough. "For giving her your name in place of my son's life," she said, her voice as sweet as sun-warmed apples. She must have been in the crowd that day. She pointed at the bucket with a long, slender hand. "My debt is paid." She disappeared through the door she'd opened, and I could have sworn I smelled roasting chestnuts and crackling fires in her wake.

It was only after the door shut that I realized I should have thanked her, and only after I looked in my bucket that I realized I'd been hiding my left arm behind my back.

I knelt beside the bucket and dipped my fingers into the water. They came out clean.

I shuddered, allowing myself a moment to slump over my knees before I dumped some of the water onto the floor and watched it wash away the muck.

✣

To the chagrin of the guards, I had completed their impossible task. But the next day, they smiled at me as they shoved me into a massive, dark bedroom, lit only by a few candles, and pointed to the looming fireplace. "Servant spilled lentils in the ash," one of the guards grunted, tossing me a wooden bucket. "Clean it up before the occupant returns, or he'll peel off your skin in strips."

A slammed door, the click of a lock, and I was alone.

Sorting lentils from ash and embers—ridiculous, wasteful, and—

I approached the darkened fireplace and cringed.

Impossible.

I cast a glance about the bedroom. No windows, no exits save the one I'd just been chucked through. The bed was enormous and neatly made, its black sheets of—of silk. There was nothing else in the room beyond basic furniture; not even discarded clothes or books or weapons.

As if its occupant never slept here. I knelt before the fireplace and calmed my breathing.

I had keen eyes, I reminded myself. I could spot rabbits hiding in the underbrush and track most things that wanted to remain unseen. Spotting the lentils couldn't be *that* hard. Sighing, I crawled farther into the fireplace and began.

✢

I was wrong.

Two hours later, my eyes were burning and aching, and even though I combed through every inch of that fireplace, there were always more lentils, more and *more* that I'd somehow not spotted. The guards had never said *when* the owner of this room would return, and so every tick of the clock on the mantel became a death knell, every footstep outside the door causing me to reach for the iron poker leaning against the hearth wall. Amarantha had never said anything about not fighting back—never specified that I wasn't allowed to defend myself. At least I'd go down swinging.

I picked through the ashes again and again. My hands were now black and stained, my clothes covered in soot. Surely there couldn't be any more; surely—

The lock clicked, and I lunged for the poker as I shot to my feet, my back to the hearth and the iron rod hidden behind me.

Darkness entered the room, guttering the candles with a snow-kissed breeze. I gripped the poker harder, pressing against the stone of the fireplace, even as that darkness settled on the bed and took a familiar form.

"As wonderful as it is to see you, Feyre, darling," Rhysand said, sprawled on the bed, his head propped up by a hand, "do I want to know why you're digging through my fireplace?"

I bent my knees slightly, preparing to run, to duck, to do anything to get to the door that felt far, far away. "They said I had to clean out lentils from the ashes, or you'd rip off my skin."

"Did they now." A feline smile.

"Do I have you to thank for this idea?" I hissed. He wasn't allowed to kill me, not with my bargain with Amarantha, but . . . there were other ways to hurt me.

"Oh, no," he drawled. "No one's learned of *our* little bargain yet—and you've managed to keep it quiet. Shame riding you a bit hard?"

I clenched my jaw and pointed to the fireplace with one hand, still keeping the poker tucked behind me. "Is this clean enough for you?"

"Why were there lentils in my fireplace to begin with?"

I gave him a flat look. "One of your mistress's *household chores*, I suppose."

"Hm," he said, examining his nails. "Apparently she or her cronies think I'll find some sport with you."

My mouth dried up. "Or it's a test for you," I managed to get out. "You said you bet on me during my first task. She didn't seem pleased about it."

"And what could Amarantha possibly have to test me about?"

I didn't balk from that violet stare. *Amarantha's whore*, Lucien had once called him. "You lied to her. About Clare. You knew very well what I looked like."

Rhysand sat up in a fluid movement and braced his forearms on his thighs. Such grace contained in such a powerful form. *I was slaughtering on the battlefield before you were even born*, he'd once said to Lucien. I didn't doubt it. "Amarantha plays her games," he said simply, "and I play mine. It gets rather boring down here, day after day."

"She let you out for Fire Night. And you somehow got out to put that head in the garden."

"She asked me to put that head in the garden. And as for Fire Night . . ." He looked me up and down. "I had my reasons to be out then. Do not think, Feyre, that it did not cost me." He smiled again, and it didn't meet his eyes. "Are you going to put down that poker, or can I expect you to start swinging soon?"

I swallowed my curse and brought it out—but didn't put it down.

"A valiant effort, but useless," he said. True—so true, when he didn't even need to take his hands out of his pockets to grip Lucien's mind.

"How is it that you have such power still and the others don't? I thought she robbed all of you of your abilities."

He lifted a groomed, dark brow. "Oh, she took my powers. This . . ." A caress of talons against my mind. I jerked back a step, slamming into the fireplace. The pressure on my mind vanished. "This is just the remnant. The scraps I get to play with. Your Tamlin has brute strength and shape-shifting; my arsenal is a far deadlier assortment."

I knew he wasn't bluffing—not when I'd felt those talons in my mind. "So you can't shape-shift? It's not some High Lord specialty?"

"Oh, all the High Lords can. Each of us has a beast roaming beneath our skin, roaring to get out. While your Tamlin prefers fur, I find wings and talons to be more entertaining."

A lick of cold kissed down my spine. "Can you shift now, or did she take that, too?"

"So many questions from a little human."

But the darkness that hovered around him began to writhe and twist and flare as he rose to his feet. I blinked, and it was done.

I lifted the iron poker, just a little bit.

"Not a full shift, you see," Rhysand said, clicking the black razor-sharp talons that had replaced his fingers. Below the knee, darkness stained his skin—but talons also gleamed in lieu of toes. "I don't particularly like yielding wholly to my baser side."

Indeed, it was still Rhysand's face, his powerful male body, but flaring out behind him were massive black membranous wings—like a bat's, like the Attor's. He tucked them in neatly behind him, but the single claw at the apex of each peeked over his broad shoulders. Horrific, stunning—the face of a thousand nightmares and dreams. That again-useless part of me stirred at the sight, the way the candlelight shone through the wings, illuminating the veins, the way it bounced off his talons.

Rhysand rolled his neck, and it all vanished in a flash—the wings, the talons, the feet, leaving only the male behind, well-dressed and unruffled. "No attempts at flattery?"

I had made a very, very big mistake in offering my life to him.

But I said, "You have a high-enough opinion of yourself already. I doubt the flattery of a little human matters much to you."

He let out a low laugh that slid along my bones, warming my blood. "I can't decide whether I should consider you admirable or very stupid for being so bold with a High Lord."

Only around him did I have trouble keeping my mouth shut, it seemed. So I dared to ask, "Do you know the answer to the riddle?"

He crossed his arms. "Cheating, are you?"

"She never said I couldn't ask for help."

"Ah, but after she had you beaten to hell, she ordered us not to help you." I waited. But he shook his head. "Even if I felt like helping you, I couldn't. She gives the order, and we all bow to it." He picked a fleck of dust off his black jacket. "It's a good thing she likes me, isn't it?"

I opened my mouth to press him—to beg him. If it meant instantaneous freedom—

"Don't waste your breath," he said. "I can't tell you—no one here can. If she ordered us all to stop breathing, we would have to obey that, too." He frowned at me and snapped his fingers. The soot, the dirt, the ash vanished off my skin, leaving me as clean as if I'd bathed. "There. A gift—for having the balls to even ask."

I gave him a flat stare, but he motioned to the hearth.

It was spotless—and my bucket was filled with lentils. The door swung open of its own accord, revealing the guards who'd dragged me here.

Rhysand waved a lazy hand at them. "She accomplished her task. Take her back."

They grabbed for me, but he bared his teeth in a smile that was anything but friendly—and they halted. "No more household chores, no more tasks," he said, his voice an erotic caress. Their yellow eyes went glazed and dull, their sharp teeth gleaming as their mouths slackened. "Tell the others, too. Stay out of her cell, and don't touch her. If you do, you're to take your own daggers and gut yourselves. Understood?"

Dazed, numb nods, then they blinked and straightened. I hid my trembling. Glamour, mind control—whatever it was he had done, it worked. They beckoned—but didn't dare touch me.

Rhysand smiled at me. "You're welcome," he purred as I walked out.

CHAPTER 39

From that point on, each morning and evening, a fresh, hot meal appeared in my cell. I gobbled it down but cursed Rhysand's name anyway. Stuck in the cell, I had nothing to do but ponder Amarantha's riddle—usually only to wind up with a pounding headache. I recited it again and again and again, but to no avail.

Days passed, and I didn't see Lucien or Tamlin, and Rhysand never came to taunt me. I was alone—utterly alone, locked in silence—though the screaming in the dungeons still continued day and night. When that screaming became too unbearable and I couldn't shut it out, I would look at the eye tattooed on my palm. I wondered if he'd done it to quietly remind me of Jurian—a cruel, petty slap to the face indicating that perhaps I was well on my way to belonging to him just as the ancient warrior now belonged to Amarantha.

Every once in a while, I'd say a few words to the tattoo—then curse myself for a fool. Or curse Rhysand. But I could have sworn that as I dozed off one night, it blinked.

If I was counting the schedule of my meals correctly, about four days after I'd seen Rhysand in his room, two High Fae females arrived in my cell.

They appeared through the cracks from slivers of darkness, just as Rhysand had. But while he'd solidified into a tangible form, these faeries remained mostly made of shadow, their features barely discernable, save for their loose, flowing cobweb gowns. They remained silent when they reached for me. I didn't fight them—there was nothing to fight them with, and nowhere to run. The hands they clasped around my forearms were cool but solid—as if the shadows were a coating, a second skin.

They had to have been sent by Rhysand—some servants of his from the Night Court. They could have been mutes for all they said to me as they pressed close to my body and we stepped—physically stepped—*through* the closed door, as if it wasn't even there. As if I had become a shadow, too. My knees buckled at the sensation, like spiders crawling down my spine, my arms, as we walked through the dark, shrieking dungeons. None of the guards stopped us—they didn't even look in our direction. We were glamoured, then; no more than flickering darkness to the passing eye.

The faeries brought me up through dusty stairwells and down forgotten halls until we reached a nondescript room where they stripped me naked, bathed me roughly, and then—to my horror—began to paint my body.

Their brushes were unbearably cold and ticklish, and their shadowy grips were firm when I wriggled. Things only worsened when they painted more intimate parts of me, and it was an effort to keep from kicking one of them in the face. They offered no explanation for why—no hint of whether this was another torment sent by Amarantha. Even if I fled, there was nowhere to escape to—not without damning Tamlin further. So I stopped demanding answers, stopped fighting back, and let them finish.

From the neck up, I was regal: my face was adorned with cosmetics—rouge on my lips, a smearing of gold dust on my eyelids, kohl lining my eyes—and my hair was coiled around a small golden diadem imbedded with lapis lazuli. But from the neck down, I was a heathen god's plaything. They had continued the pattern of the tattoo on my arm, and once the blue-black paint had dried, they placed on me a gauzy white dress.

If you could call it a dress. It was little more than two long shafts of gossamer, just wide enough to cover my breasts, pinned at each shoulder with gold brooches. The sections flowed down to a jeweled belt slung low across my hips, where they joined into a single piece of fabric that hung between my legs and to the floor. It barely covered me, and from the cold air on my skin, I knew that most of my backside was left exposed.

The cold breeze caressing my bare skin was enough to kindle my rage. The two High Fae ignored my demands to be clothed in something else, their impossibly shadowed faces veiled from me, but held my arms firm when I tried to rip the shift off.

"I wouldn't do that," a deep, lilting voice said from the doorway. Rhysand was leaning against the wall, his arms crossed over his chest.

I should have known it was his doing, should have known from the matching designs all over my body. "Our bargain hasn't started yet," I snapped. The instincts that had once told me to be quiet around Tam and Lucien utterly failed me when Rhysand was near.

"Ah, but I need an escort for the party." His violet eyes glittered with stars. "And when I thought of you squatting in that cell all night, alone . . ." He waved a hand, and the faerie servants vanished through the door behind him. I flinched as they walked through the wood—no doubt an ability everyone in the Night Court possessed—and Rhysand chuckled. "You look just as I hoped you would."

From the cobwebs of my memory, I recalled similar words Tamlin had once whispered into my ear. "Is this necessary?" I said, gesturing to the paint and clothing.

"Of course," he said coolly. "How else would I know if anyone touches you?"

He approached, and I braced myself as he ran a finger along my shoulder, smearing the paint. As soon as his finger left my skin, the paint fixed itself, returning the design to its original form. "The dress itself won't mar it, and neither will your movements," he said, his face close to mine. His teeth were far too near to my throat. "And I'll remember precisely where *my* hands have been. But if anyone else touches you—let's say a certain High Lord who enjoys springtime—I'll know." He flicked my nose. "And, Feyre," he added, his voice a caressing murmur, "I don't like my belongings tampered with."

Ice wrapped around my stomach. He owned me for a week every month. Apparently, he thought that extended to the rest of my life, too.

"Come," Rhysand said, beckoning with a hand. "We're already late."

✢

We walked through the halls. The sounds of merriment rose ahead of us, and my face burned as I silently bemoaned the too-sheer fabric of my dress. Beneath it, my breasts were visible to everyone, the paint hardly leaving anything to the imagination, and the cold cave air raised goose bumps on my skin. With my legs, sides, and most of my stomach exposed save for the slender shafts of fabric, I had to clench my teeth to keep them from chattering. My bare feet were half-frozen, and I hoped that wherever we were going would have a giant fire.

Queer, off-kilter music brayed through two stone doors that I immediately recognized. The throne room. *No.* No, anyplace but here.

Faeries and High Fae gawked as we passed through the entrance. Some bowed to Rhysand, while others gaped. I spied several of Lucien's older brothers gathered just inside the doors. The smiles they gave me were nothing short of vulpine.

Rhysand didn't touch me, but he walked close enough for it to be obvious that I was with him—that I *belonged* to him. I wouldn't have been surprised if he'd attached a collar and leash around my neck. Maybe he would at some point, now that I was bound to him, the bargain marked on my flesh.

Whispers snaked under the shouts of celebrating, and even the music quieted as the crowd parted and made a path for us to Amarantha's dais. I lifted my chin, the weight of the crown digging into my skull.

I'd beaten her first task. I'd beaten her menial chores. I could keep my head high.

Tamlin was seated beside her on that same throne, in his usual clothing, no weapons sheathed anywhere on him. Rhysand had said that he wanted to tell him at the right moment, that he'd wanted to *hurt* Tamlin by revealing the bargain I'd made. Prick. Scheming, wretched prick.

"Merry Midsummer," Rhysand said, bowing to Amarantha. She wore a rich gown of lavender and orchid-purple—surprisingly modest. I was a savage before her cultivated beauty.

"What have you done with my captive?" she said, but her smile didn't reach her eyes.

Tamlin's face was like stone—like stone, save for the white-knuckled grip on the arms of his throne. No claws. He was able to keep that sign of his temper at bay, at least.

I'd done such a foolish thing in binding myself to Rhysand. Rhysand, with the wings and talons lurking beneath that beautiful, flawless surface; Rhysand, who could shatter minds. *I did it for you*, I wanted to shout.

"We made a bargain," Rhysand said. I flinched as he brushed a stray lock of my hair from my face. He ran his fingers down my cheek—a gentle caress. The throne room was all too quiet as he spoke his next words to Tamlin. "One week with me at the Night Court every month in exchange for my healing services after her first task." He raised my left arm to reveal the tattoo, whose ink didn't shine as much as the paint on my body. "For the rest of her life," he added casually, but his eyes were now upon Amarantha.

The Faerie Queen straightened a little bit—even Jurian's eye seemed fixed on me, on Rhysand. *For the rest of my life*—he said it as if it were going to be a long, long while.

He thought I was going to beat her tasks.

I stared at his profile, at the elegant nose and sensuous lips. Games—Rhysand liked to play games, and it seemed I was now to be a key player in whatever this one was.

"Enjoy my party" was Amarantha's only reply as she toyed with the bone at the end of her necklace. Dismissed, Rhysand put a hand on my back to steer us away, to turn me from Tamlin, who still gripped the throne.

The crowd kept a good distance, and I couldn't acknowledge any of them, out of fear I might have to look at Tamlin again, or might spy Lucien—glimpse the expression on his face when he beheld me.

I kept my chin up. I wouldn't let the others notice that weakness—wouldn't let them know how much it killed me to be so exposed to them, to have Rhysand's symbols painted over nearly every inch of my skin, to have Tamlin see me so debased.

Rhysand stopped before a table laden with exquisite foods. The High Fae around it quickly cleared away. If there were any other members of the Night Court present, they didn't ripple with darkness the way Rhysand and his servants did; didn't dare approach him. The music grew loud enough to suggest there was probably dancing somewhere in the room. "Wine?" he said, offering me a goblet.

Alis's first rule. I shook my head.

He smiled, and extended the goblet again. "Drink. You'll need it."

Drink, my mind echoed, and my fingers stirred, moving toward the goblet. No. No, Alis said not to drink the wine here—wine that was different from that joyous, freeing solstice wine. "No," I said, and some faeries who were watching us from a safe distance chuckled.

"Drink," he said, and my traitorous fingers latched onto the goblet.

⸸

I awoke in my cell, still clad in that handkerchief he called a dress. Everything was spinning so badly that I barely made it to the corner before I vomited. Again. And again. When I'd emptied my stomach, I crawled to the opposite corner of the cell and collapsed.

Sleep came fitfully as the world continued to twirl violently around me. I was tied to a spinning wheel, going around and around and around—

Needless to say, I was sick a fair amount that day.

I'd just finished picking at the hot dinner that had appeared moments before when the door creaked and a golden fox-face appeared—along with a narrowed metal eye. "Shit," said Lucien. "It's freezing in here."

It was, but I was too nauseated to notice. Keeping my head up was an effort, let alone keeping the food down. He unclasped his cloak and set it around my shoulders. Its heavy warmth leaked into me. "Look at all this," he said, staring at the paint on me. Thankfully, it was all intact, save for a few places on my waist. "Bastard."

"What happened?" I got out, even though I wasn't sure I truly wanted the answer. My memory was a dark blur of wild music.

Lucien drew back. "I don't think you want to know." I studied the few smudges on my waist, marks that looked like hands had held me.

"Who did that to me?" I asked quietly, my eyes tracing the arc of the spoiled paint.

"Who do you think?"

My heart clenched and I looked at the floor. "Did—did Tamlin see it?"

Lucien nodded. "Rhys was only doing it to get a rise out of him."

"Did it work?" I still couldn't look Lucien in the face. I knew, at least, that I hadn't been violated beyond touching my sides. The paint told me that much.

"No," Lucien said, and I smiled grimly.

"What—what was I doing the whole time?" So much for Alis's warning.

Lucien let out a sharp breath, running a hand through his red hair. "He had you dance for him for most of the night. And when you weren't dancing, you were sitting in his lap."

"What *kind* of dancing?" I pushed.

"Not the kind you were doing with Tamlin on Solstice," Lucien said, and my face heated. From the murkiness of my memories of last night, I recalled the closeness of a certain pair of violet eyes—eyes that sparkled with mischief as they beheld me.

"In front of everyone?"

"Yes," Lucien replied—more gently than I'd heard him speak to me before. I stiffened. I didn't want his pity. He sighed and grabbed my left arm, examining the tattoo. "What were you thinking? Didn't you know I'd come as soon as I could?"

I yanked my arm from him. "I was *dying*! I had a fever—I was barely able to keep conscious! How was I supposed to know you'd come? That you even understood how quickly humans can die of that sort of thing? You told me you *hesitated* that time with the naga."

"I swore an oath to Tamlin—"

"I had no other choice! You think I'm going to trust you after everything you said to me at the manor?"

"I risked my neck for you during your task. Was that not enough?" His metal eye whirred softly. "You offered up your name for me—after all that I said to you, all I did, you still offered up your name. Didn't you realize I would help you after that? Oath or no oath?"

I hadn't realized it would mean anything to him at all. "I had no other choice," I said again, breathing hard.

"Don't you understand what Rhys *is*?"

"I do!" I barked, then sighed. "I do," I repeated, and glared at the eye in my palm. "It's done with. So you needn't hold to whatever oath you swore to Tamlin to protect me—or feel like you owe me anything for saving you from Amarantha. I would have done it just to wipe the smirk off your brothers' faces."

Lucien clicked his tongue, but his remaining russet eye shone. "I'm glad to see you didn't sell your lively human spirit or stubbornness to Rhys."

"Just a week of my life every month."

"Yes, well—we'll see about *that* when the time comes," he growled, that metal eye flicking to the door. He stood. "I should go. The rotation's about to shift."

He made it a step before I said, "I'm sorry—that she still punished you for helping me during my task. I heard—" My throat tightened. "I heard what she made Tamlin do to you." He shrugged, but I added, "Thank you. For helping me, I mean."

He walked to the door, and for the first time I noticed how stiffly he moved. "It's why I couldn't come sooner," he said, his throat bobbing. "She used her—used *our* powers to keep my back from healing. I haven't been able to move until today."

Breathing became a little difficult. "Here," I said, removing his cloak and standing to hand it to him. The sudden cold sent gooseflesh rippling over me.

"Keep it. I swiped it off a dozing guard on my way in here." In the dim light, the embroidered symbol of a sleeping dragon glimmered. Amarantha's coat of arms. I grimaced, but shrugged it on.

"Besides," Lucien added with a smirk, "I've seen enough of you through that gown to last a lifetime." I flushed as he opened the door.

"Wait," I said. "Is—is Tamlin all right? I mean . . . I mean that spell Amarantha has him under to make him so silent . . ."

"There's no spell. Hasn't it occurred to you that Tamlin is keeping quiet to avoid telling Amarantha which form of your torment affects him most?"

No, it hadn't.

"He's playing a dangerous game, though," Lucien said, slipping out the door. "We all are."

✠

The next night, I was again washed, painted, and brought to that miserable throne room. Not a ball this time—just some evening entertainment.

Which, it turned out, was me. After I drank the wine, though, I was mercifully unaware of what was happening.

Night after night, I was dressed in the same way and made to accompany Rhysand to the throne room. Thus I became Rhysand's plaything, the harlot of Amarantha's whore. I woke with vague shards of memories—of dancing between Rhysand's legs as he sat in a chair and laughed; of his hands, stained blue from the places they touched on my waist, my arms, but somehow, never more than that. He had me dance until I was sick, and once I was done retching, told me to begin dancing again.

I awoke ill and exhausted each morning, and though Rhysand's order to the guards had indeed held, the nightly activities left me thoroughly drained. I spent my days sleeping off the faerie wine, dozing to escape the humiliation I endured. When I could, I contemplated Amarantha's riddle, turning over every word—to no avail.

And when I again entered that throne room, I was allowed only a glimpse of Tamlin before the drug of the wine took hold. But every time, every night, just for that one glance, I didn't hide the love and pain that welled in my eyes when they met his.

✢

I had finished being painted and dressed—my gossamer gown a shade of blood orange that night—when Rhysand entered the room. The shadow maids, as usual, walked through the walls and vanished. But rather than beckon me to come with him, Rhysand closed the door.

"Your second trial is tomorrow night," he said neutrally. The gold-and-silver thread in his black tunic shone in the candlelight. He never wore another color.

It was like a stone to the head. I'd lost count of the days. "So?"

"It could be your last," he said, and leaned against the door frame, crossing his arms.

"If you're taunting me into playing another game of yours, you're wasting your breath."

"Aren't you going to beg me to give you a night with your beloved?"

"I'll have that night, and all the ones after, when I beat her final task."

Rhysand shrugged, then flashed a grin as he pushed off the door and stepped toward me. "I wonder if you were this prickly with Tamlin when you were his captive."

"He never treated me like a captive—or a slave."

"No—and how could he? Not with the shame of his father and brothers' brutality always weighing on him, the poor, noble beast. But perhaps if he'd bothered to learn a thing or two about cruelty, about what it means to be a true High Lord, it would have kept the Spring Court from falling."

"Your court fell, too."

Sadness flickered in those violet eyes. I wouldn't have noticed it had I not . . . *felt* it—deep inside me. My gaze drifted to the eye etched in my palm. What manner of tattoo, exactly, had he given me? But instead I asked, "When you were roaming freely on Fire Night—at the Rite—you said it cost you. Were you one of the High Lords that sold allegiance to Amarantha in exchange for not being forced to live down here?"

Whatever sadness had been in his eyes vanished—only cold, glittering calm remained. I could have sworn a shadow of mighty wings stained the wall behind him. "What I do or have done for my Court is none of your concern."

"And what has she been doing for the past forty-nine years? Holding court and torturing everyone as she pleases? To what end?" *Tell me about the threat she poses to the human world*, I wanted to beg—*tell me what all of this means*, why *so many awful things had to happen*.

"The Lady of the Mountain needs no excuses for her actions."

"But—"

"The festivities await." He gestured to the door behind him.

I knew I was on dangerous ground, but I didn't care. "What do you want with me? Beyond taunting Tamlin."

"Taunting him is my greatest pleasure," he said with a mock bow. "And as for your question, why does any male need a reason to enjoy the presence of a female?"

"You saved my life."

"And through *your* life, I saved Tamlin's."

"Why?"

He winked, smoothing his blue-black hair. "That, Feyre, is the real question, isn't it?"

With that, he led me from the room.

We reached the throne room, and I braced myself to be drugged and disgraced again. But it was Rhysand the crowd looked at—Rhysand whom Lucien's brothers monitored. Amarantha's clear voice rang out over the music, summoning him.

He paused, glancing at Lucien's brothers stalking toward us, their attention pinned on me. Eager, hungry—wicked. I opened my mouth, not too proud to ask Rhysand not to leave me alone with them while he dealt with Amarantha, but he put a hand on my back and nudged me along.

"Just stay close, and keep your mouth shut," he murmured in my ear as he led me by the arm. The crowd parted as if we were on fire, revealing all too soon what was before us.

Not us, I amended, but Rhysand.

A brown-skinned High Fae male was sobbing on the floor before the dais. Amarantha was smiling at him like a snake—so intently that she didn't even spare me a glance. Beside her, Tamlin remained utterly impassive. A beast without claws.

Rhysand flicked his eyes to me—a silent command to stay at the edge of the crowd. I obeyed, and when I lifted my attention to Tamlin, waiting for him to look—just *look* at me—he did not, his focus wholly on the queen, on the male before her. Point taken.

Amarantha caressed her ring, watching every movement that Rhysand made as he approached. "The summer lordling," she said of the male cowering at her feet, "tried to escape through the exit to the Spring Court lands. I want to know why."

There was a tall, handsome High Fae male standing at the crowd's edge—his hair near-white, eyes of crushing, crystal blue, his skin of richest mahogany. But his mouth was drawn as his attention darted between Amarantha and Rhysand. I'd seen him before, during that first task—the High Lord of the Summer Court. Before, he'd been shining—almost leaking golden light; now he was muted, drab. As if Amarantha had leeched every last drop of power from him while she interrogated his subject.

Rhysand slid his hands into his pockets and sauntered closer to the male on the ground.

The Summer faerie cringed, his face shining with tears. My own bowels turned watery with fear and shame as he wet himself at the sight of Rhysand. "P-p-please," he gasped out.

The crowd was breathless, too silent.

His back to me, Rhysand's shoulders were loose, not a stitch of clothing out of place. But I knew his talons had latched onto the faerie's mind the moment the male stopped shaking on the ground.

The High Lord of Summer had gone still, too—and it was pain, real pain, and fear that shone in those stunning blue eyes. Summer was one of the courts that had rebelled, I remembered. So this was a new, untested High Lord, who had not yet had to make choices that cost him lives.

After a moment of silence, Rhysand looked at Amarantha. "He wanted to escape. To get to the Spring Court, cross the wall, and flee south into human territory. He had no accomplices, no motive beyond his own pathetic cowardice." He jerked his chin toward the puddle of piss beneath the male. But out of the corner of my eye I saw the Summer High Lord sag a bit—enough to make me wonder . . . wonder what sort of choice Rhys had made in that moment he'd taken to search the male's mind.

But Amarantha rolled her eyes and slouched in her throne. "Shatter him, Rhysand." She flicked a hand at the High Lord of the Summer Court. "You may do what you want with the body afterward."

The High Lord of the Summer Court bowed—as if he'd been given a gift—and looked to his subject, who had gone still and calm on the floor, hugging his knees. The male faerie was ready—relieved.

Rhys slipped a hand out of his pocket, and it dangled at his side. I could have sworn phantom talons flickered there as his fingers curled slightly.

"I'm growing bored, Rhysand," Amarantha said with a sigh, again fiddling with that bone. She hadn't looked at me once, too focused on her current prey.

Rhysand's fingers curled into a fist.

The faerie male's eyes went wide—then glazed as he slumped to the side in the puddle of his own waste. Blood leaked from his nose, from his ears, pooling on the floor.

That fast—that easily, that irrevocably . . . he was dead.

"I said shatter his mind, not his brain," Amarantha snapped.

The crowd murmured around me, stirring. I wanted nothing more than to fade back into it—to crawl back into my cell and burn this from my mind. Tamlin hadn't flinched—not a muscle. What horrors had he witnessed in his long life if this hadn't broken that distant expression, that control?

Rhysand shrugged, his hand sliding back into his pocket. "Apologies, my queen." He turned away without being dismissed, and didn't look at me as he strode for the back of the throne room. I fell into step beside him, reining in my trembling, trying not to think about the body sprawled behind us, or about Clare—still nailed to the wall.

The crowd stayed far, far back as we walked through it. "Whore," some of them softly hissed at him, out of her earshot; "Amarantha's whore." But many offered tentative, appreciative smiles and words—"Good that you killed him; good that you killed the traitor."

Rhysand didn't deign to acknowledge any of them, his shoulders still loose, his footsteps unhurried. I wondered whether anyone but he and the High Lord of the Summer Court knew that the killing had been a mercy. I was willing to bet that there *had* been others involved in that escape plan, perhaps even the High Lord of the Summer Court himself.

But maybe keeping those secrets had only been done in aid of whatever games Rhysand liked to play. Maybe sparing that faerie male by killing him swiftly, rather than shattering his mind and leaving him a drooling husk, had been another calculated move, too.

He didn't pause once on that long trek across the throne room, but when we reached the food and wine at the back of the room, he handed me a goblet and downed one alongside me. He didn't say anything before the wine swept me into oblivion.

Chapter 40

My second task arrived.

Its teeth gleaming, the Attor grinned at me as I stood before Amarantha. Another cavern—smaller than the throne room, but large enough to perhaps be some sort of old entertaining space. It had no decorations, save for its gilded walls, and no furniture; the queen herself only sat on a carved wooden chair, Tamlin standing behind her. I didn't gaze too long at the Attor, who lingered on the other side of the queen's chair, its long, slender tail slashing across the floor. It only smiled to unnerve me.

It was working. Not even gazing at Tamlin could calm me. I clenched my hands at my sides as Amarantha smiled.

"Well, Feyre, your second trial has come." She sounded so smug—so certain that my death hovered nearby. I'd been a fool to refuse death in the teeth of the worm. She crossed her arms and propped her chin on a hand. Within the ring, Jurian's eye turned—*turned* to face me, its pupil dilating in the dim light. "Have you solved my riddle yet?"

I didn't deign to make a response.

"Too bad," she said with a moue. "But I'm feeling generous tonight." The Attor chuckled, and several faeries behind me gave hissing laughs that snaked their way up my spine. "How about a little practice?" Amarantha said, and I forced my face into neutrality. If Tamlin was playing indifferent to keep us both safe, so would I.

But I dared a glance at my High Lord, and found his eyes hard upon me. If I could just hold him, feel his skin for just a moment—smell him, hear him say my name . . .

A slight hiss echoed across the room, dragging my gaze away. Amarantha was frowning up at Tamlin from her seat. I hadn't realized we'd been staring at each other, the cavern wholly silent.

"Begin," Amarantha snapped.

Before I could brace myself, the floor shuddered.

My knees wobbled, and I swung my arms to keep upright as the stones beneath me began sinking, lowering me into a large, rectangular pit. Some faeries cackled, but I found Tamlin's stare again and held it until I was lowered so far down that his face disappeared beyond the edge.

I scanned the four walls around me, looking for a door, for any sign of what was to come. Three of the walls were made of a single sheet of smooth, shining stone—too polished and flat to climb. The other wall wasn't a wall at all, but an iron grate splitting the chamber in two, and through it—

My breath caught in my throat. "Lucien."

Lucien lay chained to the center of the floor on the other side of the chamber, his remaining russet eye so wide that it was surrounded with white. The metal one spun as if set wild; his brutal scar was stark against his pale skin. Again he was to be Amarantha's toy to torment.

There were no doors, no way for me to get to his side except to climb over the gate between us. It had such thick, wide holes that I could probably climb it to jump onto his side. I didn't dare.

The faeries began murmuring, and gold clinked. Had Rhysand bet on me again? In the crowd, red hair gleamed—four heads of red hair—and I stiffened my spine. I knew his brothers would be smiling at Lucien's predicament—but where was his mother? His father? Surely the High Lord of the Autumn Court would be present. I scanned the crowd. No sign of them. Only Amarantha, standing with Tamlin at the edge of the pit, peering in. She bowed her head to me and gestured with an elegant hand to the wall beneath her feet.

"Here, Feyre darling, you shall find your task. Simply answer the question by selecting the correct lever, and you'll win. Select the wrong one to your doom. As there are only three options, I think I gave you an unfair advantage." She snapped her fingers, and something metallic groaned. "That is," she added, "if you can solve the puzzle in time."

Not too high above, the two giant, spike-encrusted grates I'd dismissed as chandeliers began lowering, slowly descending toward the chamber—

I whirled to Lucien. That was the reason for the gate cleaving the chamber in two—so I would have to watch as he splattered beneath, just as I myself was squashed. The spikes, which had been supporting candles and torches, glowed red—and even from a distance, I could see the heat rippling off them.

Lucien wrenched at his chains. This would not be a clean death.

And then I turned to the wall that Amarantha had gestured to.

A lengthy inscription was carved into its smooth surface, and beneath it were three stone levers with the numbers *I*, *II*, and *III* engraved above them.

I began to shake. I recognized only basic words—useless ones like *the* and *but* and *went*. Everything else was a blur of letters I didn't know, letters I'd have to slowly sound out or research to understand.

The spiked grate was still descending, now level with Amarantha's head, and would soon shut off any chance I stood of getting out of this pit. The heat from the glowing iron already smothered me, sweat starting to bead at my temples. Who had told her I couldn't read?

"Something wrong?" She raised an eyebrow. I snapped my attention to the inscription, keeping my breathing as steady as I could. She hadn't mentioned reading as an issue—she would have mocked me more if she'd known about my illiteracy. Fate—a cruel, vicious twist of fate.

The chains rattled and strained, and Lucien cursed as he beheld what was before me. I turned to him, but when I saw his face, I knew he was too far to be able to read it aloud to me, even with his enhanced metal eye. If I could hear the question, I might stand a chance at solving it—but riddles weren't my strong point.

I was going to be skewered by burning-hot spikes and then crushed on the ground like a grape.

The grate now passed over the lip of the pit, filling it entirely—no corner was safe. If I didn't answer the question before the grate passed the levers—

My throat closed up, and I read and read and read, but no words came. The air became thick and stank of metal—not magic but burning, unforgiving steel creeping toward me, inch by inch.

"Answer it!" Lucien shouted, his voice hitched. My eyes stung. The world was just a blur of letters, mocking me with their turns and shapes.

The metal groaned as it scraped against the smooth stone of the chamber, and the faeries' whispers grew more frenzied. Through the holes in the grate, I thought I saw Lucien's eldest brother chuckle. Hot—so unbearably hot.

It would hurt—those spikes were large and blunt. It wouldn't be quick. It would take some force to pierce through my body. Sweat slid down my neck, my back as I stared at the letters, at the *I*, *II*, and *III* that had somehow become my lifeline. Two choices would doom me—one choice would stop the grate.

I found numbers in the inscription—it must be a riddle, a logic problem, a maze of words worse than any worm's labyrinth.

"*Feyre!*" Lucien cried, panting as he stared at the ever-lowering spikes. The gleeful faces of the High Fae and lesser faeries sneered at me above the grate.

Three . . . grass . . . grasshope . . . grasshoppers . . .

The gate wouldn't stop, and there wasn't a full body length between my head and the first of those spikes. I could have sworn the heat devoured the air in the pit.

. . . were . . . boo . . . bow . . . boon . . . king . . . sing . . . bouncing . . .

I should say my good-byes to Tamlin. Right now. This was what my life amounted to—these were my last moments, this was it, the final breaths of my body, the last beatings of my heart.

"*Just pick one!*" Lucien shouted, and some of those in the crowd laughed—his brothers no doubt the loudest.

I reached a hand toward the levers and stared at the three numbers beyond my trembling, tattooed fingers.

I, II, III.

They meant nothing to me beyond life and death. Chance might save me, but—

Two. Two was a lucky number, because that was like Tamlin and me—just two people. One had to be bad, because one was like Amarantha, or the Attor—solitary beings. One was a nasty number, and three was too much—it was three sisters crammed into a tiny cottage, hating each other until they choked on it, until it poisoned them.

Two. It was two. I could gladly, willingly, fanatically believe in a Cauldron and Fate if they would take care of me. I believed in two. Two.

I reached for the second lever, but a blinding pain racked my hand before I could touch the stone. I hissed, withdrawing. I opened my palm to reveal the slitted eye tattooed there. It narrowed. I had to be hallucinating.

The grate was about to cover the inscription, barely six feet above my head. I couldn't breathe, couldn't think. The heat was too much, and metal sizzled, so close to my ears.

I again reached for the middle lever, but the pain paralyzed my fingers.

The eye had returned to its usual state. I extended my hand toward the first lever. Again, pain.

I reached for the third lever. No pain. My fingers met with stone, and I looked up to find the grate not four feet from my head. Through it, I found a star-flecked violet gaze.

I reached for the first lever. Pain. But when I reached for the third lever . . .

Rhysand's face remained a mask of boredom. Sweat slipped down my brow, stinging my eyes. I could only trust him; I could only give myself up again, forced to concede by my helplessness.

The spikes were so enormous up close. All I had to do was lift my arm above my head and I'd burn the flesh off my hands.

"*Feyre, please!*" Lucien moaned.

I shook so badly I could scarcely stand. The heat of the spikes bore down on me.

The stone lever was cool in my hand.

I shut my eyes, unable to look at Tamlin, bracing myself for the impact and the agony, and pulled the third lever.

Silence.

The pulsing heat didn't grow closer. Then—a sigh. *Lucien.*

I opened my eyes to find my tattooed fingers white-knuckled beneath the ink as they gripped the lever. The spikes hovered not inches from my head.

Unmoving—stopped.

I had won—I had . . .

The grate groaned as it lifted toward the ceiling, cool air flooding the chamber. I gulped it down in uneven breaths.

Lucien was offering up some kind of prayer, kissing the ground again and again. The floor beneath me rose, and I was forced to release the lever that had saved me as I was brought to the surface again. My knees wobbled.

I couldn't read, and it had almost killed me. I hadn't even won properly. I sank to my knees, letting the platform carry me, and covered my face in my shaking hands.

Tears burned just before pain seared through my left arm. I would never beat the third task. I would never free Tamlin, or his people. The pain shot through my bones again, and through my increasing hysteria, I heard words inside my head that stopped me short.

Don't let her see you cry.

Put your hands at your sides and stand up.

I couldn't. I couldn't move.

Stand. Don't give her the satisfaction of seeing you break.

My knees and spine, not entirely of my own will, forced me upright, and when the ground at last stopped moving, I looked at Amarantha with tearless eyes.

Good, Rhysand told me. *Stare her down. No tears—wait until you're back in your cell.* Amarantha's face was drawn and white, her black eyes like onyx as she beheld me. I had won, but I should be dead. I should be squashed, my blood oozing everywhere.

Count to ten. Don't look at Tamlin. Just stare at her.

I obeyed. It was the only thing that kept me from giving in to the sobs trapped within my chest, thundering to get out.

I willed myself to meet Amarantha's gaze. It was cold and vast and full of ancient malice, but I held it. I counted to ten.

Good girl. Now walk away. Turn on your heel—good. Walk toward the door. Keep your chin high. Let the crowd part. One step after another.

I listened to him, let him keep me tethered to sanity as I was escorted back to my cell by the guards—who still kept their distance. Rhysand's words echoed through my mind, holding me together.

But when my cell door closed, he went silent, and I dropped to the floor and wept.

⸸

I wept for hours. For myself, for Tamlin, for the fact that I should be dead and had somehow survived. I cried for everything I'd lost, every injury I'd ever received, every wound—physical or otherwise. I cried for that trivial part of me, once so full of color and light—now hollow and dark and empty.

I couldn't stop. I couldn't breathe. I couldn't beat her. She won today, and she hadn't known it.

She'd won; it was only by cheating that I'd survived. Tamlin would never be free, and I would perish in the most awful of ways. I couldn't read—I was an ignorant, human fool. My shortcomings had caught up with me, and this place would become my tomb. I would never paint again; never see the sun again.

The walls closed in—the ceiling dropped. I wanted to be crushed; I wanted to be snuffed out. Everything converged, squeezing inward, sucking out air. I couldn't keep myself in my body—the walls were forcing me out of it. I was grasping for my body, but it hurt too much each time I tried to maintain the connection. All I had wanted—all I had dared want, was a life that was quiet, easy. Nothing more than that. Nothing extraordinary. But now . . . now . . .

I felt the ripple in the darkness without having to look up, and didn't flinch at the soft footsteps that approached me. I didn't bother hoping that it would be Tamlin. "Still weeping?"

Rhysand.

I didn't lower my hands from my face. The floor rose toward the lowering ceiling—I would soon be flattened. There was no color, no light here.

"You've just beaten her second task. Tears are unnecessary."

I wept harder, and he laughed. The stones reverberated as he knelt before me, and though I tried to fight him, his grip was firm as he grasped my wrists and pried my hands from my face.

The walls weren't moving, and the room was open—gaping. No colors, but shades of darkness, of night. Only those star-flecked violet eyes were bright, full of color and light. He gave me a lazy smile before he leaned forward.

I pulled away, but his hands were like shackles. I could do nothing as his mouth met with my cheek, and he licked away a tear. His tongue was hot against my skin, so startling that I couldn't move as he licked away another path of salt water, and then another. My body went taut and loose all at once and I burned, even as chills shuddered along my limbs. It was only when his tongue danced along the damp edges of my lashes that I jerked back.

He chuckled as I scrambled for the corner of the cell. I wiped my face as I glared at him.

He smirked, sitting down against a wall. "I figured that would get you to stop crying."

"It was disgusting." I wiped my face again.

"Was it?" He quirked an eyebrow and pointed to his palm—to the place where my tattoo would be. "Beneath all your pride and stubbornness, I could have sworn I detected something that felt differently. Interesting."

"Get out."

"As usual, your gratitude is overwhelming."

"Do you want me to kiss your feet for what you did at the trial? Do you want me to offer another week of my life?"

"Not unless you feel compelled to do so," he said, his eyes like stars.

It was bad enough that my life was forfeited to this Fae lord—but to have a bond where he could now freely read my thoughts and feelings and communicate . . .

"Who would have thought that the self-righteous human girl couldn't read?"

"Keep your damned mouth shut about it."

"Me? I wouldn't dream of telling anyone. Why waste that kind of knowledge on petty gossip?"

If I'd had the strength, I would have leaped on him and ripped him apart. "You're a disgusting bastard."

"I'll have to ask Tamlin if this kind of flattery won his heart." He groaned as he stood, a soft, deep-throated noise that traveled along my bones. His eyes met with mine, and he smiled slowly. I exposed my teeth, almost hissing.

"I'll spare you the escort duties tomorrow," he said, shrugging as he walked to the cell door. "But the night after, I expect you to be looking your finest." He gave me a grin that suggested my finest wasn't very much at all. He paused by the door, but didn't dissolve into darkness. "I've been thinking of ways to torment you when you come to my court. I'm wondering: Will assigning you to learn to read be as painful as it looked today?"

He vanished into shadow before I could launch myself at him.

I paced through my cell, scowling at the eye in my hand. I spat every curse I could at it, but there was no response.

It took me a long while to realize that Rhysand, whether he knew it or not, had effectively kept me from shattering completely.

Chapter 41

What followed the second trial was a series of days that I don't care to recall. A permanent darkness settled over me, and I began to look forward to the moment when Rhysand gave me that goblet of faerie wine and I could lose myself for a few hours. I stopped contemplating Amarantha's riddle—it was impossible. Especially for an illiterate, ignorant human.

Thinking of Tamlin made everything worse. I'd beaten two of Amarantha's tasks, but I knew—knew it deep in my bones—that the third would be the one to kill me. After what had happened to her sister, what Jurian had done, she would never let me leave here alive. I couldn't entirely blame her; I doubted I would ever forget or forgive something like that being done to Nesta or Elain, no matter how many centuries had passed. But I still wasn't going to leave here alive.

The future I'd dreamed of was just that: a dream. I'd grow old and withered, while he would remain young for centuries, perhaps millennia. At best, I'd have decades with him before I died.

Decades. That was what I was fighting for. A flash in time for them—a drop in the pool of their eons.

So I greedily drank the wine, and I stopped caring about who I was and what had once mattered to me. I stopped thinking about color, about light, about the green of Tamlin's eyes—about all those things I had still wanted to paint and now would never get to.

I wasn't going to leave this mountain alive.

⁜

I was walking to the dressing chamber with Rhysand's two shadow-servants, staring at nothing and thinking of even less, when a hissing noise and the flap of wings sounded from around an upcoming corner. The Attor. The faeries beside me tensed, but their chins rose slightly.

I'd never become accustomed to the Attor, but I had come to accept its malignant presence. Seeing my escorts stiffen awakened a dormant dread, and my mouth turned dry as we neared the bend. Even though we were veiled and hidden by shadow, each step brought me closer to that winged demon. My feet turned leaden.

Then a lower, guttural voice grunted in response to the hissing of the Attor. Nails clicked on stone, and my escorts swapped glances before they swung me into an alcove, a tapestry that hadn't been there a moment before falling over us, the shadows deepening, solidifying. I had a feeling that if someone pulled back that tapestry, they would see only darkness and stone.

One of them covered my mouth with a hand, holding me tightly to her, shadows slithering down her arm and onto mine. She smelled of jasmine—I'd never noticed that before. After all these nights, I didn't even know their names.

The Attor and its companion rounded the bend, still talking—their voices low. It was only when I could understand their words that I realized we weren't merely hiding.

"Yes," the Attor was saying, "good. She'll be most pleased to hear that they're ready at last."

"But will the High Lords contribute their forces?" the guttural voice replied. I could have sworn it snorted like a pig.

They came closer and closer, unaware of us. My escorts pressed in tighter to me, so tense that I realized they were holding their breath. Handmaidens—and spies.

"The High Lords will do as she tells them," the Attor gloated, and its tail slithered and slashed across the floor.

"I heard talk from soldiers in Hybern that the High King is not pleased regarding this situation with the girl. Amarantha made a fool's bargain. She cost him the War the last time because of her madness with Jurian; if she turns her back on him again, he will not be so willing to forgive her. Stealing his spells and taking a territory for her own is one thing. Failure to aid in his cause a second time is another."

There was a loud hiss, and I trembled as the Attor snapped its jaws at its companion. "Milady makes no bargains that are not advantageous to her. She lets them claw at hope—but once it is shattered, they are her beautifully broken minions."

They had to be passing right before the tapestry.

"You had better hope so," the guttural voice replied. What manner of creature was this thing to be so unmoved by the Attor? My escort's shadowy hand clamped tighter around my mouth, and the Attor passed on.

Don't trust your senses, Alis's voice echoed through my mind. The Attor had caught me once before when I thought I was safe . . .

"And you had better hold your tongue," the Attor warned. "Or Milady will do so for you—and her pincers are not kind."

The other creature snorted that pig noise. "I am here on a condition of immunity from the king. If your *lady* thinks she's above the king because she rules this wretched land, she'll soon remember who can strip her powers away—without spells and potions."

The Attor didn't reply—and a part of me wished for it to retort, to snap back. But it was silenced, and fear hit my stomach like a stone dropped into a pool.

Whatever plans the King of Hybern had been working on for these long years—his campaign to take back the mortal world—it seemed he was no longer content to wait. Perhaps Amarantha would soon receive what she wanted: destruction of my entire realm.

My blood went cold. Nesta—I trusted Nesta to get my family away, to protect them.

Their voices faded, and it wasn't until a good extra minute had passed that the two females relaxed. The tapestry vanished, and we slipped back into the hall.

"What *was* that?" I said, looking from one to the other as the shadows around us lightened—but not by much. "*Who* was that?" I clarified.

"Trouble," they answered in unison.

"Does Rhysand know?"

"He will soon," one of them said. We resumed our silent walk to the dressing room.

There was nothing I could do about the King of Hybern, anyway—not while trapped Under the Mountain, not when I hadn't even been able to free Tamlin, much less myself. And with Nesta prepared to flee with my family, there was no one else to warn. So day after day passed, bringing my third trial ever closer.

I suppose I sank so far into myself that it took something extraordinary to pull me out again. I was watching the light dance along the damp stones of the ceiling of my cell—like moonlight on water—when a noise traveled to me, down through the stones, rippling across the floor.

I was so used to the strange fiddles and drums of the faeries that when I heard the lilting melody, I thought it was another hallucination. Sometimes, if I stared at the ceiling long enough, it became the vast expanse of the starry night sky, and I became a small, unimportant thing that blew away in the wind.

I looked toward the small vent in the corner of the ceiling through which the music entered my cell. The source must have been far away, for it was just a faint stirring of notes, but when I closed my eyes, I could hear it more clearly. I could . . . see it. As if it were a grand painting, a living mural.

There was beauty in this music—beauty and goodness. The music folded over itself like batter being poured from a bowl, one note atop another, melting together to form a whole, rising, filling me. It wasn't wild music, but there was a violence of passion in it, a swelling kind of joy and sorrow. I pulled my knees to my chest, needing to feel the sturdiness of my skin, even with the slime of the oily paint upon it.

The music built a path, an ascent founded upon archways of color. I followed it, walking out of that cell, through layers of earth, up and up—into fields of cornflowers, past a canopy of trees, and into the open expanse of sky. The pulse of the music was like hands that gently pushed me onward, pulling me higher, guiding me through the clouds. I'd never seen clouds like these—in their puffy sides, I could discern faces fair and sorrowful. They faded before I could view them too clearly, and I looked into the distance to where the music summoned me.

It was either a sunset or sunrise. The sun filled the clouds with magenta and purple, and its orange-gold rays blended with my path to form a band of shimmering metal.

I wanted to fade into it, wanted the light of that sun to burn me away, to fill me with such joy that I would become a ray of sunshine myself. This wasn't music to dance to—it was music to worship, music to fill in the gaps of my soul, to bring me to a place where there was no pain.

I didn't realize I was weeping until the wet warmth of a tear splashed upon my arm. But even then I clung to the music, gripping it like a ledge that kept me from falling. I hadn't realized how badly I didn't want to tumble into that deep dark—how much I wanted to stay here among the clouds and color and light.

I let the sounds ravage me, let them lay me flat and run over my body with their drums. Up and up, building to a palace in the sky, a hall of alabaster and moonstone, where all that was lovely and kind and fantastic dwelled in peace. I wept—wept to be so close to that palace, wept from the need to be there. Everything I wanted was there—the one I loved was there—

The music was Tamlin's fingers strumming my body; it was the gold in his eyes and the twist of his smile. It was that breathy chuckle, and the way he said those three words. It was *this* I was fighting for, *this* I had sworn to save.

The music rose—louder, grander, faster, from wherever it was played—a wave that peaked, shattering the gloom of my cell. A shuddering sob broke from me as the sound faded into silence. I sat there, trembling and weeping, too raw and exposed, left naked by the music and the color in my mind.

When the tears had stopped but the music still echoed in my every breath, I lay on my pallet of hay, listening to my breathing.

The music flittered through my memories, binding them together, making them into a quilt that wrapped around me, that warmed my bones. I looked at the eye in the center of my palm, but it only stared right back at me—unmoving.

Two more days until my final trial. Just two more days, and then I would learn what the Eddies of the Cauldron had planned for me.

CHAPTER 42

It was a party like any other—even if it would likely be my last. Faeries drank and lounged and danced, laughing and singing bawdy and ethereal songs. No glimmer of anticipation for what might occur tomorrow—what I stood to alter for them, for their world. Perhaps they knew I would die, too.

I lurked by a wall, forgotten by the crowd, waiting for Rhysand to beckon me to drink the wine and dance or do whatever it was he wished of me. I was clothed in my typical attire, tattooed from the neck down with that blue-black paint. Tonight my gossamer gown was a shade of sunset pink, the color too bright and feminine against the whorls of paint on my skin. Too cheery for what awaited me tomorrow.

Rhysand was taking longer than usual to summon me—though it was probably because of the supple-bodied faerie perched in his lap, caressing his hair with her long greenish fingers. He'd tire of her soon.

I didn't bother to look at Amarantha. I was better off pretending she wasn't there. Lucien never spoke to me in public, and Tamlin . . . It had become difficult to look at him in recent days.

I just wanted it done. I wanted that wine to carry me through this last night and bring me to my fate. I was so intent on anticipating Rhysand's order to serve him that I didn't notice that someone stood beside me until the heat from his body leaked onto mine.

I went rigid when I smelled that rain and earthen scent, and didn't dare to turn to Tamlin. We stood side by side, staring out at the crowd, as still and unnoticeable as statues.

His fingers brushed mine, and a line of fire went through me, burning me so badly that my eyes pricked with tears. I wished—wished he wasn't touching my marred hand, that his fingers didn't have to caress the contours of that wretched tattoo.

But I lived in that moment—my life became beautiful again for those few seconds when our hands grazed.

I kept my face set in a mask of cold. He dropped his hand, and, as quickly as he had come, he sauntered off, weaving through the crowd. It was only when he glanced over his shoulder and inclined his head ever so slightly that I understood.

My heart beat faster than it ever had during my trials, and I made myself look as bored as possible before I pushed off the wall and casually strolled after him. I took a different route, but headed toward the small door half hidden by a tapestry near which he lingered. I had only moments before Rhysand would begin looking for me, but a moment alone with Tamlin would be enough.

I could scarcely breathe as I moved nearer and nearer to the door, past Amarantha's dais, past a group of giggling faeries . . . Tamlin disappeared through the door as quick as lightning, and I slowed my steps to a meandering pace. These days no one really paid attention to me until I became Rhys's drugged plaything. All too quickly, the door was before me, and it swung open noiselessly to let me in.

Darkness encompassed me. I saw only a flash of green and gold before the warmth of Tamlin's body slammed into me and our lips met.

I couldn't kiss him deeply enough, couldn't hold him tightly enough, couldn't touch enough of him. Words weren't necessary.

I tore at his shirt, needing to feel the skin beneath one last time, and I had to stifle the moan that rose up in me as he grasped my breast. I didn't want him to be gentle—because what I felt for him wasn't at all like that. What I felt was wild and hard and burning, and so he was with me.

He tore his lips from mine and bit my neck—bit it as he had on Fire Night. I had to grind my teeth to keep myself from moaning and giving us away. This might be the last time I touched him, the last time we could be together. I wouldn't waste it.

My fingers grappled with his belt buckle, and his mouth found mine again. Our tongues danced—not a waltz or a minuet, but a war dance, a death dance of bone drums and screaming fiddles.

I wanted him—here.

I hooked a leg around his middle, needing to be closer, and he ground his hips harder against me, crushing me into the icy wall. I pried the belt buckle loose, whipping the leather free, and Tamlin growled his desire in my ear—a low, probing sort of sound that made me see red and white and lightning. We both knew what tomorrow would bring.

I tossed away his belt and started fumbling for his pants. Someone coughed.

"Shameful," Rhysand purred, and we whirled to find him faintly illuminated by the light that broke in through the doorway. But he stood behind us—farther into the passage, rather than toward the door. He hadn't come in through the throne room. With that ability of his, he had probably walked through the walls. "Just shameful." He stalked toward us. Tamlin remained holding me. "Look at what you've done to my pet."

Panting, neither of us said anything. But the air became a cold kiss upon my skin—upon my exposed breasts.

"Amarantha would be greatly aggrieved if she knew her little warrior was dallying with the human help," Rhysand went on, crossing his arms.

"I wonder how she'd punish you. Or perhaps she'd stay true to habit and punish Lucien. He still has one eye to lose, after all. Maybe she'll put it in a ring, too."

Ever so slowly, Tamlin removed my hands from his body and stepped out of my embrace.

"I'm glad to see you're being reasonable," Rhysand said, and Tamlin bristled. "Now, be a clever High Lord and buckle your belt and fix your clothes before you go out there."

Tamlin looked at me, and, to my horror, did as Rhysand instructed. My High Lord never took his eyes off my face as he straightened his tunic and hair, then retrieved and fastened his belt again. The paint on his hands and clothes—paint from *me*—vanished.

"Enjoy the party," Rhysand crooned, pointing to the door.

Tamlin's green eyes flickered as they continued to stare into mine. He softly said, "I love you." Without another glance at Rhysand, he left.

I was temporarily blinded by the brightness that poured in when he opened the door and slipped out. He did not look back at me before the door snicked shut and darkness returned to the dim hall.

Rhysand chuckled. "If you're that desperate for release, you should have asked me."

"Pig," I snapped, covering my breasts with the folds of my gown.

With a few easy steps, he crossed the distance between us and pinned my arms to the wall. My bones groaned. I could have sworn shadow-talons dug into the stones beside my head. "Do you actually intend to put yourself at my mercy, or are you truly that stupid?" His voice was composed of sensuous, bone-breaking ire.

"I'm not your slave."

"You're a fool, Feyre. Do you have any idea what could have happened had Amarantha found you two in here? Tamlin might refuse to be her lover, but she keeps him at her side out of the hope that she'll break him—dominate him, as she loves to do with our kind." I kept silent.

"You're both fools," he murmured, his breathing uneven. "How did you not think that someone would notice you were gone? You should thank the Cauldron Lucien's delightful brothers weren't watching you."

"What do you care?" I barked, and his grip tightened enough on my wrists that I knew my bones would snap with a little more pressure.

"What do I care?" he breathed, wrath twisting his features. Wings—those membranous, glorious wings—flared from his back, crafted from the shadows behind him. "What do *I* care?"

But before he could go on, his head snapped to the door, then back to my face. The wings vanished as quickly as they had appeared, and then his lips were crushing into mine. His tongue pried my mouth open, forcing himself into me, into the space where I could still taste Tamlin. I pushed and thrashed, but he held firm, his tongue sweeping over the roof of my mouth, against my teeth, claiming my mouth, claiming me—

The door was flung wide, and Amarantha's curved figure filled its space. Tamlin—Tamlin was beside her, his eyes slightly wide, shoulders tight as Rhys's lips still crushed mine.

Amarantha laughed, and a mask of stone slammed down on Tamlin's face, void of feeling, void of anything vaguely like the Tamlin I'd been tangled up with moments before.

Rhys casually released me with a flick of his tongue over my bottom lip as a crowd of High Fae appeared behind Amarantha and chimed in with her laughter. Rhysand gave them a lazy, self-indulgent grin and bowed. But something sparked in the queen's eyes as she looked at Rhysand. Amarantha's whore, they'd called him.

"I knew it was a matter of time," she said, putting a hand on Tamlin's arm. The other she lifted—lifted so Jurian's eye might see as she said, "You humans are all the same, aren't you."

I kept my mouth shut, even as I could have died for shame, even as I ached to explain. Tamlin *had* to realize the truth.

But I wasn't given the luxury of learning whether Tamlin understood as Amarantha clicked her tongue and turned away, taking her entourage with her. "Typical human trash with their inconstant, dull hearts," she said to herself—nothing more than a satisfied cat.

Following them, Rhys grabbed my arm to drag me back into the throne room. It was only when the light hit me that I saw the smudges and smears on my paint—smudges along my breasts and stomach, and the paint that had mysteriously appeared on Rhysand's hands.

"I'm tired of you for tonight," Rhys said, giving me a light shove toward the main exit. "Go back to your cell." Behind him, Amarantha and her court smiled with glee, their grins widening when they beheld the marred paint. I looked for Tamlin, but he was stalking for his usual throne on the dais, keeping his back to me. As if he couldn't stand to look.

✣

I don't know what time it was, but hours later, footsteps sounded inside my cell. I jolted into a sitting position, and Rhys stepped out of a shadow.

I could still feel the heat of his lips against mine, the smooth glide of his tongue inside my mouth, even though I'd washed my mouth out three times with the bucket of water in my cell.

His tunic was unbuttoned at the top, and he ran a hand through his blue-black hair before he wordlessly slumped against the wall across from me and slid to the floor.

"What do you want?" I demanded.

"A moment of peace and quiet," he snapped, rubbing his temples.

I paused. "From what?"

He massaged his pale skin, making the corners of his eyes go up and down, out and in. He sighed. "From this mess."

I sat up farther on my pallet of hay. I'd never seen him so candid.

"That damned bitch is running me ragged," he went on, and dropped his hands from his temples to lean his head against the wall. "You hate me. Imagine how you'd feel if I made you serve in my bedroom. I'm High Lord of the Night Court—not her harlot."

So the slurs were true. And I could imagine very easily how much I would hate him—what it would do to me—to be enslaved to someone like that. "Why are you telling me this?"

The swagger and nastiness were gone. "Because I'm tired and lonely, and you're the only person I can talk to without putting myself at risk." He let out a low laugh. "How absurd: a High Lord of Prythian and a—"

"You can leave if you're just going to insult me."

"But I'm so good at it." He flashed one of his grins. I glared at him, but he sighed. "One wrong move tomorrow, Feyre, and we're all doomed."

The thought struck a chord of such horror that I could hardly breathe.

"And if you fail," he went on, more to himself than to me, "then Amarantha will rule forever."

"If she captured Tamlin's power once, who's to say she can't do it again?" It was the question I hadn't yet dared voice.

"He won't be tricked again so easily," he said, staring up at the ceiling. "Her biggest weapon is that she keeps our powers contained. But she can't access them, not wholly—though she can control us through them. It's why I've never been able to shatter her mind—why she's not dead already. The moment you break Amarantha's curse, Tamlin's wrath will be so great that no force in the world will keep him from splattering her on the walls."

A chill went through me.

"Why do you think I'm doing this?" He waved a hand to me.

"Because you're a monster."

He laughed. "True, but I'm also a pragmatist. Working Tamlin into a senseless fury is the best weapon we have against her. Seeing you enter into a fool's bargain with Amarantha was one thing, but when Tamlin saw my tattoo on your arm . . . Oh, you should have been born with my abilities, if only to have felt the rage that seeped from him."

I didn't want to think much about his abilities. "Who's to say he won't splatter you as well?"

"Perhaps he'll try—but I have a feeling he'll kill Amarantha first. That's what it all boils down to, anyway: even your servitude to me can be blamed on her. So he'll kill her tomorrow, and I'll be free before he can start a fight with me that will reduce our once-sacred mountain to rubble." He picked at his nails. "And I have a few other cards to play."

I lifted my brows in silent question.

"Feyre, for Cauldron's sake. I drug you, but you don't wonder why I never touch you beyond your waist or arms?"

Until tonight—until that damned kiss. I gritted my teeth, but even as my anger rose, a picture cleared.

"It's the only claim I have to innocence," he said, "the only thing that will make Tamlin think twice before entering into a battle with me that would cause a catastrophic loss of innocent life. It's the only way I can convince him I was on your side. Believe me, I would have liked nothing more than to enjoy you—but there are bigger things at stake than taking a human woman to my bed."

I knew, but I still asked, "Like what?"

"Like my territory," he said, and his eyes held a far-off look that I hadn't yet seen. "Like my remaining people, enslaved to a tyrant queen who can end their lives with a single word. Surely Tamlin expressed similar sentiments to you." He hadn't—not entirely. He hadn't been able to, thanks to the curse.

"Why did Amarantha target you?" I dared ask. "Why make you her whore?"

"Beyond the obvious?" He gestured to his perfect face. When I didn't smile, he loosed a breath. "My father killed Tamlin's father—and his brothers."

I started. Tamlin had never said—never told me the Night Court was responsible for that.

"It's a long story, and I don't feel like getting into it, but let's just say that when she stole our lands out from under us, Amarantha decided that she especially wanted to punish the son of her friend's murderer—decided that she hated me enough for my father's deeds that I was to suffer."

I might have reached a hand toward him, might have offered my apologies—but every thought had dried up in my head. What Amarantha had done to him . . .

"So," he said wearily, "here we are, with the fate of our immortal world in the hands of an illiterate human." His laugh was unpleasant as he hung his head, cupping his forehead in a hand, and closed his eyes. "What a mess."

Part of me searched for the words to wound him in his vulnerability, but the other half recalled all that he had said, all that he had done, how his head had snapped to the door before he'd kissed me. He'd known Amarantha was coming. Maybe he'd done it to make her jealous, but maybe . . .

If he hadn't been kissing me, if he hadn't shown up and interrupted us, I would have gone out into that throne room covered in smudged paint. And everyone—especially Amarantha—would have known what I'd been up to. It wouldn't have taken much to figure out whom I'd been with, especially not once they saw the paint on Tamlin. I didn't want to consider what the punishment might have been.

Regardless of his motives or his methods, Rhysand was keeping me alive. And had done so even before I set foot Under the Mountain.

"I've told you too much," he said as he got to his feet. "Perhaps I should have drugged you first. If you were clever, you'd find a way to use this against me. And if you had any stomach for cruelty, you'd go to Amarantha and tell her the truth about her whore. Perhaps she'd give you Tamlin for it." He slid his hands into the pockets of his black pants, but even as he faded into shadow, there was something in the curve of his shoulders that made me speak.

"When you healed my arm . . . You didn't need to bargain with me. You could have demanded every single week of the year." My brows knit together as he turned, already half-consumed by the dark. "Every single week, and I would have said yes." It wasn't entirely a question, but I needed the answer.

A half smile appeared on his sensuous lips. "I know," he said, and vanished.

CHAPTER 43

For my final task, I was given my old tunic and pants—stained and torn and reeking—but despite my stench, I kept my chin high as I was escorted to the throne room.

The doors were flung open, and the silence of the room assaulted me. I waited for the jeers and shouts, waited to see gold flash as the onlookers placed their bets, but this time the faeries just stared at me, the masked ones especially intently.

Their world rested on my shoulders, Rhys had said. But I didn't think it was worry alone that was spread across their features. I had to swallow hard as a few of them touched their fingers to their lips, then extended their hands to me—a gesture for the fallen, a farewell to the honored dead. There was nothing malicious about it. Most of these faeries belonged to the courts of the High Lords—had belonged to those courts long before Amarantha seized their lands, their lives. And if Tamlin and Rhysand were playing games to keep us alive . . .

I strode up the path they'd cleared—straight for Amarantha. The queen smiled when I stopped in front of her throne. Tamlin was in his usual place beside her, but I wouldn't look at him—not yet.

"Two trials lie behind you," Amarantha said, picking at a fleck of dust on her blood-red gown. Her hair shone, a gleaming crimson river that threatened to swallow her golden crown. "And only one more awaits. I wonder if it will be worse to fail now—when you are so close." She gave me a pout, and we both awaited the laughter of the faeries.

But only a few laughs hissed from the red-skinned guards. Everyone else remained silent. Even Lucien's miserable brothers. Even Rhysand, wherever he was in the crowd.

I blinked to clear my burning eyes. Perhaps, like Rhysand's, their oaths of allegiance and betting on my life and nastiness had been a show. And perhaps now—now that the end was imminent—they, too, would face my potential death with whatever dignity they had left.

Amarantha glared at them, but when her gaze fell upon me, she smiled broadly, sweetly. "Any words to say before you die?"

I came up with a plethora of curses, but I instead looked at Tamlin. He didn't react—his features were like stone. I wished that I could glimpse his face—if only for a moment. But all I needed to see were those green eyes.

"I love you," I said. "No matter what she says about it, no matter if it's only with my insignificant human heart. Even when they burn my body, I'll love you." My lips trembled, and my vision clouded before several warm tears slipped down my chilled face. I didn't wipe them away.

He didn't react—he didn't even grip the arms of his throne. I supposed that was his way of enduring it, even if it made my chest cave in. Even if his silence killed me.

Amarantha said sweetly, "You'll be lucky, my darling, if we even have enough left of you to burn."

I stared at her long and hard. But her words were not met with jeers or smiles or applause from the crowd. Only silence.

It was a gift that gave me courage, that made me bunch my fists, that made me embrace the tattoo on my arm. I had beaten her until now, fairly or not, and I would not feel alone when I died. I would not die alone. It was all I could ask for.

Amarantha propped her chin on a hand. "You never figured out my riddle, did you?" I didn't respond, and she smiled. "Pity. The answer is so lovely."

"Get it over with," I growled.

Amarantha looked at Tamlin. "No final words to her?" she said, quirking an eyebrow. When he didn't respond, she grinned at me. "Very well, then." She clapped her hands twice.

A door swung open, and three figures—two male and one female—with brown sacks tied over their heads were dragged in by the guards. Their concealed faces turned this way and that as they tried to discern the whispers that rippled across the throne room. My knees bent slightly as they approached.

With sharp jabs and blunt shoves, the red-skinned guards forced the three faeries to their knees at the foot of the dais, but facing me. Their bodies and clothes revealed nothing of who they were.

Amarantha clapped her hands again, and three servants clad in black appeared at the side of each of the kneeling faeries. In their long, pale hands, they each carried a dark velvet pillow. And on each pillow lay a single polished wooden dagger. Not metal for a blade, but ash. Ash, because—

"Your final task, Feyre," Amarantha drawled, gesturing to the kneeling faeries. "Stab each of these unfortunate souls in the heart."

I stared at her, my mouth opening and closing.

"They're innocent—not that it should matter to you," she went on, "since it wasn't a concern the day you killed Tamlin's poor sentinel. And it wasn't a concern for dear Jurian when he butchered my sister. But if it's a problem . . . well, you can always refuse. Of course, I'll take your life in exchange, but a bargain's a bargain, is it not? If you ask me, though, given your history with murdering our kind, I do believe I'm offering you a gift."

Refuse and die. Kill three innocents and live. Three innocents, for my own future. For my own happiness. For Tamlin and his court and the freedom of an entire land.

The wood of the razor-sharp daggers had been polished so expertly that it gleamed beneath the colored glass chandeliers.

"Well?" she asked. She lifted her hand, letting Jurian's eye get a good look at me, at the ash daggers, and purred to it, "I wouldn't want you to miss this, old friend."

I couldn't. I couldn't do it. It wasn't like hunting; it wasn't for survival or defense. It was cold-blooded murder—the murder of them, of my very soul. But for Prythian—for Tamlin, for all of them here, for Alis and her boys . . . I wished I knew the name of one of our forgotten gods so that I might beg them to intercede, wished I knew any prayers at all to plead for guidance, for absolution.

But I did not know those prayers, or the names of our forgotten gods—only the names of those who would remain enslaved if I did not act. I silently recited those names, even as the horror of what knelt before me began to swallow me whole. For Prythian, for Tamlin, for their world and my own . . . These deaths would not be wasted—even if it would damn me forever.

I stepped up to the first kneeling figure—the longest and most brutal step I'd ever taken. Three lives in exchange for Prythian's liberation—three lives that would not be spent in vain. I could do this. I could do this, even with Tamlin watching. I could make this sacrifice—sacrifice them . . . I could do this.

My fingers trembled, but the first dagger wound up in my hand, its hilt cool and smooth, the wood of the blade heavier than I'd expected. There were three daggers, because she wanted me to feel the agony of reaching for that knife again and again. Wanted me to *mean* it.

"Not so fast." Amarantha chuckled, and the guards who held the first kneeling figure snatched the hood off its face.

It was a handsome High Fae youth. I didn't know him, I'd never seen him, but his blue eyes were pleading. "That's better," Amarantha said, waving her hand again. "Proceed, Feyre, dear. Enjoy it."

His eyes were the color of a sky I'd never see again if I refused to kill him, a color I'd never get out of my mind, never forget no matter how many times I painted it. He shook his head, those eyes growing so large that white showed all around. He would never see that sky, either. And neither would these people, if I failed.

"Please," he whispered, his focus darting between the ash dagger and my face. "Please."

The dagger shook between my fingers, and I clenched it tighter. Three faeries—that's all that stood between me and freedom, before Tamlin would be unleashed upon Amarantha. If he could destroy her . . . *Not in vain*, I told myself. *Not in vain.*

"Don't," the faerie youth begged when I lifted the dagger. *"Don't!"*

I took a gasping breath, my lips shaking as I quailed. Saying "I'm sorry" wasn't enough. I'd never been able to say it to Andras—and now . . . now . . .

"Please!" he said, and his eyes lined with silver.

Someone in the crowd began weeping. I was taking him away from someone who possibly loved him as much as I loved Tamlin.

I couldn't think about it, couldn't think about who he was, or the color of his eyes, or any of it. Amarantha was grinning with wild, triumphant glee. Kill a faerie, fall in love with a faerie, then be forced to kill a faerie to keep that love. It was brilliant and cruel, and she knew it.

Darkness rippled near the throne, and then Rhysand was there, arms crossed—as if he'd moved to better see. His face was a mask of disinterest, but my hand tingled. *Do it*, the tingling said.

"Don't," the young faerie moaned. I began shaking my head. I couldn't

listen to him. I had to do it now, before he convinced me otherwise. *"Please!"* His voice rose to a shriek.

The sound jarred me so much that I lunged.

With a ragged sob, I plunged the dagger into his heart.

He screamed, thrashing in the guards' grip as the blade cleaved through flesh and bone, smooth as if it were real metal and not ash, and blood—hot and slick—showered my hand. I wept, yanking out the dagger, the reverberations of his bones against the blade stinging my hand.

His eyes, full of shock and hate, remained on me as he sagged, damning me, and that person in the crowd let out a keening wail.

My bloody dagger clacked on the marble floor as I stumbled back several steps.

"Very good," Amarantha said.

I wanted to get out of my body; I had to escape the stain of what I'd done; I had to get out—I couldn't endure the blood on my hands, the sticky warmth between my fingers.

"Now the next. Oh, don't look so miserable, Feyre. Aren't you having fun?"

I faced the second figure, still hooded. A female this time. The faerie in black extended the pillow with the clean dagger, and the guards holding her tore off her hood.

Her face was simple, and her hair was gold-brown, like mine. Tears were already rolling down her round cheeks, and her bronze eyes tracked my bloody hand as I reached for the second knife. The cleanness of the wooden blade mocked the blood on my fingers.

I wanted to fall to my knees to beg her forgiveness, to tell her that her death wouldn't be for naught. Wanted to, but there was such a rift running through me now that I could hardly feel my hands, my shredded heart. What I'd done—

"Cauldron save me," she began whispering, her voice lovely and even—like music. "Mother hold me," she went on, reciting a prayer similar to one I'd heard once before, when Tamlin eased the passing of that lesser faerie who'd died in the foyer. Another of Amarantha's victims. "Guide me to you." I was unable to raise my dagger, unable to take the step that would close the distance between us. "Let me pass through the gates; let me smell that immortal land of milk and honey."

Silent tears slid down my face and neck, where they dampened the filthy collar of my tunic. As she spoke, I knew I would be forever barred from that immortal land. I knew that whatever Mother she meant would never embrace me. In saving Tamlin, I was to damn myself.

I couldn't do this—couldn't lift that dagger again.

"Let me fear no evil," she breathed, staring at me—into me, into the soul that was cleaving itself apart. "Let me feel no pain."

A sob broke from my lips. "I'm sorry," I moaned.

"Let me enter eternity," she breathed.

I wept as I understood. *Kill me now*, she was saying. *Do it fast. Don't make it hurt. Kill me now*. Her bronze eyes were steady, if not sorrowful. Infinitely, infinitely worse than the pleading of the dead faerie beside her.

I couldn't do it.

But she held my gaze—held my gaze and nodded.

As I lifted the ash dagger, something inside me fractured so completely that there would be no hope of ever repairing it. No matter how many years passed, no matter how many times I might try to paint her face.

More faeries wailed now—her kinsmen and friends. The dagger was a weight in my hand—my hand, shining and coated with the blood of that first faerie.

It would be more honorable to refuse—to die, rather than murder innocents. But . . . but . . .

"Let me enter eternity," she repeated, lifting her chin. "Fear no evil," she whispered—just for me. "Feel no pain."

I gripped her delicate, bony shoulder and drove the dagger into her heart.

She gasped, and blood spilled onto the ground like a splattering of rain. Her eyes were closed when I looked at her face again. She slumped to the floor and didn't move.

I went somewhere far, far away from myself.

The faeries were stirring now—shifting, many whispering and weeping. I dropped the dagger, and the knock of ash on marble roared in my ears. Why was Amarantha still smiling, with only one person left between myself and freedom? I glanced at Rhysand, but his attention was fixed upon Amarantha.

One faerie—and then we were free. Just one more swing of my arm.

And maybe one more after that—maybe one more swing, up and inward and into my own heart.

It would be a relief—a relief to end it by my own hand, a relief to die rather than face this, what I'd done.

The faerie servant offered the last dagger, and I was about to reach for it when the guard removed the hood from the male kneeling before me.

My hands slackened at my sides. Amber-flecked green eyes stared up at me.

Everything came crashing down, layer upon layer, shattering and breaking and crumbling, as I gazed at Tamlin.

I whipped my head to the throne beside Amarantha's, still occupied by my High Lord, and she laughed as she snapped her fingers. The Tamlin beside her transformed into the Attor, smiling wickedly at me.

Tricked—deceived by my own senses again. Slowly, my soul ripping further from me, I turned back to Tamlin. There was only guilt and sorrow in his eyes, and I stumbled away, almost falling as I tripped over my feet.

"Something wrong?" Amarantha asked, cocking her head.

"Not . . . Not fair," I got out.

Rhysand's face had gone pale—so, so pale.

"Fair?" Amarantha mused, playing with Jurian's bone on her necklace. "I wasn't aware you humans knew of the concept. You kill Tamlin, and he's free." Her smile was the most hideous thing I'd ever seen. "And then you can have him all to yourself."

My mouth stopped working.

"Unless," Amarantha went on, "you think it would be more appropriate to forfeit your life. After all: What's the point? To survive only to lose him?" Her words were like poison. "Imagine all those years you were going to spend together . . . suddenly alone. Tragic, really. Though a few months ago, you hated our kind enough to butcher us—surely you'll move on easily enough." She patted her ring. "Jurian's human lover did."

Still on his knees, Tamlin's eyes turned so bright—defiant.

"So," Amarantha said, but I didn't look at her. "What will it be, Feyre?"

Kill him and save his court and my life, or kill myself and let them all live as Amarantha's slaves, let her and the King of Hybern wage their final war against the human realm. There was no bargain to get out of this—no part of me to sell to avoid this choice.

I stared at the ash dagger on that pillow. Alis had been right all those weeks ago: no human who came here ever walked out again. I was no exception. If I were smart, I would indeed stab my own heart before they could grab me. At least then I would die quickly—I wouldn't endure the torture that surely awaited me, possibly a fate like Jurian's. Alis had been right. But—

Alis—Alis had said something . . . something to *help* me. A final part of the curse, a part they couldn't tell me, a part that would aid me . . . And all she'd been able to do was tell me to *listen*. To *listen* to what I'd heard—as if I'd already learned everything I needed.

I slowly faced Tamlin again. Memories flashed, one after another, blurs of color and words. Tamlin was High Lord of the Spring Court—what did that do to help me? The Great Rite was performed—no.

He lied to me about everything—about why I'd been brought to the manor, about what was happening on his lands. The curse—he hadn't been allowed to tell me the truth, but he hadn't exactly pretended that everything was fine. No—he'd lied and explained as best he could and made it painfully obvious to me at every turn that something was very, very wrong.

The Attor in the garden—as hidden from me as I was from it. But Tamlin had hidden me—he'd told me to stay put and then *led* the Attor right toward me, *let* me overhear them.

He'd left the dining room doors open when he'd spoken with Lucien about—about the curse, even if I hadn't realized it at the time. He'd spoken in public places. He'd *wanted* me to eavesdrop.

Because he wanted me to know, to *listen*—because this knowledge . . . I ransacked each conversation, turning over words like stones. A part of the curse I hadn't grasped, that they couldn't explicitly tell me, but Tamlin had needed me to know . . .

Milady makes no bargains that are not advantageous to her.

She would never kill what she desired most—not when she wanted Tamlin as much as I did. But if I killed him . . . she either knew I couldn't do it, or she was playing a very, very dangerous game.

Conversation after conversation echoed in my memory, until I heard Lucien's words, and everything froze. And that was when I knew.

I couldn't breathe, not as I replayed the memory, not as I recalled the conversation I'd overheard one day. Lucien and Tamlin in the dining room, the door wide open for all to hear—for *me* to hear.

"For someone with a heart of stone, yours is certainly soft these days."

I looked at Tamlin, my eyes flicking to his chest as another memory flashed. The Attor in the garden, laughing.

"Though you have a heart of stone, Tamlin," the Attor said, "you certainly keep a host of fear inside it."

Amarantha would never risk me killing him—because she knew I *couldn't* kill him.

Not if his heart couldn't be pierced by a blade. Not if his heart had been turned to stone.

I scanned his face, searching for any glimmer of truth. There was only that bold rebellion within his gaze.

Perhaps I was wrong—perhaps it was just a faerie turn of phrase. But all those times I'd held Tamlin . . . I'd never felt his heartbeat. I'd been blind to everything until it came back to smack me in the face, but not this time.

That was how she controlled him and his magic. How she controlled all the High Lords, dominating and leashing them just as she kept Jurian's soul tethered to that eye and bone.

Trust no one, Alis had told me. But I trusted Tamlin—and more than that, I trusted myself. I trusted that I had heard correctly—I trusted that Tamlin had been smarter than Amarantha, I trusted that all I had sacrificed was not in vain.

The entire room was silent, but my attention was upon only Tamlin. The revelation must have been clear on my face, for his breathing became a bit quicker, and he lifted his chin.

I took a step toward him, then another. I was right. I had to be.

I sucked in a breath as I grabbed the dagger off the outstretched pillow. I could be wrong—I could be painfully, tragically wrong.

But there was a faint smile on Tamlin's lips as I stood over him, ash dagger in hand.

There was such a thing as Fate—because Fate had made sure I was there to eavesdrop when they'd spoken in private, because Fate had whispered to Tamlin that the cold, contrary girl he'd dragged to his home would be the one to break his spell, because Fate had kept me alive just to get to this point, just to see if I had been listening.

And there he was—my High Lord, my beloved, kneeling before me.

"I love you," I said, and stabbed him.

Chapter 44

Tamlin cried out as my blade pierced his flesh, breaking bone. For a sickening moment, when his blood rushed onto my hand, I thought the ash dagger would go clean through him.

But then there was a faint thud—and a stinging reverberation in my hand as the dagger struck something hard and unyielding. Tamlin lurched forward, his face going pale, and I yanked the dagger from his chest. As the blood drained away from the polished wood, I lifted the blade.

Its tip had been nicked, turned inward on itself.

Tamlin clutched his chest as he panted, the wound already healing. Rhysand, at the foot of the dais, grinned from ear to ear. Amarantha climbed to her feet.

The faeries murmured to one another. I dropped the blade, sending it clattering across the red marble.

Kill her now, I wanted to bark at Tamlin, but he didn't move as he pushed his hand against his wound, blood dribbling out. Too slowly—he was healing too slowly. The mask didn't fall off. *Kill her now.*

"She won," someone in the crowd said. "Free them," another echoed.

But Amarantha's face blanched, her features contorting until she looked truly serpentine. "I'll free them whenever I see fit. Feyre didn't specify *when* I had to free them—just that I had to. At some point. Perhaps when you're dead," she finished with a hateful smile. "You assumed that when I said instantaneous freedom regarding the riddle, it applied to the trials, too, didn't you? Foolish, stupid human."

I stepped back as she descended the steps of the dais. Her fingers curled into claws—Jurian's eye was going wild within the ring, his pupil dilating and shrinking. "And you," she hissed at me. *"You."* Her teeth gleamed—turning sharp. *"I'm going to kill you."*

Someone cried out, but I couldn't move, couldn't even try to get out of the way as something far more violent than lightning struck me, and I crashed to the floor.

"*I'm going to make you pay for your insolence*," Amarantha snarled, and a scream ravaged my throat as pain like nothing I had known erupted through me.

My very bones were shattering as my body rose and then slammed onto the hard floor, and I was crushed beneath another wave of torturous agony.

"Admit you don't really love him, and I'll spare you," Amarantha breathed, and through my fractured vision, I saw her prowl toward me. "Admit what a cowardly, lying, inconstant bit of human garbage you are."

I wouldn't—I wouldn't say that even if she splattered me across the ground.

But I was being ripped apart from the inside out, and I thrashed, unable to out-scream the pain.

"*Feyre!*" someone roared. No, not someone—Rhysand.

But Amarantha still neared. "You think you're worthy of him? A *High Lord*? You think you deserve anything at all, human?" My back arched, and my ribs cracked, one by one.

Rhysand yelled my name again—yelled it as though he cared. I blacked out, but she brought me back, ensuring that I felt everything, ensuring that I screamed every time a bone broke.

"What are you but mud and bones and worm meat?" Amarantha raged. "What are you, compared to our kind, that you think you're worthy of us?"

Faeries began calling foul play, demanding Tamlin be released from the curse, calling her a cheating liar. Through the haze, I saw Rhysand crouching by Tamlin. Not to help him, but to grab the—

"You are all pigs—all scheming, filthy *pigs*."

I sobbed between screams as her foot connected with my broken ribs. Again. And again. "Your mortal heart is *nothing* to us."

Then Rhysand was on his feet, my bloody knife in his hands. He launched himself at Amarantha, swift as a shadow, the ash dagger aimed at her throat.

She lifted a hand—not even bothering to look—and he was blasted back by a wall of white light.

But the pain paused for a second, long enough for me to see him hit the ground and rise again and lunge for her—with hands that now ended in talons. He slammed into the invisible wall Amarantha had raised around herself, and my pain flickered as she turned to him.

"You traitorous piece of filth," she seethed at Rhysand. "You're just as bad as these human beasts." One by one, as if a hand were shoving them in, his talons pushed back into his skin, leaving blood in their wake. He swore, low and vicious. "You were planning this all along."

Her magic sent him sprawling, and it then hurled into Rhysand again—so hard that his head cracked against the stones and the knife dropped from his splayed fingers. No one made a move to help him, and she struck him once more with her power. The red marble splintered where he hit it, spiderwebbing toward me. With wave after wave she hit him. Rhys groaned.

"Stop," I breathed, blood filling my mouth as I strained a hand to reach her feet. "Please."

Rhys's arms buckled as he fought to rise, and blood dripped from his nose, splattering on the marble. His eyes met mine.

The bond between us went taut. I flashed between my body and his, seeing myself through his eyes, bleeding and broken and sobbing.

I snapped back into my own mind as Amarantha turned to me again. "Stop? *Stop?* Don't pretend you care, human," she crooned, and curled her finger. I arched my back, my spine straining to the point of cracking, and Rhysand bellowed my name as I lost my grip on the room.

Then the memories began—a compilation of the worst moments of my life, a storybook of despair and darkness. The final page came, and I wept, not entirely feeling the agony of my body as I saw that young rabbit, bleeding out in that forest clearing, my knife through her throat. My first kill—the first life I'd taken.

I'd been starving, desperate. Yet afterward, once my family had devoured it, I had crept back into the woods and wept for hours, knowing a line had been crossed, my soul stained.

"*Say that you don't love him!*" Amarantha shrieked, and the blood on my hands became the blood of that rabbit—became the blood of what I had lost.

But I wouldn't say it. Because loving Tamlin was the only thing I had left, the only thing I couldn't sacrifice.

A path cleared through my red-and-black vision. I found Tamlin's eyes—wide as he crawled toward Amarantha, watching me die, and unable to save me while his wound slowly healed, while she still gripped his power.

Amarantha had never intended for me to live, never intended to let him go.

"Amarantha, stop this," Tamlin begged at her feet as he clutched the gaping wound in his chest. "*Stop*. I'm sorry—I'm sorry for what I said about Clythia all those years ago. Please."

Amarantha ignored him, but I couldn't look away. Tamlin's eyes were so green—green like the meadows of his estate. A shade that washed away the memories flooding through me, that pushed aside the evil breaking me apart bone by bone. I screamed again as my kneecaps strained, threatening to crack in two, but I saw that enchanted forest, saw that afternoon we'd lain in the grass, saw that morning we'd watched the sunrise, when for a moment—just one moment—I'd known true happiness.

"*Say that you don't truly love him*," Amarantha spat, and my body twisted, breaking bit by bit. "*Admit to your inconstant heart.*"

"Amarantha, *please*," Tamlin moaned, his blood spilling onto the floor. "I'll do anything."

"I'll deal with you later," she snarled at him, and sent me falling into a fiery pit of pain.

I would never say it—never let her hear that, even if she killed me. And if it was to be my downfall, so be it. If it would be the weakness that would break me, I would embrace it with all my heart. If this was—

For though each of my strikes lands a powerful blow,
When I kill, I do it slow . . .

That's what these three months had been—a slow, horrible death. What I felt for Tamlin was the cause of this. There was no cure—not pain, or absence, or happiness.

But scorned, I become a difficult beast to defeat.

She could torture me all she liked, but it would never destroy what I felt for him. It would never make Tamlin want her—never ease the sting of his rejection.

The world became dark at the borders of my vision, taking the edge off the pain.

But I bless all those who are brave enough to dare.

For so long, I had run from it. But opening myself to him, to my sisters—that had been a test of bravery as harrowing as any of my trials.

"*Say it, you vile beast*," Amarantha hissed. She might have lied her way out of our bargain, but she'd sworn differently with the riddle—instantaneous freedom, regardless of her will.

Blood filled my mouth, warm as it dribbled out between my lips. I gazed at Tamlin's masked face one last time.

"*Love*," I breathed, the world crumbling into a blackness with no end. A pause in Amarantha's magic. "The answer to the riddle . . . ," I got out, choking on my own blood, "is . . . love."

Tamlin's eyes went wide before something forever cracked in my spine.

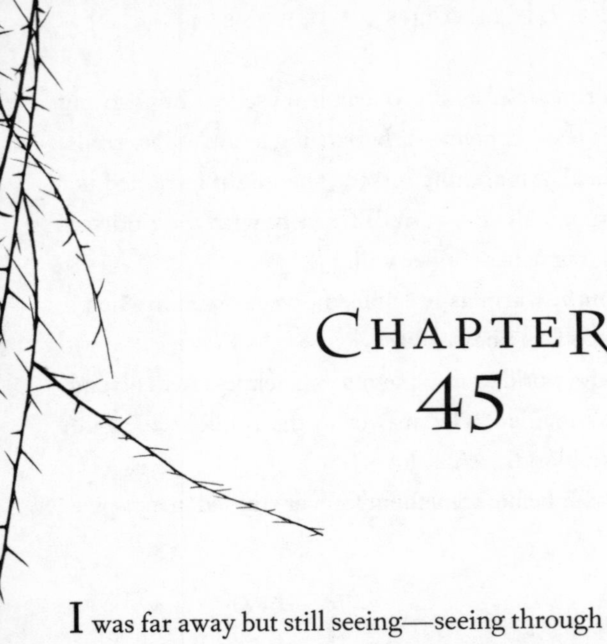

CHAPTER 45

I was far away but still seeing—seeing through eyes that weren't mine, eyes attached to a person who slowly rose from his position on a cracked, bloodied floor.

Amarantha's face slackened. There my body was, prostrate on the ground, my head snapped to one side at a horribly wrong angle. A flash of red hair in the crowd. Lucien.

Tears shone in Lucien's remaining eye as he raised his hands and removed the fox mask.

The brutally scarred face beneath was still handsome—his features sharp and elegant. But my host was looking at Tamlin now, who slowly faced my dead body.

Tamlin's still-masked face twisted into something truly lupine as he raised his eyes to the queen and snarled. Fangs lengthened.

Amarantha backed away—away from my corpse. She only whispered "Please" before golden light exploded.

The queen was blasted back, thrown against the far wall, and Tamlin let out a roar that shook the mountain as he launched himself at her. He shifted into his beast form faster than I could see—fur and claws and pound upon pound of lethal muscle.

She had no sooner hit the wall than he gripped her by the neck, and the stones cracked as he shoved her against it with a clawed paw.

She thrashed but could do nothing against the brutal onslaught of Tamlin's beast. Blood ran down his furred arm from where she scratched.

The Attor and the guards rushed for the queen, but several faeries and High Fae, their masks clattering to the ground, jumped into their path, tackling them. Amarantha screeched, kicking at Tamlin, lashing at him with her dark magic, but a wall of gold encompassed his fur like a second skin. She couldn't touch him.

"Tam!" Lucien cried over the chaos.

A sword hurtled through the air, a shooting star of steel.

Tamlin caught it in a massive paw. Amarantha's scream was cut short as he drove the sword through her head and into the stone beneath.

And then closed his powerful jaws around her throat—and ripped it out.

Silence fell.

It wasn't until I was again staring down at my own broken body that I realized whose eyes I'd been seeing through. But Rhysand didn't come any closer to my corpse, not as rushing paws—then a flash of light, then footsteps—filled the air. The beast was already gone.

Amarantha's blood had vanished from his face, his tunic, as Tamlin slammed to his knees.

He scooped up my limp, broken body, cradling me to his chest. He hadn't removed his mask, but I saw the tears that fell onto my filthy tunic, and I heard the shuddering sobs that broke from him as he rocked me, stroking my hair.

"No," someone breathed—Lucien, his sword dangling from his hand. Indeed, there were many High Fae and faeries who watched with damp eyes as Tamlin held me.

I wanted to get to Tamlin. I wanted to touch him, to beg for his forgiveness for what I'd done, for the other bodies on the floor, but I was so far away.

Someone appeared beside Lucien—a tall, handsome brown-haired man with a face similar to his own. Lucien didn't look at his father, though he stiffened as the High Lord of the Autumn Court approached Tamlin and extended a clenched hand to him.

Tamlin glanced up only when the High Lord opened his fingers and tipped over his hand. A glittering spark fell upon me. It flared and vanished as it touched my chest.

Two more figures approached—both handsome and young. Through my host's eyes, I knew them instantly. The brown-skinned one on the left wore a tunic of blue and green, and atop his white-blond head was a garland of roses—the High Lord of the Summer Court. His pale-skinned companion, clad in colors of white and gray, possessed a crown of shimmering ice. The High Lord of the Winter Court.

Chins raised, shoulders back, they, too, dropped those glittering kernels upon me, and Tamlin bowed his head in gratitude.

Another High Lord approached, also bestowing upon me a drop of light. He glowed brightest of them all, and from his gold-and-ruby raiment, I knew him to be High Lord of the Dawn Court. Then the High Lord of the Day Court, clad in white and gold, his dark skin gleaming with an inner light, presented his similar gift, and smiled sadly at Tamlin before he walked away.

Rhysand stepped forward, bringing my shred of soul with him, and I found Tamlin staring at me—at us. "For what she gave," Rhysand said, extending a hand, "we'll bestow what our predecessors have granted to few before." He paused. "This makes us even," he added, and I felt the twinkle of his humor as he opened his hand and let the seed of light fall on me.

Tamlin tenderly brushed aside my matted hair. His hand glowed bright as the rising sun, and in the center of his palm, that strange, shining bud formed.

"I love you," he whispered, and kissed me as he laid his hand on my heart.

CHAPTER 46

Everything was black, and warm—and thick. Inky, but bordered with gold. I was swimming, kicking for the surface, where Tamlin was waiting, where *life* was waiting. Up and up, frantic for air. The golden light grew, and the darkness became like sparkling wine, easier to swim through, the bubbles fizzing around me, and—

I gasped, air flooding my throat.

I was lying on the cold floor. No pain—no blood, no broken bones. I blinked. A chandelier dangled above me—I'd never noticed how intricate the crystals were, how the hushed gasp of the crowd echoed off them. A crowd—meaning I was still in that throne room, meaning I . . . I truly wasn't dead. Meaning I had . . . I had killed those . . . I had . . . The room spun.

I groaned as I braced my hands against the floor, readying myself to stand, but—the sight of my skin stopped me cold. It gleamed with a strange light, and my fingers seemed *longer* where I'd laid them flat on the marble. I pushed to my feet. I felt—felt *strong*, and fast and sleek. And—

And I'd become High Fae.

I went rigid as I sensed Tamlin standing behind me, smelled that rain and spring meadow scent of him, richer than I'd ever noticed. I couldn't turn around to look at him—I couldn't . . . couldn't move. A High Fae—immortal. What had they done?

I could hear Tamlin holding his breath—hear as he loosed it. Hear the breathing, the whispering and weeping and quiet celebrating of everyone in that hall, still watching us—watching *me*—some chanting praise for the glorious power of their High Lords.

"It was the only way we could save you," Tamlin said softly. But then I looked to the wall, and my hand rose to my throat. I forgot about the stunned crowd entirely.

There, beneath Clare's decayed body, was Amarantha, her mouth gaping as the sword protruded from her brow. Her throat gone—and blood now soaked the front of her gown.

Amarantha was dead. They were free. I was free. Tamlin was—

Amarantha was dead. And I had killed those two High Fae; I had—

I shook my head slowly. "Are you—" My voice sounded too loud in my ears as I pushed back against that wall of black that threatened to swallow me. Amarantha was dead.

"See for yourself," he said. I kept my eyes on the ground as I turned. There, on the red marble, lay a golden mask, staring at me with its hollow eyeholes.

"Feyre," Tamlin said, and he cupped my chin between his fingers, gently lifting my face. I saw that familiar chin first, then the mouth, and then—

He was exactly how I dreamed he would be.

He smiled at me, his entire face alight with that quiet joy I had come to love so dearly, and he brushed my hair aside. I savored the feel of his fingers on my skin and raised my own to touch his face, to trace the contours of those high cheekbones and that lovely, straight nose—the clear, broad brow, the slightly arching eyebrows that framed his green eyes.

What I had done to get to this moment, to be standing here . . . I shoved against the thought again. In a minute, in an hour, in a day, I would think about that, force myself to face it.

I put a hand on Tamlin's heart, and a steady beat echoed into my bones.

✢

I sat on the edge of a bed, and while I'd thought being an immortal meant a higher pain threshold and faster healing, I winced a good deal as Tamlin inspected my few remaining wounds, then healed them. We'd scarcely had a moment alone together in the hours that followed Amarantha's death—that followed what I had done to those two faeries.

But now, in this quiet room . . . I couldn't look away from the truth that sounded in my head with each breath.

I'd killed them. Slaughtered them. I hadn't even seen their bodies being taken away.

For it had been chaos in the throne room in the moments after I'd awakened. The Attor and the nastier faeries had disappeared instantly, along with Lucien's brothers, which was a clever move, as Lucien wasn't the only faerie with a score to settle. No sign of Rhysand, either. Some faeries had fled, while others had burst into celebration, and others just stood or paced—eyes distant, faces pale. As if they, too, didn't quite feel like this was real.

One by one, crowding him, weeping and laughing with joy, the High Fae and faeries of the Spring Court knelt or embraced or kissed Tamlin, thanking him—thanking *me*. I kept far enough back that I would only nod, because I had no words to offer them in exchange for their gratitude, the gratitude for the faeries I'd butchered to save them.

Then there had been meetings in the frenzied throne room—quick, tense meetings with the High Lords Tamlin was allied with to sort out next steps; then with Lucien and some Spring Court High Fae who introduced themselves as Tamlin's sentries. But every word, every breath was too loud, every smell too strong, the light too bright. Keeping still throughout it all was easier than moving, than adjusting to the strange, strong body that was now mine. I couldn't even touch my hair without the slight difference in my fingers jarring me.

On and on, until every newly heightened sense was chafing and raw, and Tamlin at last noticed my dull eyes, my silence, and took my arm. He escorted me through the labyrinth of tunnels and hallways until we found a quiet bedroom in a distant wing of the court.

"Feyre," Tamlin said now, looking up from inspecting my bare leg. I had been so accustomed to his mask that the handsome face surprised me each time I beheld it.

This—this was what I had murdered those faeries for. Their deaths had not been in vain, and yet . . . The blood on me had been gone when I'd awoken—as if becoming an immortal, as if surviving, somehow earned me the right to wash their blood off me.

"What is it?" I said. My voice was—quiet. Hollow. I should try—try to sound more cheerful, for him, for what had just happened, but . . .

He gave me that half smile. Had he been human, he might have been in his late twenties. But he wasn't human—and neither was I.

I wasn't certain whether that was a happy thought or not.

It was one of my smallest concerns. I should be begging for his forgiveness, begging the families and friends of those faeries for their forgiveness. I should be on my knees, weeping with shame for all that I had done—

"Feyre," he said again, lowering my leg to stand between my knees. He caressed my cheek with a knuckle. "How can I ever repay you for what you did?"

"You don't need to," I said. Let that be that—let that dark, dank cell fade away, and Amarantha's face forever disappear from my memory. Even if those two dead faeries—even if *their* faces would never fade for me. If I could ever bring myself to paint again, I would never be able to stop seeing those faces instead of the colors and light.

Tamlin held my face in his hands, leaning close, but then released me and grasped my left arm—my tattooed arm. His brows narrowed as he studied the markings. "Feyre—"

"I don't want to talk about it," I mumbled. The bargain I had with Rhysand—another small concern compared to the stain on my soul, the pit inside it. But I didn't doubt I'd see Rhys again soon.

Tamlin's fingers traced the marks of my tattoo. "We'll find a way out of this," he murmured, and his hand traveled up my arm to rest on my shoulder. He opened his mouth, and I knew what he would say—the subject he would try to broach.

I couldn't talk about it, about them—not yet. So I breathed "Later" and hooked my feet around his legs, drawing him closer. I placed my hands on his chest, feeling the heart beating beneath. This—I needed *this* right now. It wouldn't wash away what I'd done, but . . . I needed him near, needed to smell and taste him, remind myself that he was real—*this* was real.

"Later," he echoed, and leaned down to kiss me.

It was soft, tentative—nothing like the wild, hard kisses we'd shared in the hall of throne room. He brushed his lips against mine again. I didn't want apologies, didn't want sympathy or coddling. I gripped the front of his tunic, tugging him closer as I opened my mouth to him.

He let out a low growl, and the sound of it sent a wildfire blazing through me, pooling and burning in my core. I let it burn through that hole in my chest, my soul. Let it raze through the wave of black that was starting to press around me, let it consume the phantom blood I could still feel on my hands. I gave myself to that fire, to him, as his hands roved across me, unbuttoning as he went.

I pulled back, breaking the kiss to look into his face. His eyes were bright—hungry—but his hands had stopped their exploring and rested firmly on my hips. With a predator's stillness, he waited and watched as I traced the contours of his face, as I kissed every place I touched.

His ragged breathing was the only sound—and his hands soon began roaming across my back and sides, caressing and teasing and baring me to him. When my traveling fingers reached his mouth, he bit down on one, sucking it into his mouth. It didn't hurt, but the bite was hard enough for me to meet his eyes again. To realize that he was done waiting—and so was I.

He eased me onto the bed, murmuring my name against my neck, the shell of my ear, the tips of my fingers. I urged him—faster, harder. His mouth explored the curve of my breast, the inside of my thigh.

A kiss for each day we'd spent apart, a kiss for every wound and terror, a kiss for the ink etched into my flesh, and for all the days we would be together after this. Days, perhaps, that I no longer deserved. But I gave myself again to that fire, threw myself into it, into him, and let myself burn.

✣

I was pulled from sleep by something tugging at my middle, a thread deep inside.

I left Tamlin sleeping in the bed, his body heavy with exhaustion. In a few hours, we would be leaving Under the Mountain and returning home, and I didn't want to wake him sooner than I had to. I prayed I would ever get to sleep that peacefully again.

I knew who summoned me long before I opened the door to the hall and padded down it, stumbling and teetering every now and then as I adjusted to my new body, its new balance and rhythms. I carefully, slowly took a narrow set of stairs upward, up and up, until, to my shock, a trickle of sunlight poured into the stairwell and I found myself on a small balcony jutting out of the side of the mountain.

I hissed against the brightness, shielding my eyes. I'd thought it was the middle of the night—I'd completely lost all sense of time in the darkness of the mountain.

Rhysand chuckled softly from where I could vaguely make him out standing along the stone rail. "I forgot that it's been a while for you."

My eyes stung from the light, and I remained silent until I could look at the view without a shooting pain going through my head. A land of violet snowcapped mountains greeted me, but the rock of this mountain was brown and bare—not even a blade of grass or a crystal of ice gleamed on it.

I looked at him finally. His membranous wings were out—tucked behind him—but his hands and feet were normal, no talons in sight. "What do you want?" It didn't come out with the snap I'd intended. Not as I remembered how he'd fought, again and again, to attack Amarantha, to save me.

"Just to say good-bye." A warm breeze ruffled his hair, brushing tendrils of darkness off his shoulders. "Before your beloved whisks you away forever."

"Not forever," I said, wiggling my tattooed fingers for him to see. "Don't you get a week every month?" Those words, thankfully, came out frosty.

Rhys smiled slightly, his wings rustling and then settling. "How could I forget?"

I stared at the nose I'd seen bleeding only hours before, the violet eyes that had been so filled with pain. "Why?" I asked.

He knew what I meant, and shrugged. "Because when the legends get written, I didn't want to be remembered for standing on the sidelines. I want my future offspring to know that *I* was there, and that I fought against her at the end, even if I couldn't do anything useful."

I blinked, this time not at the brightness of the sun.

"Because," he went on, his eyes locked with mine, "I didn't want you to fight alone. Or die alone."

And for a moment, I remembered that faerie who had died in our foyer, and how I'd told Tamlin the same thing. "Thank you," I said, my throat tight.

Rhys flashed a grin that didn't quite reach his eyes. "I doubt you'll be saying that when I take you to the Night Court."

I didn't bother to reply as I turned toward the view. The mountains went on and on, gleaming and shadowed and vast under the open, clear sky.

But nothing in me stirred—nothing cataloged the light and colors.

"Are you going to fly home?" I said.

A soft laugh. "Unfortunately, it would take longer than I can afford. Another day, I'll taste the skies again."

I glanced at the wings tucked into his powerful body, and my voice was hoarse as I spoke. "You never told me you loved the wings—or the flying." No, he'd made his shape-shifting seem . . . base, useless, boring.

He shrugged. "Everything I love has always had a tendency to be taken from me. I tell very few about the wings. Or the flying."

Some color had already come into that moon-white face—and I wondered whether he might once have been tan before Amarantha had kept him belowground for so long. A High Lord who loved to fly—trapped under a mountain. Shadows not of his own making still haunted those violet eyes. I wondered if they would ever fade.

"How does it feel to be a High Fae?" he asked—a quiet, curious question.

I looked out toward the mountains again, considering. And maybe it was because there was no one else to hear, maybe it was because the shadows in his eyes would also forever be in mine, but I said, "I'm an immortal—who has been mortal. This body . . ." I looked down at my hand, so clean and shining—a mockery of what I'd done. "This body is different, but this"—I put my hand on my chest, my heart—"this is still human. Maybe it always will be. But it would have been easier to live with it . . ." My throat welled. "Easier to live with what I did if my heart had changed, too. Maybe I wouldn't care so much; maybe I could convince myself their deaths weren't in vain. Maybe immortality will take that away. I can't tell whether I want it to."

Rhysand stared at me for long enough that I faced him. "Be glad of your human heart, Feyre. Pity those who don't feel anything at all."

I couldn't explain about the hole that had already formed in my soul—didn't want to, so I just nodded.

"Well, good-bye for now," he said, rolling his neck as if we hadn't been talking about anything important at all. He bowed at the waist, those wings vanishing entirely, and had begun to fade into the nearest shadow when he went rigid.

His eyes locked on mine, wide and wild, and his nostrils flared. Shock—pure shock flashed across his features at whatever he saw on my face, and he stumbled back a step. Actually *stumbled.*

"What is—" I began.

He disappeared—simply disappeared, not a shadow in sight—into the crisp air.

✠

Tamlin and I left the way I'd come in—through that narrow cave in the belly of the mountain. Before departing, the High Fae of several courts destroyed and then sealed Amarantha's court Under the Mountain. We were the last to leave, and with a wave of Tamlin's arm, the entrance to the court crumbled behind us.

I still didn't have the words to ask what they'd done with those two faeries. Maybe someday, maybe soon, I would ask who they were, what their names had been. Amarantha's body, I'd heard, had been hauled off to be burned—though Jurian's bone and eye were somehow missing. As much as I wanted to hate her, as much as I wished I could have spat on her burning body . . . I understood what had driven her—a very small part of her, but I understood it.

Tamlin gripped my hand as we strode through the darkness. Neither of us said anything when a glimmer of sunlight appeared, staining the damp cave walls with a silvery sheen, but our steps quickened as the sunlight grew brighter and the cave warmer, and then both of us emerged onto the spring-green grass that covered the bumps and hollows of his lands. Our lands.

The breeze, the scent of wildflowers hit me, and despite the hole in my chest, the stain on my soul, I couldn't stop the smile that spread as we mounted a steep hill. My faerie legs were far stronger than my human ones, and when we reached the top of the knoll, I wasn't nearly as winded as I might once have been. But the breath was knocked from my chest when I beheld the rose-covered manor.

Home.

In all my imaginings in Amarantha's dungeons, I'd never allowed myself to think of this moment—never allowed myself to dream that outrageously. But I'd made it—I'd brought us both home.

I squeezed his hand as we gazed down at the manor, with its stables and gardens, two sets of childish laughter—true, free laughter—coming from somewhere inside its grounds. A moment later, two small, shining figures darted into the field beyond the garden, shrieking as they were chased by a taller, chuckling figure—Alis and her boys. Safe and out of hiding at last.

Tamlin slipped an arm around my shoulders, tucking me close to him as he rested his cheek on my head. My lips trembled, and I wrapped my arm around his waist.

We stood atop the hill in silence, until the setting sun gilded the house and the hills and the world and Lucien called us to dinner.

I stepped out of Tamlin's arms and kissed him softly. Tomorrow—there would be tomorrow, and an eternity, to face what I had done, to face what I shredded into pieces inside myself while Under the Mountain. But for now . . . for today . . .

"Let's go home," I said, and took his hand.

Acknowledgments

To be honest, I'm not quite sure where to begin these acknowledgments, because this book exists thanks to so many people working on it over so many years. My eternal gratitude and love to:

Susan Dennard, my jaeger copilot and Threadsister, the Leonardo to my Raphael, the Gus to my Shawn, the Blake to my Adam, the Scott to my Stiles, the Aragorn to my Legolas, the Iseult to my Safi, the Schmidt to my Jenko, the Senneth to my Kira, the Elsa to my Anna, the Sailor Jupiter (or Luna!) to my Sailor Moon, the Moss to my Roy, the Martin to my Sean, the Alan Grant to my Ian Malcolm, the Brennan to my Dale, and the Esqueleto to my Nacho: I literally don't know what I'd do without you. Or our inside jokes. Our friendship is the definition of Epic—and I'm pretty sure it was written in the stars. (Like a thousand years before the dinosaurs. It's the prophecy.) See also: Imhotep, Tiny Cups For Tiny Hands, *Ohhhh you do??*, Cryssals, Henry Cavill, Sam Heughan, Claaaassic Peg, and everything ever from Nacho Libre. Sarusan Forever.

To Alex Bracken, who was one of the first friends I made in this industry, and remains one of my best friends to this day. There are moments when it still feels like we're fresh out of college with our first book deals, wondering what is next for us—I'm so happy that we've gotten to share this insane journey with each other. Thank you for all the amazing feedback, the multiple reads (on this book and so many others), and always, always, having my back. I can't tell you how much that means to me. Thanks for believing in this story for so many years.

To Biljana Likic, who read this pretty much as I wrote it chapter by chapter, helped me write all those riddles and limericks, and made me believe this story might not actually sit in a drawer for the rest of my life. So proud to now see you kicking ass and taking names, dude.

To my agent, Tamar Rydzinski, who took a chance on an unpublished twenty-two-year-old writer and changed my life forever with one phone call. You are a supreme badass. Thank you for everything.

To Cat Onder—you are such a delight to work with, and I'm honored to call you my editor. To Laura Bernier—thank you so, so much for helping me transform this book into something that I'm truly proud of. I couldn't have done it without your brilliant feedback.

To the entire worldwide team at Bloomsbury: I cannot tell you how thrilled I am that this series found a home with you. You guys are the ultimate best. Thank you for your hard work, your enthusiasm, and making my dreams come true. I can't imagine being in better hands. Thank you, thank you, thank you.

To Dan Krokos, Erin Bowman, Mandy Hubbard, and Jennifer Armentrout—thank you for being there for everything and anything. I don't know what I would do without you.

To Brigid Kemmerer, Andrea Maas, and Kat Zhang, who read various early drafts of this book and provided such crucial feedback and enthusiasm. I owe you one.

To Elena of NovelSounds, Alexa of AlexaLovesBooks, Linnea of Linneart, and all the *Throne of Glass* Ambassadors: Thank you guys so much for your support and dedication. Getting to know you all has been such a highlight and pleasure.

To my parents: it took me a while to realize it, but I'm tremendously blessed to have you as my Number One fans—and to have you as parents. To my family: thank you for the unconditional love and support.

To Annie, the greatest dog in the history of canine companions: I love you forever and ever and ever.

And lastly, to my husband, Josh—this book is for you. It's always been yours, the same way my heart has been yours from the moment I saw you on the first day of freshman orientation at college. Considering the way our lives mysteriously wove together before we ever set eyes on each other, I have a hard time believing it wasn't fate. Thanks for proving to me that true love exists. I'm the luckiest woman in the world to get to spend my life with you.

Pronunciation Guide

CHARACTERS

Feyre: Fay-ruh

Tamlin: Tam-lin

Lucien: Loo-shien

Rhysand: Ree-sand (Rhys: Reese)

Alis: Alice

Amarantha: Am-a-ran-tha

PLACES

Prythian: Prith-ee-en

Hybern: Hi-burn

OTHER

Attor: At-tor

Suriel: Sur-ee-el

Bogge: Boh-ghi

Puca: Pu-kah

Naga: Nah-gah

Calanmai: Cal-an-may

FEYRE'S STORY REACHES NEW HEIGHTS IN THIS SPELLBINDING SEQUEL

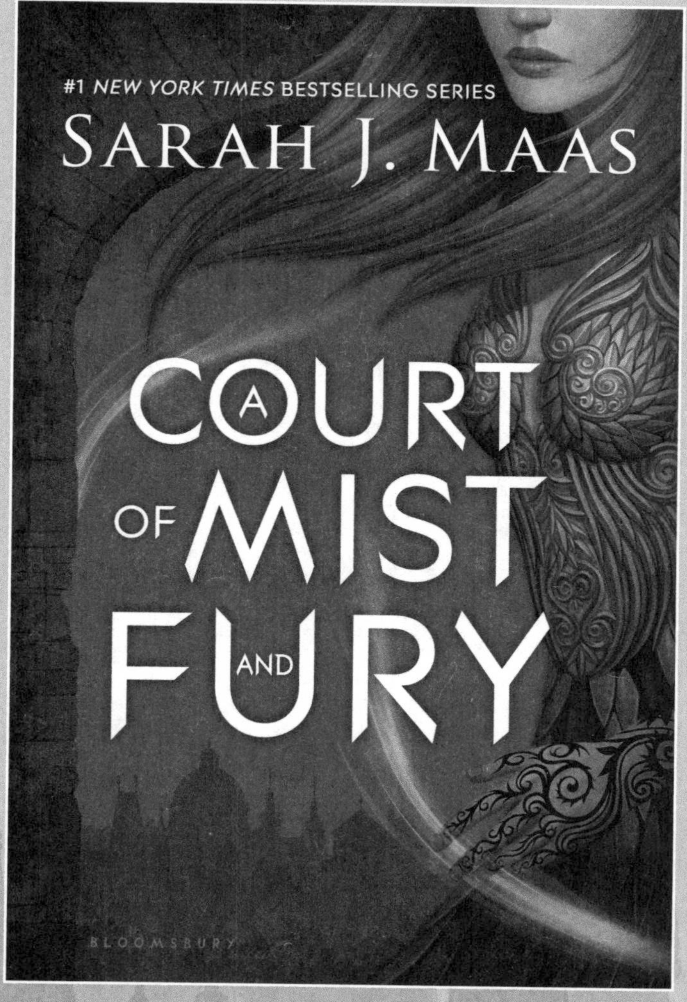

READ ON FOR A SNEAK PEEK AS THE JOURNEY THROUGH PRYTHIAN CONTINUES . . .

I agreed to sit at the long, wooden table in a curtained-off alcove only because he had a point. Not being able to read had almost cost me my life Under the Mountain. I'd be damned if I let it become a weakness again, his personal agenda or no. And as for shielding . . . I'd be a damned fool not to take up the offer to learn from him. The thought of anyone, especially Rhys, sifting through the mess in my mind, taking information about the Spring Court, about the people I loved . . . I'd never allow it. Not willingly.

But it didn't make it any easier to endure Rhysand's presence at the wooden table. Or the stack of books piled atop it.

"I know my alphabet," I said sharply as he laid a piece of paper in front of me. "I'm not that stupid." I twisted my fingers in my lap, then pinned my restless hands under my thighs.

"I didn't say you were stupid," he said. "I'm just trying to determine where we should begin." I leaned back in the cushioned seat. "Since you've refused to tell me a thing about how much you know."

My face warmed. "Can't you hire a tutor?"

He lifted a brow. "Is it that hard for you to even try in front of me?"

"You're a High Lord—don't you have better things to do?"

"Of course. But none as enjoyable as seeing you squirm."

"You're a real bastard, you know that?"

Rhys huffed a laugh. "I've been called worse. In fact, I think you've called me worse." He tapped the paper in front of him. "Read that."

A blur of letters. My throat tightened. "I can't."

"Try."

The sentence had been written in elegant, concise print. His writing, no doubt. I tried to open my mouth, but my spine locked up. "What, *exactly*, is your stake in all this? You said you'd tell me if I worked with you."

"I didn't specify *when* I'd tell you." I peeled back from him as my lip curled. He shrugged. "Maybe I resent the idea of you letting those sycophants and war-mongering fools in the Spring Court make you feel inadequate. Maybe I indeed enjoy seeing you squirm. Or maybe—"

"I get it."

Rhys snorted. "Try to read it, Feyre."

Prick. I snatched the paper to me, nearly ripping it in half in the process. I looked at the first word, sounding it out in my head. "Y-you . . . " The next I figured out with a combination of my silent pronunciation and logic. "Look . . . "

"Good," he murmured.

"I didn't ask for your approval."

Rhys chuckled.

"Ab . . . Absolutely." It took me longer than I wanted to admit to figure that out. The next word was even worse. "De . . . Del . . . "

I deigned to glance at him, brows raised.

"Delicious," he purred.

My brows now knotted. I read the next two words, then whipped my face toward him. "*You look absolutely delicious today, Feyre*?! That's what you wrote?"

He leaned back in his seat. As our eyes met, sharp claws caressed my mind and his voice whispered inside my head: *It's true, isn't it?*

I jolted back, my chair groaning. "*Stop that*!"

But those claws now dug in—and my entire body, my heart, my lungs, my *blood* yielded to his grip, utterly at his command as he said, *The fashion of the Night Court suits you.*

I couldn't move in my seat, couldn't even blink.

This is what happens when you leave your mental shields down. Someone with my sort of powers could slip inside, see what they want, and take your mind for themselves. Or they could shatter it. I'm currently standing on the threshold of your mind . . . but if I were to go deeper, all it would take would be half a thought from me and who you are, your very self, would be wiped away.

Distantly, sweat slid down my temple.

You should be afraid. You should be afraid of this, and you should be thanking the gods-damned Cauldron that in the past three months, no one with my sorts of gifts has run into you. Now shove me out.

I couldn't. Those claws were everywhere—digging into every thought, every piece of self. He pushed a little harder.

Shove. Me. Out.

I didn't know where to begin. I blindly pushed and slammed myself into him, into those claws that were everywhere, as if I were a top loosed in a circle of mirrors.

His laughter, low and soft, filled my mind, my ears. *That way, Feyre.*

In answer, a little open path gleamed inside my mind. The road out.

It'd take me forever to unhook each claw and shove the mass of his presence out that narrow opening. If I could wash it away—

A wave. A wave of self, of *me*, to sweep all of him out—

I didn't let him see the plan take form as I rallied myself into a cresting wave and struck.

The claws loosened—reluctantly. As if letting me win this round. He merely said, "Good."

My bones, my breath and blood, they were mine again. I slumped in my seat.

"Not yet," he said. "Shield. Block me out so I can't get back in."

I already wanted to go somewhere quiet and sleep for a while—

Claws at that outer layer of my mind, stroking—

I imagined a wall of adamant snapping down, black as night and a foot thick. The claws retracted a breath before the wall sliced them in two.

Rhys was grinning. "Very nice. Blunt, but nice."

I couldn't help myself. I grabbed the piece of paper and shredded it in two, then four. "You're a pig."

"Oh, most definitely. But look at you—you read that whole sentence, kicked me out of your mind, *and* shielded. Excellent work."

"Don't condescend to me."

"I'm not. You're reading at a level far higher than I anticipated."

That burning returned to my cheeks. "But mostly illiterate."

"At this point, it's about practice, spelling, and more practice. You could be reading novels by Nynsar. And if you keep adding to those shields, you might very well keep me out entirely by then, too."

Nynsar. It'd be the first Tamlin and his court would celebrate in nearly fifty years. Amarantha had banned it on a whim, along with a few other small, but beloved Fae holidays that she had deemed *unnecessary*. But Nynsar was months from now. "Is it even possible—to truly keep you out?"

"Not likely, but who knows how deep that power goes? Keep practicing and we'll see what happens."

"And will I still be bound by this bargain at Nynsar, too?"

Silence.

I pushed, "After—after what happened—" I couldn't mention specifics on what had occurred Under the Mountain, what he'd done for me during that fight with Amarantha, what he'd done after— "I think we can agree that I owe you nothing, and you owe *me* nothing."

His gaze was unflinching.

I blazed on, "Isn't it enough that we're all free?" I splayed my tattooed hand on the table. "By the end, I thought you were different, thought that it was all a mask, but taking me away, *keeping* me here . . . " I shook my head, unable to find the words vicious enough, clever enough to convince him to end this bargain.

His eyes darkened. "I'm not your enemy, Feyre."

"Tamlin says you are." I curled the fingers of my tattooed hand into a fist. "Everyone else says you are."

"And what do *you* think?" He leaned back in his chair again, but his face was grave.

"You're doing a damned good job of making me agree with them."

"Liar," he purred. "Did you even tell your friends about *what I did to you* Under the Mountain?"

So that comment at breakfast *had* gotten under his skin. "I don't want to talk about anything related to that. With you or them."

"No, because it's so much easier to pretend it never happened and let them coddle you."

"I don't *let* them coddle me—"

"They had you wrapped up like a present yesterday. Like you were *his* reward."

"So?"

"So?" A flicker of rage, then it was gone.

"I'm ready to be taken home," I merely said.

"Where you'll be cloistered for the rest of your life, especially once you start punching out heirs. I can't wait to see what Ianthe does when she gets her hands on *them*."

"You don't seem to have a particularly high opinion of her."

Something cold and predatory crept into his eyes. "No, I can't say that I do." He pointed to a blank piece of paper. "Start copying the alphabet. Until your letters are perfect. And every time you get through a round, lower and raise your shield. Until *that* is second nature. I'll be back in an hour."

"What?"

"Copy. The. Alphabet. Until—"

"I heard what you said." Prick. Prick, prick, *prick*.

"Then get to work." Rhys uncoiled to his feet. "And at least have the decency to only call me a prick when your shields are back up."

He vanished into a ripple of darkness before I realized that I'd let the wall of adamant fade again.

✠

By the time Rhys returned, my mind felt like a mud puddle.

I spent the entire hour doing as I'd been ordered, though I'd flinched at every sound from the nearby stairwell: quiet steps of servants, the flapping of sheets being changed, someone humming a beautiful and winding melody. And beyond that, the chatter of birds that dwelled in the unnatural warmth of the mountain or in the many potted citrus trees. No sign of my impending torment. No sentries, even, to monitor me. I might as well have had the entire place to myself.

Which was good, as my attempts to lower and raise that mental shield often resulted in my face being twisted or strained or pinched.

"Not bad," Rhys said, peering over my shoulder.

He'd appeared moments before, a healthy distance away, and if I hadn't known better, I might have thought it was because he didn't want to startle me. As if he'd known about the time Tamlin had crept up behind me, and panic had hit me so hard I'd knocked him on his ass with a punch to his stomach. I'd blocked it out—the shock on Tam's face, how *easy* it had been to take him off his feet, the humiliation of having my stupid terror so out in the open . . .

Rhys scanned the pages I'd scribbled on, sorting through them, tracking my progress.

Then, a scrape of claws inside my mind—that only sliced against black, glittering adamant.

I threw my lingering will into that wall as the claws pushed, testing for weak spots . . .

"Well, well," Rhysand purred, those mental claws withdrawing. "Hopefully I'll be getting a good night's rest at last, if you can manage to keep the wall up while you sleep."

I dropped the shield, sent a word blasting down that mental bridge between us, and hauled the walls back up. Behind it, my mind wobbled like jelly. I needed a nap. Desperately.

"Prick I might be, but look at you. Maybe we'll get to have some fun with our lessons after all."

✢

I was still scowling at Rhys's muscled back as I kept a healthy ten steps behind him while he led me through the halls of the main building, the sweeping mountains and blisteringly blue sky the only witnesses to our silent trek.

I was too drained to demand where we were now going, and he didn't bother explaining as he led me up, up—until we entered a round chamber at the top of a tower.

A circular table of black stone occupied the center, while the largest stretch of uninterrupted gray stone wall was covered in a massive map of our world. It had been marked and flagged and pinned, for whatever reasons I couldn't tell, but my gaze drifted to the windows throughout the room—so many that it felt utterly exposed, breathable. The perfect home, I supposed, for a High Lord blessed with wings.

Rhys stalked to the table, where there was another map spread, figurines dotting its surface. A map of Prythian—and Hybern.

Every court in our land had been marked, along with villages and cities and rivers and mountain passes. Every court . . . but the Night Court.

The vast, northern territory was utterly blank. Not even a mountain range had been etched in. Strange, likely part of some strategy I didn't understand.

I found Rhysand watching me—his raised brows enough to make me shut my mouth against the forming question.

"Nothing to ask?"

"No."

A feline smirk danced on his lips, but Rhys jerked his chin toward the map on the wall. "What do you see?"

"Is this some sort of way of convincing me to embrace my reading lessons?" Indeed, I couldn't decipher any of the writing, only the shapes of things. Like the wall, its massive line bisecting our world.

"Tell me what you see."

"A world divided in two."

"And do you think it should remain that way?"

I whipped my head toward him. "My family—" I halted on the word. I should have known better than to admit to having a family, that I cared for them—

"Your human family," Rhys finished, "would be deeply impacted if the wall came down, wouldn't they? So close to its border . . . If they're lucky, they'll flee across the ocean before it happens."

"*Will* it happen?"

Rhysand didn't break my stare. "Maybe."

"Why?"

"Because war is coming, Feyre."

She stole a life. Now she must pay with her heart.

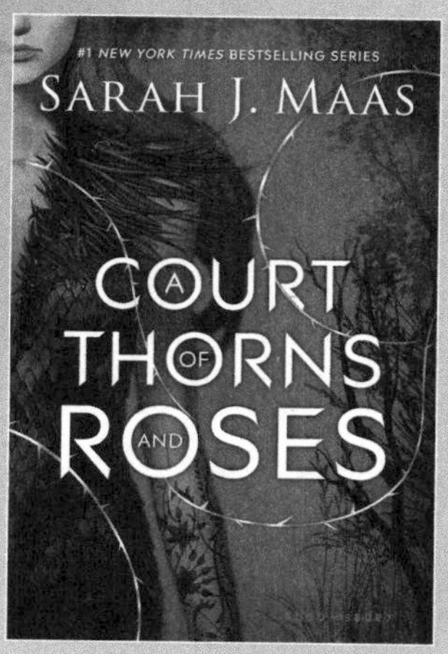

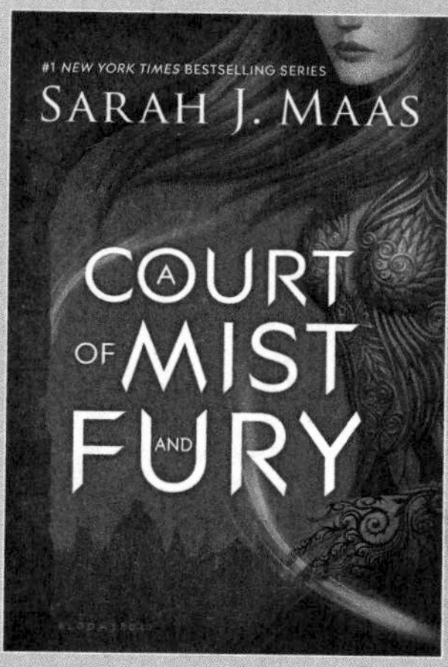

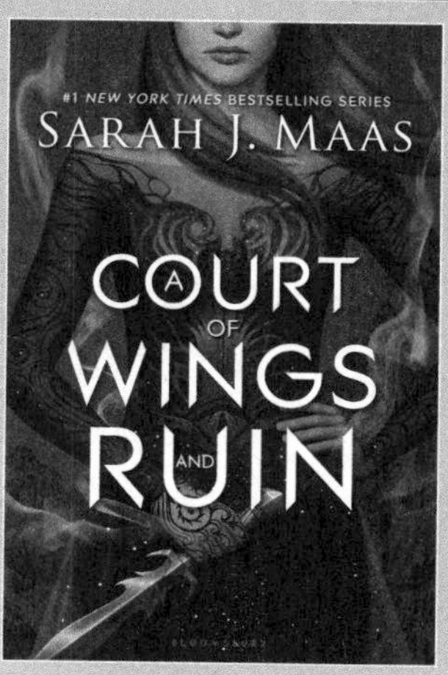

Don't miss this captivating #1 *New York Times* bestselling series from author Sarah J. Maas, which blends "Beauty and the Beast" and faerie lore.

www.bloomsbury.com
Twitter: BloomsburyKids
Snapchat: BloomsburyYA

Praise for the *New York Times* and *USA Today* bestselling Throne of Glass series

THRONE OF GLASS

A *Kirkus Reviews* Best Teen Book
An Amazon Best Book
A YALSA-ALA Best Fiction for Young Adults Book

★ "A thrilling read." —*Publishers Weekly*, starred review

"A must-read for lovers of epic fantasy and fairy tales." —*USA Today*

"Fans of Tamora Pierce and George R.R. Martin, pick up this book!" —*RT Book Reviews*, Top Pick

CROWN OF MIDNIGHT

★ "An epic fantasy readers will immerse themselves in and never want to leave." —*Kirkus Reviews*, starred review

"Series fans will be . . . thrilled by the prospect of deepening adventures in the next volume." —*Booklist*

"With assassinations, betrayal, love and magic, this novel has something to match everyone's interests." —*RT Book Reviews*, Top Pick

HEIR OF FIRE

"I was afraid to put the book down!"
—*New York Times* bestselling author Tamora Pierce

"Readers will devour Maas's latest entry. . . . A must-purchase." —*SLJ*

"Maas shines as a brilliant storyteller. . . . The most exhilarating installment yet." —*RT Book Reviews*, Top Pick

QUEEN OF SHADOWS

The Goodreads Choice Award Winner for Best Young Adult Fantasy and Science Fiction for 2015

"Character motivations and interactions . . . are always nuanced and on point, especially as Aelin's growing maturity offers her new perspectives on old acquaintances. . . . Impossible to put down." —*Kirkus Reviews*

"Fans of the high-fantasy series likely won't mind the protracted story at all, packed as it is with brooding glances, simmering sexual tension, twisty plot turns, lush world building, and snarky banter. . . . The final chapters of this installment promise more epic adventures and badder bad guys to defeat in forthcoming volumes." —*Booklist*

EMPIRE OF STORMS

An Amazon Best Book
A Buzzfeed Best Book

"Fans devoted to the series (and there are many) will be eager for this installment's cinematic action, twisty schemes, and intense revelations of secrets and legacies." —*Booklist*

"Tightly plotted, delightful escapism." —*Kirkus Reviews*

THE ASSASSIN'S BLADE

"Fans will delight in this gorgeous edition. . . . Action-packed and full of insight into Celaena's character. . . . What a ride!" —*Booklist* online

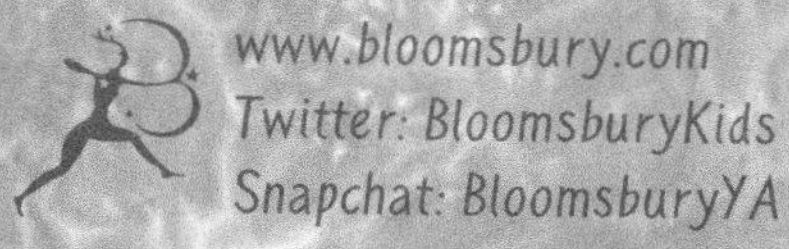

SHE IS HER KINGDOM'S MOST FEARLESS ASSASSIN

DON'T MISS ANY OF THIS **EPIC SERIES** FROM **SARAH J. MAAS**

WWW.WORLDOFSARAHJMAAS.COM

Josh Wasserman

SARAH J. MAAS is the author of the #1 *New York Times* bestselling Court of Thorns and Roses series—*A Court of Thorns and Roses*, *A Court of Mist and Fury*, *A Court of Wings and Ruin*, and *A Court of Thorns and Roses Coloring Book*. She is also the #1 *New York Times* bestselling author of the Throne of Glass series—*Throne of Glass*; *Crown of Midnight*; *Heir of Fire*; *Queen of Shadows*; *Empire of Storms* and its parallel novel, *Tower of Dawn*; the series' prequel, *The Assassin's Blade*; and *The Throne of Glass Coloring Book*. A New York native, Sarah lives in Pennsylvania with her husband and dog.

www.worldofsarahjmaas.com
facebook.com/throneofglass
instagram.com/therealsjmaas
@SJMaas